PAST REMEMBERING

In this enthralling sequel to *'Such Sweet Sorrow'*, the community in Pontypridd struggle with rationing, rumour and speculation. Ronnie Ronconi's return from Italy in 1941, without his beloved Maud, exposes the cracks in Diana Powell's marriage to Wyn Rees. Haydn Powell, star of BBC Radio, is desperate to convince his wife that she must evacuate from blitzed London to Wales before it's too late. In the valleys, meanwhile, employment in munitions factories and collieries has given women a new-found freedom. And through it all, the Ronconi cafés keep going, giving the fractured town its one and only sense of continuity.

PAST REMEMBERING

PAST REMEMBERING

by

Catrin Collier

Magna Large Print Books
Long Preston, North Yorkshire,
England.

British Library Cataloguing in Publication Data.

Collier, Catrin
  Past remembering.

  A catalogue record for this book is
  available from the British Library

  ISBN 0-7505-1236-9

First published in Great Britain by Century Books, Random House
UK Ltd., 1997

Published in Large Print 1998 by arrangement with Century, one
of the publishers in Random House UK.

Magna Large Print is an imprint of
Library Magna Books Ltd.
Printed and bound in Great Britain by
T.J. International Ltd., Cornwall, PL28 8RW.

To Les and Wendy Watkins,
who married one perfect June day in 1996

ACKNOWLEDGEMENTS

I would like to thank those people who have so generously shared their memories with me during the year I spent writing and researching this book.

A special thank-you to Deirdre Beddoe, Professor of History at the University of Glamorgan, Pontypridd, who is doing such sterling work recording local women's history, and the history of women during the Second World War.

As always I would also like to acknowledge a great debt of gratitude to Mrs Lindsay Morris and the staff of Pontypridd Library, especially the archivist, Mrs Penny Pugh, and Mr Brian Davies and the staff of Pontypridd Historical Centre for their unstinting professional assistance.

My parents Glyn and Gerda Jones, my husband John, and my children, Ralph, Sophie and Ross for their love, and for giving me the time to write this book.

Margaret Bloomfield for her friendship and continued help.

Everyone at Random House for their support and kindness, especially Mike Morgan, Tracey Jennings, Tess Tattersall, and above all my editor Mary Loring for her patience, encouragement, suggestions and being on the end of the telephone whenever I needed to talk, and my agent, Michael Thomas, for his continued faith in me.

And while gratefully acknowledging the assistance of everyone I would like to stress that any errors are entirely mine.

Catrin Collier
Swansea June 1996

NOTES

The characters in *Past Remembering* are creations of my imagination. The traumatic events they lived through are not.

There are women living in the Welsh valleys now, who still bear the scars and cope with the loss of limbs and blindness that occurred as a result of 'minor incidents' in munitions factories during the war. In one accident alone between thirty and forty workers were killed, two-thirds of them women.

Up until September 1942 more civilians than servicemen had been killed and injured as a result of the war.

Past Remembering is their story.

CHAPTER 1

'Soon be in Pontypridd.' The corporal shouted
to make himself heard above the roar of the
lorry's engine as he glanced across at the
passenger huddled into an army blanket in the
corner of the cab. If the request to take the
shady-looking traveller had come from anyone
other than a wing commander he would have
told the hiker to shove off and use shanks's
pony to get from the south coast to Wales. He
not only looked disreputable, but foreign, and
in the eleven months since France had fallen,
the corporal, like most of the population of
beleaguered Britain, had learned to look on all
foreigners as Hitler's henchmen.

His passenger's accent had the lilt of the
valleys but there was something odd about it
that suggested other, stronger influences, and
on the few occasions he hadn't been able to
avoid answering questions, his speech had been
slow as though he'd had to carefully consider
every word before he said it. The man's dark
eyes and black hair were common enough in
Wales, but his skin looked as though it had been
burned by a hotter sun than the one that had
shone in the south of England during the last
few fine April days. He was thinner and taller
than most locals; drawn and wasted as though
he hadn't eaten properly in a year. And then

13

there were his clothes—his linen shirt was more hole than cloth, and his black trousers had been bled grey by wear and washing. Both were too thin for early spring. He had no jacket or coat, and no luggage. Not even a haversack. Only the blanket, and the corporal had seen a sergeant hand him that. It was all very well the wing commander vouching for him, but then the wing commander might be a spy too. The newspapers were full of stories of German agents infiltrating all ranks, high and low, in the services as well as civilian life.

His passenger could have come in by boat, shipwrecked even, which would explain the state of his clothes and his injured leg. After all, Dover was just across the Channel from France, and a man in the Home Guard had told him they could see the German guns trained on the English coast on a clear day.

'You know anyone in Pontypridd?' The driver tried to make the enquiry casual, wanting to hear the man's voice again just in case he could pick up on a trace of an accent. German or Italian? That was it! His passenger resembled the Mussolini Fascists he had seen on the newsreels. To think he'd carried a potential saboteur to Pontypridd, slap bang in the middle of one of the largest concentrations of munitions factories in the country.

'A few people,' came the guarded reply.

'You haven't been there for a while?'

'Over four years.'

'Well, the town isn't what it used to be since the war broke out. God forgive me for

14

saying so, but it's better. More money about. Every spare room in the place is packed to bursting with evacuees and war workers,' he added cautiously, giving away nothing that wasn't already common knowledge. 'You got somewhere to stay?'

'There's a few houses I can try.'

'You haven't written to tell anyone you're coming?'

'No.'

'A lot have moved on since the war started, what with the call-ups and labour shortages. There's no saying whether your friends will still be in the town. We won't be pulling in much before midnight. If you don't want to disturb anyone, you could try Jacobsdal,' he suggested slyly, knowing the house was under the direct supervision of the police.

'Never heard of it.'

'Big house up by the boys' grammar school. It was bought back in '37 by German Jews. Rumour has it they intended to make their home there but they returned to Germany to pick up their furniture ... or perhaps it was their relatives ... either way they didn't come back. Council took it over last year. They use it as a hostel for foreigners. Refugees and immigrants and those sort of people,' he hinted heavily, hoping to spark a revelation.

'You think I'll get a bed there?'

'Bound to. Don't mind me asking, but have you been overseas?'

The man's lips twisted into a parody of a smile, and the driver concentrated on the road.

15

His passenger's smile held more menace than the scowl he'd worn for most of the journey.

'Of course I know Ponty inside out,' the driver continued nervously, keeping an eye on the sturdy wooden crutch the man had jammed between the bench seat and the passenger door. If he *was* a foreigner there was no saying what violence he was capable of. 'My missus was born in Hopkinstown. We live in Aberdare now, which is why I'm driving through, but her mother's still in Ponty, and we like to go down for tea on the Sundays I'm home to catch up on all the news. My wife's four brothers are in the army. My three sisters too.'

'We should win, then.'

'I should bloody well think so,' the corporal retorted hotly, missing the intended irony. 'Anyone special you thinking of visiting?' he hazarded another question.

'No one special.' There was a bitterness in the man's voice that finally silenced the driver. Peering into the blackout he rolled the heavy wagon to the end of Broadway before sliding back his window to check for oncoming traffic at the Tumble crossroads. Ahead loomed the blackout-shrouded centre of the town.

'You can drop me off here.'

'Suit yourself.' The corporal lifted his foot from the accelerator to the brake, grinding to a halt outside the New Theatre in the narrowest part of Taff Street.

'Thanks for the lift.' His passenger opened the door.

'You know the forces: the officers shout, the

16

squaddies jump. What the wing commander says, goes on that particular base. You good friends?'

'Not really.' The stranger offered his hand and the driver took it briefly. 'You ever in the town?' he asked as he lowered his wooden crutch out of the cab.

'Now and then.'

'Eat in any of the cafés?'

'Used to. They shipped out most of the Italians back last year about the time of Dunkirk. They said they were enemy aliens. Couldn't see it myself. After all, most of them have lived here for donkey's years.'

'Know the Ronconis?'

'Who doesn't? A couple of the girls are still in town. They married local fellows so they were allowed to stay. Look I can't stop here any longer. If a copper comes he'll nab me for blocking the road.' The driver revved his engine as the man lowered himself gingerly from the cab, clutching the door until he could ease his weight on to the crutch. 'Say, you're not one of them, are you?' the corporal asked suddenly, taking his foot off the accelerator.

'A Ronconi or an enemy alien?' he asked as he wrapped the blanket around his shoulders. The night air was fresh and chilly after the close, petrol-ridden atmosphere of the cab.

The driver had the grace to remain silent.

'It's all right, I am on your side.'

'You've hardly said a bloody word in all the fifteen hours we've been on the road, and now you want to talk?'

17

'Not really. Thanks for the lift.'

The driver stared into his rearview mirror, watching the shadowy figure limp through the darkness back up towards the Tumble and Ronconi's café. Finally he released the handbrake. He'd seen enough Sherlock Holmes films to put together a description if the police wanted one.

The traveller stood outside the café until he could no longer hear the thunder of the lorry's engine as it rumbled on down Taff Street. The building was in darkness, but then, courtesy of the blackout, so was the entire Tumble. He walked to the door and knocked.

'We're closed.'

He leaned against the café window in relief. There was someone he knew in Pontypridd after all. 'Open up, Tina, it's me.'

'Who's me?' The bolts were drawn back before he had time to answer. A face peered out, then the door opened a crack. He pushed aside the curtain.

'Careful, the blackout ...' Tina stared in bewilderment. 'Ronnie?' she ventured tentatively.

'I used to go by that name.'

'You look awful.'

'Trust me to have a sister who always tells the truth.'

'But you do. That blanket's filthy and your clothes ... you look as though you haven't seen a square meal in years.'

'Has anyone, since this war started?' Untangling his crutch from the curtain he stumbled

18

inside, locking the door behind him. As he turned Tina flung herself into his arms. He lost his balance and crashed backwards into the wall.

'Ronnie, it's so good to see you ... We didn't know if you were alive or dead ... I have so much to tell you ... Gina is going to be out of her mind when she sees you ... You've hurt your leg ... How did you do it? Come here, sit down. I'll get you something to eat ...'

Scarcely hearing Tina's babbling, he scrutinised the deserted café, automatically checking that the linoleum that covered the floor had been swept and washed and the wooden chairs cleaned before they'd been lifted on to the tables. Old habits died hard, he reflected grimly. 'You run this place by yourself now?' he interrupted.

'Of course.'

'But Tina it's the roughest ...'

'So? You want me to put Gina in charge?'

'Gina run a café? Don't be ridiculous, she's a baby.'

'She's managing the restaurant we opened in Taff Street, and managing it well.'

'God help the business. And Papa's café?'

'Laura took care of it until a week ago. Then Trevor got a posting to a hospital in Sussex. He found rooms near the hospital so she took the baby down there to be near him.'

'You closed our place in High Street!'

'You haven't changed have you, Ronnie? Still business before family.'

'I spent years building up the cafés ...'

'And they're all standing, and making a profit. Not as much as when you were in charge, but then there's a war on. I put a girl into Papa's old café in High Street. It was never that busy. I keep an eye on the two.'

Propping his crutch against a table, he lifted down a chair and sat on it.

'What am I doing standing here talking? You must be starved.'

'I'm not sure I could eat anything.' The driver had made three stops on the long journey down, but apart from coffee Ronnie hadn't eaten or drunk anything. Even now, he felt queasy, nauseated by the rich smells of cocoa and fried food that lingered in the air.

'I have some eggs hidden in the back, and ...'

'After what I've eaten for the last year, better make it dry toast and tea. I can't keep much else down.'

'Ronnie, I have so much to tell you.'

'I know most of it. Papa drowned on the *Arandora Star* when they were shipping internees to Canada. Someone said the boat was torpedoed.'

'That's what we heard too, but Mama and the little ones are safe in Birmingham. They had to relocate to an area more than a hundred miles from the sea.'

'I'm surprised any place is that far from the sea on this island.'

'Tony's in the army. He was wounded before Dunkirk. As far as we know he's still stationed somewhere in this country, and Angelo ...'

20

'Was taken prisoner when France fell. Two sons in the army and they thought Papa was an enemy alien. What do we have to do to convince people we're not Fascists?'

'It's not the people around here who need convincing but the government.'

'I hear you're married.'

'William Powell last summer.'

'You wouldn't have married him if I'd been home. He's nowhere near good enough for you.'

'Then it's just as well you weren't around,' she bit back tartly. 'And before we go any further you may as well know Gina's married too.'

'What! She's only sixteen.'

'The same age Maud was when she married you. Anyway she's seventeen now. Her husband's only a couple of years older than her. He's a conscientious objector, so they sent him down the pit.'

'Sensible fellow. I tried to opt out of the war, but I didn't quite manage it.'

'That covers everyone except you, Ronnie. We never thought you and Maud would get out of Italy once Mussolini came down on the side of the Germans ...' She looked at her brother's face. 'Something's happened to Maud, hasn't it? You never would have left her otherwise. Ronnie ...'

'She's dead, Tina.' He'd meant to break the news gently, but now the moment had arrived, there didn't seem any other way to tell her.

'Oh, Ronnie! I'm sorry, so sorry.' Memories

21

of her brother's wedding flooded into her mind. Had it really been only five years ago? So much had happened since then, it seemed like half a lifetime and another world away.

Ronnie rose wearily to his feet. Wrapping his arms around his sister's shoulders, he held her close while she sobbed hot, salt tears on to his ragged shirt. He would have given a great deal to have been able to cry with her. His heart had turned to stone the day Maud had died. Eighteen months later he was still too numb to weep.

He began to wonder what he was doing in Pontypridd. He'd crawled home like a wounded animal needing to lick its sores. How had that corporal put it 'Anyone special you thinking of visiting?' There was no one special person left in the world, not for him. He should never have allowed the British pilots he'd guided over the mountains into Switzerland to talk him into returning to England with them so he could draw maps for British Intelligence. He should have ignored the bullets in his leg and gone back to the hills and the Resistance. Better to have died fighting in Italy. That way at least he would have stood a chance of sharing Maud's grave.

'It's more like midsummer than spring. Real holiday weather.' Jane Powell slowed her steps as her husband hesitated in front of a park bench.

'Lovely weather for the countryside. I'm not too sure about the city, though. If it's like this now we'll be able to fry eggs on the pavement in a week or two.' Finally deciding that the bench commanded as fine a view of the small park as they were likely to get, and a better vista of the blitzed London suburbs that surrounded it than he desired, Haydn jammed his foot against the brake on the pram he'd been pushing and sat down.

'And where do you suggest we get eggs other than powdered to fry?'

'In Pontypridd. Plenty of people keep chickens there. Remember how cool it was in the woods around Shoni's pond last August? It would be even prettier now, the bluebells would be out and—'

'... and just as soon as you get leave we'll go back there for a visit,' Jane interrupted, deliberately ignoring yet another hint that she should take herself and the baby out of London and Hitler's bomb path. Bending over the pram she folded back the covers and lifted up their eight-week-old daughter. Haydn was already holding out his arms. She suppressed a small smile of triumph as she handed him the shawl-wrapped bundle. It hadn't been easy to fend off Haydn's demands that she evacuate to his father's house in Wales before Anne's birth, but since the baby's arrival he had become as malleable as bread dough—until last night.

She wondered if he'd heard something in work that had prompted him to renew his badgering that she leave London for the comparative safety of Pontypridd. Usually all it took to weaken his resolve was for her to twine her arms around his neck, look into his eyes and plant a kiss on his lips, and if he still wavered, give him Anne to cuddle; but today, for some reason she hadn't yet fathomed, he appeared impervious to her coaxings.

'You could go ahead of me. I'll follow as soon as I get leave.'

'And travel on the train by myself with Anne? I'd never cope.'

'Of course you would,' he snapped with uncharacteristic brusqueness, closing his eyes against the horrific images that had haunted him since his bus had been held up next to a cordoned-off bomb site yesterday afternoon. Only three houses had been left standing in a sea of rubble that had been a heavily populated street a couple of months ago. While he'd sat on the top deck and idly watched ARP wardens and Home Guard veterans comb the wreckage for salvageable objects, a tin-hatted warden had emerged from the hole he'd been digging in, to blow his whistle. Just before the bus had moved off a pathetically small, dust-coated corpse had been lifted out of the crater. A body that had suddenly, unaccountably, become Anne's in Haydn's mind's eye.

The child must have lain there, forgotten and unmourned since the last bombing raid weeks ago. Haydn couldn't help wondering about the parents. Had they been killed in the same raid, or was there a father fighting somewhere who carried a photograph of a wife and child he didn't even know were dead? Had the child died instantly, or had it lived for hours, days even, trapped, frightened and alone, all the while slowly dying of thirst ...

He clutched Anne closer, shivering despite the sunshine. The nights had been quiet for so long they were almost getting used to the peace, but that didn't mean the bombing had stopped. Now that the winter storms had died in the Channel, everyone was waiting for Hitler to invade. The precursor to the Nazis' spring campaign would undoubtedly be a resumption of the blitz, and next time Anne might be the one buried beneath the ruins. It was a horrific scenario he hated himself for even daring to imagine, because Anne, like Jane, had become too precious to contemplate losing. He crossed his fingers superstitiously lest even the thought of such tragedy precipitate it.

'The bombing could start again, and I'd never forgive myself if anything happened to Anne, or you,' he murmured, softening his voice in the hope it would atone for his outburst.

'Nothing is going to happen to either of us.'

'How can you say that?'

'Do you really think we'd be any safer in Pontypridd with Cardiff docks just down the road?'

'They're twelve miles away.'

'And the munitions factories in Treforest?' she whispered, after checking no fifth columnist was close enough to overhear their conversation. 'And don't bring up America again,' she warned. 'Not after that last ship of refugees was sunk by a U-boat.'

'I wasn't going to, but can't you see you'd be

safer in Pontypridd? No matter what, it has to be less of a target than London. Please, love, if you won't go for your own sake, then go for Anne's.'

She moved closer to him, lifting the shawl from the baby's face. 'Do you think I'd ever put Anne at risk? I always go down the cellar the minute the siren sounds, and the walls are as thick as anything you'll find in the underground, at least that's what Mrs Allen says, and she should know. She's lived in the place for over seventy years. We are better off down there than we would be in any Anderson or Morrison shelter.'

'And if there's a direct hit?'

'Do you know the odds against that happening?'

'It happens,' he reiterated stubbornly.

'If I'd gone to Wales when you'd wanted me to, Anne would have been born there. I doubt you'd have even been given leave to come down and see us.'

'Of course I would have.'

'A day or two at most, if anything. Your radio show is popular, you're doing wonders for the morale of the troops. The powers that be won't let you go until the war's over, and by then Anne could be old enough to be married. Don't you want to see your daughter grow up?' she pleaded.

'Her safety has to come first.'

'Safe is with us. I want every advantage for our child that I never had, especially a family. And that means a father as well as a mother.'

'Do you think I like the idea of you leaving?' He wrapped his arm around Jane's shoulders as he dropped a kiss on Anne's forehead.

'No. So that's settled,' she smiled triumphantly.

'It is not.'

'You just said you didn't want us to go, I don't want to, and Anne certainly doesn't.'

'Jane!' he exclaimed in exasperation.

'It's time for her feed,' she declared, effectively closing the argument. Taking the baby from his arms she held Anne's face close to her own for a moment, before tucking her back into her pram. Refusing to be mollified, the baby fought free from the covers. Pounding the air with her small fists she screwed her face into the wrinkled, crimson ball that generally preceded an outburst.

'She was perfectly happy where she was.' Haydn kicked the brake free on the pram.

'In her father's arms? If you have your way she'll have to get used to doing without your cuddles.'

'I'd come down to see you every chance I'd get.'

'That wouldn't be very often when you work every day.'

'I'd demand a weekend off a month,' Haydn asserted unconvincingly, glancing at his watch. He had a busy afternoon ahead of him in the studio. Requests and letters from the troops to wade through with the researchers; an ENSA tour of the North African front to plan that he hadn't dared mention to Jane—yet; three new songs to rehearse, and that was before he even began his four-hour broadcasting stint on the Overseas Service.

When he'd been commissioned into the army as a second lieutenant purely on the strength of his singing voice and popularity, and 'temporarily' assigned to the BBC's Overseas Service, the idea of talking to the men who were actually doing the fighting had been awesome and exciting, but familiarity had long since extinguished any sense of wonder; and since Anne's arrival even the excitement had worn off. It wasn't that he was disenchanted with his work, rather that he was more enchanted with family life. An enchantment that must have overcome his common sense, he reflected soberly as he pushed the pram towards the spot where the park gates would have been, if they hadn't been salvaged for scrap iron. How else could he explain to himself, or his family, why he hadn't frogmarched his pregnant wife to Paddington and put her on the first train to Wales when France had fallen and the blitz had started in earnest.

'I really want you to go this time, Jane,' he murmured, deciding that the dripping tap principle of wearing her objections down was the best option left open to him.

'We'll talk about it.'

He remembered the tiny corpse. 'There's no more talking to be done.'

'Just look at your daughter. How can you bear to send her away?'

'Because I love her. And her mother's not

too bad either.' He slipped his arm around Jane's waist as they walked past the vegetable and potato beds that had replaced last year's geraniums. 'I hate working afternoons, but there's nothing I can do about it. You promise, the minute the siren sounds ...'

'We'll go down the cellar. But I can't understand why you're so edgy, there hasn't been a raid in weeks. Besides, you're the one taking all the risks by travelling through London, not us. We'll be as safe as houses, won't we, sweetheart?' Jane rocked the pram handle in an attempt to still Anne's whimpering.

Haydn glanced up at the jagged, roofless houses silhouetted against the skyline like hollowed-out, rotted teeth. He wished Jane hadn't used the hackneyed expression. It had an ironic ring to it now that so many of London's buildings had been reduced to rubble.

'Looks like we've had the quietest part of the day.' Jane said the first thing that came into her head in an attempt to divert Haydn's attention from the subject of evacuation. The park was filling up with people on lunch breaks, the streets outside clogging with queues that snaked out of the shops; all of London seemed to be engaged in the endless quest for increasingly rare foodstuffs, preferably off the ration books.

'One of the advantages of Madam getting us up at the crack of dawn.' He wheeled the pram across the road to the block that housed their two-roomed flat. When he had first arrived in London it had seemed comfortable. Even Jane had thought so before Anne had put in

29

an appearance. Now he could only marvel that such a small scrap of humanity could commandeer such a vast expanse of living and storage space.

Leaning on the handle, Haydn lifted the front wheels and manoeuvred the coach pram into the hallway. Distrusting the lift, Jane took the baby from the pram while he dragged it up the stairs to the first floor.

'You have time for tea?' she asked as they walked into the room that did duty as hall, living room and kitchen rolled into one.

'Tea is about all I do have time for. I'll make it while you see to Madam.'

'I'm amazed you can even think of anything else after the breakfast you ate this morning.' Jane carried Anne over to a Rexine-covered sofa, so firmly stuffed with horsehair its surface was as solid as the sideboard. She changed the baby while Haydn disappeared behind the curtain that hid the sink and cooker.

The flat was blessed with a small bathroom. The sink was cracked and the bath had lost its enamel in places, but after Jane's upbringing in orphanages and workhouses, she considered it the height of luxury. But with Anne already grizzling there wasn't time to linger. She plunged the nappy into the bucket, washed her hands, unbuttoned her blouse, and was lifting Anne to her breast when Haydn reappeared with a tray loaded with cups, saucers, plates and the last two slices of an eggless sponge she had made two days ago.

'Mock duck all right for supper?' Jane pulled

30

Anne back slightly to stop her from choking on the initial glut of milk.

'I'd rather you ate early and went to bed in the cellar. You look exhausted.'

'It's only this heat. After the winter it's come as a shock.' She gently caressed the small body pressed against her own, wiping away the froth of milk that spilled out of Anne's mouth with a clean handkerchief. 'Besides, cooking makes the time pass more quickly. I think I have enough dripping left to make some Welsh cakes.'

'I'm not even going to ask what goes into mock duck, but please leave the carrots out of the Welsh cakes this time.' Haydn walked over to Jane, unable to resist the temptation to stroke the baby's soft, downy cheek with his little finger. Anne opened one deep blue eye and squinted at him sideways.

'How can anyone say babies can't see properly?' he asked. Anne's mouth relaxed; she loosened her hold on Jane's nipple as she continued to stare at him. 'If ever there's a knowing look it's that one.'

'Don't distract her. She won't take her full feed, then she'll get cross, wake again in half an hour and there'll be no supper for either of us.'

'Sorry.' He returned to the table. 'But you promise, no carrots, or any other peculiar ingredients in my Welsh cakes?'

Jane stared at him, a tantalising smile curving the corners of her generous, full-lipped mouth, her eyes enormous dark pools in her sun-flushed face, reminding him exactly why he had fallen in love with her.

'I have a recipe for pea purée pancakes.'

'Now I know why the Germans are biding their time before invading. They've heard of Lord Woolton and they're waiting until we all die from malnutrition or food poisoning.'

'The kettle,' she reminded.

He dived behind the curtain and made the tea. When he turned around, Jane was lifting their daughter from her breast. Head lolling, milk bubbling on her lips, Anne was already asleep.

'Can I put her down?'

'If you don't wake her.'

Carrying Anne to the pram, he folded back the blankets and gently laid the baby on her side, tucking the covers securely around her small figure. 'Shall I pour your tea?'

'I'd better wash first.' Jane returned to the bathroom and filled the sink with water. Haydn followed, standing behind her as she slipped off her blouse. 'You looking to see if I'm getting fat?' she asked as she sponged herself down.

'No.' His breath caught in his throat as she glanced up and saw him watching her in the mirror. 'Just admiring my very beautiful wife.' Reaching out, he caressed her shoulders and nuzzled the back of her neck.

'I'm all wet,' she remonstrated.

'Soap and water will soon dry off.'

'I'm amazed you have the energy after last night.'

'Anne needs a brother or sister. And the sooner the better. An only child invariably gets spoilt.'

'Not much chance of her being an only child with you around.'

He bent his head to hers.

'Don't you have to be in work?'

'Work can wait for ten minutes.'

'Haydn ...'

The half-hearted protest faded into silence as he pulled her round to face him. His lips sought hers as he unfastened the button on her skirt. It fell around her ankles in a soft swish of cotton.

'Please, don't ask me to leave you,' she whispered.

'It won't be for long.' Slipping her petticoat and bloomers over her hips, he explored her naked body with his hands, pulling her even closer.

'And in the meantime you'd find someone else to do this with?' She needed reassurance, not only because her body hadn't yet recovered from the demands pregnancy had made on it, but because she'd met some of the women he worked with. Beautiful women, like Ruth and Marilyn Simmonds who sang chorus for all the radio stars. She knew they'd like nothing better than an affair with a celebrity as good-looking and famous as Haydn in the hope that some of his success would rub off on them.

'You and Anne are the only women I want in my life.'

'I need to spend part of every day with you to believe it.'

'Why, when you know I love you?'

'Because you're blue-eyed, blond and handsome, and I'm mousy and ugly; and because I saw the way the chorus girls in the Town Hall fought over you before you married me.' Haydn's roving eye and numerous affairs had been legendary, and not only in Pontypridd.

'I promised you on our wedding day that I'd never stray again, and I meant it.' Taking her weight in his arms, he pushed her gently on to the rug in front of the sink, staring at her while he stripped off his uniform. They would have been more comfortable in the bedroom, but his need was too great, too urgent. His last thought before entering her body was how incredibly, wonderfully kind the fates had been in giving him a loving wife, a beautiful daughter and a home in England at a time when so many other couples had been forcibly separated with no hope of knowing when, if ever, they'd see, let alone live with one another again.

Perhaps Jane was right. Perhaps they should stay together and brave the bombs. After all, who, other than Hitler, knew where they were going to fall next?

CHAPTER 2

'She's buried beneath a tree in a corner of the cemetery in Bardi. When the war's over I'd like to go back there and erect a headstone. Perhaps you could help me pick out a suitable inscription. It's a quiet spot, pretty in spring and summer when the flowers bloom.' And desolate in winter, Ronnie thought, keeping the last observation to himself.

'We all knew the tuberculosis could return at any time.' Evan Powell didn't want to dwell on his youngest daughter's deathbed, but the images conjured up by his son-in-law insisted on intruding into his mind. He laid his gnarled and battered miner's hand on Ronnie's shoulder. 'She loved you very much. You gave her hope and extra years, which was more than the rest of us could do. I can understand you not wanting to move in with us, but Maud's death doesn't alter the fact that you're part of our family, Ronnie. Don't be a stranger. I know how happy you made her, because she wrote and told us. I've kept all her letters. You're welcome to call in and read them any time you want.'

'Thank you.' Ronnie had no intention of doing anything of the kind. Tina and Gina had meant well when they'd organised this supper so everyone who had loved Maud could mourn her passing, but it was proving pure purgatory.

Facing Maud's father and sister and receiving condolences stirred bitter, painful memories and a guilt that was never far below the surface. Not for the first time he wondered what was the point in carrying on, when all he loved and cared for was buried in the cemetery in Bardi, and he was responsible for putting it there.

'She loved Italy, and we all knew how much you sacrificed to take her there,' Bethan John, Maud's sister murmured.

Ronnie nodded briefly before looking away.

'Have you decided where you're going to live?' Bethan asked, sensing he couldn't take much more sympathy.

'I came in so late last night I slept on the floor of Tina's living room, but I moved into Laura's house today. From what Tina says she'll be away for some time, and there's no way the authorities will allow any house to stand empty with the demand for accommodation for evacuees and munition workers, so it's probably just as well I'm there to keep an eye on the place. Although in my opinion it's Tina who should be living in Laura's, not me, but she absolutely refuses to leave the café.'

'She's done wonders with those two rooms.'

'Wonders or not, it's hardly the sort of place a young girl should be living in alone.'

'She's not a young girl any more, Ronnie, she's a married woman who has taken on responsibilities a lot of men would have run from.'

He looked over to the other side of the room where his younger sister, Gina was clinging to the arm of her husband Luke. 'I'm going to need time to adjust to the idea of my two little sisters being married.'

'They may be young, but they've got their heads screwed on and their priorities sorted,' Evan observed. 'And Luke's been a great help. He puts in a full six-day week in the pit, and then spends his Sundays doing the heavy work in the cafés.'

'I hope to take over some of that.'

'Not before you've given yourself time to recover,' Bethan warned, glancing at the crutch propped next to him. 'Old Dr Evans told me you'd called into the surgery this morning. He was appalled at the state of the wounds in your legs. If you don't rest and eat a lot better than you have been, you'll run the risk of gangrene setting in.'

'Nice to know my medical condition is being discussed in detail.'

'Only by the staff in the surgery. Dr Evans has put you down for daily district nurse visits.'

'And you're the district nurse?'

'Someone had to take the position.'

'But you've got two babies.'

'And help to look after them. I didn't have much choice in the matter. There's such a shortage of nurses, no one applied for the post, so they approached me. But I caution you now brother-in-law or not, I do a thorough job. I've seen your notes. You're in a terrible state, and unless you do exactly what I tell you to, you'll find yourself in hospital under the loving care of a ward sister who'll make Hitler look like a fairy godmother.'

'I'm beginning to regret coming home. Is that Diana over there?' he asked, noticing a slight resemblance between the attractive young woman sitting next to Tina, and the young girl who had been Maud's best friend as well as cousin.

'You see a change?'

'It's incredible. Not just her appearance. She seems so confident and sophisticated. When I last saw her she was afraid to look me in the eye.'

'Few people dared to in those days,' Bethan reminded. 'You had a ferocious temper, and a reputation for driving anyone who worked in the cafés to the point of exhaustion.'

'I did, didn't I?' His voice was flat, devoid of emotion, almost as though they were discussing someone else.

'Ronnie, I'm sorry, I have to go.' Alma Raschenko crossed the room, already wearing her hat and coat. 'I just wanted to offer my condolences. Maud was a lovely girl. Everyone who knew her was fond of her.'

Ronnie averted his eyes as he murmured the inevitable 'thank you'. Alma had not only worked for him when he'd run the Tumble café for his father, she'd also been his mistress until he'd fallen head over heels in love with Maud. The last time he had seen her she'd flung a coffee cup at his head, and screamed that she hated him and wished him and Maud dead. He wondered if she remembered the ugly scene.

She'd had every right to be angry with him at the time. He only hoped she wasn't going to dredge up the memory now. He couldn't cope with his own guilt, let alone anyone else's.

Evan left his chair and drew Bethan aside. 'I wrote to Haydn after work, but someone will have to tell your mother.'

'I went to see her this afternoon. I thought the news of Ronnie's return would soon travel up from the café to the Rhondda and better she hear it from me than someone else.'

'How did she take it?'

'She knows that I visit you and Phyllis, so she wouldn't let me into Uncle Joseph's house. I told her on the doorstep. It wasn't pleasant.'

'I'm sorry, Beth. I should have done it myself.'

'If she wouldn't let me over the doorstep what makes you think she would have let you into the street?'

He tried to smile at her poor joke and failed. He had thought nothing could compare with the pain of losing his son Eddie at Dunkirk. He'd been wrong. When he'd come home from work to find Ronnie sitting in his back kitchen with the news that Maud had died a year and a half ago he felt as though someone had physically wrenched the heart from his body. All that time when he had believed Maud was if not entirely safe, because of the war, at least well and happy with her husband, she'd been dead. Even now he was conscious of Bethan watching him with a professional eye. He gripped her hand briefly before leaving her to join Phyllis,

39

his common-law wife.

Ronnie was still talking to Alma, so Bethan went to find Tina and Diana. She had never needed their company more. Maud's death had been a wretched shock; her mother's response to the news even more so. She could still hear the bitter angry words Elizabeth Powell had flung after her as she'd fled to her car.

' "As ye sow so shall ye reap." When I married your father I took the Devil into my bed. I tried to fight his sinful ways, to bring my children to the paths of righteousness, but I failed. And how I failed. Maud's lung sickness was just one manifestation of the birthright of evil your father bestowed on all of you. Maud deserved to die for living out her life in a land of papists and heathens, just as Eddie deserved to die by the sword for seeking violence in the boxing ring. Your time will come, my girl. As will Haydn's. Mark my words. I know both of you consort with the Satan who spawned you. You sit at his table with his whore, you recognise his bastard, but God sees. He'll punish you by damning you to hell, along with Maud and Eddie. And perhaps then, when you're all writhing in the eternal fires, I'll finally get some peace.'

'Good God, Charlie? Is it you?' the stationmaster asked, as a broad-built, stocky figure with pale hair that gleamed silver in the blackout, stepped closer to the puddle of torchlight he was using to read tickets.

'It is,' Charlie Raschenko replied flatly in his

guttural Russian accent, as he shouldered his kitbag.

'So they finally gave you leave?'

'A few days,' Charlie replied noncommittally as he retrieved his rail pass and stowed it in his breast pocket. Closing his ears against the guard's whistle that was signalling the train to move out, he turned and negotiated the wide stone flight of steps that led from the platform of Pontypridd Station into station yard. Standing in the light of a half-moon that seemed unnaturally bright after months of winter blackout, he breathed in the cool, night air and looked out over the Tumble.

The scene before him had remained wonderfully, absurdly unchanged in a world gone mad. Like a reassuring glimpse of normality after a horrific nightmare. The darkened silhouette of the last bus rattling out of the old tram road towards Broadway; a flash of light from the doorway of Ronconi's café opposite as someone lifted the blackout curtain too wide; the high-pitched cry of Joey Rees the retired boxer, calling 'Echo' as he left the White Hart in an attempt to sell his last copies of the wartime-thinned pages of the Cardiff evening paper.

Turning away from the women touting for trade behind him, he closed his eyes and gripped the cord of his kitbag until it cut into the palm of his hand. He was home! For the first time in thirteen months, one week, three days and nine hours his wife was within reach, and he was determined that for the next seventy-two

41

hours they would forget there was a war. And afterwards—best not to think about afterwards.

Setting his sights on Taff Street, he pushed his cap to the back of his head and headed for the gap in the low, red-brick wall that marked the boundary of the yard. Listening warily for traffic, he stepped off the pavement on to the road. As he kicked a ball of paper from his path, the fishy, vinegary smell of cockles wafted to his nostrils, bringing with it a flood of nostalgia for the old, uneventful, pre-war Pontypridd days.

It was a Wednesday—market day—and if he knew the locals, not even a war would be allowed to interrupt Pontypridd market. Although it was late, he heard footsteps echoing along the street, and laughter, the deep resonant tones of a man's voice joined by high-pitched feminine giggles. He drew his breath in sharply before remembering where he was. No one other than the Germans had laughed in the country he had just left since the autumn of 1939, but then he'd forgotten that the war that had annihilated freedom in most of Europe and rained devastation on London and the Home Counties, where he was theoretically stationed, had brought munitions factories and work to the Welsh valleys; an employment that was finally putting an end to the deprivation of the depression.

The clock on St Catherine's church struck the hour as he passed Rivelin's and crossed the road from Woolworth's to the New Inn. His step quickened as he hurried past the entrance to Market Square, heading for the

42

fountain and the shop with the comfortable flat above. Would Alma be sitting in the living room listening to the radio? Or would she be in bed? He only hoped that Alma's mother hadn't changed her lifetime habit of early nights. He had been dreaming about this homecoming for months, and couldn't bear the thought of anyone, not even his mother-in-law, witnessing his first moments with his wife.

He and Alma had what was left of tonight. And tomorrow? It was half-day. Alma had written to tell him that she had taken on four assistants since he'd left to join the army. He hadn't understood why she'd needed so many for just one cooked meat and pie shop when meat was so heavily rationed, but surely the paid help would be able to manage the business between them tomorrow. Thursday morning had never been a busy one, which was why he'd urged his CO to include a Thursday in his leave pass.

He slowed his step when he saw the Gothic outline of the Victorian fountain gleaming palely ahead. Stepping on to the plinth surrounding it, he swung his bag from his shoulder and leaned against the stonework, staring up at the blacked-out windows of the shop and the flat above.

He would have given a great deal to have been allowed a glimpse beyond the curtains before he walked in. Perhaps if he crept up the stairs quietly? He patted his jacket trying to remember if he'd tossed his keys into his kitbag when he'd packed, or slipped them into one of his many pockets. Balking at the idea of emptying his bag out on the pavement, he began searching for them in his uniform.

A door opened in the wall of shops across the road. He turned as a low murmur of voices drifted out of Ronconi's restaurant. It was way past normal opening hours and he could only wonder that Pontypridd had remained so unscathed by war and the presence of Hitler's army camped across the Channel that people could think of holding a party.

A couple drifted ghost-like out of the shadows and crossed the street. The man was swinging himself forward with the aid of a crutch, the woman walking at his side, their heads close together. The woman's hair was drained grey by the moonlight, but Charlie didn't need to exercise his imagination to picture the flame-coloured tints in her curls, or the depth of colour that glowed in her sea-green eyes. The couple paused in front of the fountain, the man balancing awkwardly while the woman embraced him. She murmured something too low for Charlie to catch, but the man's voice was louder.

'It happened a long time ago. We're both different people now. Forget it, Alma.'

'I'm sorry, Ronnie. So very sorry.' Resting her hands on his shoulders she stood on tiptoe and kissed his cheek.

Charlie's back stiffened. Ronnie Ronconi back from Italy! He stepped out of the shadows.

Alma looked up and saw him. 'Charlie ...'

He sidestepped her embrace as she ran,

arms outstretched towards him. 'You haven't introduced me to your friend,' he said.

'You remember, Ronnie.' Alma hung back as Charlie ignored the hand Ronnie offered. Suddenly she realised how the scene must have looked. 'If you'll excuse us, Charlie hasn't been home in over a year.'

'Of course, you must have things to talk about. Congratulations on marrying Alma ...' A door opened and closed and Ronnie found himself talking to the empty street.

Cocooned in a soundproof studio, his thoughts concentrated on putting out a good show that would give the serving troops a taste of home and a momentary escape from the harsher realities of war, while observing the official line of 'not too strong lest it bring on homesickness and undermine morale' Haydn managed to push his anxieties about Jane to the back of his mind; but the minute transmission ceased and the door opened he heard it—the sickening roar of what sounded like thousands of planes flying overheard. Before he could speak, the guns opened up in a barrage that made speech unintelligible and thought impossible. With the whole building shuddering around him, he retreated into the booth with Joe, his sound engineer.

'I don't remember it being this noisy before,' Joe complained.

'Probably because it wasn't.' Hands shaking, Haydn pulled a packet of cigarettes from his pocket and offered them to Joe.

'We can't stay here. You game to make a run down to the basement?'

'You go if you want to, I'm for home.'

'Home! Don't be an ass. You'll never get there in one piece.'

The tea lady burst through the door, dragging her trolley behind her. 'It's like bonfire night in the OK Corral out there,' she announced cheerfully, as soon as the door shut out the din. 'I've never seen anything like the size of the flares, and you should have heard the gun barrage—'

'We did,' Joe interrupted, instinctively ducking as the room shook and a chunk of plaster fell from the ceiling. Missing his head by a few inches it landed on the floor, shattering into crumbs on the polished cork tiles.

'Good, I thought I saw the tea trolley heading this way.' A sub-editor from the newsroom joined them. 'If I'd known it was this quiet in here I would have made a beeline for a studio when the sirens started.'

'Any word on where they're targeting yet?' Haydn asked as the tea lady started filling cups from a lukewarm teapot.

'We've had the first unofficial estimates. It looks as though there's at least five hundred and fifty enemy planes up there, so you tell me, where aren't they targeting?' The news hound turned Haydn's question back on him.

'The river? The East End?'

'That's a fair guess. They always come a cropper.'

'Come on, Haydn, you know it's too early to

say for certain.' Joe took his arm. 'Let's go down to the basement and sit it out. I know where we can find a bottle of whisky.'

'I'd rather try to get home.'

'You got a death wish?' the sub-editor enquired tactlessly as he picked up his tea and left.

'It's not far,' Haydn protested to Joe, as soon as the door closed and he could be heard.

'Far enough for you to get blown to bits on the streets? And how do you expect me to explain that to a nice, sensible girl like Jane? "Sorry, love, but he insisted on viewing the blitz first hand?" '

'But she could be ...'

'In the cellar, tucked up fast asleep with the baby.'

It was Joe's voice, calm, matter-of-fact, that finally broke Haydn's resolve to tear out of the building right then and there.

'You really think she will be all right?'

'As all right as anyone can be in this God-forsaken city tonight. Come on, let's find that whisky, go downstairs, and get plastered. At least we've a bloody good excuse this time.'

'She's still awake ...' Mrs Lane faltered when she saw a man walking up the stairs behind Alma. 'Oh it's you, Mr Charlie,' she stammered in relief, embarrassment scorching her cheeks. But then, it was hardly her fault for thinking the worst. Not when Ronnie Ronconi was back and everyone was waiting to see if he and Alma would pick up where they had left off, now that poor Maud was dead and Charlie away soldiering. And it wasn't just Alma. It was practically all the young women in town. Munitions money had given them the wherewithal to visit pubs—and drink. An unheard-of phenomenon before the war. Morality was being flung out of the window as all the unmarried girls and half the married ones used the war, their husbands' absence, and loneliness as an excuse to comfort any and every soldier who passed through Pontypridd.

'Mrs Lane.' Charlie touched his cap as he swung his kitbag down on to the landing.

'Thank you for sitting with Mam. I'll go in and see to her now.' Alma pushed past Mrs Lane and went into her mother's room, closing the door behind her.

'It's nice to see you home.' Mrs Lane reached for her coat. 'These past months have been hard on Alma. You away, her mother on her last legs, all the responsibility of trying to run two shops at opposite ends of the town ...'

The news of Alma's mother's illness and a second shop came as a complete surprise to Charlie, but skilled in the art of concealing his emotions, he gave Mrs Lane no indication that Alma hadn't written to inform him of all the happenings.

'... and of course it's only a matter of time. Days, or so old Dr John told us this morning. That's why I was so pleased when that nice Nurse John persuaded Alma to go to the restaurant tonight. Not that it was really a party. More of a wake for poor Maud Ronconi,

48

Powell that was. To think of her being dead and buried for over a year and a half, and her own father and sister not knowing a thing about it. God only knows, none of us have much to be happy about these days, but poor Nurse John has less than most. One brother dead at Dunkirk, now her sister gone, and her husband in a prison camp for the duration. And then there's the Ronconi girls. What with the rest of the family being enemy aliens and forced to leave Pontypridd, and now their brother coming home a widower ...' Alma's mother's bedroom door opened and Mrs Lane started guiltily. 'Well, listen to me going on when you're on leave. You got long, Mr Charlie?' she asked, utilising Charlie's nickname as both Christian and surname, because like the majority of people in Pontypridd she couldn't get her tongue around his Russian names.

'A couple of days,' he answered briefly, glancing at Alma.

'I'll see you to the door, Mrs Lane.' Alma preceded Mrs Lane down the stairs, leaving the woman no option but to follow her. 'Constable Davies is waiting in Ronconi's to walk you home.'

'There's no need. I'll be fine.'

'He insisted. You know his ideas on preventative policing in the blackout. Thank you again.'

Silencing her old neighbour's protests with a kiss on the cheek, Alma ushered her into the street. She slammed the bolts across the door then she mounted the stairs, hearing her mother's querulous voice crying out before she even reached the first floor.

'You didn't tell me your mother was ill,' Charlie admonished.

'There was no point when you couldn't do anything about it.'

'What else haven't you told me?'

'I'm sorry, I have to see to my mother.' Ignoring his question she laid her hand on the bedroom door. 'I told her you were here.' Without waiting for him to reply she walked into the room, leaving the door ajar for her husband to follow. Her mother was lying, a smaller, more shrunken figure than Charlie remembered, in the centre of a vast double bed. Alma walked towards her. 'Charlie's home, Mam. Here he is, come to see you.'

The old woman's eyes, the only part of her that seemed alive, although she had been blind ever since Charlie had known her, moved restlessly in their sockets.

'Mrs Moore,' Charlie greeted her softly as he wrapped his fingers around the old woman's hand.

'We think she can hear, but she can't talk. It's a stroke.'

Charlie kissed the old woman's forehead before retreating into the living room. Leaving the light burning in the passage he closed the door, opened the blackout and looked down on the moonlit street. Ronconi's restaurant was open, the room behind it in darkness. He stared at the crowd milling outside, picking out Ronnie, Bethan John's arm locked into his. Understandable, he allowed grudgingly, considering Maud had been her sister. There were other men behind Ronnie, one a tall, fair-haired fellow he recognised as a conscientious objector who'd been given a job in the pit. He had his arms around the shoulders of two girls, neither of whom appeared to be unduly concerned by his familiarity.

Hearing Alma's step in the passageway he pulled down the blind and switched on the lamp as she walked through the door.

'I'm sorry, she's very restless. She hasn't slept through a night in over six months now,' Alma apologised as she stood before Charlie, staring at him as though she couldn't believe he was really there.

'You should have written to tell me she was ill.'

'Even if I had, you couldn't have done anything except worry. Besides, we both know you can't always read my letters when I send them.'

'Mrs Lane told me you'd opened another shop,' he broke in harshly. 'Didn't you have enough to do with running one?'

'It was too good an opportunity to miss. I've gone into partnership with Wyn and Diana Rees. When he closed his sweetshop in High Street we restocked it with our pies and reopened it. It's doing so well we're thinking of opening another, perhaps in Treforest or Rhydyfelin.'

'You've become quite the businesswoman.'

'I thought you'd be pleased.'

'At finding my wife in another man's arms?'

He raised his eyes to meet her steady gaze.
'Ronnie only came back late last night. Maud's dead.'

'Mrs Lane told me.'

'He's heartbroken, Charlie.'

'And he needs you to comfort him?'

She took a deep breath, squared her shoulders and faced him head on. 'You of all people should know that my relationship with Ronnie ended when he fell in love with Maud.'

'But now Maud's dead he's looking to you for consolation?'

'No more than from any of his other friends. And that's all we are to one another now, Charlie. Friends,' she emphasised, pitching her voice deliberately low in an effort to keep her temper. 'It's you I married, and you I love.'

'And if I hadn't come home just now?'

'I would have held Ronnie's hand, kissed his other cheek and sent him on his way. Please, Charlie, I don't want to waste whatever time we've got talking about Ronnie.' Slowly, tentatively she walked over to him. When he didn't step away from her she wrapped her arms around his chest. 'It's been so long. I was beginning to wonder if you were ever coming back.'

Despite the jealousy that seeped like poison through his mind, Charlie returned her embrace, but there was an awkwardness between them that was rooted as much in their long separation and the reason for his leave as in the incident he had witnessed between Alma and Ronnie. Before either of them had time to ask any

52

more questions, a soft moan echoed down the passage.

'That's Mam again.' Alma reluctantly pulled away from him. 'I'm sorry, I'll be back as soon as I can.'

Charlie unlaced his shoes and shrugged off his jacket. Stretching out in what had been his favourite chair, he laid his head against the backrest watching the minutes tick by on the clock on the mantelpiece. One minute ... two ... was it wrong of him to be angry with the men who'd stayed at home? Men who'd been given work in the pits and the munitions factories, as Ronnie probably would be. Work that enabled them to make free and easy with his wife, and not only his wife. Bethan John's husband, Andrew, was in a German POW camp for the duration, just like Angelo Ronconi. And William Powell and Tony Ronconi were away on active service somewhere. Tony and Angelo weren't married, but he had recognised William's wife, Tina, and Jenny, Eddie Powell's widow, in the crowd.

Would William and Andrew be greeted on their return by wives who'd become accustomed to receiving the attentions of other men? Wives who'd made lives for themselves that no longer included husbands? Even aside from the incident with Ronnie, Alma had seemed like a stranger. All he had was seventy-two hours, less travelling time, to make her remember who she was married to—but knowing what he did about his future, did he have a right to?

Woken by the whine of the all-clear, Haydn wondered why the bed was so hard. He reached out for Jane and his arm hit the empty whisky bottle. Disorientated, he opened his eyes in alarm as it clattered noisily, rolling over the stretch of concrete between the straw mattress Joe occupied and his own. A chorus of disgruntled voices rose around him, protesting at the din, then he remembered the raid that had driven him to take refuge in the basement.

He peered into the gloom. A candle flickered forlornly in the corner of the cellar. The effort it took to focus hurt his eyes. It had been months since he had experienced this kind of morning-after feeling. Just lifting his head off the makeshift pillow he had concocted out of his jacket brought a sickening tide of nausea. The last thing he recalled was watching Joe drain the dregs from the bottle, and thinking that as the whisky had gone, he might as well leave the building, raid or no raid, as he'd never be able to sleep for worrying about Jane and Anne.

'What time is it?' Joe mumbled thickly.

Haydn held up his wrist in the direction of the candlelight and peered at his watch. 'Just after four-thirty.'

'Bring me tea and shaving water at nine.' Joe pulled the improvised bedding over his head and burrowed down as deep as the thin layer of straw would allow.

Haydn threw off the army surplus blanket, sending a shower of dust over Joe as he climbed to his feet.

'Where are you going?' Joe's head appeared

54

over the edge of his overcoat.

'Home. See you later?'

'At showtime. No offence intended, but I'd prefer to limit our relationship to work and social from now on. No more all-nighters. You snore a bloody sight louder than my wife.'

'Only when I'm fed whisky.' Haydn stooped and picked up the empty bottle.

'Your turn to supply the goods tonight.'

'I'll be happy to lay one down for the future, but I'm hoping the Luftwaffe has run out of bombs after last night.'

He slipped on his uniform jacket when he reached street level. The air was bracing after the close, humid atmosphere of the cellar, but London seemed unnaturally quiet, even for early morning. There wasn't a milk cart, policeman or paper boy in sight. He dropped the empty whisky bottle into a glass salvage bin set by the door, turned up his collar and walked to the corner. Stunned, he stopped, looked, and looked again, his mind refusing to believe the evidence of his eyes.

What had been a street when he'd gone into work, was now a smoking ruin. Blackened men in the boiler suits and tin hats of ARP wardens worked stolidly against a backdrop of dying flames and smouldering rubble.

'They need help down at the FAP, mate.'

'FAP?' Haydn repeated dully.

'First aid post. You all right, mate? Haven't been hit by falling masonry or anything like that?'

'Is it like this down by the river?'

'Who knows? It's as much as we can do to keep up with what's happening here, without worrying about what's happening down the road.'

Haydn's only thought was of Jane and Anne. Turning on his heel he started to run, recklessly, blindly, in the direction of the flat he had left the afternoon before. He lost count of the number of times he was turned back at barricades that fenced off burning streets, bomb craters and UXB sites. The sun rose somewhere above the smoke and destruction, bathing what was left of the city in a pale, grey light that wasn't as kind as the fire-lit darkness. People were crawling out of shelters into a sea of desolation and dereliction. He passed them, scarcely registering their pale, numbed faces as they searched for something—anything—that was unscathed and familiar. Ahead was a patch of green. He thought he recognised the park opposite his street. Quickening his pace he raced towards it.

When he reached the area he had to stop. Bending double he clutched his knees, fighting for breath. After a few moments he heaved himself upright, pushed his hair back from his eyes and ran his tongue over his lips. They were dry, covered with dust and ashes. He moved off again feeling as though he were struggling against elastic bands that bound his chest and tugged him back in the direction he had come from. His mind was suffused with images of Jane and the baby. All he could think of was reaching them and holding them tight. Two more steps. He rounded the curve that hid their block from view.

His heart stopped. His mind froze. He closed his eyes but when he opened them moments later nothing had changed. There it was again, the square, solid building that had been home, with the smashed roof and smouldering, skeletal walls that signalled a direct hit.

CHAPTER 3

Alma woke with a start, opening her eyes to see the lamp still burning on her mother's bedside table. She lifted her head from the eiderdown, straightened her back against the chair she'd slept in and read the clock. Six! She should have been up and supervising the baking in the kitchen of the shop an hour ago. She had no clear recollection of falling asleep, only her mother moaning every time she had tried to leave the room. Pain and confusion had kept the old lady awake for most of the night, but now that morning had finally arrived she lay quiet and peaceful. Alma checked she was still breathing before creeping out on to the landing. It was then she remembered Charlie—was he really home—or had she dreamed it?

She pushed open the door to the living room and saw her husband deep in sleep, stretched out on his easy chair, his feet resting on the brass log box she used to keep her knitting in. For the first time in her life she found herself actually resenting her mother's frailty. If Charlie had mentioned how much leave he had been given, she couldn't recall him telling her. His only free time in over a year and her mother had to be seriously ill.

The doorbell rang. Was that the sound that had woken her? Straightening her skirt and combing her curls with her fingers she closed the door softly behind her and tiptoed along the passage and down the stairs lest she wake either of the sleepers.

Bethan John was standing on the doorstep, neat in her district nurse's uniform, her cousin Diana behind her.

'We heard Charlie's home.'

Alma opened the door wider to let them in. 'He's asleep upstairs,' she whispered.

'And you haven't had a wink all night by the look of you?' Bethan shook her head at the creased silk blouse and crêpe skirt Alma had worn to the restaurant.

'Mam was very restless,' Alma murmured by way of an apology. 'Would you like a cup of tea?'

'We're not here to make work, but to do it,' Diana announced briskly. 'I'm taking over the management of the shop and Bethan is going to look after your mother.'

'But ...' Alma looked to Bethan in bewilderment.

'It's my day off, and after the news about Maud I'd rather be kept busy.'

'What about your children?'

'I've left mine with Phyllis, and Megan's caring for Diana's baby. It's half-day in all the shops so Diana will easily cope, especially as Wyn's offered to run their shops on his own. She'll sit with your mother now while I take you and Charlie home.'

'Home?'

'To my house,' Bethan answered.

'I couldn't leave Mam.'

'You've a husband home on leave, or so Ronnie told us last night. I know he's been away for a long time, but I didn't think it was long enough to forget Charlie. Go on off with you. Pack a case. You can have a bath and change your clothes at my place. I don't know how long Charlie's got, but Liza Clark's taken all my evacuees down to Phyllis's for the day. The older ones are going to school from Graig Avenue, and Liza's organised a picnic for the little ones, so you'll have the house to yourself until teatime, and Maisie and Liza will see that the children don't disturb you when they come home. They've been ordered to stay out of my bedroom and sitting room. It's hardly the most romantic place to spend a leave, but it's the best we can come up with at short notice.'

Bethan fell silent as Charlie appeared at the top of the stairs. He'd always been superbly fit, and while he'd run his butcher's stall he'd developed muscles like a wrestler's, but he was leaner than she remembered and harder, and there was a look in his ice-blue eyes that she hadn't seen before. She recalled something her father had said when they had been worried about the boys at the time of Dunkirk. That wherever Charlie was, he wasn't on the French coast. The war was proving difficult for all of them, but the strain mirrored on Charlie's face told her that it was proving more difficult for him than most.

'Is something wrong?' Charlie asked.

'Only that we've decided that you two should

spend whatever leave you have at my house. It will give Alma the break she needs from caring for her mother. I'll take over nursing Mrs Moore, and Diana will help in between looking after the shops.'

'You've got good staff, they won't need much supervising,' Diana declared, minimising her own contribution.

'I still don't know whether I should leave my mother ...' Alma began doubtfully.

'Penycoedcae is hardly the ends of the earth,' Bethan reminded her. 'If there is any change, or your mother comes round, I'll drive up there and bring you down.'

'You promise?'

'I promise,' Bethan agreed solemnly. 'Come on, hurry up. Both of you look as though you could do with a good rest.'

Charlie hesitated but only for a moment. 'I'll get my kitbag.'

Alma went upstairs. She checked on her mother before throwing a few things into an overnight case. It was only when they were walking out through the door that she realised she still didn't know exactly how much leave Charlie had been given.

'Sorry, mate, this street is closed. You'll have to walk around through Empress Avenue.'

'You don't understand!' Haydn confronted the ARP warden who was standing guard over the ruined block.

'You live here?' the man asked with a gentleness that irritated Haydn more than his

61

earlier refusal to allow him to pass.

'Of course I bloody well live here. Why else would I be trying to get in?'

'The walls are unstable. They're likely to fall in at any moment, Sir ... Sir ... you can't go in there ...'

Haydn pushed the man aside and walked over the shattered, splintered remains of the front door and windows, into what had been the hallway of the block of flats. A crash was followed by a cloud of dust and ashes that billowed out over the expanse of rubble that covered the street. The warden put a whistle to his lips.

'I couldn't stop him, sir,' he apologised to the senior officer who came running in response to his signal. 'I tried—'

A second crash sent the rescuers back choking, coughing and spluttering for breath. An ominous silence settled over the area, punctuated only by the creak of timbers, crackle of flames and distant screams and shouts.

'Right, start digging,' the senior officer commanded. 'Anyone left in this house before that silly bugger went inside?'

'We're not sure, sir.'

'Then ask someone! I've a feeling that this is going to be the usual story. Family safe in the nearest shelter while the idiot home on leave kills himself by rushing into a blitzed house.' The senior warden looked at what was left of the building. It had been a long night, and it promised to be an even longer day. Taking off his helmet he wiped his forehead with the back of his hand, then set to work.

'Fourth right at the top of the stairs on the first floor. When I took in the evacuees I turned Andrew's dressing room into a sitting room so I'd have somewhere quiet to retreat to when I needed it. It's small but cosy, and it's next door to the bedroom and bathroom. Maisie knows you're coming, she's already changed the bed and she'll bring up breakfast.' Bethan stopped the car on the gravel drive that swept round to the front door.

'Where are you going to sleep?' Charlie asked.

'When I'm not with Alma's mother, in my children's room.'

'I wanted to tell you how sorry I was about Eddie and Maud.' He reached out for her hand, sympathy etched on his face and in his eyes, and she understood something of the pain Ronnie had felt at receiving so many condolences the night before.

'Thank you, but if you don't mind we'll talk about them later, Charlie. How much leave have you got?'

'Three days.'

'They could have given you longer after all this time.'

'Some men in my unit haven't had any leave since the beginning. I'm lucky to get this much.'

Bethan turned to Alma in the back seat. 'Then you'd better see he makes the most of it. You're going back on Saturday morning, Charlie?'

'First thing.'

'If you don't mind us taking up your time, we could have a small party here Friday night. I'll invite Phyllis and my father, and anyone else you want to see. Think about it? Let me know tomorrow morning.'

'I will, and thank you,' he responded mechanically as he heaved his kitbag and Alma's small case out of the car. Maisie must have heard them coming because the door was already open.

'Mrs John said you'd be tired so I carried the toaster and chafing dishes up to her sitting room. There's porridge, scrambled eggs, bread, blackberry jam and tea. It's all ready. Would you like me to take your coats?'

'Thank you, Maisie.' Alma followed her into the house that Andrew John had bought for his wife when he had returned to Pontypridd after working in a London hospital. Bethan had altered it beyond all recognition during the last two years. The fine lawns had been dug up and turned into vegetable and potato gardens. The once elegant, tiled hall was awash with children's coats, prams, bicycles and rubber boots. Answering the plea for homes for evacuees, Bethan had put her name down to take four, but the hard pressed authorities had prevailed on her good nature, and she had ended up with six, plus a young girl who helped her to keep the brood in order. The maid Andrew had engaged before the war had long since departed to earn four times what Bethan could afford to pay her in the munitions factory, so she had taken an unmarried mother, Maisie Crockett, from the workhouse to help out, and feeling sorry for her, had ended up with Maisie's child as well. Three women and nine children, including Bethan's two, made for a very full house, but there was no sign of anyone except Maisie.

'Just stack the breakfast dishes when you've finished with them, Mrs Charlie. I'll get them when I come in. It's my morning for putting our order into Griffiths' shop and Pegler's Stores, so you'll have the house to yourself until the children finish school, and even then they won't come near Mrs John's rooms,' Maisie reassured them shyly as they walked across the hall.

'Mrs John said Liza Clark had taken the children down to Graig Avenue.' Alma glanced into what had been Andrew's pride and joy, the spacious formal drawing room. Bethan had packed the best furniture into the old groom's accommodation above the stables, and a threadbare, faded carpet, a couple of sagging sofas, and overflowing baskets of home-made wooden and rag toys were all the furnishings that adorned the once expensively decorated room.

'The weather's so fine, Mrs John thought the little ones would benefit from some fresh air. So Liza offered to take them over the mountain for a picnic.' Maisie led the way up the stairs.

Alma was amazed at Bethan's powers of organisation at such short notice, unless she'd sacrificed a quiet day she'd arranged for herself to Charlie's unexpected leave.

All the windows in the house had been

opened wide to the beautiful spring morning. She paused on the landing and gazed out over the fields. Barely two miles outside the town and they could have been in the heart of the countryside. The scent of apple and cherry blossom mixed with bluebells and newly ploughed earth wafted in on the warm, fresh air. Birds were singing. In the distance she could hear a dog barking and sheep bleating, and she suddenly realised that it had been a long time since she'd taken the leisure to enjoy the simple things in life.

Sensing Charlie waiting behind her she climbed up the final half a dozen steps. Bethan had been right. Andrew's dressing room was tiny but, just as she'd promised, it was also cosy. Two small easy chairs stood either side of the window, a round table between them set with chafing dishes warmed by candles, an electric toaster, bread, jam, sugar, milk and a scraping of butter in a small pot that Alma hoped Charlie wouldn't touch in case it was the last of Bethan's ration. Charlie dropped his kitbag by the door and in two strides was at the window.

'I'll bring up the boiling water for the tea and anything else you want, then I'll be off,' Maisie said.

'There's no need to wait on us, Maisie, I know where the kitchen is.'

'You sure, Mrs Charlie? Mrs John said you were to rest.'

'We'll be fine, Maisie. Thank you for all this.'

'It was nothing. Besides, I enjoyed doing it.'

Maisie bristled with pleasure at the praise before closing the door.

Charlie unbuttoned his jacket and sank into one of the chairs as Alma went downstairs to get the water for the tea.

'Seems to me Bethan has thought of everything,' Charlie observed when she returned.

'She always has been thoughtful, more so if anything since the war started. It can't be easy, knowing Andrew's stuck in a German prison camp for the duration and working as a district nurse. I don't know how she does it. She has a houseful of evacuees as well as her own two children, and little Eddie's only four months old.' Alma was grateful to Charlie for mentioning Bethan. It was easier to talk about her than it was to talk about themselves.

'There's a new baby?'

'Born seven months after Andrew was captured. She named him after Eddie. You got my letter?'

'Yes.'

They fell silent, remembering. Bethan's brother Eddie had worked for Charlie in the shop and they had both been fond of him. His death fighting with the rearguard in Dunkirk was one piece of news she hadn't kept from Charlie. She looked up at her husband, tracing the familiar lines of his face and features, thinking of all the nights she had lain awake dreaming of their reunion—a moment just like this—and now that it had actually arrived, all she could do was sit in strained silence.

As she reached across the table to lift the

lids on the chafing dishes, her hand accidentally brushed against Charlie's. He jerked back as though he'd been scalded.

'You're not still angry with me over Ronnie?' she asked, fighting back tears. Exhaustion and his sudden, unexpected return had made her vulnerable to emotions she usually kept firmly in check.

'No.'

'Bethan talked to you?'

He shook his head. 'I saw the look on his face last night. Before Mrs Lane told me about Maud I thought it was because he'd seen me. You were right, he is heartbroken.'

'As I'd be if anything happened to you,' she whispered.

He picked up the tea she'd poured.

'I'm sorry, Charlie, this probably isn't the homecoming you expected. My mother ill, the extra shop ...'

'You should have told me more in your letters. Even if I can't answer them right away, I read them as soon as I can.'

'I don't want to burden you with my problems when you have more serious things to think about.'

'If it concerns the shop, they are not your problems. They used to be mine; now I suppose I have to accept that they're ours.'

She didn't answer him. She didn't even know how to begin to tell him that she hadn't written about her difficulties because she clung to the irrational hope that if he had nothing else to think about, he'd have to concentrate all his energies on staying alive and coming back to her in one piece. But then what was the point in him returning to her when there was this awful gulf between them?

'Charlie?' she faltered, and lost courage. 'Shall I dish out for you?'

He nodded, reminding her of his infuriating habit of speaking only when absolutely necessary. When he began to eat, she left the room and went into the bathroom. She bathed and changed into the light summer dress she had brought, taking care over brushing out her hair, putting on cold cream, touching her lips with the remains of the last lipstick she had hoarded against Charlie's return. Dabbing scent behind her ears and powder on her nose, she left the room and walked into the bedroom. Charlie had unlaced his boots, taken off his jacket and was lying on the bed in his shirt-sleeves and braces. His eyes were closed. She went to the window and pulled the curtains. He didn't move. She returned to the bed and lay on it carefully, so as not to touch him. She longed to reach out, place her hand over his, whisper his name, but the chill between them froze the conciliatory gestures before she summoned the courage to make them. Afraid of a rebuff she closed her eyes and pretended to sleep, and soon there was no need for pretence.

'Here's the idiot who ran past me.' The ARP warden straightened his back as he raised the doorpost that had fallen on Haydn.

'He all right?' his colleague asked.

'He's breathing.' He crouched down and checked Haydn's vital signs, 'but out cold. There doesn't appear to be a mark on him.'

'Thank God for that. We've had enough fatalities for one day. Call for a stretcher to carry him over to the FAP.'

'That a baby crying?'

Leaving Haydn lying on the rubble the two men picked their way gingerly through the debris to the back corner of the house.

'It's strongest here.'

They began to move scattered and smashed planking and bricks in the slow, methodical manner of workers accustomed to their task. The cry heightened, reaching a crescendo that permeated Haydn's subconscious. Dazed, he clambered to his feet. Rushing over to where the men were working he began to tear into the wreckage with his bare hands.

'Steady, lad, or you'll have the whole lot down on top of us, not to mention that poor little scrap,' one of the men complained. 'Slowly does it. Slow and steady ...'

Dizzy from concussion, hangover and lack of sleep, Haydn continued to snatch at the stones that covered the area where the stairwell to the cellar had been. The wardens worked quietly, straining their ears for a repetition of the cry that had died before they had cleared the top step. As soon as he was able, the senior warden moved into the hole they had dug, and inspected the mass of shattered masonry that blocked his path.

'It must have been a cat. Nothing larger could

have survived this,' he asserted authoritatively, eyeing the craters in the floor that were now on a level with his head.

'There's a door at the bottom,' Haydn pleaded insistently. 'A strong metal door.'

'A door's no use when the ceiling doesn't hold, lad. Can't you see how it's caved in over there ... and there ...' The more he looked, the more holes he saw.

'You heard the cry. I know you did. We all heard it.' Grey-faced from dust and anxiety, Haydn continued to burrow into the masonry. The skin hung in threads from his fingers, dripping blood with every movement, his nails were cracked, split to the quick, but he continued to delve with his bare hands. The wardens glanced at one another. The senior one nodded.

'Keep going, shout when you finally break through, but for heaven's sake watch that beam up there doesn't come crashing down on both of you. I'll go back to the ARP post and see if I can organise a hoist and tackle.'

Haydn didn't even glance at the beam: all he could think of was that last, faint cry. He had never been a religious man, but as he dug he made a bargain with some vague, remote deity.

'Please God let them be all right, and if they are, I swear I'll send them back to Wales. I won't keep them with me. Just let them be alive. Please God ...'

Alma woke to see Charlie standing over her with

71

a tray in his hands. He cleared a space on the dressing table and set it down.

'I've made tea and toast. You didn't eat any breakfast.'

'I was too tired.' She sat up on the bed as he passed her a cup. 'I'm sorry, I should be waiting on you.'

'Why?'

'You're the fighting man. You only have three days' rest and I've wasted one of them by sleeping.' She glanced out of the window. The light had turned from silver to gold. Even if the small hand on the alarm clock on the bedside cabinet hadn't pointed to four, she would have known it was late afternoon.

Charlie took his tea over to the window, and drank it looking down the valley at the oaks and chestnuts budding into life.

'What would you like to do with what's left of the day?' Alma ventured.

'We could go for a walk before the light fades.'

'I'll wash my face.' She finished her tea and swung her legs over the side of the bed.

'Alma?'

She turned and smiled.

'Nothing.' He watched her leave the room, not knowing how to breach the wall between them, despising himself for resenting the fact that life had gone on in Pontypridd without him. It was obvious Alma didn't need him any more, not even to cope with the trauma of her mother's final illness or the stress of expanding the business he had set up. And where did that leave him? A pawn on the chessboard of the secret war no one, least of all him, dare mention? An irritating disruption to his wife's daily routine when he was given leave? But then, wasn't that what he had wanted? He had come home with the intention of telling her to get on with her life no matter what happened to him. But now, when he was faced with an independent Alma and a newly returned and bereaved Ronnie Ronconi, it was unbelievably hard knowing he wouldn't even be missed.

'If you don't take a break, you're not going to be any good to man or beast, let alone whoever's buried under this lot,' an elderly cockney 'helper' warned, as Haydn stopped digging to wipe the blood from his split and shredded fingers.

'Quiet!' the warden ordered abruptly.

Haydn sat half-way down the steps they had cleared and strained his ears. He heard it again. Could it be the mewing of a trapped cat his wishful thinking had transformed into Anne's cry? Neither of the wardens ventured an opinion. He picked up a chunk of masonry and handed it to the cockney who in turn handed it to a warden.

He drove himself on, hauling more and more debris to the surface. Finally he reached the steel door that had closed off the cellar. It was leaning drunkenly in its frame, the hinges and the surround buckling beneath the weight of shattered stonework. Beyond it lay a mass of rubble interspersed with splintered wood—and a severed arm—a woman's arm complete with rings and wristwatch.

He tried to cry out, but his mouth was caked with dust. The urgency that had sustained him suddenly ebbed and his knees gave way, pitching him forward. The warden behind him blew his whistle to summon help.

'Leave it to us now, lad. We'll do everything that can be done. Stand down and go and get yourself a cup of tea. We need all the room we can get here.'

Haydn retreated to the ruins of what had been the ground-floor apartment and waited while others fought to free his wife and child. His family were his entire world, he would have willingly laid down his life for them, and yet here he was, sitting impotently on a blasted window-ledge, framing prayers he hadn't the strength to utter while others dug them out.

'Steady ... easy ... here we go. You recognise her?'

Haydn closed his eyes not wanting to look, clinging to the absurd thought that as long as he didn't see Jane dead, she would still be alive.

'We need to identify her. Come on, there's a good lad.'

He opened his eyes and scrutinised the corpse laid out on the ground. She had been young and pretty, but now she was motionless, her hair and skin overlaid by a fine layer of powdered mortar that had transformed her flesh to stone. Apart from a thread of crimson that ran from her temple down to her eye she was perfect. So perfect he had the peculiar notion that she ought to be exhibited like a sculpture in a gallery.

'It's Mrs Allen's granddaughter from upstairs. Her name was Nancy. She worked in the canteen at the War Office.'

'You sure, lad?'

'I'm sure.' Haydn staggered to the hole that marked the boundary between house and street. He clung to a fragment of wall, leaned outside and was horribly and thoroughly sick. A young, pretty girl he had known and liked, one who had her whole life in front of her, was dead, and the only feeling he could muster was fervent and sincere gratitude, that it was Nancy Allen not Jane Powell who was being rolled on to a collapsible mortuary stretcher.

'Bethan's got quite a little farm going here,' Alma commented, needing to break the interminable silence that had fallen between her and Charlie. Even impersonal, commonplace remarks seemed better than nothing.

Charlie ran an appraising eye over the pig pen and chicken run that closed off one end of the garden, and the hutches that housed hares and rabbits bordering the vegetable plots.

'It's the same everywhere. People do whatever it takes to survive.'

'Even where you've been?' Alma risked asking a question she knew she shouldn't.

'Food's scarce all over Europe.' He went to the chicken run and clicked his tongue against the roof of his mouth. The hens came running.

'I almost forgot. You told me you'd grown up in the country.'

'Don't you know the saying, scratch a Russian and find a peasant?'

'Would you like to farm after the war?'

'I can't look that far ahead.'

'Why not?'

'How can we plan a future we may not have?'

'Then you think the Germans will invade us?' she asked, deliberately choosing to interpret his remark on a global not personal level.

'I listened to the news when I made the tea. London's been bombed again. They delivered the usual propaganda about the undefeated cockney spirit, but I've been caught in a raid and I don't mind admitting I was petrified. There's only so much people can take.'

'We can't lose now. Not after all the lives this war has already cost.'

'People in Germany are saying the same thing.'

'You've been there?'

'You know I can't talk about where I've been.'

'Charlie—' she blocked his path feeling like a nervous child waylaying a rather formidable headmaster—'I love you,' she blurted out uneasily. 'I don't know what's happening between us, but everything I do, the shops, work, everything, it's for you after the war. If I didn't think it was going to end and that you were coming back I wouldn't want to go on.'

'You'll survive,' he reassured her gravely.

'Look at you, expanding the business, taking care of the shops and your mother ...'

'Nothing means anything without you.' She stepped closer and laid her head against his chest. After a few moments she felt the warmth of his powerful arms around her shoulders. 'We've wasted one whole day. I want to go back up to the bedroom, close the door and shut out the entire world. Please, Charlie, just for tonight?'

He looked down into her eyes. She locked her arms around his neck and pulled his head to hers. He kissed her. It was simpler than trying to grapple with the mixed emotions whirling through his mind.

When she released him he led her towards the house. She trembled at her own audacity and the prospect of making love for the first time in over a year to a man who seemed more like a stranger than her husband.

'This is a fine place.' She stood back, pretending to admire the house.

He studied the triple bays that swept up to the turreted roof and row of attic windows. 'Andrew John knew what he was doing when he persuaded Bethan to let him buy it for her. It's the right sort of place to bring up a family.'

'We'll be a family one day,' she declared, embarrassed because she suspected that he'd seen through her delaying tactics.

'Perhaps.' He put his arm around her, hugging her in an attempt to soften the pain he knew his vague answer had caused. He had lost his family home, his first wife and unborn child in Russia, and all reason told him he was about to lose Alma and the life he had built in Pontypridd. But just like the last time, he could do nothing to prevent it from happening. He, along with thousands of other men across Europe, was no longer master of his own destiny. The day after tomorrow he would leave Alma and board a train. And knowing what he did about his destination and the life expectancy of people in his line of work it would more than likely be for ever.

Earlier he had been angry because she had built a life for herself that excluded him; now he knew he should be grateful for her self-reliance. He would ask Bethan to organise that party. It might be as well to remind Evan Powell that he held his will, and perhaps add a letter to tell Alma all the things he couldn't bring himself to say to her face.

CHAPTER 4

'Someone take him from me.'

The dome of the warden's tin hat appeared above the hole that hid the cellar steps. He handed out a blackened, dust-encrusted shawl, a shawl Haydn recognised. It moved, and the cry came again, thin, weak and wailing. Haydn stumbled over the wreckage and grabbed the baby.

'It's a her, not a him.'

'Reckon she knows her father.' The warden smiled in relief as he relinquished his hold on Anne. He rarely pulled live victims from the wreckage wrought by the blitz, especially babies. Haydn unwrapped his daughter gently and carefully, checking every limb and inch of skin as he brushed clumps of black mortar from her hair and face.

'My wife?' Haydn's voice sounded strange. Hoarse and rusty as though he hadn't used it in years.

'There's two women close by.'

'Are they alive?'

'Can't tell yet, lad.'

Haydn knew from the tone of the warden's voice that they weren't.

'Take care of the little one while we get them out. There should be powdered milk and nappies down at the centre.'

Haydn rose to his feet just as the cockney 'helper' dragged a second lifeless body to the surface.

'Jane!' The anguished cry turned to a sob. He clutched Anne tightly, before realising that the woman was too old and too fat to be Jane.

'This your wife?'

Haydn shook his head. 'Mrs Collins from downstairs.'

'Can you give us an idea of how many were down here?'

'There were twelve flats in the building. We didn't know everyone.'

'Hazard a guess?' the warden pressed impatiently.

'The last time I was home during a raid there were twenty people in the cellar.'

'Keep looking, boys.'

'I've picked up on a voice over here,' the cockney shouted.

Anne began to cry but Haydn remained rooted to the spot. Rocking his daughter in his arms he watched the senior warden climb to the surface and tie a rope around his waist.

'When I tug the rope twice, pull me back, but mind you do it slowly,' he warned the cockney before lowering himself down the hole again. Haydn was aware of the blood rushing to his head and his heart thundering erratically against his ribcage. A shout came from below. He stepped forward, someone—he didn't notice who—took Anne from him. He turned to see a VAD standing behind him.

'The baby's dehydrated, we have to get her to the first-aid post.'

'Please, can you hold on for just two minutes, I'm waiting for them to bring out my wife.'

The nurse took Anne out of the shadow of the crumbling walls into the comparative safety of the street. Haydn watched her go but his attention remained riveted on the rubble around the hole. The tin hat appeared again, and Haydn saw that the warden was carrying a woman over his shoulder. A woman in a dark skirt and light blouse.

'Jane?' He knelt beside them.

'Go easy, lad. She's alive, but she's in shock and she may be hurt.'

Haydn cradled Jane in his arms as the warden heaved her to the surface. Her eyes flickered as she closed them against the strong afternoon sunlight.

'Anne?' she pleaded urgently.

'She's here, she's fine.'

'I told you we would be, didn't I? My handbag?'

'I've got it.' The warden pushed it into her hand.

'I've saved the ration books, and the bank book.' Dazed she opened her eyes and looked around the ruins of the block. 'We've lost everything ...'

'Nothing that can't be replaced,' Haydn reassured, holding her close.

'Best get her and the little one down to the centre as quick as you can, lad.'

Haydn lifted Jane high in his arms, picking his

way cautiously over the debris into the street, before stopping and turning back. 'I can't thank you enough. All of you.' He looked from the wardens to the old cockney.

'It's all in a day's work, thanks to bloody Hitler. I only hope our RAF boys are giving them what for over there, that's all I can say,' the cockney groused as he continued to dig.

'I can walk,' Jane protested as he nodded to the VAD who was carrying Anne.

'After you've seen a doctor.' He followed the VAD towards the centre. 'And then any walking you do will be in the direction of Paddington station.'

'Haydn ...'

'No arguments.'

His face was grim, set, and she realised no amount of coaxing, cajoling or lovemaking would sway him. Not this time.

Alma and Charlie lay wrapped in one another's arms in Bethan's bed, watching the sun sink slowly over the hills.

'I've been dreaming about that for a long time.' He pulled her even closer, locking his hands around her waist.

'It's probably wrong for a woman to say so, but so have I.' She ran her fingertips over the smooth skin of his shoulders, wishing that it had been like this between them from the first moment of his leave.

'Why is it wrong for a woman?'

'I don't know. Welsh chapel morality, maybe? Didn't you know that women aren't supposed to like lovemaking, only put up with it for their husbands' sake?' She smiled at him. 'It is going to be all right between us, isn't it?'

'It's always been all right between us.' He reached for the jacket he'd flung down next to the bed. Fumbling in the pockets he pulled out a packet of cigarettes and the lighter she had given him the last Christmas before the war. A lighter that lay in his locker in base camp in between 'jobs' because he dare not take anything of English manufacture where he went.

'I don't just mean bed.'

'I know, Alma.'

'I was being silly and selfish earlier when I said I wouldn't want to go on without you. You mustn't worry about me. Especially when you are away.'

'I'll never stop worrying about you, that's a husband's prerogative.' Turning his back to her, he leaned on his elbow and lit a cigarette.

'Charlie, I need to say something and, please, don't interrupt me before I've finished, because I'll never pluck up enough courage to bring this up again. I think I know where they send you, and you told me once that your first wife and baby may still be alive somewhere in Russia ...'

'You have no idea how vast Russia is.'

'Please, Charlie, I said no interruptions.' She sat up and looked earnestly into his ice-blue eyes, cold no longer, but warm with love and tenderness. 'What I'm trying to say is that if you do find her, and want to stay with her after the war, that's all right.'

'Alma ...'

'I won't pretend to like it, but I'll understand. You warned me before we married that Masha had prior claim on you.'

'Just as Ronnie Ronconi had on you.'

'Ronnie was my lover, not my husband, Charlie, it's not the same thing. I want our relationship to be built on honesty and trust, that's why I told you everything about me before we married. We were truthful with one another then, and I want no secrets between us now. Neither of us could have imagined anything like this war happening. We both thought we would live out our lives quietly in Pontypridd. That Masha would remain somewhere where you couldn't reach her, and Ronnie would stay in Italy with Maud, but now things are different. This has nothing to do with Ronnie,' she emphasised. 'I will never go back to him no matter what happens. I promise ...'

'No.' He laid his finger across her lips. 'Don't make promises you may find yourself unable to keep. You were right to say that we had no idea how this war would affect us. We have even less idea what else is coming our way.'

'I promise,' she reiterated fervently. 'There will *never* be anything between me and Ronnie Ronconi ever again. But I mean it about Masha. If you do find her and decide to stay with her, I will be all right here. But please, Charlie, I beg you, let me know you're alive. That's all I ask. Don't let me go on believing you're dead, if you are alive and happy somewhere.'

Charlie drew on his cigarette, and exhaled

thoughtfully. 'If by some miracle I do find Masha, I think that after twelve years, she, like me, will have a new life.'

'And if there's room in it for you?'

'How do you expect me to answer that? I don't know what Masha and I will think of each other after twelve years. Yesterday you felt like a stranger after only a year's separation.'

'But we're not strangers now,' she whispered, curling her body around his and burying her fingers in the hair on his chest.

'If I don't come back, you'll be free to marry again.'

'Free, maybe, but I won't marry.'

'You can't say that.'

'I can. Just look at Ronnie. There was only one woman for him, now she's dead he'll go on living, but all the joy has gone from his life. He's a broken man. He'll never marry again.'

Charlie turned aside and tapped his cigarette into the ashtray at the side of the bed. Alma wholeheartedly believed in what she was telling him, but no one knew better than him that 'never' was a long time. Ronnie was heartbroken—now. If he didn't return he knew that Alma would be too—for a while. Just as he had been when he'd returned to his village and found his pregnant wife and entire family gone. The pain of that loss was with him still, but it was a grief that he had learned to endure and live with. His sorrow hadn't prevented him from marrying Alma and finding happiness a second time. Just as he suspected Alma and Ronnie might if he was killed. They had been lovers once, why not again? And why did the idea of Ronnie and Alma taking solace in one another, and building a future together, hurt him so much? He hardly had the right to object when he wouldn't even be around to see it happen.

It was after ten o'clock when Diana Rees walked up the steps to the front door of her father-in-law's substantial, semi-detached villa in Tyfica Road. Like every other house in Pontypridd since the influx of evacuees and munitions workers, it was full, only in their case with family. She and her husband, Wyn, shared a bedroom with their six-month-old baby. Her mother Megan, and Wyn's spinster sister Myrtle each had a bedroom that was more like a box room, and her invalid father-in-law slept downstairs in what had been the front parlour.

Occasionally, she would have given a great deal to have been able to walk through the door and retreat into a space that was wholly and solely hers. Especially after a hectic day like today, when she had divided her time between watching over Alma's mother's deathbed, and checking on Alma's shop, takings and staff. But peace, quiet and privacy were luxuries that existed only in the memory, like bananas and slab chocolate.

'You look as though you're sleeping on your feet, love.' Wyn greeted her at the front door.

'I am. How did you manage without me?'

'You're not indispensable yet.' He said as he helped her off with her coat.

'You ready for your supper now, Wyn?'

Megan called from the kitchen.

'Both of us are. Diana's just arrived.'

Diana removed the pearl-headed pins from her black velvet hat and hung it on the stand before following Wyn into the back kitchen where Megan was presiding over a simmering pot of cawl.

'How has he been?' Diana leaned over the day cot pushed into a corner next to the range.

'As good as gold.'

'He didn't notice you'd gone,' Wyn's father added from the depths of the sofa. He pulled the blanket that covered him to the chest higher, and shook the rocker on the cradle as the baby began to snuffle. 'He knows his grandfather.'

'Then you've terrified him into silence.' Wyn had meant the quip to sound lighthearted, but the remark fell heavily into the strained atmosphere. Relations between him and his father had improved since he'd married Diana, and her mother had moved in with them, but only because the introduction of extra people into the household had forced his father to temper his constant criticism of every single thing he said or did.

'Myrtle went to bed early. The shifts have been extended at the factory. They'll be working twelve-hour days next week.' Megan sliced a loaf of soda bread into quarters and set it on the table.

'Fine hours and work for your sister to be doing, while you ponce around like a sissy serving up sweets in the New Theatre,' the old man grouched from the corner.

'I sieved some stew for the baby and tried him with a few spoonfuls at the six o'clock feed,' Megan broke in, hoping that Wyn would ignore his father's taunting.

'Did he like it?' Diana asked.

'Lapped it up.'

'Good, the sooner he gets used to ordinary food the better for me and anyone who looks after him.'

'Sit down and eat up while it's hot.' Megan carried the pot to the table and ladled out two bowlfuls.

'How is Mrs Moore, Diana?' Wyn's father asked.

'Unconscious most of the time and incoherent when she does wake. Bethan says she hasn't eaten in days.'

'Then she'll not last long. And to think she's a good ten years younger than me,' the old man cackled gleefully.

'The way you're going, Mr Rees, you'll outlast us all.' Megan handed the old man his supper of bread and cheese on a tray. She and Wyn's father were the only ones who were able to eat at regular meal-times. Myrtle generally ate in the factory canteen to save bother, while Diana and Wyn usually only managed breakfast and supper at home, filling up in between on pies from the shop and tea in Ronconi's café.

'Strong constitution to begin with.' The old man smiled, which made him look more sickly than ever, reminding Diana that Alma Moore's mother wasn't the only one who had been given a death sentence.

'How is Bethan?' Megan sat down opposite her daughter and son-in-law at the table.

'You know Beth, looking after all the sick in the town, her evacuees, running errands for all and sundry.'

'Anything not to think about Eddie, and now Maud,' Megan frowned. 'She heard from Andrew lately?'

'She didn't say.'

'That means she hasn't. Sometimes it feels as though letters are the scarcest commodities of all.' It had been a month since Megan had heard from her son, William, who as far as she could make out was 'somewhere in North Africa'. The closest she could get to him were the daily trips his wife, Tina, made from the Tumble café to see if her mother-in-law had received any news she hadn't.

'This is the best cawl I've ever eaten, Megan. Just what I needed.' Wyn pushed back his chair and stretched his legs out to the fire.

'It always tastes better after the second boil. There's plenty more if you want another bowl.'

'No thanks, I wouldn't be able to move, let alone climb the stairs.'

'Tea?'

'I'll give Diana a hand to bath the baby and put him to bed.'

'Women's work,' his father sneered.

'With this war keeping three-quarters of the men in the town away from home, it's good to know there's at least one poor mite in Pontypridd who knows who his father is,' Megan countered briskly, in an attempt to let the old man know that Wyn wasn't the only one who resented his constant carping.

Diana went to the cot and lifted out the boy they'd named William after her father who'd been killed in the Great War. 'You take Billy.' She handed him over to Wyn. 'Put your feet up, Mam. I'll do the dishes.'

'What dishes?' her mother scoffed as she cleared the table. 'Two bowls and four bread plates. Go on, off with you, I'll have the tea made by the time you've finished.'

Wyn followed Diana up the stairs. This was his favourite time of day. The only time he could be alone with his wife and baby when they were awake.

'Did you really cope in the shops without me today?' Diana asked.

'Is that a "Can you cope without me tomorrow" question?'

'Bethan thought it might be nice if Alma and Charlie could spend the whole of Charlie's leave in her house to give Alma a break from caring for her mother. She's also thinking of having a small "welcome home and goodbye again" party for Charlie tomorrow evening. If it comes off, we're invited.'

'I can just about manage the banking without you,' he assured with mock gravity.

'I won't be needed after tomorrow. Charlie's leaving on Saturday morning.'

'They didn't give him much time.'

'That's why Bethan thinks he and Alma should spend what little he has in peace and quiet.' She sat on the edge of the bath and put the plug in the sink they used to wash the baby.

'If it hadn't been for that damned van mowing me down, I'd be where Charlie is now, and then I'd be doing something a sight more useful than running a sweet shop and a pie shop.'

She glanced at him as he sat on the linen bin, his stick resting against the wall, his wooden leg extended at an awkward angle. 'It's your father again, isn't it, Wyn? How many times do I have to tell you not to listen to him, he's ...'

'Right?'

'We've been through all this before. You're medically unfit. It's a fact. I know it can't be easy for you ...'

'Erik called into the shop this afternoon.'

'What did he want?' she asked uneasily as she turned on the taps.

'To tell me they desperately need men in the munitions factory. Even one-legged cripples.'

'And what did you say?'

'That I'd think about it.'

'And the shops?'

'You could manage those if we took on an extra girl to cover the second house in the one in the cinema.'

'It won't be easy to find someone we can trust, not at wages we can afford. Tina told me they're upping the pay to three pounds a week in the munitions factories, and that's for untrained girls.'

'Look at the shifts Myrtle's working. Not everyone can cope with a hundred hours a week when there's a push on. We'll find someone.

Perhaps a mother with children at school and a grandmother living close by who can look after them in the evening. I'll start looking tomorrow.'

'You've already made up your mind about this, haven't you?'

'I may have lost a leg, but there's still plenty of things I could do that are a sight more important than running a damned sweet shop. I know better than anyone how unpleasant my father can be, but this time he's hit the nail on the head. No man should be running a shop in wartime. I want to contribute more like your brother, and the Ronconi boys and Andrew John.'

'Fat lot Andrew and Angelo Ronconi are contributing to the war effort stuck in a German prison camp.'

'At least they tried,' he asserted softly.

She forced herself to look at him. 'I'm not stupid, Wyn. I know what Erik is, and I don't mean a Polish refugee. If this arrangement between us isn't working out for you, just say the word and my mother and I will take the baby back to my Uncle Evan's house.'

'Don't you know that you and Billy are the two most important people in my life?'

'But that's why you want the job, isn't it? To be near Erik?'

'No. It's to contribute more to the war effort than I'm doing now.'

'It's not Billy and myself I'm thinking about, but you. I know how unhappy you were before we married.'

'And I'm unhappy now, because I don't feel I'm pulling my weight. My sister works twelve-hour shifts in a factory doing a man's job, and I'm playing at shop assistant and nursemaid.' He undressed the baby on his lap, feeling all fingers and thumbs with such a tiny, wriggling mite.

'If it will help, you could bring Erik home. I really wouldn't mind.'

'How can I bring him home with my father in the house?'

'Perhaps we should try to find our own place?'

'And then who would look after Dad? Let's face it, Diana, he has us trapped.'

'Not us, Wyn. Me. I'm the one with the baby. Your father is no real trouble to me or my mother except in the way he treats you. Why don't you see Dr Evans tomorrow and ask him if there's any medical reason why you shouldn't register for war work, if that's what you want to do? I think that's a better way of going about things than trusting to Erik's recommendation.' After testing the water she took Billy from Wyn, lowered him into the sink and splashed him gently.

'If I registered they could send me anywhere.'

'That's not likely when the factories are so desperate here. As you said, we can try to get another girl to help out in the shops. There may even be one in the workhouse. Maisie turned out well for Bethan.'

'A workhouse girl would have to sleep somewhere, and there's no room here.' He held out a towel and she wrapped Billy in it.

'If I do end up working with Erik it would be just friendship, nothing more, Diana, I swear it. I made you a promise when we married, and I've stuck to it. I won't break it, or risk any scandal that will affect you or Billy.'

'As if I could care less about gossip. I owe you everything. You've given me and Billy a home and a name. You've been a good friend when I needed one most. I just couldn't bear to see you getting hurt, or worse still, being arrested and sent to prison.'

'Don't worry, I won't be. And once I'm doing work I can be proud of, I'll be a lot happier, you'll see.' He took Billy from her and carried him through to their bedroom.

She heard him talking to the baby as he wrestled with the nappy he'd never learned to fasten properly. She knew that a new job wouldn't really solve anything for Wyn, because he wasn't the only one who felt there was something missing from his life.

Outwardly she had everything a woman could want. A beautiful baby, a mother who took all the domestic drudgery off her hands and a kind and thoughtful husband. She should be content, and generally was until she sensed Wyn's restlessness, or intercepted a look between husband and wife like the one Charlie had given Alma that morning. A look that told her there was more. Much, much more than she could ever hope to find in marriage to a man like Wyn Rees, for all his gentle kindness.

'Two cracked ribs, bit shaken, but otherwise

she's in one piece. The baby's come through the experience with no ill-effects that I can see. We'll keep them in overnight as a precautionary measure, but they'll be able to go home first thing tomorrow.' The doctor's smile was genuine. It was the only good news he'd had to deliver all day.

'We have no home left to go to,' Haydn said drily. 'That's why I'd like to take my family to Wales tomorrow.'

'If you can get the travel warrants, go ahead. We've strapped up your wife's ribs. Provided she takes it easy and doesn't do any heavy lifting she should be fine. In fact it would probably be better to get them into the country than a place in a temporary shelter here. Would you like to see them for a few minutes?'

'Please.' Haydn gathered his jacket from the corridor bench.

'The sister will show you the way. Good luck, to you and your family, young man.'

Haydn followed the sister down the stairs into a gloomy, windowless basement.

'We try to keep as many of our short-stay patients in the cellars as we can, it saves on evacuation time,' she explained.

Jane was lying on a bed at the end of a very long row of camp beds. There was a canvas cot at her side but she'd lifted the baby in with her, and was feeding her from a bottle when Haydn arrived. He'd stayed with Jane while they'd cleaned her and Anne up at the first-aid post, travelled with her to hospital, but he was still shocked at her

95

ashen complexion and the dark shadows beneath her eyes.

'My milk's dried up,' she explained.

'A few days' rest and it will come back.'

'That's what the sister said. Only by then Anne probably won't want me to feed her any more.' A tear rolled down her cheek, and Haydn reached for his handkerchief.

'She'll want you,' he reassured her awkwardly, conscious of the other patients' eyes fixed in their direction.

'I'm not crying about that, but what you said. You're determined to send us to Wales, aren't you?'

'Not send, take. I called into the studio when the doctor was checking you over. I have tomorrow off. I don't have to be back until late Saturday.'

'And that's supposed to make it all right?'

'Jane, please.' He looked around for a chair. There wasn't one so he crouched awkwardly beside the iron bedstead. 'We were lucky once, don't tempt fate a second time. I didn't want to tell you until it was all organised, but it looks as though we wouldn't have been together much longer anyway. My producer has arranged a tour of the fronts so we can broadcast a series of shows from the serving troops. You and Anne couldn't have come with me, and I wouldn't have been happy leaving you on your own in London.'

'But I'm supposed to be happy with you going to the front?' Her eyes widened in a mixture of fear and indignation.

'The fronts I'll be visiting will be nowhere near the fighting. Nothing's going to happen to me.'

'And what am I supposed to do back in Pontypridd?'

'Look after Anne.'

'For how long, Haydn? How long are we going to have to live without you?'

'Only Hitler can answer that question, love. It's the same for everyone. Please, can't you see I'm doing this for you and Anne?'

'You're doing it for yourself. Hiving us off so you won't have to worry about us.'

'Hey, whatever happened to the independent girl I married?'

'It's easy to be independent when you've no one to care about. Now I have you, I can't bear the thought of losing you.'

'And I wouldn't want to go on living without you, which is why I have to get you out of London. But it's Pontypridd you're going to, not China. You'll have my father and Phyllis and Bethan ...'

'And Eddie's widow to remind me I could lose you.' She concentrated all her attention on Anne, refusing to look into his eyes.

He tried one last time. 'Think of my sister. Andrew's in a prison camp in Germany, she knows she won't see him until the end of the war—whenever that will be. And Jenny will never see Eddie walking through the door again.'

'At least she can get on with her life.' Jane regretted the words the instant they were out of her mouth, but once said, they couldn't be retracted.

He rose from his knees, kissed her on the cheek and stroked the baby's head. 'You're tired, get some sleep. Don't worry about clothes, or replacing the baby's things. I've organised the essentials, and anything I haven't got, you can pick up in Pontypridd. I'll be here first thing in the morning to take you to my father's house.'

She watched him walk down the ward, wishing she could turn the clock back just twenty-four hours. Couldn't he understand just how terrified she was of losing him? Because, apart from Anne, he was all the family she'd ever had.

Constable Huw Davies walked along Tyfica Road, one of the most select and salubrious streets in Pontypridd, hardly the place to find trouble, even at four-thirty in the morning. But he wasn't looking for trouble. He lit a match and checked his watch—any minute now. Then he heard the sound he'd been waiting for. The light tap of footsteps walking towards him in the darkness.

'Careful, Miss Rees. You've plenty of time. Go slowly and you won't risk tripping up in the blackout.'

'Constable Davies, how kind,' a disembodied voice floated back, 'but I'm sure I'm putting you out. You don't have to walk me to the station every morning, you know.'

'It's part of my beat. Besides, you can never be too sure who you'll run into in the blackout.'

'Wyn's offered to walk me, but I won't let him. It's bad enough I have to get up at this hour in the morning, without disturbing the whole household. He and Diana don't get much sleep as it is.'

'How is the baby?' Huw asked, although he already knew the answer to his question. He made a point of calling in to see his sister, Megan, at least once a day.

'He's fine, thank you.'

'And your father?'

'Much the same.' She lowered her voice although the street was silent and deserted. 'To be truthful, as difficult as ever.'

He laughed, before apologising. 'I'm sorry, it's only funny when you don't have to live with someone like him.'

'I'm all right because working the shifts I do, I hardly ever see him. Sometimes I feel very selfish taking this job in munitions.'

'Selfish? Working the hours and the way you do in that factory?'

'It's hard work, but the girls are friendly and everyone's given set tasks, so in a way it's much easier than staying home with Dad. A meal break in the factory is just that. A break. No one's going to ask me to get a cup of tea, or run upstairs ... I'm sorry, I should never have said that. I sound so ungrateful. My father's been good to me and Wyn.'

Huw grunted. He knew exactly how good a father Wyn Rees senior had been to his son and daughter. Most men of his means were kinder to their kitchen skivvies.

'I wouldn't have taken the job if Megan and Diana hadn't insisted they could cope without me.'

'My sister can cope with anything,' Huw observed wryly.

'And it's always been poor Wyn who's borne the brunt of my father's temper.'

'I've noticed.'

'It's the pain. He has to take it out on someone.' She excused her father's behaviour out of habit, because he never apologised for it himself. 'Although he hasn't gone on at Wyn quite so much since Billy was born.'

'He's a bonny baby.'

'Isn't he?' she enthused. 'I never thought there'd be any babies in our house. It's wonderful being an auntie and Diana's so generous. She lets me monopolise his waking time when I'm home ...' Her voice tailed away as she realised she was gushing.

'It's nice being an uncle too. I try to forget the "great".'

'You don't look like a great-uncle.' She was glad the blackout hid her face. She could feel her cheeks burning. What had she been thinking of? The comment could so easily be misconstrued as a compliment, and as her father would have undoubtedly pointed out, Huw Davies's connection to her was hardly close enough for such familiarity.

They crossed Gelliwastad Road and walked down Church Street into Market Square in silence, she, squirming because she believed she'd embarrassed him by having been too personal, he, desperately searching for something to say. Myrtle was thirty-eight years old to his forty-five, and at times like this he wished he had the impetuosity and confidence of his nephew William. In the last year he and Myrtle had witnessed half the young people in their respective circles of friends and relations rush into war marriages, but he still lacked the courage to ask her to share his life and the house he'd inherited from his father in Bonvilston Road. Even now, when she worked in a factory full of what her father referred to as 'common tarts' she had retained her middle-class reserve, a reserve he felt put her way out of the reach of an ordinary working-class man like himself.

'Myrtle, what a time to get up in the morning, eh?' Judy Crofter, a blonde maneater from Leyshon Street accosted them in station yard. Huw would have known her voice anywhere, and he thought her a most unsuitable acquaintance for a refined lady like Myrtle.

'You get used to it like everything else, Judy.'

'Myrtle, over here,' another voice called.

'I'll leave you now.' The milling crowd of women was too much for him, even when he was wearing his uniform.

'Thank you for walking me down, Constable Davies.'

Huw straightened his helmet and beat a hasty retreat. Judy's shrill tones followed him.

'Seems to me we're going to be hearing wedding bells soon, eh,' her cackle echoed around the yard.

'Constable Davies is a friend of the family.'

'Friend? I've seen the look in his eye. Can't wait to get his leg over like every other man ...'

Huw crossed the road quickly. Whenever he daydreamed of Myrtle it was always in chaste terms. Sitting companionably either side of the fire in his parlour, miraculously transformed into a warm and cosy room by Myrtle's delicate, womanly touch, or going shopping arm in arm, visiting his sister on a Sunday, all the small everyday trivia of family life he saw and envied in other households, and hadn't been a part of since his father had died and his brothers moved away.

How dare Judy Crofter reduce his feelings for Myrtle Rees to a disgusting term more suited to what went on between sluts and their customers in station yard. How dare she!

CHAPTER 5

It was morning when Bethan next drove up the hill to Penycoedcae. Bright, beautiful sunny morning without a cloud in the sky, but she wasn't in a mood to appreciate the sparkling, spring light, or the buds breaking into flower in the fields and hedgerows. The night spent closeted in Alma's mother's bedroom had been a long one and the old lady had been confused and restless for most of it. Mrs Moore persisted in defying all logic and Dr John and Dr Evans's predictions of imminent demise by lingering on when her heart should have given out weeks ago. The strain on Alma had been enormous, even before Charlie had come home.

This morning, she had urged the relief nurse to do all she could to keep the old lady going for the next twenty-four hours, but she still had a presentiment that Mrs Moore was going to die at the most inopportune moment, right in the middle of Charlie's leave.

She parked the car in the old coachhouse Andrew had converted into a garage, and walked into the kitchen. Liza Clark was doling out mugs of milk and porridge to the rows of children ranged on benches at the kitchen table. Maisie had washed and dressed Rachel, and was giving Eddie his morning bottle.

'I'll do that for you, Maisie, about all I'm fit

for is sitting down.'

'You look fagged, Nurse John,' Liza observed in her strong London accent. 'Rough night?'

'No rougher than Alma's been having for the last couple of months. Any sign of our guests?'

'I took them up some supper last night. Mrs Charlie brought down the dishes before we went to bed, but we haven't seen them this morning,' Maisie answered as she wiped a dribble of porridge from one of the younger mouths.

'Alma needs the lie-in. She's been working all day in the shops and sitting up all night with her mother for months now. No one can stand that kind of strain for any length of time.'

Liza began to lift the children who'd finished their breakfast from the table, and shepherd them to the downstairs cloakroom to brush their teeth in salt. She had taken it upon herself to relieve Bethan of as much of the work of looking after the evacuees as she could. With her mother killed in the bombing raid that had destroyed their house in East London, and her father away in the army, she had assumed full responsibility for her three younger sisters. They hadn't been anyone's ideal guests. Some people in Pontypridd had been prepared to take one evacuee child, a few had been imposed upon to make room for two, but no one had been prepared to take in four.

Bethan had arrived late at the station to find all the clean and tidy children already gone. The only ones left in the waiting room had flea bites, impetigo, or ringworm beneath the layers of grime that covered their hands and faces, and sitting, caring for them as well as her own sisters, had been a tearful Liza Clark, protesting in between sobs that she wouldn't be separated from her sisters because she'd promised her parents she'd look after them no matter what.

Bethan had taken one look at the young girl who appeared even younger than her sixteen years, imagined herself in the same predicament and offered Liza and her family a home on condition Liza pulled her weight. It hadn't taken the girl long to work out what 'pulling her weight' meant as Mrs Llewellyn Jones, bank manager's wife and WVS autocrat, had set aside the two worst cases of impetigo for Bethan 'because nurses are used to that sort of thing'.

Gratitude had led Liza to do much more than anyone could have reasonably expected of her. Friendly with Maisie, she insisted on deferring to her hostess as the 'lady' of the house, which highly amused Bethan. The cockney was what most people on the Graig called a rough diamond with the emphasis on the 'rough', but Bethan couldn't imagine getting through a day now without her warmth, sympathy, practical help and constantly flowing cups of tea.

She brought one over as soon as Bethan took her baby and sat in the chair Maisie had vacated. Rachel, who was perched in her high chair at the head of the table in between Liza's eight- and ten-year-old sisters, looked across at her mother.

'Want to go and see Auntie Phyllis today, Rachel?'

The toddler nodded solemnly, lowering her brown ringlets into her enamel mug of milk.

'I can look after Eddie and Rachel if you want to go to bed, Mrs John,' Maisie offered as she dried Rachel's hair with a tea towel.

'You have enough to do. I can sleep just as well down there, and it will give you a chance to get on with the baking for the weekend.'

Liza laid a plate of toast spread with blackberry jam next to Bethan's tea.

'Thank you, I don't know what I'd do without you two.'

'Have a quieter life and a tidy house,' Liza suggested.

'I'd still have the children.' Hearing a creak overhead, Bethan realised that either Alma or Charlie was stirring. 'I'm going into Daddy's study. Would you like to come with me, Rachel?'

The child nodded, and Maisie lifted her down. She trailed after Bethan as she crossed the hall. Conscious that her children were growing up without their father, Bethan was doing her utmost to make them feel that he was still part of the household. Andrew's photograph was prominently displayed in every room, especially the bedroom the children shared, and she kept his study exactly as he'd left it apart from the addition of photographs and the special toys her mother-in-law had given her. Toys that had been his.

Sitting on the sofa in front of Andrew's desk

she resumed Eddie's interrupted feed. His tiny hands reached for the bottle as she stroked the soft down of dark hair on his head. She looked for a resemblance between the baby's unformed features and those of his namesake, but there was already an auburn sheen to his hair that was pure Andrew and the eyes that had been blue had darkened: not to the deep brown of her own and Eddie's eyes, more the tawny shade of her husband's.

She leaned back and propped her feet up on a footstool. She had to stop looking for a likeness. Keeping her brother and sister's memory alive was one thing; saddling the living with an ideal of the dead they couldn't possibly live up to, quite another.

'Good morning.'

Alma was standing in the doorway.

'Come in, how's Charlie?'

'Fine, how's my mother?'

'The same. She hasn't regained consciousness since you left, and she hasn't a clue who is sitting with her, so you may as well stay here until Charlie has to go back.'

'I couldn't possibly do that.'

'Don't forget there's a telephone here. The relief nurse promised to phone the minute there's any change. Even if I'm not here, you could call a taxi and be with her in a quarter of an hour at the most.'

'I'd still like to see her.'

'Then I'll take you down later on, but only if you promise to come right back. Diana has everything under control in the shops. She's right, you do have good staff.'

'I know.'

'If you'd like breakfast, just call Maisie.'

'She has enough to do with the children. I'll make something for Charlie and me later. I left him sleeping.'

Bethan looked at her closely. 'Nothing wrong, is there?'

Alma stepped into the room and sat next to Bethan on the sofa. 'Not exactly.'

'You haven't seen him in over a year. Things are bound to be strange between you. Sometimes I wonder if I'll recognise Andrew when he eventually comes home.'

'Before Charlie even walked into the house he saw me leave the restaurant with Ronnie.'

'Come on, Charlie knows you. He loves you. He'd never think that you and Ronnie ...'

'He made it clear that he didn't like the idea of me getting too friendly with Ronnie again, but even when he was being the masterful, jealous husband I had the feeling that his thoughts were elsewhere. As though he'd left his mind wherever he's been, instead of bringing it home with him.'

'I've known Charlie a long time. He's always been quiet, you know that, particularly when he's bothered about something. We don't know what he's going back to—'

'That could be it, couldn't it?' Alma broke in eagerly. 'He's not allowed to say where he's been or what he's been doing, but given the languages he speaks, it stands to reason that he fights behind enemy lines.'

Bethan fell silent. She knew Alma was thinking the same as her. That people who were sent into enemy territory were out of uniform and if caught, shot as spies. She couldn't begin to imagine the pressure of living with the knowledge that one wrong move meant a death sentence. Her own problems paled into insignificance beside those Charlie must face every minute of his working life.

'I'm taking the children down to Phyllis's for the day so I can get some sleep. Maisie's going to be busy baking for the weekend, the others won't go near my rooms, so why don't you stay here again tonight?' she offered. 'You'd have all day to yourselves. Try and talk to him, Alma. I know Charlie: if you feel something's wrong between you, he will too.'

'You're right.' She looked at Rachel who was playing on the floor with a dozen green and red wooden blocks, and the baby who had just finished his feed and was sleeping, curled contently in Bethan's arms. 'I really envy you.'

'And I you. I'd give a great deal to spend an hour with Andrew right now.'

'Can I?' Alma held out her arms and Bethan deposited Eddie in them. 'Both of them are absolutely beautiful,' Alma said for Rachel's benefit, who seeing her mother's lap empty, promptly climbed on to it.

'Aren't they?' Bethan wrapped her arms around Rachel and dropped a kiss on the top of her head. 'And Rachel and I have decided that Eddie looks just like his father, haven't we, poppet? I only wish I knew how long this war was going to last.'

'Don't we all,' Charlie agreed as he walked in. For the first time since his return he'd abandoned his uniform. Dressed in a pair of dark trousers and a thick, ribbed sweater, his fair hair tousled and uncombed, he reminded Bethan of the fishermen she'd seen setting off from the quaysides of west Wales.

'I hope I didn't wake you when I left,' Alma said.

'I was only dozing. It's too beautiful a day to waste sleeping. I thought we might go for a walk down Shoni's pond.'

'After I've seen my mother?'

'We could pick up a couple of pies from the shop for a picnic lunch.'

'In that case I'll get us some breakfast now. Here, cuddle your godson.'

'My godson?' He looked to Bethan in surprise as Alma passed the baby to him.

'I asked Alma if you'd like to be his godparents. It seemed appropriate, considering his name. Eddie was fond of both of you; he used to say you were the best boss he ever had.'

'He was a good friend.'

'So,' she continued a little too brightly, 'when this Eddie was christened, Alma stood godmother and my father stood in for you. Jenny and Haydn are the other godparents.'

'Haydn was home?'

'He had a forty-eight-hour Christmas leave, so he brought Jane down for the day.'

110

'Lucky devil. And before I forget, thank you for this leave. I imagined snatched moments in between serving customers.' He sat down and laid the baby on his knees. Eddie snuggled sideways and continued sleeping.

'Most men hold babies out at arm's length as though they're likely to explode. You look as though you've handled them all your life.'

'Does that surprise you?'

'I just never thought of you with children.'

'I was the eldest of six, but none of them were as quiet and well behaved as these two.'

'I'm glad you approve. Have you thought any more about tonight?'

'I'd like to see your father and Phyllis, Megan and Diana if you're sure it's not too much trouble for you.'

'No trouble. I'll stretch my district nurse's petrol ration and bring them up. Would you mind if Wyn, Ronnie Ronconi, Tina and Jenny come as well? We try to include Jenny and Tina in all the family things for Eddie and William's sake, and Ronnie's only just got back from Italy.'

'No,' he replied evenly, 'I wouldn't mind at all.'

'You look a bit brighter than you did last time I saw you, but those clothes do nothing for you,' Jenny Griffiths greeted Ronnie as he hobbled into her shop wearing a pair of trousers that were three inches too short and a pullover that barely skimmed his waist.

'I raided Tony and Angelo's wardrobes up at

the house. They both seem to be a foot shorter than me, especially in the arms and legs, but as Tina confiscated the only rags I possess to fumigate them, these will have to do until I can get some clothing coupons.'

'Eddie was about your height, but heavier,' she said thoughtfully. 'You've lost a lot of weight.'

'The way Tina is feeding me I'll soon put it back on.'

'I've kept Eddie's clothes. He moved them down from Graig Avenue on his last leave. I'd be grateful if you took them off my hands.'

'I couldn't do that. Think how you, Evan and Bethan would feel seeing me walk around town in Eddie's things.'

'We'd be thankful that they were being put to some use, instead of mouldering away in a wardrobe. Please, Ronnie, I wouldn't have offered if I hadn't meant it. I've almost taken them down to Wilf's stall a couple of times, but I couldn't bring myself to do it. It didn't seem right to sell them and they didn't fit anyone in the family. I'd rather you had them than strangers.'

'I don't know what to say.'

'You'd be doing me a favour by taking them. I need the space and if you don't mind me saying so, it's obvious you couldn't bring much from Italy.'

'I couldn't bring anything from Italy. Not that there was much to bring,' he added ruefully.

'Come upstairs and look them over. If they fit and you can use them, I'll pack everything

112

up and ask Bethan to drop the parcel off at Laura's house the next time she passes. That is where you're living?'

'It is,' he answered, surprised that she'd taken the trouble to find out.

She opened the flap in the counter and threw the bolt across the shop door. 'I daren't leave the shop unlocked when I'm not here. George Collins delivered the cheese and butter rations this morning, and there's always people looking for a bit extra. Generally the same ones who aren't too fussy where it comes from.'

'You might lose customers.'

'They know the service here is worth waiting for.' Opening the door that led to the living quarters upstairs, she ran ahead of him. As he used his crutch to clamber up awkwardly behind her, her skirt flared high around her legs. They were long, slim and elegant, like the rest of her. He hated himself for even noticing. He hadn't as much as looked at a woman since Maud had died. But Jenny exuded a warm, seductive sensuality that disturbed him, threatening his arid, monk-like existence. Just being alone with her was enough to make him feel as though he was committing adultery, which was ridiculous considering he no longer even had a wife.

'They're in here.' Apparently oblivious to the impact she was having on him, she walked along the landing and ushered him into the front bedroom. 'This was our room. After I had the telegram I couldn't bear to sleep in here, too many memories I suppose, so I moved into my parents' old bedroom in the back. What do you

113

think?' She unlocked the door of a cumbersome, old-fashioned oak wardrobe and started lifting out coat-hangers.

He looked around. The bed had been dismantled. The mattress wrapped in dust sheets and propped on its side. The smell of damp, disuse and mothballs was overwhelming.

'He was quite a dresser,' he complimented as she peeled back the muslin protector on a suit to show him the cloth.

'He spent a lot of his boxing prize money on clothes,' she boasted proudly, 'and the last couple of years before the war he earned good money in Charlie's shop. There's a dozen almost new shirts, braces, sock suspenders, two caps, a hat, ties, a couple of pullovers and cardigans, a sports coat, blazer and three pairs of trousers as well as three suits, and his underclothes of course, that's if you don't mind wearing them. Could you use them, Ronnie?' she asked, her face darkly serious as she fought back tears evoked by the clothes.

'I have one torn shirt, one pair of worn trousers and these—' he put his hands in the pockets of the trousers he was wearing—'which as you so astutely pointed out, don't fit. So if you really don't mind, I could use them.'

'What size shoes do you take?'

'Ten.'

'Same as Eddie. They're all in boxes at the bottom of the wardrobe. Why don't you try some of the things on now, then I'll pack up what's left this evening.'

'You sure about this? I don't know how I'd

114

feel if I saw another woman wearing Maud's clothes.'

'If it was someone in the family who'd lost everything the way you have, you wouldn't mind.'

'Perhaps not.' He lifted a shirt from a shelf in the wardrobe and fingered the fine cotton. It had been a long time since he had seen clothes laid out in this kind of domestic order. Why did everything, especially the small things, always remind him of his life with Maud? 'Thank you, Jenny.'

'There's nothing to thank me for. Are you staying on in Pontypridd?'

'I don't see that I've got much option at the moment, with this—' he held up his crutch.

'What are you going to do? Go back to running the cafés?'

'I don't know.'

'It's difficult to make plans when it feels as though your world has come to an end.'

'You understand that too?'

'They need workers in the munitions factories. I start next week.'

'What about the shop?'

'I've found a girl in Leyshon Street who is prepared to run it for me. I've wanted to do something to help the war effort ever since Eddie got killed.'

'I would have thought you were doing enough in managing this place.'

'With the Germans about to invade at any minute?'

He would have liked to contradict her, but

the one question on everyone's lips at the RAF base where he had been debriefed, was 'what are the bastards waiting for?'

'I want to make the bullets and shells that will kill the men who murdered Eddie. It was murder, you know. William was there and he told us about it. Eddie's whole unit was shot by German soldiers after they surrendered their weapons.'

'I didn't know.' He shuddered, not at her story but at the venom in her voice. He'd long since discovered that it wasn't only those who were killed who had been destroyed by the war.

'You must come around one evening. I could make supper for us. It would be nice to talk to someone who understands what I'm going through.' She gave him a sad little smile as the shop door rattled. 'I'd better go and open up, before whoever that is breaks something.'

He stripped off down to Tony's underpants, changed into the shirt and one of the suits, and looked around for a mirror. There was a full-length cheval in Jenny's bedroom. Turning his back on the feminine clutter of hairpins, cold cream, scent bottles and brushes on the dressing table that reminded him too acutely of his wife, he studied his image in the glass. The suit hung loosely on his skeletal frame, and the trousers would have fallen down without the braces, but Jenny was right about his and Eddie's height. The length of the trousers and sleeves was perfect. Bundling Tony's clothes under his arm, he limped down the stairs into the shop and straight into Mrs Richards, Evan Powell's neighbour and the Graig gossip.

She raised her eyebrows as he closed the door that led to Jenny's private quarters. 'Well, I see you've wasted no time in visiting old friends, Ronnie?'

'Ronnie's been helping me with something upstairs,' Jenny intervened.

'It's handy for a widow to have a man to call on,' Mrs Richards smirked knowingly. 'And good to see someone home in one piece,' she added in an acidic tone that implied she would much rather have seen her own son, Glan, home from the POW camp he'd been consigned to for the duration.

'Not quite one piece, Mrs Richards.' Ronnie lifted his crutch.

'You're alive, aren't you, and you'll mend. Sorry to hear about Maud, but then she always was sickly.'

He nodded, not trusting himself to reply.

'You two have a lot in common now, both married to Powells who've passed on. Nice to see you consoling one another like this.'

Ronnie took half a crown from his pocket and pushed it across the counter. 'Twenty Players please, Jenny.'

'She was serving me,' Mrs Richards snapped.

'Ronnie only wants cigarettes and he is in a hurry.' Jenny turned to the tobacco shelves above the till. Handing Ronnie his change and cigarettes, she said, 'I won't forget to give those things to Bethan, and your rations. Gina dropped your coupons in this morning.'

He knew perfectly well Gina had done no such thing, because his food coupons were snarled up in the same bureaucratic web as his clothing coupons. 'Thank you for everything, Jenny. See you soon.' Nodding to Mrs Richards he opened the door and left.

'Well, it's easy to see what's on his mind,' Mrs Richards declared in a loud voice before he managed to pull his crutch out behind him.

'Do you have a list, Mrs Richards?'

'Here it is. I'm putting a food parcel together for my Glan in the prison camp. They have it rough, you know. According to his letters they have nothing to eat except potatoes, swedes and black bread. All I can say is, I hope it's not black from mould. Disgraceful the way those Jerries are treating our boys.'

'At least your Glan is still alive to be treated disgracefully, Mrs Richards.' Jenny bit down hard on her bottom lip as she watched the back of Eddie's suit disappear across the road and down the hill towards Laura's house.

'Constable Davies, how nice to see you,' Myrtle greeted him as she opened the door to his tentative knock.

'Just thought I'd call in and see how Megan's doing.'

'I'm sorry, you've missed her. Mrs Lane called in to let us know that Pegler's have had a consignment of tinned fruit in, but if you'd like to wait, she shouldn't be much longer.'

'I wasn't expecting to find you home at this hour.'

'My section finished two hours earlier than usual today. We ran out of materials, which probably means we'll have to put in extra time tomorrow when the supplies arrive. Please, come on through to the living room. Would you like some tea?'

'I should go on into town to pick up my rations.'

'I've just made a fresh pot. My father always takes a cup when he goes for his afternoon nap.'

'Myrtle? Myrtle? Who's there?' the old man called peevishly from the front parlour.

'Only Constable Davies for Megan, Dad.'

'Turn up the radio will you? You're making such a racket I can't hear it.'

Myrtle went into his room and did as he asked before returning to the hall. 'Please, do come through. I need someone to keep me awake until Megan gets back. I'm looking after Billy and I'm so tired I could easily fall asleep and not hear him crying.'

'From what I recall of the noise he makes, there's not much danger of that.' He followed her into the living room.

'Please, sit down. I'll pour the tea.'

'Your shift begins the same time as usual in the morning?'

'I'll be leaving on the five o'clock train, but really, you don't have to walk me down.'

'It's easy to time my beat to coincide with the departure of the munitions special.' He summoned his courage as he took the tea she handed him. There'd never be a better time.

He'd been rehearsing the speech he was about to make all morning when he had been lying in his bed, trying to sleep. 'I'm off on Sunday. If you are too, I thought we could go for a walk in the park,' he blurted out. He leaned back in the chair, weak with relief. He'd done it. He'd finally breached the barrier that marked the dividing line between friendship and courtship.

'I'm sorry, I'm working on Sunday.'

'It doesn't matter.' His heart sank. He should have braced himself to take disappointment. What right had he to think that a woman like Myrtle would want to bother with him?

'My next day off isn't until a week Monday. Because the production line is kept flat out twenty-four hours day, seven days a week we can't pick and choose our time off.'

'I have a week Monday off too.' He didn't, but as there were a few officers in the station who owed him a favour, he didn't envisage any difficulties in changing shifts.

'Perhaps we could go for a walk then?' she suggested shyly.

'Or Cardiff,' he hazarded boldly. 'There's more to do there. We could go to a matinée in the pictures and have tea in a Lyons afterwards.'

'I'd like that.'

'I'll pick you up here about twelve, give you a chance to have a bit of a lie-in.'

'No,' she answered swiftly, thinking of her father. It was one thing to have Huw Davies visiting Megan, quite another to have him calling to take her out. 'I'll meet you at the station.'

'I'll get the tickets.'

'About twelve, then.'

'I'll be waiting in the booking office.'

The door opened and closed. As Myrtle helped Megan unpack the tins she'd queued an hour for, he sat back and drank his tea, his triumph marred by the thought that Myrtle didn't see the outing in the same light as him. How could she, when she didn't want anyone else in the house to know that he was taking her out?

'The postman saw your car outside, and dropped this in.' Phyllis set down the tea she'd brought for Bethan on the bedside cabinet, and laid the letter on the bed.

Bethan picked up the blue and white envelope and turned it over. 'It's from Andrew.'

'Take your time reading it, Rachel's having a nap and I've just changed and fed Eddie.'

'Thank you.' Bethan glanced at the alarm clock next to the bed. She'd asked Phyllis to wake her at two and it was five to the hour. She could steal ten minutes. As soon as Phyllis closed the door she tore open the envelope.

Dear Bethan,

Thank you for your letter and the photograph of our son which I had yesterday, eight weeks after you sent them. What do you want me to say? That I'm grateful to you for keeping this pregnancy from me? You say you didn't want to worry me, but as I've nothing to do here except think about you and Rachel, all you've succeeded in doing is making me feel excluded from your life more than ever.

I don't mind if you name our son Eddie ...

She picked up her tea and sipped it slowly, wondering if Andrew hated the idea of naming their son after her brother. He had never really got on with Eddie, but by the time he'd had the letter telling him of the birth it would have been too late for him to have made a contribution to the name anyway.

Perhaps he was right, perhaps she should have told him about her pregnancy before Eddie's birth; only after the complications she'd had in her first pregnancy, she couldn't bear the thought of him sitting in a prison camp, day in, day out, with nothing to do except worry about her, the way she worried about him and the survival of their marriage during the few odd moments when she was free to think at all.

I hope you are taking it easy and looking after the children ...

She started guiltily, glancing at the date on his letter. It had taken nine weeks to get to her, and it was obvious hers took just as long to reach him. She hadn't even had an address for him until four months after he'd been captured. Although she'd written to him four and sometimes five times a week since, the missive in which she'd dropped the bombshell that she had taken the district nurse's job had to be stuck in a mailbag somewhere.

Things here are the same as ever—crushingly boring. I have set up a small infirmary to treat the sick and wounded, but infirmary is a grand name for an eight by twelve wooden hut, with three bunks and no xxxxxxxxxxxxxxxxxxxxxxxxxxxxxxx

She studied the thick black lines, but it was hopeless. The German censor had done a thorough job. There was no deciphering the words beneath the crossings out. She guessed that Andrew had written: drugs, medical supplies and bandages.

We do all kinds of crazy things to keep up our spirits. Some of the boys are building a theatre. The entertainments committee make an effort to put on a variety show at least once a week and it will be good to have a place where everyone can congregate to watch, instead of a small number of us squashing into the largest barracks. The chorus of our sergeants in drag has to be seen to be believed. We also have a few good singers, although none of them are up to Haydn's standard. I hope he is still singing somewhere through all of this. As I said before, being a POW, or KRIEGIES as we're known to the guards (my German is better than I'd like it to be) is not too onerous, but when you can spare the money, rations and the time, food parcels are very desirable and books even more so.

Thank you for the socks and mittens. It is still unbelievably cold here, but rumour has it spring is on the way and I hope I'll never have to spend another winter away from you, Rachel—and Eddie. My son—it's strange to have a child I've never seen. Little did I think when I left you that last morning that we would end up being separated with no hope of seeing one another again until the war is over. Please keep writing, you can have no idea bow much your letters mean to me.

Re-reading this I realise I've allowed my anger to show through in the beginning, but I am still finding it difficult to get used to the idea of suddenly becoming a father for the second time. If only I could hold you. Then it would be easy to tell you how I feel. Furious—but only because I love you and worry about you having to bring up the children on your own.

I love and miss you so very much. Kiss Rachel and Eddie for me, and pray with me every night that this war will soon come to an end.

Your devoted husband Andrew.

PS Mother has written to me. Thank her for the socks and scarf and explain that I can't write as many letters as I'd like. And try to get up to see her with the children more often. I know things have been difficult between you, but she does adore Rachel, and with me here, and Fiona and Alex in Scotland, you and my father are all the family she has.

Bethan re-read the letter while she finished her tea. The censor hadn't blacked out any important bits, so she supposed she should be grateful for that much, but she found herself wishing that he'd blacked out the postscript. It infuriated her to think that her mother-in-law could still get to her through Andrew, even when he was in a POW camp in the heart of Germany. What did she care for Andrew's sister Fiona, and her doctor husband Alex who'd pulled every string he could reach to get a posting to a hospital in Edinburgh the minute war had been declared?

She clutched the letter, scanning for more in between the words. Andrew seemed so remote. The only time she had to miss him in her hectic days was the increasingly brief time between going to bed and sleeping, and even then she was not always alone, because since Eddie's birth, Rachel had taken to climbing out of her cot and joining her.

A year—a whole year since she'd seen him. How much longer? And what would they both be like when it finally ended?

CHAPTER 6

'Heard you paid Jenny Powell a visit,' Tina greeted Ronnie as he limped into the café. Gina had walked up to the Tumble from the restaurant lower down Taff Street to pass on the gossip. She was far too wary of her older brother to dare mention any scandal concerning him to his face, but Tina had no such qualms.

Ronnie perched on a stool and unfolded the copy of the *Pontypridd Observer* he'd bought off a boy manning the pitch outside the Clarence. 'I called into her shop for a packet of cigarettes, and as you can see,' he fingered the lapel on the suit he was wearing, 'she offered me Eddie's clothes. As beggars can't be choosers in these days of rationing, coupons and shortages, I took them.'

'Rumour has it you've a lot more in common than most brother and sister-in-laws.'

'Mama Mia! You sound just like Mrs Richards,' he complained as she dumped two cups on the counter and reached for the coffee jug.

'I can see you've just come back from Italy. It used to be "bloody hell" before you went.'

'Our grandmother objected to anything stronger, and she understood just enough English to know when I was swearing. Haven't people anything better to do than talk about me? For pity's sake

126

I've just lost my wife.'

'Which means you're available. And virile, eligible men are at such a premium in the town at the moment, you'll have half the women, married as well as single, flinging themselves at you. So you may as well get used to the attention now.' She poured out the coffee too vigorously, slopping it into the saucers as well as the cups. 'And then again, you did have to go and pick on Jenny Powell to talk to, didn't you?'

'It's a bit difficult to buy anything in her shop without talking to her.'

'Everything Jenny Powell does is of interest to the gossips. She can't even brush her hair and put on a dab of lipstick without someone spreading the rumour she's after a new husband. But then, young widows are expected to lead racy lives to entertain their neighbours. As are young widowers,' she added pointedly.

'What I can't understand is how she ended up marrying Eddie Powell,' he said in an attempt to draw Tina's attention away from himself. 'The last I remember she and Haydn were courting strong.'

'She might have been courting Haydn, but she left your wedding breakfast to go up the mountain with Eddie.'

'Frankly I was too busy looking at Maud at the time to care what her brothers and their girlfriends were doing.'

'Then when Haydn left Pontypridd to go on stage, she well and truly sank her claws into Eddie.'

' "Sank her claws?" Since when have you joined Mrs Richards's gossipers' club?' he asked as she handed him the milk jug and sugar shaker.

'I'd hate to see you get tarnished by Jenny's reputation.'

'Her reputation? Have I missed something here, like Jenny forcing Eddie to marry her at gunpoint?'

'No one really knows what happened except that she kissed Haydn outside the church after she married Eddie in a way no sister-in-law should. And everyone, including me, saw it. Tony told me the next day that he saw Eddie drinking until two in the morning. Jenny was nowhere in sight, and considering it was their wedding night—'

'More fool Tony,' Ronnie broke in, 'because there's nowhere legal you can drink until that hour.'

'You never stop playing the big brother, do you?' Tina complained, irritated by his interruption.

'Someone has to with our tribe.'

'Our tribe is in Birmingham with our mother. Gina and I are married women. Responsible adults who work and run businesses as well as homes.'

'You were telling me about Eddie and Jenny,' he reminded her, refusing to quarrel.

'And you weren't listening. God! I'd forgotten just how infuriating you can be!' The steamer began to hiss, she opened it up, took out the pie inside, slapped it on to a plate and carried it into the back room for a customer.

'I'm listening now, always presuming there's a point to this story of yours,' he said when she returned.

'There is a point, and it concerns you. The day after the wedding, Eddie left Jenny with her parents and returned to live in his father's house in Graig Avenue. A couple of days after that he attacked Haydn, punching him through a plate-glass window in town, breaking his leg and cutting his face and head really badly. Haydn was in the cottage hospital for days. Trevor and Andrew said he was lucky to have survived. Before Haydn even left hospital, Eddie disappeared. We found out afterwards he'd joined the Guards. He only came back once on leave before he was killed, and that was when Jenny's mother died.'

'Thank you for the news report, but what's all this got to do with me?'

Tina narrowed her eyes and repeated the gossip exactly as she'd heard it. ' "Ronnie Ronconi was seen taking off his clothes in Jenny Powell's front bedroom this morning. And the shop door was locked. Something Jenny has never done before during opening hours." '

'And where did you hear that bit of spicy tittle-tattle?' His voice was soft, controlled, but his hands trembled as he picked up the coffee in front of him.

'Old Mrs Evans who lives above the fruit shop opposite saw you in the bedroom, she told Mrs Richards, who caught you coming out of Jenny's private rooms. Mrs Evans went to the restaurant this morning to order a cake for Mrs Jones's daughter's wedding ...'

'And no doubt by now all three ladies have relayed the story, with embellishments, to the entire Graig. Did Mrs Evans also say that the bed in the room I was in was dismantled, and Jenny was only with me for a few minutes? I told you, Jenny offered me Eddie's clothes. She took me upstairs to see them. Amazing as this may sound, they were in a wardrobe in a bedroom, not one of the kitchen cupboards.'

'But you undressed?'

'Not in front of Jenny. Eddie might be dead, but as far as I could tell from my brief visit, Jenny was nowhere near frustrated enough to sink her claws into my battered body. Of course if I'd known Mrs Evans was watching I might have removed my underpants as well as my shirt to give her a real thrill.'

'I doubt she would have survived the experience.'

'I needed clothes,' he reiterated. 'Jenny offered me Eddie's. There was no point in taking them if they didn't fit, so I tried them on, and it's difficult to do that without undressing.'

'I'm only telling you to be more careful in future. You know how people talk.'

'Apparently even my own sister.'

'Don't say I didn't warn you,' she snapped back.

'What's to warn me about? Jenny offered me clothes, which I gratefully accepted.'

'Just as long as it is only Eddie's clothes she's expecting you to fill.'

130

'That's not the kind of remark I ever expected to hear from a sister of mine.'

'I told you, Ronnie, we've grown up since you went away.'

'Crudely.'

'Save the lectures for the little ones when they come home. Gina and I don't take kindly to being told what to do, say or think any more.'

'What do you mean, "any more"? You never did a damned thing Papa and I told you to do when I was home.'

'Can you blame us when you expected us to behave like nuns?' She picked up a rag and began polishing the tea urn.

'You may as well finish what you started so we can get it over with,' he advised, hoping to diffuse her anger before it erupted into a full-blown argument.

'Considering the reception you've given my warnings, I rather think I have.'

'Come on, get it out in the open.'

'It's nothing I can prove, so I'd rather not say anything.'

'You've gone this far, what's another bit of scandal?'

'I've heard that Jenny's carrying on with Alexander Forbes, Evan Powell's conchie lodger. Some even say she was doing it before Eddie was killed.'

'She's a widow, she's entitled to see anyone she wants to.' He didn't know why he was defending Jenny. Eddie'd been killed at Dunkirk, the telegram couldn't have come much before nine months ago. Maud had been dead twice as long and he couldn't imagine 'carrying on' with anyone.

'That's just it, she isn't seeing him.'

'So how can she be carrying on with him? Through radio waves or out-of-body experiences?'

'Mrs Evans spotted a man with fair hair sneaking around the Factory Lane side of the shop late at night, and ...'

'You believe her?'

'It was obvious that things had gone wrong between Jenny and Eddie. If it hadn't been for the state of their marriage, Eddie would never have volunteered to join the Guards in the first place.'

'Thousands are dying every day,' he asserted harshly. 'If Eddie hadn't died at Dunkirk, there's no guarantee he would have survived the war.'

'I just don't want to see you fall for someone like Jenny Powell who's already ruined one man's life.'

'The only ruin I can see is Jenny's reputation at the hands of Mrs Richards and Mrs Evans.'

'You're my brother. Much as you irritate me, I wouldn't like to see you get hurt.'

'I've managed to live the last thirty-two years without your help, and I have every intention of avoiding Jenny's and any other designing woman's claws.'

'I'm serious, Ronnie. You've no idea how starved of male company the women are in this town. A lot of girls are going to be looking your way. And a widower, even one in your condition, has to be a better proposition than those too old or young to be called up.'

'You're missing William that much?' he asked perceptively.

'Every minute of every day. It's bad enough for me and Alma; it's worse for women like Bethan who are trying to bring up children without their fathers. The hardest is not even knowing where our husbands are. Every time there's fighting I imagine William and Tony lying injured somewhere, with no one to care for them.'

'Look at it logically, Tina. When it comes to self-preservation, comfort and caring for number one, William's an expert. If there's fighting, he's got enough sense to keep his head down, and you told me Tony's probably still somewhere in this country. Can't you see that because everyone's under a lot of strain in the town, they're generating this doom-laden atmosphere?'

'I suppose you're right.'

'And I'm here now, so you don't have to go on doing everything yourself. Use me to take some of the load off your shoulders.'

She gazed at him earnestly, seeking re-assurance. 'You've lived in Europe, you know what it's like over there. The war can't go on much longer, can it?'

'If we don't get help, it might be over sooner than we'd like.'

'You don't think we're going to lose!'

'How long do you think this one small island can hold out against the rest of the world? I've

133

lived under the Fascists, seen London flattened by bombs. Our troops are stretched on every front.'

'There's talk of the Americans coming in on our side.'

'Why should they, when there's nothing in it for them?'

'So what do you suggest we do? Surrender?'

'Of course not. We'll go on fighting as best we can, because it's the only real option open to us. Which is why I went to see Dr Evans this morning. Thanks to the papers I had from the RAF I'm no longer regarded as an enemy alien. They're allowing me to work in the munitions factory.'

'Not with your wounds, surely?'

'I can start as soon as my injuries have healed. And it's my hands not my legs they want. Like me with Eddie's clothes, they're grateful for what they can get.' He finished his coffee and pushed his cup across the counter. 'Until then I'm offering you my services as a counter hand.'

'You work for me?' she scoffed.

'Why not?'

'Fine, you can start right now. There's a mountain of potatoes that need peeling in the kitchen,' she ordered, not expecting him to make a move. She wasn't disappointed.

'First thing tomorrow morning, after we've negotiated my wages.'

'All meals plus a pound a week?'

'That will do until I start in the munitions factory.'

'My God, you really are serious, aren't you?'

'About helping out, yes.'

'Maud changed you that much?'

'She gave me the happiest years of my life,' he said simply. 'But do me a favour, Tina. No more gossip. Since Maud died I'm not sure who I am, or where I'm going, but one thing I do know is that there's no room for another woman in my life. Not now, and not ever.'

'In that case you'd better go up to Bethan's with me tonight. And before you ask, Gina and Luke are taking over the café.'

'Why do I have to go to Bethan's?'

'She's having a party for Charlie, and Alma and Jenny will be there. If you start treating both of them as family, it might silence the gossips on two counts.'

Her conscience pricked by Andrew's letter, Bethan waited only as long as it took Rachel to wake from her afternoon nap. After washing and dressing both children in their best clothes, she packed Rachel and the baby into the back of the car and drove slowly through the town and up the hill to the Common and Andrew's father's house.

She had timed her visit to coincide with afternoon tea, because she knew Dr John made an effort to be home at that hour. Her relationship with Andrew's mother had never been cordial for the simple reason that Mrs John considered a miner's daughter an unsuitable wife for her son. His father was different. One of only two doctors left in the town, their newly won mutual respect was founded as much in their present, professional association as their personal relationship. But unfortunately for her, Andrew's parents weren't the only ones sitting in the overfurnished drawing room the maid showed her into. Her mother-in-law's close friend, Mrs Llewellyn Jones, and her spoilt, but extremely fashionable and attractive daughter, Anthea, were taking tea with them.

The first time Andrew had taken her home, Mrs John had gone to great pains to let her know that Anthea Llewellyn Jones had been earmarked as her prospective daughter-in-law. Even now, Bethan occasionally had the feeling that Mrs John hadn't quite given up on the hope that she would die young, or have an affair, so Andrew could divorce her and marry a woman of his own class. Someone just like Anthea.

All four of them were sipping tea and eating slices of sponge cake smothered in jam and butter icing as though they hadn't even heard there was a war on.

'Bethan, how wonderful to see you and the little angels,' Andrew's mother gushed, overdoing the welcome for the benefit of her guests. 'And how kind of you to spare the time to visit us. I know how busy you must be with the evacuees and your nursing. Come in, sit down. May I hold the baby?'

Bethan dutifully handed Eddie over, wondering why everything her mother-in-law said to her always sounded insincere.

'Tea?' Her father-in law's hand was on the bell ready to summon the maid. It would never have occurred to him to fetch the extra crockery himself.

'No thank you, I've just had a cup.' Bethan sat down with Rachel on her lap. The little girl who was at home enough in Phyllis and Evan's back kitchen to crawl on to whoever's lap happened to be the closest, invariably clung to Bethan during her visits to Andrew's parents. 'I came to tell you I've just had a letter from Andrew.'

'How is he?' his mother enquired swiftly, her eyes darkening in a genuine anxiety that made Bethan ashamed of her critical thoughts.

'He says fine. He wanted me to thank you for your letters and all the things you sent him, and to tell you he can't write as often as he'd like.'

'We know that, the silly boy. He really is all right?'

'Apart from boredom.'

'I can understand that,' Anthea drawled. 'Andy was always so active—tennis, driving, swimming, riding—nothing was too much for him. You remember that time he borrowed a boat and we sailed from Mumbles Bay to Oxwich, Mummy? We went to a party afterwards at Penrice Manor and danced until dawn, and he still didn't want to go to bed.' She beamed at Bethan in an attempt to emphasise just how much fun she and Andrew had shared in his bachelor days. 'It must be absolute hell for him to be holed up in a prison camp and not be able to move around. And it must be almost as unpleasant for you, Bethan, not knowing when, if ever, he's coming home.'

'The war won't last for ever,' Mrs John broke in sharply.

'Of course not,' Anthea conceded hastily, upset that Andrew's mother had taken offence at a remark she'd directed at Bethan. 'But it must be dreadful for him to be stuck in a cell, forced into idleness while others do the fighting, covering themselves with medals and glory that should have been his.'

'I don't think Andrew gave a thought to medals and glory when he signed up, and he has certainly served his country better than most,' Dr John answered, before Bethan could. 'It takes a special kind of courage to remain with the wounded in a field hospital, knowing that the enemy is about to overrun the area at any moment, and that you can't even risk firing a shot in your own defence because in doing so, you'd be putting your patients in the front line.'

'I couldn't be prouder of Andrew.' Bethan regretted the words the instant they were out of her mouth. All she'd succeeded in doing was sounding as pompous as Anthea was foolish.

'We heard that you've gone back to work, Bethan?'

'I'm afraid the medical board press-ganged her.' Andrew's father intervened again on her behalf. 'The shortage of nurses in the town is absolutely desperate.'

'Desperate enough to take on a new mother?' Mrs Llewellyn Jones clucked disapprovingly. 'I must say, national emergency or not, I can't condone working wives let alone working mothers. I don't know what the world is coming to when women abandon their homes and their children. It's bad enough that our young men have to suffer all the privations of war without our children having to grow up without any semblance of family life.'

'I have help in the house, and my family and friends are only too happy to take care of the children for me whenever I'm busy, Mrs Llewellyn Jones.' Bethan could have kicked herself for feeling the need to explain.

'Really?' Mrs Llewellyn Jones questioned sceptically. 'And, as though nursing isn't enough, you've taken in all those evacuees.'

'I meant to thank you for billeting such a helpful girl with me.' Bethan swallowed her pride and forced a smile. She'd learned from bitter experience that no one ever won an argument with Mrs Llewellyn Jones. The woman had influence in every sphere of Pontypridd life, and never hesitated to make things difficult for people who crossed her. 'I hardly know the evacuee children are in the house. Liza Clark takes care of them beautifully.'

'Not your own I hope, dear. It wouldn't do to have them picking up that dreadful accent.' When Bethan didn't answer, she continued: 'I simply don't know how you cope. It's all very well the government telling us that we all have to do our bit, but they're not the ones who have to give up their privacy and goodness only knows what else. I was just telling Dr and Mrs John that Mr Llewellyn Jones and I have been forced to take in the headmaster of one of the evacuee schools. He's no trouble really, except that the house doesn't seem to be our own any more.'

'He's so old and finicky,' Anthea grumbled, giving Bethan the impression that she wouldn't be complaining if he were young and handsome.

'At least our headmaster is civilised,' her mother chimed in. 'I've heard down at the WVS that some of the evacuee children don't even know how to eat. Would you believe that they've never held a knife and fork? Used to running wild all day and living off slices of bread and jam eaten in their fists in the street. And the diseases on the labels! Over half the children had impetigo, scabies, vermin, hair nits and I wouldn't like to say what else,' she whispered *sotto voce* to Mrs John. 'Some of them, great big lumps of children too, even wet the bed. But then as a nurse, Bethan, you're accustomed to dealing with the unpleasant side of life.'

'That doesn't mean I like it any more than you, Mrs Llewellyn Jones. But thanks to the efforts of Dr Evans and Dr John—'

'And the town's nurses,' her father-in-law interrupted, 'all the evacuees are now guaranteed disease free.'

'Disease free or not, they're still nasty little savages who have no idea how to behave. All I can say is I'm glad not many people on the Common took them in. They're rife down in town and Trallwn, and the number of criminal incidents involving them escalates every day. Things like playing ball in the street, which in

140

my experience always ends in broken windows, and disturbing people by knocking on doors and running away. One of the teachers over at Maesycoed School told me that the situation there is quite impossible.'

'It will quieten down now they've settled in,' Bethan said in the hope that Mrs Llewellyn Jones would change the subject.

'Have you had much trouble with your four?'

'Six actually; seven, if you include Liza Clark, but then as I said she's a real help, and in answer to your question, no I haven't had any trouble with them.'

'Six as well as your own two, and decent help as impossible as it is to get today, whatever were you thinking of? Poor Andrew's children will suffer so. And going out to work as well ... Oh dear is that the time?' she asked as a horn sounded outside. 'It's been wonderful, but we have to go. Hurry up Anthea, we can't keep your father waiting. We promised to visit his mother, poor dear. All this war business is such an upset for her. It's so difficult to get butter, ham and cheese these days. Dinner parties are becoming quite impossible, and her maid of ten years left her at a day's notice to work in munitions. Have you any idea what they're paying untrained girls in the factories? It will be the ruination of the working class, mark my words. They'll be spending it all on drink, and cheap finery and ...'

'Be sure to give my regards to Andy the next time you write, Bethan,' Anthea instructed as she followed her mother out of the french

141

windows and across the lawn.

'I will,' Bethan agreed hollowly as she took the baby from her mother-in-law, who wanted to see her guests out. By the time she returned, Rachel had thawed enough to sit on her grandfather's knee.

'I do wish you'd bring the children up here one or two days a week, dear.' Andrew's mother rang the bell for the maid to clear the tea things. 'We hardly see them. It would help you as you're so busy, and we would get to know our own grandchildren.'

'They're a lot of work at this age,' Bethan warned.

'Don't I know it. There's barely fifteen months between Andrew and Fiona, and they were little monkeys.'

'That was a long time ago,' her husband reminded her.

'It isn't as though I haven't any help. If they got too much for me, the maid could take them.'

Bethan thought of her father's cosy back kitchen where Phyllis allowed the housework to pile up while she played with Rachel and her own small son, Brian, contrasting it with Andrew's mother's neat sterile kitchen that was geared for the maid's convenience, not children's.

'I can manage, really, but if I ever need help, you'll be the first I'll call on. I'm sorry, I have to go. My father is coming up tonight. Charlie and Alma have been spending his leave with me, and I thought it might be fun to have a family get-together.'

'You really do seem to be doing far too much, dear. You look exhausted.'

'I'm fine, just missing Andrew.'

'As I'm sure he's missing you.' Mrs John put her hand on Bethan's arm and looked down at baby Eddie. 'Just remember if there is anything ...'

'You could try praying for the war to end so Andrew can come home.'

'I think we're all doing enough of that already. The problem is, no one up there seems to be listening. They must be all out on tea-break,' her father-in-law observed irreverently as he reached for the brandy bottle.

Diana climbed the Graig hill to Laura's house in Graig Street swinging a brown paper and string carrier bag in each hand. One held meat, the other cooked savouries from the shop Alma and Wyn had opened at the bottom of the hill. Even with the café supplies to fall back on, she suspected that Ronnie's sudden arrival without ration cards had put a strain on Tina's housekeeping, and as the food in the bags hadn't been earmarked for anyone, no one would miss what she'd taken except Wyn and Alma when they counted up their profits at the end of the month. She knew, since she'd taken over the books when Alma's mother had fallen ill, that the shop could easily withstand the small gift.

She nodded to Mrs Richards who was heading into town, and walked on determinedly, pretending not to see her signalling to her to

143

stop. She was enjoying her solitude far too much to indulge her old neighbour's fondness for tittle-tattle. After a morning spent helping Wyn interview Vera Collins's sister, Harriet, and checking and banking the takings in Alma's shops as well as Wyn's, before the three o'clock bank closing, and then putting her weekly order into Jenny's shop and sitting with Alma's mother to give the relief nurse time to pick up her own rations, she felt she'd earned half an hour's peace. Usually the only thing she had to look forward to that wasn't work, was bathing Billy at the end of the day, and Wyn and her mother's company, but tonight was going to be different. Tonight there was Bethan's party. An occasion she was looking forward to with mixed feelings, because every gathering emphasised the empty chairs. William's, Haydn's, Eddie's, Andrew's—she knew she should be grateful that she had Wyn. Or did she?

Her marriage had given her material comfort, but not the security she craved. She couldn't help wondering how long the quiet, safe world she and Wyn had built for themselves and Billy could last. Wyn's mention of Erik and his determination to work with him in the munitions factory had continued to prey on her mind, feeding an ominous sense of impending disaster. Their marriage had been built on a web of lies, not to each other, but to everyone connected with them, making her feel like a conspirator—a criminal who was about to be caught and punished. But where and how—the workhouse?

She shivered as she passed the high grey walls, superstitiously crossing the road to escape their shadow. Instead of dwelling on all the things that could go wrong, she tried to concentrate on all the things that were right: like the complete honesty that marked her relationship with Wyn, and the pleasure Billy's arrival had given both of them. She and Wyn had made such plans. Opening a bank account in Billy's name, an embryonic nest egg, so that unlike her and her brother, William, he would be able to stay on in grammar school until matriculation. Wyn had already decided he was so bright, intelligent and forward for his age he was bound to pass the entrance examination. During one rash flight of fancy, Wyn had even mentioned college and university. She imagined Billy grown up, passing through college gates, something tall and imposing like the ones she'd seen in *Goodbye Mr Chips*. A dark, attractive, young man—everyone complimented her on him inheriting her colouring, but then they didn't know the truth.

She turned left, crossing a triangular patch of grass to the pavement outside Laura's house. She turned the key and stepped inside, walking straight down the stone-flagged passage into the kitchen.

'I'm sorry, I thought you'd be at the café,' she apologised, as she crashed into Ronnie's outstretched legs.

'I wasn't expecting anyone.' He looked as though he'd been sleeping. His black hair was ruffled, his eyes heavy, the dark shadows beneath them more prominent than when she had last seen him in the restaurant. It was obvious he hadn't expected to be disturbed. When he'd lived in Pontypridd she had never seen him in anything less formal than a jacket, collar and tie; now he was in shirt-sleeves and braces, his collar hanging loose from one stud. He shifted the stool he'd rested his feet on so she could edge her way around him. 'But seeing as how you're here, you can make me a cup of tea.'

'You haven't changed a bit, but I warn you now, everyone else around here has.'

'So I've noticed. The women aren't anywhere near as obliging as when I left.'

'If by that you mean we can't be bullied into waiting hand and foot on you men any more, we can't spare the time.' She opened the door to the pantry and unpacked the food she had brought. When she'd finished she returned to the kitchen, lifted the kettle from the range, and went into the washhouse to fill it.

'You don't have to make tea,' he murmured, half apologising. 'I'm so used to teasing my sisters, I can't get out of the habit.'

'It's all right, you're no different from William.' She picked up the hooked metal bar that opened the hotplate, and put the kettle on to boil.

'I'm not so helpless that I can't make tea for myself, so don't feel that you have to stay on my account. I know it probably upsets you to see me without Maud.'

'No it doesn't,' she answered thoughtfully.

146

'Because you married so quickly I have very few memories of you together.'

'I suppose it was a rush wedding.' He drifted into the comforting world of memory. It was easy to slip into the past in this house. His wedding breakfast had been held in the front parlour and, because of the confines of space, virtually every other room. He and Maud had sat here together. If only he could reach out and tear down the curtain of time they could be together again ...

'Do you want anything to eat? I brought up a couple of pasties.'

Jerked back to the present, he struggled to regain his composure. 'Half a pasty might be nice. My appetite isn't up to Pontypridd standards yet.'

'I was hoping to catch you alone some time.' She lifted down cups, saucers and a plate from the dresser.

'It was good of Tina and Gina to organise that get-together, but I was tired, and there were just too many people there.'

'Have you thought what you're going to do with yourself now?'

'The munitions factory is desperate enough to take me on once my injuries have healed.'

'Tina said you'd been shot.'

'The Germans like to use non-Aryans for target practice.' Something in his voice warned her not to trespass further.

'As it looks like you've done more than your fair share towards the war effort, perhaps you should forget munitions and take things easy for a while, and then later on, when you're up to it, you could go back to running the cafés?'

'You might think that's a good idea. I'm not too sure Tina and Gina would agree with you.'

'They surprised everyone when they took over. Both of them have worked incredibly hard.'

'You don't have to tell me. I know exactly how much graft is involved in running a café.'

She leaned across him to reach the teapot, giving a small start as she glanced down and noticed his slippers.

'I'm sorry, these are Eddie's.'

'I know. I should have expected it. Jenny told me she'd given his clothes to you. Both of us thought it was a good idea. Far better than lying mothballed in a wardrobe.'

'I know he was more like a brother to you than a cousin.'

'Just as Maud was more like a sister. We shared the same room when we worked in the Infirmary and I helped to look after her when we came home after she'd been taken ill, but we can't go pussyfooting around their memories for the rest of our lives, Ronnie. Both of them would have hated the idea. They were real people, not saints to have their names whispered in reverence by the living.'

'In the case of Eddie, a very real person.'

'Uncle Evan used to dread the sight of my Uncle Huw in his police uniform. I wanted to see you to tell you that we all know how much you did for Maud. Did you know that we used to write to one another every week before the war broke out? Her letters were full of your life together. You made her so happy ...'

'Diana, please.'

'I'm sorry. I'm being selfish. It's just that ever since you told us she was dead, I've felt this need to talk about her. It must be painful for you, almost like reliving her death again for our benefit.'

'It's not that.' He covered his mouth with his hand, but his eyes were anguished, full of pain and something else, something she couldn't quite decipher.

'Ronnie, what is it?'

'You—Bethan—Evan—Pontypridd.'

'I'm sorry ...'

'For Christ's sake stop apologising. Don't you understand that I can't take any more of this "you saved Maud's life by taking her to Italy", "she had happy years she never would have had if you hadn't married her". If I don't tell someone what really happened I'll go mad.'

'But ... but ... the tuberculosis returned,' she stammered in bewilderment. 'You said as much, and Andrew and Trevor warned us that it might ...'

'Forget the tea, Diana. Sit down, and then I'll tell you exactly how good a husband I was to Maud.'

CHAPTER 7

'To think of an old married couple like us getting carried away like that,' Alma murmured as she straightened her clothes.

'Must be the sun.' Charlie lay back, locked his hands beneath his head and stared up at the wispy clouds drifting above the trees. 'There were times when I thought last winter was never going to end.'

'It was a hard winter where you were?'

'Freezing,' he replied shortly. Reaching out he picked a long stem of grass and pushed it into his mouth. Below them the stream frothed and gurgled into the top end of Shoni's pond. Dragonflies hovered low over the water. The croaking of a frog joined in with the birdsong. He felt contented and at peace with himself, Alma, and the world, for the first time since he had come home. But it couldn't last. This evening there would be other people; afterwards just one final night together. The talking that had to be done had to be done now, or not at all. And he still had to make amends for the harsh things he had said when he had arrived.

'This High Street shop of yours, it's doing well?'

'It averages ten pounds a week clear profit after all the overheads have been accounted for,' she said proudly.

'That much?'

'Of course it's split between us and Wyn and Diana.'

'If you too can increase production enough to supply more shops, perhaps you should go ahead and open up in Treforest as well as Rhydyfelin. If they show a profit, you could use our savings to give you the capital you'll need to open more. There's Cilfynydd, Ynysybwl and the valleys. Cardiff even, if you feel like venturing that far.'

'You trust me with your savings?'

'Our savings. If you can trade successfully during wartime with all the restrictions imposed by rationing, you'll do even better in peacetime.'

'And if the Germans invade?'

'Not even the Nazis can shut a country down. Look at France. The people there still have to buy food.'

'You were the one who thought I had enough to do with running one shop.'

'You seem to have a good partner in Wyn.'

'It's not Wyn who has the business head. It's Diana.'

'Diana? But she has a baby.'

'Having a baby doesn't affect a woman's brain. She was the one who did all the costings and kept an eye on the stock for the first couple of months the shop opened, but if you think we mere females can handle it, we'll expand.'

He sat up and looked at her. His heart skipped a beat just as it had the first time he had gazed into her sea-green eyes. It wasn't just the after-effects of separation or the uncertainty

151

of war. He knew he would feel this way about her until the day he died. 'I'm beginning to think you can handle anything you want, Mrs Raschenko.'

'The only thing I want to handle right now is you, Feodor,' she addressed him by his Russian name before returning his kiss.

There were many things that needed to be resolved between them, but time was so short, so precious, she felt they couldn't afford to waste a single minute—not in talk.

The clock ticked like a metronome into the stillness of Laura's kitchen. Ronnie filched a packet of cigarettes from the pocket of his shirt. It was empty. Before he could reach for his jacket and the packet he had bought in Jenny's shop, Diana opened her handbag and offered him one of hers.

'Since when have you smoked?'

'Since the retreat from France.' She leaned forward and lit her cigarette on the match he struck.

'Poor Eddie.'

'From what William said, it was quick. He never knew what hit him. As Uncle Evan said, there are worse ways to die.' She looked into his troubled eyes, willing him to start telling her about Maud, but he continued to sit, white-faced, shivering, staring into the fire. A barely recognisable shell of the handsome, cynical Ronnie Ronconi who had swept Maud off to Italy before the war.

Summoning all her patience she forced herself

to remain still and wait for him to begin. It wasn't easy. Like Bethan, Tina, Alma and all the women she knew, since war had been declared she lived out her days in an escalating sense of urgency, trying to cram more and more into every minute. Sometimes she felt as though she was chained to a treadmill that she had to keep turning at all costs, because if she stopped, she'd have time to think about what she was doing and then she might fall apart.

Her son—the single most important being in her world—spent more of his waking hours with her mother than he did with her. Anything extra like this time with Ronnie ate into the precious minutes she set aside for him.

'When the war broke out and Italy remained neutral we seemed to have no other option but to lie low and sit it out,' he began hesitantly. 'Apart from worrying about everyone here, I can't pretend I was devastated at the thought of not being able to do more. Maud had always come first with me, and what was happening in Britain and the rest of Europe seemed remote from our life on my grandfather's farm. Then, when Mussolini ordered the registration and call-up of all men of military age, Maud and I left my grandfather's house. I was damned if I was going to fight for the Fascists and there was no way I was going to leave her. And, Maud was British,' his mouth twisted wryly. 'In Fascist Italy *she* was the enemy alien. So, rather than wait for the government officials to come and get me and intern her, we went up into the hills.'

153

'You joined the Resistance?'

'That's a rather grand name for a rag-tag collection of men and women whose only thought was to get out of the war and into some peace and quiet. Don't forget Mussolini didn't even declare war on the Allies until after Dunkirk, and by then Maud had been dead for seven months.' He drew heavily on his cigarette as he continued to stare into the fire. 'After the depression Wales was in bad shape, Italy even worse. Do you know Mussolini's soldiers were marched barefoot into Greece? The Italian army has no money for boots, let alone guns. The country's bankrupt. Everything is in short supply—food, clothes, money. Government troops could at least live off the land because there were enough of them to terrorise the farmers into handing over what little they'd hidden to feed their families. Anti-Fascists like us simply starved. That winter of '39 was damned cold, and we had to keep moving to stay one step ahead of the police and the army. We took refuge in caves and shepherds' huts, and when there were none, we made shelters out of turf and whatever wood was to hand. At night a few of us would go down into the valleys to scavenge for food. Sometimes we struck lucky, sometimes we stole. I'm not proud of it, there wasn't enough for the peasants, they couldn't really spare any for us, but no matter how bad things were, Maud never complained, not once. All the time I thought I was being so damned careful, but as it turned out I wasn't careful enough. I got Maud pregnant.'

'She told me in her letters that she wanted your child.'

'Wanted! It was an impossible dream. We both knew a baby could kill her. Andrew and Trevor warned me before we left here, the doctors in Italy told her as well, but once it happened she wouldn't do anything about it, or allow anyone to help her. A combination of cold, hunger and the filthy conditions we were living in proved too much. The tuberculosis flared up again. I took her back down to my grandfather's house, but it was too late. She died two days after we reached there.'

'Ronnie, you can't blame yourself for that, it wasn't your fault.'

'No? Then whose fault was it? I was the one who took her to Italy. We became fugitives to save my hide ...'

'And hers? How long do you think she would have lasted in an internment camp?'

'I got her pregnant,' he stated bitterly.

'What did you do after she died?' she questioned, not knowing how else to respond to his self-recriminations.

'Buried her in the cemetery in Bardi before returning to the hills.'

'To fight?' she asked, thinking of his wounds.

'Fight?' he sneered derisively. 'What with? Ploughs and hoes? After the battles in Greece last winter some of us took it in turns to guide people through the mountains into Switzerland. Downed Allied pilots, Communists, Jews, intellectuals, anyone who was trying to flee

Mussolini's particular brand of Fascism. I got out with a group of pilots, and as you can see, here I am, safe and sound.'

The anguish in Ronnie's eyes was almost more than Diana could bear. She put her hands over his in an attempt to still his trembling. Despite the fire and the warmth of the room he was as cold as a corpse.

'Maud's death wasn't your fault, Ronnie.'

'I knew how ill she was. I should never have touched her.'

'She loved you very much.' Diana desperately wanted to offer consolation, but she had never been more conscious of her ignorance of passionate love or physical desire. 'I can understand why Maud wanted to carry your child,' she comforted him clumsily. 'Somehow, in the middle of all this mess of war and killing, babies are more important than ever.'

'You sound just like her.'

'Is that surprising when we practically grew up together?'

'I know what you're trying to do, and I thank you for it. It helps to know that you don't blame me, but I'll never forgive myself.'

'And how do you think Maud would feel about that?'

'Have you ever seen anyone die of tuberculosis?'

'Yes.'

'Of course, you worked in Cardiff Infirmary with Maud so you must have.' He tossed his cigarette into the fire. 'It's horrible—the blood, the mess ...'

She crouched down beside him and looked up into his eyes. 'Do you think for one minute Maud would want you to remember her that way? What about the happy Maud who wrote to us sitting outside your grandfather's house in the warm Italian summers? The Maud who helped your aunt to plant begonias in the garden, the almost healthy Maud, Trevor and Laura saw when they visited you the summer after you left here? You gave her those extra years, Ronnie. Happy years. Dwell on them, not on her dying.'

'I only wish I could.'

'You have to, for her sake as well as yours.'

'There is no "her sake" any more, she's dead.'

'You can wallow in self-pity if you want to, Ronnie, but if you do, you won't be the only one to suffer. You don't have exclusive rights on Maud's life, she's a part of me, and all the other people who knew and loved her. Don't tarnish our memories by killing her a second time. And you will if you persist in dwelling on her death to the exclusion of her life. I loved Eddie and Maud,' she asserted fiercely, 'and I'm going to tell Bethan's children about the uncle and aunt they'll never know. Not as names they have to whisper in case someone starts crying, but as warm, funny, loving people who enriched all our lives.'

'And you don't want a killjoy sitting in the corner reminding them of the cruel realities of life?'

'Exactly,' she rejoined bluntly. 'You're not just

157

Maud's husband, you're Bethan and Haydn's brother-in-law. Maud left you two nieces and a nephew. So, are you going to help Bethan, Haydn and the rest of us keep Maud and Eddie's memory alive for them?' Her question echoed against the ticking of the clock.

'You don't understand. How could you?'

'I understand that while Maud lived, you loved and cared for her. You've nothing to feel guilty about, Ronnie. Only sadness that we've all lost her.'

If he heard her he gave no sign of it.

'Would you like that tea, now?'

He didn't even look at her. Instead he remained hunched in his chair staring into the fire.

She sat with him while the clock ticked on. After a while she doubted that he even knew she was there. 'Ronnie, if there's ever anything I can do?'

He shook his head. She picked up her bag and left, closing the front door quietly.

He heard her leave. The kitchen closed into silence once again. It was then that he felt a tear roll down his cheek. It was followed by another and another, the first tears he'd shed in eighteen numb, arid months.

As he lifted his hand to wipe them away a racking sob tore through his emaciated body. The paroxysm of emotion carried in its intensity some of the guilt and anguish that had tormented him since Maud's death. But even when he was done, too spent and exhausted even to weep, he wasn't sure

158

whether he'd been crying for Maud, or for himself.

'I don't know how Liza and Maisie do it,' Phyllis commented as she admired the array of sandwiches and cakes they had set out on the table in Bethan's dining room, a room that had only been opened up twice since Andrew had left home.

'I'll let you in on a secret,' Bethan confessed as she made space on the table for the curried corned beef balls and dripping cake Phyllis had brought. 'Neither do I. I just hand over the ration cards and let them get on with it.'

'I only hope you've got some food left for the rest of the week.'

Maisie came in and took Phyllis's coat, too conscious of her status as maid to do any more than answer Phyllis's polite enquiries after her and her daughter's health, although they had once lived in the same street.

'Have you invited anyone else, love?' Evan followed Megan and Diana, who carried Billy in her arms, from the hall as Brian scampered off to join the evacuees.

'Tina, Jenny and Ronnie. They're coming up together after Jenny has closed the shop.'

'And Wyn's sorry, but as we've only just moved Alice from the High Street to the New Theatre shop he wants to give her a hand to open up, but he'll be along later,' Diana apologised.

'I asked Charlie if there was anyone else he wanted to see, but as tonight's his last night

I think we're probably overwhelming enough as it is.'

'Speak of the Devil and he appears,' Megan announced as Charlie walked down the stairs with Alma.

'Thought we heard voices.' Alma kissed the women while Charlie lifted Evan off his feet in a bear hug.

'I slipped a couple of bottles of beer I've been saving into Andrew's study,' Evan said with a smile. 'Why don't we go and sample them while the women sort out the food?'

'Here, take this with you.' Bethan cradled Eddie in one arm as she took a half-empty bottle from the sideboard and handed it to her father. 'I'm sorry, Charlie, it's brandy. I know you prefer vodka.' She brought out another two bottles, home-made, elderberry wine this time. The bell rang shrilly as she placed them on the table. 'That's too early for the girls.' Bethan glanced up at the clock.

'You on duty?' Megan asked.

'The relief's on until midnight, but as she's sitting with Mrs Moore I said I'd cover for emergencies.' She followed Maisie into the outer hall and cried out in surprise. 'You're the last people I expected to see!'

'We took a taxi up from the station. There was no one in Graig Avenue, but Mrs Richards told us that Dad, Phyllis, Diana and Megan had got into your car ...'

'Nosy old so-and-so.'

'So here we are.' Haydn put an arm around a reluctant Jane and ushered her forward.

Bethan opened the door into the main hall. 'Dad, you're never going to believe in a hundred years who's here.'

'Tony's written. He's coming home soon,' Gina announced as she walked into the Tumble café with Luke. She looked past Ronnie to the kitchen. 'Tina with the cook?'

'Gone up to Jenny's. I hope to get a taxi and pick them up there. My leg isn't up to walking that far yet.'

'You'll be damned lucky to get a wheelbarrow, let alone a taxi. Haven't you heard petrol's rationed?'

'Your language is appalling,' Ronnie said.

'You going to stand by and let him talk to your wife like that?' Gina demanded of Luke.

'I'd rather get to know your brother before I try coming between the two of you.'

'Wise man.' Ronnie couldn't help thinking that Gina and Luke looked more like a couple of schoolchildren than husband and wife. He reached for the cups. 'Tea?'

'Seeing as how you're serving, yes please. I don't suppose you've got any teacakes left?' she asked, as she leaned over the counter and poked around the empty glass cake-stands.

'You suppose right.'

'I'm starving.'

'You've just eaten a huge tea,' Luke pointed out mildly.

'I'm still hungry.' Lifting the flap on the counter she went foraging.

'So when is Tony coming?' Ronnie asked, as

161

he turned the tap on the tea urn.

'A week tomorrow. Can he stay with you in Laura's? I'd offer, but one of my evacuees' husbands is coming down on embarkation leave and her children will have to move out of her bedroom so he can move in. We won't have a spare bed or room in the house.'

'He'll probably appreciate the peace in Graig Street.'

'Good, I'm glad that's settled. It's not that I don't want to see him, it's just that our house is bedlam with all the evacuees squashed in.'

'Does Mama know you've taken them in?' As a concession to Luke's status as family, Ronnie produced the sugar shaker.

'She was the one who suggested we put them up. Her landlady in Birmingham has been good to her, and Mama thought it might be a way of putting something back into the system.' Gina discovered a scraping of margarine in an end of greaseproof paper and spread it on the last slice of bread in the bread box. 'Looks like you're going to have plenty of company working in munitions.'

'I know Jenny Powell's starting in the factory on Monday.' He watched Gina carefully to see if the mention of Jenny's name would spark the same reaction in her as it had in Tina.

'And not only Jenny. Wyn Rees too.'

'Queer Wyn?'

'You'd better not let his wife catch you saying that.'

162

'Wyn Rees, married? Come on, not even I've been away that long.'

'And the father of a bouncing baby boy,' she crowed, delighting in passing on news he hadn't yet heard.

'Good God, some woman well and truly caught him.'

'He and Diana seem very happy.'

'Diana? Not Diana Powell.' He stopped polishing the pie steamer and stared at her in disbelief.

'She's Rees now.'

'I thought she worked for him.'

'She used to before they got married.'

'But she brought some food up to the house today. She never said a word. I had absolutely no idea she was married. She didn't write to Maud about it.'

'She wouldn't have been able to. It happened after the war broke out and the mail was stopped. Haven't you got anything else around here that's edible? I'm never going to last until closing time without eating something, and we haven't any coupons left for sweets.'

Without thinking what he was doing, Ronnie reached under the counter and handed her a stick of coconut ice Tina had been saving for Bethan's little girl.

'Thanks Ronnie, you're a gem. Hadn't you better start thinking about getting ready?'

He went into the back and slipped off the khaki jacket that he'd found in one of the kitchen cupboards. He simply couldn't believe it! Diana Powell married to queer Wyn and the

163

mother of a baby. Why hadn't she told him? Was she so naive she didn't know what Wyn was? Had she assumed he'd known about her marriage, or was she so ashamed of her husband she didn't want to talk about him?

She wasn't that different from Maud, and despite Gina's assertion he found it difficult to believe that any girl, let alone one like Diana Powell, could be happy married to a man like Wyn Rees.

'Why is it, that every time we have a family get-together the women end up sitting in one room and the men in another?' Megan complained as Bethan topped up their glasses.

'I've no idea, but I agree it always happens that way.' Bethan cuddled a sleepy Rachel, who'd been allowed to stay up for the occasion. The sound of splashes and shrieks of childish laughter echoed down the stairs as Liza and Maisie bathed the younger children and put them to bed.

'It's probably something to do with primitive tribal instincts,' Tina declared authoritatively. 'Like having to prove how much drink they can take while boasting about their prowess between the sheets.'

'Tina!' Jenny pretended to be shocked.

'It's true. Haven't you ever eavesdropped on their conversation? It's always about who was falling down drunk, and the smile they put on their wife's face, or if they haven't got a wife, someone else's wife. Mind you—' she dipped the edge of one of Maisie's vinegar and oatmeal

164

biscuits into her wine then nibbled it—'after nine months without William, I'd give a year's sugar and sweet-ration for a chance to have one of those smiles. Look at us.' She glanced around the table. 'Eight women and only five men next door, and one of those isn't attached. So four of us are going to be sleeping in cold, lonely beds tonight.'

'Only the lucky ones who aren't working,' Bethan broke in.

'And the ones without children,' Phyllis contended. 'Brian's at that irritating age when he sees monsters in the dark, but only in his own room. The last three weeks I've woken up beside him to find that Evan has retreated into his bed in the box room.'

'I hope Billy won't go through that phase.'

'He will,' Megan warned. 'You don't know what a disturbed night is yet.'

'And bang goes any chance of having fun with Wyn in the mornings.' Tina picked up a Welsh cake.

'You're going to be the size of a house if you eat any more,' Jenny warned.

'What does it matter when there's no one to see me naked?'

'Apart from Phyllis and Diana, we'll all be in the same boat tomorrow,' Jane contributed shyly, beginning to understand just why Haydn had insisted on bringing her back to Pontypridd. It was going to be easier to face separation with his family and friends around.

'I wish I knew how the men managed,' Tina

persisted. 'Knowing William, I bet he's found a knocking shop somewhere in Africa that sells Welsh beer.'

'A knocking shop?' Jane asked in bewilderment.

'Station yard,' Megan supplied. 'And when I last heard, my son was too busy fighting to look for girls.'

'Is it true they put something in their tea to dampen the urge?' Tina mused. 'I must admit I prefer that idea to belly dancers eager to satisfy their every whim.'

'Ask Charlie,' Bethan suggested. 'He's a serving soldier, he might know.'

'I doubt it,' Alma laughed.

'Oh, oh, we know what that laugh means, and boy am I jealous. Well if Charlie doesn't know, perhaps you could write to Andrew and ask him, Beth? He's a doctor and an officer, so he might have been ordered to solve the problem. After all he's in the worst position of all. Locked up in a camp full of men. He must be as frustrated as I am.'

'From what he says in his letters the POWs are too cold and hungry to worry about that kind of frustration. And as there's a shortage of basic supplies, I doubt they have anything extra to put in their tea.'

'From what Eddie was like on his last leave, I don't believe they use anything,' Jenny said.

'And I don't believe I'm hearing this conversation.'

'Come on, Mam,' Tina addressed her mother-in-law, 'I bet this is no different from the way you felt during the last war?'

'No,' Megan smiled, 'it isn't. Apart from the fact that once my Will went he never came back.'

'What we need is an army camp somewhere near here.'

'In Pontypridd? What for, to save us from the Home Guard?' Bethan lifted Rachel against her shoulder and reached for the bottle to replenish their glasses.

'Hitler's henchmen when they get here.'

'They've got to get through an awful lot of other places first, and even if there was one, there'd be no guarantee that William would be stationed here,' Jenny pointed out.

'What you need are cold showers, and plenty of exercise,' Megan joked.

'Come on, I can't be the only one who feels this way?' Tina looked around the table.

'No you aren't,' Jenny agreed.

'But you are the only one who talks about it all the time.' Bethan glanced at Diana, who had hardly said a word since Tina had steered the conversation on to sex.

'I suppose I'll have to settle for Errol Flynn in the White Palace like all the other abandoned wives. Anyone want to come?'

'I will,' Jenny offered. 'It might be the last time I'll be able to for a while, now I'm going into munitions.'

'You're going to work in a factory?' Jane asked.

'I want to do my bit.'

'It's good money too,' Tina chipped in. 'If

I didn't have the café to run, I'd be with you like a shot.'

'Are they taking anyone?'

'Absolutely anyone they can get. They're desperate. You thinking of applying, Jane?'

'I have Anne to look after.'

'I could take care of Anne, if you wanted to work,' Phyllis offered. 'Another baby's neither here nor there when I've already got Brian and sometimes Bethan's two.'

'Won't it be rather a lot for you?' Jane asked.

Phyllis shook her head. 'I'd like to feel that I'm pulling my weight too. The harder we all work, the sooner this war will be over.'

'Amen to that.' Tina finished the wine in her glass.

'Jane, you look exhausted, are you sure you're all right?' Diana asked as Jane's eyelids flickered.

'Just tired after the journey.'

Bethan could see tears hovering perilously close to the surface. From what little Haydn had said, Jane had every right to be emotionally drained. Depositing Rachel on Tina's lap, she slipped out through the door to Andrew's study. Charlie must have brought a bottle of vodka with him. Andrew's brandy stood untouched on the desk, while there was a suspiciously bright gleam in the eyes of all the men.

'I came to see if you wanted anything else to eat, or dare I suggest tea?'

'As you can see, we're fine,' her father grinned sheepishly.

'So I notice.' She looked to Haydn who was still shell-shocked by the news of Maud. 'Jane's tired. I gather you have to leave first thing in the morning. I could run you down the hill if you want some time alone together tonight.'

'Would you, Beth? That would be great.'

'What time are you leaving?' Charlie asked.

'Six o'clock train.'

'To London?'

Haydn nodded.

'I'll walk down to Graig Avenue in the morning and pick you up; we can travel together.'

'I'd appreciate some company.' Haydn rose to his feet.

Wyn followed suit. 'And if you don't mind, Diana and I will walk down now. I'd like to make sure Alice has locked up the New Theatre shop properly.' He held out his hand to Charlie. 'It's good to know you approve of our wives' business partnership.'

'They need a hobby to occupy themselves,' Charlie said drily.

'Do you want to leave with us now, Dad?' Bethan asked.

'There won't be room in the car as it is for Megan, Phyllis and the children as well as Haydn and Jane.'

'Yes there will, Jane can sit on Haydn's lap and we'll squash Brian, Anne and Billy in somehow.'

'The boot?' Haydn suggested.

'I'd be more likely to put you in there.'

'I'll stay on and talk to Charlie a while longer.

I'll enjoy the walk down.'

'I'll walk down with you,' Ronnie offered. 'This leg of mine needs some exercise.'

'That's not what I heard from the relief nurse,' Bethan contradicted. 'I'll be back up for you.'

'I'd prefer to walk, really. Tina will look after me. It's only as far as Laura's.'

'I'll call in to see you first thing in the morning to check just how well it's mending.'

'I'll give Maisie a hand to bath your babies,' Alma said as she began to clear the men's plates.

'Thanks, Alma. In that case I'll go straight on to your mother's after dropping off Megan and Billy. Maisie knows what to do if either of mine wake in the night, although after the day they've had today, they should sleep through.'

By the time she returned to the dining room, Jane had already wrapped Anne in a shawl and Phyllis had buttoned on her own and Brian's coat.

'Haydn's old room is all ready for you, Jane. All we have to do is air and make up the bed and carry the cot through from the other room. Bethan uses it when she comes down. It will be perfect for Anne.'

Jane nodded agreement, but she looked so tired, Bethan doubted she'd heard a word Phyllis had said. Diana came in carrying their coats, bumping into Haydn who was showing the after-effects of Charlie's vodka. He tried to kiss Megan on the cheek, but she pushed him away.

'I recognise the smell of that stuff of Charlie's even if no one else does. Come on, if Bethan isn't in too much of a hurry, I'll give you a hand to get everything sorted in the house.'

In all the bustle of filling copper warming-pans with hot coals to air the mattress on Haydn's old bed, emptying wardrobes and carrying cots across the landing, Bethan found herself alone in the kitchen with her brother for a few moments.

'You'll keep an eye on Jane for me, sis?'

'Do you need to ask?'

'It's going to take some getting used to, just the two of us from now on.' Haydn looked at the last photograph that had been taken of the four of them together. They were standing in the back garden the summer before Bethan had qualified as a nurse. She hadn't met Andrew, he hadn't left town to go on stage, Eddie had been on the dole, and Maud had still been in school. She saw what he was looking at and hugged him, burying her face in his shoulder.

'Just make sure you take care of yourself.'

'I'll be fine, they never let entertainers go near the fighting in case we frighten the enemy away before the sappers get a chance to shoot them. But I am worried about Jane. She hates the idea of us being separated. I really don't know how she'll cope without me.'

'Don't flatter yourself that she won't be able to manage. She'll cope very well, just like the rest of us have had to.' Bethan thought of Tina's conversation and how it would probably shock her brother to the core to know exactly how the women left behind kept up their spirits.

'You look a bit peaky, love,' Megan said as Bethan drove her up to Tyfica Road. 'Too much work too soon after having Eddie, if you ask me.'

'I manage, and I'd probably manage better if people didn't keep telling me how tired I looked.'

'Like what people?'

'Andrew's mother for starters.'

'How is she?'

'Missing Andrew, but not much else judging by the table she keeps. Do me a favour, stop me now, before I say something I regret.'

'If I were you I wouldn't regret anything I'd say about that woman.'

'She is my children's grandmother.'

'Poor children.' Megan had even less reason to like Mrs John than Bethan. She hadn't had as much as an acknowledging nod from her since she'd been released from prison.

'How are Wyn and Diana?' Bethan asked, deliberately changing the subject. 'Diana hardly says a word these days.'

'As you saw tonight, outwardly fine; inwardly I worry myself to death about them.'

'Is there a problem?'

'You tell me?'

'As I said, Diana seems very quiet.'

'Exactly. There's nothing concrete that I can put my finger on. Of course Wyn's father doesn't help, miserable old soul that he is.

Nothing that boy ever does is right where the old man is concerned. A couple of days ago he was nagging him to find real work instead of selling sweets. Now Wyn's found a job in munitions, he's telling him he won't be able to cut it after years of serving behind the counter like a sissy.'

'That can't be very pleasant for Diana.'

'As you noticed she doesn't say much. Wyn couldn't be kinder to her or Billy, but—' she looked across at Bethan—'you think it was a marriage of convenience too, don't you?'

'I don't know, Auntie Megan.'

'Did you see the look on her face when Tina was talking about missing William?'

'That's just Tina. I think she succeeded in shocking Phyllis and Jane.'

'What she said was right enough if you have a normal, healthy marriage. I wish I'd never got involved with the forty thieves, and I'm sorry I went to prison, but you can't change the past. I did wrong and I paid for it. Unfortunately it wasn't only me who did the paying, it was Diana too.'

'Come on, no one could have been a better mother than you.'

'When I was around.' There was no trace of self-pity in Megan's voice. 'Most of the time I was just too damned busy trying to earn a living to talk to Will and Diana. It's not easy bringing up a family without a father, but then you're beginning to find that out.'

'At least I'm not short of money and I know Andrew will be back, some day.'

'I don't suppose Diana ever went to you for advice when I was inside?'

'When she and Maud came back to Pontypridd from Cardiff Infirmary, I was living in London.'

'And your mother was still living with your father. I can imagine the way she treated Diana.'

'When I eventually came home, Diana seemed all right. She obviously liked working for Wyn. If she was a bit quiet, it was no more than any of us with Will and Eddie in the house.'

'I knew something was wrong when I was released, but I put it down to the quarrel she'd had with Tony Ronconi. William told me it was serious between them, but she insisted she didn't want to wait for a husband who might never come back.'

'Perhaps she didn't love him.'

'You think she loves Wyn?'

'They seem very fond of one another.'

'I'm fond of Tiddles the cat.'

Bethan burst out laughing. 'I think Wyn stands a little higher in Diana's estimation than Tiddles.'

'Billy arriving six months after the wedding certainly set tongues wagging.'

'People have said things to your face?'

'Mrs Richards.'

'She would.'

'She asked me why I let my daughter marry a queer. There, I've finally said the word.'

'I always assumed it was just gossip.'

'I hoped it was,' Megan said as they turned

174

the corner into Tyfica Road. 'But after living with them, I know it isn't. They're more like older brother and younger sister than husband and wife, which means Billy's father is someone else. What I'd like to know is; just why didn't he marry my daughter?'

CHAPTER 8

'Enough of the reminiscences,' Evan declared as Ronnie went to see if Tina and Jenny were ready to leave. 'How are you really faring?'

Charlie shrugged his massive shoulders as he pushed a cigarette between his lips. 'Better than you after the news you've had. I didn't want to say too much in front of Haydn, because he was obviously devastated, but it must be hard, losing two children, especially ones like Maud and Eddie.'

Evan drew on his pipe, while his mind groped for words to answer Charlie.

'I know it's no help now, but it will get easier in time.'

'I'm not so sure. I lost my brother in the last war and there isn't a day that goes by without me feeling bloody angry about it. I still don't know what that was all about and neither does anyone else. And just look at us now. Back where we were in 1916. Boys dying to satisfy the egos of politicians. Nothing changes.'

'Believe me, when this war is over everyone will know what it was about,' Charlie asserted quietly.

'Then the stories in the press aren't just propaganda?'

'Hitler's a maniac. He won't be satisfied until he's taken over the world, and made every non-Aryan a slave to his Reich.'

'That helps,' Evan reflected soberly. 'I'd hate to think that Eddie died for nothing.'

'Take a look at William and every other soldier who came back from France to fight on another front. They know what Eddie died for, and they won't forget it.'

'Do you think the Germans will invade?'

'The only question is, why are they waiting?'

'Then we'll lose.'

'Not without putting up a bloody good fight.' Charlie slipped his hand into the inside pocket of his jacket and pulled out an envelope. 'This is for Alma. You have my will; perhaps you'll be kind enough to give her this if anything happens.'

Evan took it and stowed it away in his own jacket. He knew Charlie too well to offer platitudes. 'And don't worry about Alma. We'll be here to sort everything for her when her mother goes.'

'I know you will. You've been a good friend.' He pulled the cork from the vodka bottle as Alma walked in.

'You two still at it?'

'A man needs protection against the night air at this time of year, and Evan still has to walk down the hill.'

'Evan will be rolling down Penycoedcae hill if he has any more of that.' Evan rose to his feet. 'You take care.'

'And you. I hear it's tough in the pits these days.' They looked at one another, a look more eloquent and intimate than any of the conversation they had shared.

As Charlie walked Evan, Ronnie and the girls to the lane, Alma cleared away the glasses and went up the stairs. She pulled the blackout in Bethan's tiny sitting room, lit the lamp and put the bottle of vodka and a glass on the table, together with a cup of cocoa she'd made for herself. When she heard Charlie's slow, steady tread on the stairs she sat in one of the chairs and waited.

'It was good to see old friends.'

'It was,' she smiled, thinking of Tina's conversation. Tomorrow she would be in Tina's situation, but tonight she wouldn't change places with any woman on earth.

He lifted her hand and kissed the tips of her fingers. 'You gave me good advice yesterday. No more talking, let's go to bed.'

'And make a lot of women jealous.'

'Jealous?'

'Tina was complaining how frustrated she felt with William away.'

'She talked about that?'

'You'd be surprised what we women talk about.' She switched off the light and abandoned her cocoa as she followed him into the bedroom.

'About this?' he murmured after he'd undressed her and lifted her on to the bed.

'Not this. This is just for memories, Charlie, yours and mine. And we have all night to make them.'

'Mrs Moore died an hour ago,' the relief nurse

178

announced as she opened the door of Alma's flat to Bethan. 'She didn't regain consciousness. I washed her and laid her out. I know I should have telephoned you, but I kept thinking of her daughter. Her husband told me this morning he has to go back tomorrow.' She led the way up the stairs and opened the door to the bedroom.

Bethan looked at the old lady lying peacefully on the bed.

'Did you phone the doctor?'

'No, nor the undertaker. It can wait until morning, can't it?'

'Only if we lie about the time of death. And the doctor is bound to notice.'

'I can't see either of them making a fuss under the circumstances, can you?'

'Let's hope not.' Bethan looked up at the clock. 'Why don't you go home, I'll sort everything out in the morning.'

'Do you think Mrs Raschenko will forgive us?' the nurse asked as she went into the hall to fetch her coat.

'With luck she'll never know.' Bethan opened her bag and took out one of the blue and white folding, pre-printed letters she used to write to Andrew. Corpse-sitting was a lonely task, especially at night, and after today she had a lot to tell him.

'I'm sorry, I shouldn't have gone on about missing William the way I did,' Tina apologised to Jenny as they walked down the hill ahead of Ronnie and Evan.

'Why not? I've been married. I know what it's like to live in an empty house and long for my husband to come home. I'm tired of people avoiding any mention of men when I'm around.'

'I don't know how you stand it. At least I've got William's leaves, always supposing he's ever going to get any more, to look forward to. You know Eddie's never coming back. I couldn't bear it if it was Will.'

'Sometimes, even now, I can't quite believe it. I think it's because we only really lived together for a couple of days on his last leave. Even after William told me he saw him being killed, I only felt it was true for a day or two. Then, after William went back it was just like before. I've never told anyone this, but I've actually picked up a pen a couple of times to write to Eddie.'

'What's so odd about that? When I close the café at night and start clearing up, I talk to Will for hours.'

'Then I'm not a candidate for Hensol Castle?'

'No more than I am.'

They slowed their steps as they reached the junction of Llantrisant Road and Graig Avenue. Tina turned her head. 'I can't even see Ronnie behind us.'

'He did tell us not to wait for him if we were in a hurry.'

'Which we are.' Tina quickened her step.

'You're lucky to have a brother like him,' Jenny said with all the wistful naivety of an only child.

'You can have him. I've four others and

they're all the same, even the little ones. Bossy, overbearing, typical Italian males who believe themselves so vastly superior to women it gives them the right to dictate the way their sisters live, even when they've left home to marry.'

'You don't really mean that?'

'Don't I? Ronnie's a worse tyrant than Papa ever was. When he lived at home he was always reminding us that he was the eldest by six years, and he believed that endowed him with the God-given right to stop me and Gina from doing any and everything we enjoyed, like dancing, or seeing boys. He said he would never have let me marry Will if he'd been home, and he meant it.'

'He won't stop you from going to the pictures tomorrow?'

'Let him try. Gina's offered to look after the café if Ronnie can't.'

'Then I'll come down and pick you up, same as usual?'

'Of course.' Tina halted outside the Morning Star next door to Jenny's shop.

'You sure you'll be all right walking the rest of the way down the hill by yourself?'

'You seen any men left in the town fit enough to jump out and attack me?'

'Don't joke about it.'

'I'll be fine. See you tomorrow.' Tina pushed her hands into her pocket and walked on briskly. Soon her slight figure was swallowed by the blackout.

Jenny turned the corner into Factory Lane, opened the high door set in the wall and fumbled her way across the tiny yard to the back door. Her parents had always used the side gate after hours, and she continued to do so, although it would have been more convenient to use the shop door that fronted Llantrisant Road.

The stockroom was in darkness. Locking the door she thrust the bolts across it, and felt her way into the shop. Opening the blackout she scanned the deserted road wondering how much longer it would be before Ronnie passed that way. Not long, unless he had called into Evan's for tea. Perhaps it was worth waiting just a little while.

It felt peculiar to be back home in the bedroom that had been his as a child, and even odder to share with Jane the bed that he and Eddie had slept in for all those years.

'I'm not asleep,' Jane murmured as Haydn stripped off the last of his clothes and crept in beside her.

'You should be after that horrendous journey up from London. I need warming. I'd forgotten just how cold it is to wash in a washhouse, even in spring. I'm beginning to wonder how I stood it for all those years.'

'Living in London has turned you soft. If you think your washhouse is cold, you should try a workhouse. It was never warm. Winter or summer it was always freezing inside those stone walls.'

Leaving the bedside lamp Eddie had made out of an old wooden table leg burning, Haydn pulled Jane close, tangling his hands in folds of linen as he sought her skin. 'What's this?'

'A nightie. I borrowed one from Phyllis.'

'You don't wear them.'

'I do when I sleep with you in your father's house.'

'No one is going to come in.'

'I know, but it just doesn't feel right to sleep naked when I'm not in my own home.'

'You're being silly.' He tried to pull it off her, but she moved away from him.

'How long have you known about the tour of the front?'

'There's been talk about it for a while. Are you going to help me with this?' he demanded as he grappled with the pearl buttons on the high, Victorian neck of the gown.

'How long is a while?'

Giving up on the nightdress, he rolled on his back, crossed his arms beneath his head and stared at the ceiling. 'A while is a while,' he reiterated irritably. 'I thought it was just talk until they finalised the itinerary last week.'

'You could have mentioned it.'

'Why? So we could quarrel like we are now? I knew you wouldn't like the idea.'

'I'm not angry about the tour, but I am furious that you didn't see fit to tell me it was being arranged.'

'I didn't want to spoil what we had.'

'It's spoilt good and proper now, isn't it? I thought we agreed to discuss everything when we married, and now I discover that you've been keeping something like this from me for heaven only knows how long. I just don't feel I can trust you any more.'

He turned on his side and faced her. 'I swear to you, I was going to tell you the minute I knew for certain that the tour was definitely on. So many things could have happened to cancel it. An unexpected attack, a push, the brass closing off the area to all non-essential personnel. There was no point in upsetting you over nothing.'

'Nothing ...'

'Jane, please,' he reached out and stroked the side of her face with the tips of his fingers. 'Don't let's argue. Not now.'

'If not now, then when? You'll be gone tomorrow.'

'I couldn't believe it when they pulled you and Anne out of that cellar alive,' he murmured, clenching his fists against the images of the alternative that still haunted him. 'Have you any idea what it was like for me, standing in the ruins of that block? No one, not even the wardens, thought that anyone could have possibly survived the blast that flattened our house.'

'But Anne and I did survive and everyone knows that lightning never strikes twice in the same place. How about a compromise?' she pleaded. 'I'll stay here until you finish the tour, then I'll go back to London. You'll need somewhere to live. I could find us rooms closer to the—'

'No,' he interrupted sharply.

'Haydn ...'

'You weren't the one who had to stand by

and identify our neighbours as they pulled them out of the wreckage one by one, all the time expecting your body or Anne's to be next. Don't ask me to ever go through anything like that again. And if you're angry with me because I'm leaving you in Pontypridd, then go ahead, be angry. I'd rather see you angry than dead.'

'So you intend to leave me and Anne here for the duration, no matter what?'

'The war won't last for ever.'

'I wish I had a pound for every time I've heard that lately.'

'Jane, it's our last night together for a while. Don't let's waste it by quarrelling.'

'I still can't believe you kept something like the tour from me.' She sat up in the bed, and for the first time he saw the tears on her cheeks—tears that belied her anger. He reached out to her.

'I promise, I'll come back every chance I get.'

Anne stirred restlessly, crying out in her sleep. Jane left the bed and lifted her out of the cot.

'Leave her, she'll settle,' he pleaded.

'She's really upset. First buried alive, now in a strange place, surrounded by strange people.'

'They're not strange, they're my family,' he remonstrated.

'They are strange to her.' She lifted Anne into the bed and laid her between them. The baby opened her mouth and screwed her face into an angry ball.

'I'll make her a bottle,' Haydn offered.

'I'll do it.' She picked up Anne as she left the bed.

'Jane ...'

'I'll bring her back when I'm sure she'll settle. Otherwise she'll keep you and your father awake, and you both have busy days tomorrow.'

'I'll come down with you.'

'There's no point in both of us missing our sleep. I won't be long.'

She crept downstairs on bare feet, making up a bottle with as little noise and fuss as possible. As she sat in her father-in-law's chair and fed her daughter, she thought of all the things she wanted to say to Haydn. How she knew he was thinking only of her and Anne, but how she couldn't bear the thought of living without him. Perhaps he would agree to her moving into rooms in an area of London that hadn't been as severely bombed as those around the river. It would mean more travelling time for him. Hopefully he would think that a small price to pay for them being together.

But by the time she returned to the bedroom, it was too late. His breathing had steadied to the soft, even rhythm of sleep. Fuming because he'd fallen asleep on her, and with herself for starting an argument that had woken the baby, she returned Anne to her cot. When she finally crept back into bed she took off the nightdress, loosened the ugly bandages that strapped up her ribs, and tried curling around Haydn in the hope of waking him, but emotional and physical exhaustion had taken its toll. His sleep

186

was too deep, too sound, for her to rouse him. As she shed tears of rage, frustration and fear for the future into the pillow, a feeling of desolation settled over her. A bleak, cold loneliness that she truly believed she had left behind her in the workhouse.

Ronnie was only ten minutes behind Jenny. She heard the muted tapping of the rubber tip on his crutch as he limped down the pavement towards the shop door. Rushing to waylay him, she tripped over the blackout curtain and stumbled into his path.

'I heard that women in Pontypridd were throwing themselves at men, but I never expected to see it for myself.'

'Just putting out the rubbish,' she mumbled breathlessly, hoping he wouldn't notice that her hands were empty.

'Couldn't it wait until morning?'

'The ash men always come early.' She deliberately kicked one of the bins she'd carried out before she'd left for the party, pushing it along the pavement as though she were repositioning it.

'If there's any more, perhaps I could help.'

'On crutches?'

'I like to fool myself I'm not that in-capacitated.'

'You could come in for a cup of tea if you like. I always have one before I go to bed, and I'd appreciate the company.'

'The question is, would your neighbours appreciate your company?'

'Pardon?'

'They watch every move you make.'

'I know.'

'You don't mind the gossip?'

'As they're going to talk about me anyway, I may as well give them something worth tattling about.'

Ronnie recalled Tina's warnings, and couldn't help feeling a sneaking admiration for Jenny's attitude.

'Tea would be nice, thank you. Although I'd better not stay too long.' He looked across the road where he thought he saw Mrs Evans's blackout curtain twitching. 'We don't want to keep your neighbours up.'

'Please, come on through.'

'You locking me in, or the world out?' Ronnie asked as she slid bolt after bolt across the shop door.

'Huw Davies advised me to increase security when rationing started. You wouldn't believe what some foodstuffs fetch on the black market.'

'Oh yes I would. But then you're lucky to have rationing.'

'Lucky!'

'Try living in a country where the rich can buy anything they want, and do, while the poor watch their children starve.'

'I see what you mean. I suppose fair shares for all is better, even if fair shares isn't very much.' She opened the door that led to the living quarters. 'Pull the blackout, please. I've left a light burning at the top of the stairs.'

'Very wasteful.'

'I don't usually. It must have been a momentary lapse.'

'Because you were worried about putting the rubbish out?'

'Possibly,' she answered before she realised he'd seen through her ploy. She climbed the stairs and led the way into the living room. Unbuttoning her coat she tossed it on to the sofa.

'Drink?'

She turned around and froze. Alexander Forbes was standing in front of the fireplace, a bottle of wine in one hand, two glasses in the other.

'There has to be an easier way of climbing stairs with a crutch, perhaps I should ask at the hospital ...' Ronnie walked through the door, and looked from Jenny's flustered features to Alexander's red face.

'I don't think we've met.' Leaning against the sofa, Ronnie extended his hand. 'I'm Ronnie Ronconi.'

'Alexander Forbes.' Alexander set the glasses on the table and shook his hand briefly.

'Oh yes, my father-in-law's conscientious objector lodger. I've heard a lot about you.' Unabashed by the strained atmosphere, and Jenny's mounting fury, Ronnie limped over to an easy chair and sat down. 'Two sugars in my tea please, Jenny, if you can spare it.'

'I can spare it,' she said, glad of an excuse to leave the room. 'Alexander?'

He looked down at the bottle he was holding. 'My father sent me his last case of French burgundy so I could toast my birthday. I thought you might like to join me?'

'Even better,' Ronnie smiled. 'If there's something I really enjoy, it's a good French wine.'

Bethan took a blanket from Alma's linen cupboard. Leaving the bedroom door open and a light burning next to the bed she retreated into the living room, wrapped herself in folds of Welsh flannel and curled up in Charlie's chair. The air was chilly after the warmth of the day, but it would have been too much of an extravagance to have set a match to the fire laid in the grate.

Opening her handbag she took out her pen, and looked around for a book to lean on. She found a large cookery tome. Smoothing out the blue and white sheet she'd bought in the post office, she unscrewed the top from her pen and wiped the excess ink from the nib with her handkerchief. She always kept her pen filled, because she was never sure when she'd be able to steal an odd moment to write to Andrew.

As she sat, nib poised over the paper, she was aware of absolute silence. Even the street outside was still. It was almost like working the night shift in hospital again, only this time Andrew wouldn't be walking in with a smile on his face and chocolates in his pocket.

Dear Andrew,
I had your letter today, and because it will probably take weeks for you to get this, I'd

better remind you. It's the one where you were annoyed with me because I hadn't told you I was pregnant. I wasn't trying to exclude you from my life, darling, just cope with day-to-day living, which isn't easy without you. I took the children up to your parents' house this afternoon to tell them that I'd heard from you. Mrs Llewellyn Jones and Anthea were there. Anthea asked me to send 'Andy' her love. I'm only doing so because she has decided that men in POW camps can't possibly be heroes, so I'm afraid you may have lost yourself a girlfriend there, but you can console yourself with the thought that you still have me and the children. Haydn brought Jane back today, she's staying with Dad while Haydn goes on an ENSA tour of the front. Poor Jane, she doesn't seem at all happy with the idea. Charlie's home on leave, but like Haydn he has to go back tomorrow, so I'll soon be surrounded by lonely wives again, not that we sit around miserably, there's too much to do. I know it's wrong of me, but I'm so jealous of Jane and Alma, it actually hurts. I'd give anything for just one night with you. Perhaps you could suggest instigating compassionate leave for POWS to your German commandant? You say you feel redundant, I'll cure you of that the minute you get home. I'm writing a list of jobs that need doing around the house. It's about a mile long and growing longer by the day. And of course, you'll have a lot of catching up to do with the children, who kiss your photograph every night so they'll know exactly who their daddy is when he walks through the door. Rachel holds up the frame for little Eddie now without me having to remind her. Our son is going to look exactly like you. He already has auburn hair, and his eyes have darkened to your exact shade. Instead of being angry, think how lucky we are: two beautiful children and the certain knowledge that we will be together again when this dreadful war is over.

Ronnie came back a few days ago. It doesn't matter how. Maud died eighteen months ago, and he had no way of telling us until now. Haydn was devastated when he came home to the news. It's hard for both of us knowing there's only the two of us left. But we have the comfort of knowing that Maud was loved and cared for to the last by Ronnie. So please, don't be angry with me for not telling you about Eddie until he was born. Instead keep writing and praying that in a few months we'll all be together. As you can see, although I've written as small as I possibly can, I've run out of paper. Take care of yourself, my darling, we all love and miss you.
Bethan

She sat back and read what she'd written. It was an odd mixture of reproach and love, not at all what she'd intended. His letter had made her angry, but not angry enough to take him to task for what he'd written.

Her imagination had been working overtime since he'd been captured. She'd visualised cells, daily beatings and chains, and although he'd tried to reassure her on that score, she knew from his first letter, which had taken months to reach her, that the POWs weren't being supplied with adequate food or warm clothes. Even when the situation had eased and the first Red Cross parcels had got through to the camps, he still lacked essentials. It all seemed so ridiculous. Andrew living in, at best discomfort, imprisoned and guarded by soldiers who wanted to destroy the whole of Britain, and couldn't possibly care what happened to him, while she, who so desperately needed him, had to carry on bringing up their children alone until such time as he might be released. A day that seemed no nearer now than it had ten months ago.

Sometimes, she couldn't help the disloyal, unpatriotic thought from creeping into her head that perhaps it wouldn't be so terrible if Germany did invade and Britain lost the war. Not if it meant that Andrew could finally come back to her.

'So how do you like working in the pit?' Ronnie sat back, wine in hand, apparently oblivious to Alexander's embarrassment.

'It's hard work but we all ...'

'Have to do our bit?' Ronnie suggested. Feeling sorry for him, because Jenny was still visibly seething, he drained his glass. 'Happy birthday and thank you for the wine, but I'd better be going.'

Jenny didn't bother with polite delaying tactics. She abandoned the glass she'd been nursing and went to the door.

'Don't worry,' Ronnie smiled at Alexander as

he levered himself to his feet. 'Your secret is safe with me.'

'That's good to know,' Alexander said wryly.

'Although I think it's only fair to warn you that Mrs Evans across the road has suspicions. I've only been back two days but I've already heard rumours about a tall blond man sneaking around to the stockroom entrance of the shop at night.'

'But you didn't hear who it was?'

'It was just idle gossip,' Ronnie answered, avoiding Jenny's question.

'I gave Alexander a key in the hope that he'd attract less attention by slipping in the back way,' Jenny explained.

'If I'm ever ready for another relationship I'll come to you for advice on how to conduct the courting, Jenny. Good-night, Alexander.' He walked out on to the landing and hobbled awkwardly down the stairs. Jenny followed him.

'I think I'd better go out the front way in case Mrs Evans doesn't see me leaving by the side entrance. You do realise that if she misses me she won't sleep a wink?'

'Ronnie ...'

'Good luck to you.' He bent his head and kissed her on the cheek. 'Both of you,' he smiled, as she began unbolting the door.

'Alexander is only a friend, a casual friend,' she declared emphatically as she returned his chaste kiss. 'But thank you all the same for not being shocked.'

'No one can live in the past, Jenny.'

He mulled over his own words as he walked

down the hill to Laura's house. For the first time he realised the truth behind the trite phrase. Wasn't that exactly what he'd been doing since Maud had died? Living in the past? A shadow of a man with no more substance than a spectre inhabiting a ghost world. Rightly or wrongly, he had made a decision when he had buried Maud. A decision to go on living without her. Perhaps it was time he took some of his own and Diana's advice and started doing just that.

'I wasn't expecting you.'

'Evidently,' Alexander commented as Jenny returned to the living room.

'I dread to think what might have happened if anyone other than Ronnie had seen you waiting for me in my living room. He meant what he said about not telling anyone he found you here, or that you have a key.'

'That's good of him.'

'It is. Extremely good, considering the circumstances.'

'Why did you invite him in?'

'This is my house, I'll invite in anyone I choose.'

'I thought we ...'

' "We" don't exist, Alexander. There is no "we". You're my friend at the moment, but I warn you now, you're taking far too much for granted.'

'You walk in with another man ...'

'Ronnie is an old friend. I haven't seen him for five years so I invited him in for tea and a chat to catch up on what we've been doing with our lives.'

'Nothing more?' He raised one finely sculpted, sceptical eyebrow.

'No,' she reiterated firmly. 'Besides, as well as being an old friend, Ronnie also happens to be my brother-in-law.'

'Your husband's brother-in-law.'

'Same thing,' she disputed testily.

'Hardly a blood relation.'

'We've both lost people we loved ...'

'So you thought you'd console one another.'

'And what's wrong with that?'

'Depends on what consolation you were prepared to offer him.'

'I think you'd better go.' She held the door open.

He left his seat and looked at her for a moment. 'I'm sorry,' he apologised. 'I shouldn't have said that. I don't know what's got into me. It's just that you're the only thing that makes life in this God-forsaken backwater bearable.'

'That's my home town you're insulting.'

'Jenny there's a whole world out there. One day I'd like to show it to you.'

'But in the meantime we have a war to win.'

'Don't remind me. This is turning out to be a lousy birthday.'

'If I'd known, I would have got you a present,' she said, relenting slightly.

'There's still one thing you can give me.' He moved over to the door. Shutting it, he pulled her close, slipping the pins from her chignon

196

until her fair hair tumbled down her back.

'We should finish the wine. It would be a pity to waste it.'

'Later.' He closed his mouth over hers, and kissed her. She bit down hard on his lower lip, drawing blood.

'Ouch!'

'That's for walking in here uninvited.'

'I won't do it again.'

'I know you won't, I'm taking my key back.'

'Jenny, I love you. I want to be with you ...'

She silenced him with a kiss. A gentler one than before. He ran his fingers over her breasts, caressing her nipples through the thin silk of her blouse. She moaned softly as he moved closer, meshing his body with hers.

'The wine can keep until midnight. That's when my birthday really begins.' He turned his attention to the buttons on her skirt. 'And I know exactly how we can occupy ourselves until then.'

CHAPTER 9

'I could go to the station with you,' Alma suggested as she left the bed and slipped on her nightdress.

'No.' Charlie shook his head as he buttoned on his uniform.

'It would give us another couple of hours together,' she pleaded.

'I'd rather remember you as you are here and now.'

'But ...'

'Ssh,' he laid a finger across her lips. 'Take care of yourself until I come back.'

'Only if you promise you will do the same.'

'I promise.' They both tried not to think just how empty that promise might be. He kissed her for the last time, pushed a box into her hand, slung his kitbag over his shoulder and left the room.

She went to the window, listening to his footsteps as he descended the stairs. The front door opened and closed. She followed the crunch of gravel as he walked over the drive to the lane. She watched, trying to pick out the shadow of his hat above the hedgerows. It was impossible, the darkness was too dense. She returned to the bed where the sheets were still warm from his body and the pillow bore the imprint of his head. Curling into the spot where he had slept such a short time before, she opened the small leather box he had given her. Nestling on a bed of pink cotton wool was a gold locket forged in the shape of a tiny book. She pressed the minuscule catch. It flew open and Charlie's face smiled up at her. Then, and only then, did she allow her tears to fall.

'The birds are singing.'

'So?' Alexander wrapped his legs around Jenny's, trapping her beneath him.

'Time you left. People will soon be up and about.'

'No one's up and about in Factory Lane before four in the morning. And I could leave a lot later if you'd let me keep my pit clothes here.'

'You'd be seen by the milkman. I can't risk my father-in-law finding out about us. I'm not at all sure how he'd react to the idea of his lodger in my bed.'

'Ronnie wasn't shocked.'

'He didn't see us like this.'

'He gave me the impression that even if he had, he wouldn't have been.'

'You don't know the people around here. They'd create a right stir if they found out for certain that I'd allowed you into the house, let alone my bedroom. I've only been widowed ten months.'

'And for six of those you've been sleeping with me. I'm tired of sneaking around, Jenny. I want to marry—'

'Not yet,' she broke in sharply, wriggling out from under him.

'Then when?'

'When I'm ready.'

He slumped face down into the pillows. 'Sometimes I think you're only using your status as a widow as an excuse to keep me dangling on a string.'

'Ten months is nothing in Welsh valley mourning terms. And it really is time you made a move.' She gave him a push to help him on his way.

'Just answer one question. How much longer do I have to wait before I can buy you an engagement ring?'

'Five years is considered a suitable lapse of time in chapel terms.'

'Five years! This is wartime. No one can expect a woman of your age to live like a nun.'

'They may expect it,' she smiled mischievously, 'but thanks to you I don't.' She stretched out languorously as he finally left the bed and reached for his clothes. He was right. She was using her widowhood as an excuse to keep their relationship secret. People would be shocked, but not all that shocked.

As he had pointed out, it was wartime and the world was changing, even in Pontypridd. For a start women no longer had to rely on their husbands and fathers to keep them, which in theory meant they could disregard the safe, steady and invariably dull men and pick more exciting partners. The only problem was, there were hardly any men left to pick from. Alexander was definitely the best of the bunch on the Graig: witty, charming, attractive and crache to boot. She was only too happy to spend time with him, but she didn't love him. And, after Eddie, the one thing she was certain of was that she never wanted another man to put a ring on her finger again.

Before Alexander had taken to calling into the shop on his way to and from work, she, like Tina, had burned with frustration. Her marriage to Eddie had been fraught with difficulties, but the nights they had spent together had aroused a sexual need that had begun to obsess her waking moments. Knowing how a public 'courtship' would excite gossip and her neighbours' expectations, she'd turned down Alexander's offer of a trip to the cinema, only to slip him a key to the storeroom in his change, and under the pretence of asking him to help her empty a sack of potatoes, she suggested that he call on her after blackout.

Since then she had enjoyed the best of both single and married life. Her house and her business were solely hers. She had a lover only too willing to call whenever she needed company, a lover she didn't have to cook, or wash and iron clothes for, and perhaps most important of all, a worldly, educated lover who knew all about birth control, so there'd be no little 'accidents' to upset her new, liberated lifestyle.

'The thought of you in a convent goes beyond the realms of my imagination.' He picked up his underwear from the chair where he'd hung his clothes. One of the first things Jenny had noticed about him was how meticulous and fastidious he was in everything he did. When Eddie had made love to her, he had thrown his clothes everywhere, and generally taken clean ones out of the drawer afterwards, which meant that she'd had to go searching for socks and pants under the tallboy, bed and dressing table. But then Alexander was much older than Eddie—and her. Thirty-four to her twenty-one. A difference that had initially made her feel like a pupil to his master, especially when it came to lovemaking. He had taught her more in the first hour they'd spent in her bed than she had learned from Eddie in six months of unrestrained, passionate courtship.

'I think I'd make a very good nun.' She reached for her robe.

'If you're an example of a nun, lead me to the convent.' He caught the robe and tugged it from her hands. Stripping back the bedclothes he gazed at her.

Unabashed, she looked into his eyes, basking in his approbation. 'You can barely handle me. A convent would finish you off.'

'Don't be too sure.' He caught sight of the brass alarm clock on the bedside table and reluctantly pulled on his trousers. Jenny allowed him to stay over only on condition he sneaked out of the Factory Lane entrance to her shop after the munitions workers had walked down the hill, and before the miners headed for the morning shift in the Maritime.

For all her precautions, Evan Powell had given Alexander some odd looks lately, although his landlord had never questioned the identity of the 'friends' he claimed to visit until midnight, and occasionally stay overnight with. But he still had to get up to Graig Avenue to change for work. 'How about I meet you in Shoni's on Sunday? I could bring another bottle of wine. If there's anyone about we could make it look as though we'd met by accident.'

'I've invited Ronnie Ronconi, Alma, Diana and Wyn up for Sunday dinner,' she lied. Alexander had brought up the subject of going out together too often in the past month for her peace of mind. The last thing she wanted was a public proclamation of their relationship that would introduce domestic responsibility and kill all the delicious sense of excitement.

'You know I won't be around next week,' he reminded her, hoping to induce her to change her mind.

'You're taking your six days' leave?'

'I either take them, or lose them. I have a warrant for the early train on Monday. Can't I persuade you to come with me? We wouldn't have to travel together, my mother would make you very welcome, and no one knows you in Sussex.'

'And what do you suggest I tell people around here?'

'That you're visiting family or friends.'

'Everyone on the Graig not only knows my family, they know my grandfather's family, and as for friends, I've never left Ponty to make any elsewhere.'

'Then tell them you're taking a holiday.'

'A holiday around here is a day trip to Porthcawl or Barry Island. Besides, I can't go anywhere, I'm starting in munitions on Monday.'

He stopped buttoning his shirt. 'This is the first I've heard about it.'

'I told you.'

'No you did not. I distinctly remember you saying you couldn't possibly leave the shop to go to Sussex with me, and now I find that you're giving up ...'

'I am not giving up. A girl in Leyshon Street is going to run the shop for me. The whole thing was a bit of a rush. I only applied to the Employment Exchange last week.'

'Jenny ...'

'I bet you have a girl back home.' She sidestepped what she sensed was going to be another reproach.

'A girl? Any girl I might have had, I haven't seen in over a year. No one would wait that long for me.'

'Bethan's waited that long for Andrew and it looks as though she might have to wait at least as long again.'

'Bethan John is a saint, and as you well know, I've never managed to lure the devout and virtuous between the sheets.' He ran his hands up her legs, caressing the soft skin at the top of her thighs.

'Your hands are rough,' she complained,

moving out of his reach.

'That's mining for you.' He held out his fingers and studied them ruefully. 'They're honourable scars, and hard won. I only hope the damage isn't permanent.'

'You were dressing,' she prompted.

He donned a beautifully tailored waistcoat and wool jacket. Even a slight sheen on the cuffs and elbows couldn't disguise its quality, or his. He'd been a museum curator and university lecturer before the war. A man she could never have hoped to have met in normal circumstances. After he had registered as a conscientious objector, the Ministry of Labour had sent him to the Maritime Colliery.

It had taken time, but eventually he'd won the respect of his fellow miners, but not the acceptance he'd hoped for. Labelled as 'crache' because of his refined voice, manners and pacifist views, the only times he didn't feel lonely and isolated were the evenings he spent with Jenny. But even during his most optimistic moments he was aware that he valued their relationship far more than she did.

'So, when will I see you again?' he pressed.

'I have no idea. I don't even know what shifts I'll be working.'

'If I catch a late train back on Sunday, I could call in on the way up. I'll make sure no one sees me.'

'No, don't. I could be working, and even if I'm not, I might have company.'

'Ronnie Ronconi, again?' His voice was heavy with resentment.

'Perhaps,' she answered airily, 'or I might invite some of the girls I'll be working with back for supper. There's Judy Crofter from Leyshon Street, and Myrtle Rees and ...'

'I understand. This is goodbye.'

'No. Can't you see I'm only trying to be sensible for both our sakes? Ronnie said Mrs Evans had seen you coming in here.'

'A blond man,' he corrected. 'She didn't know it was me.'

'It won't be much longer before she puts two and two together, and I don't want any more scandal about me than there has been already.' She left the bed and retrieved the robe he'd hung on a hook at the back of the door.

The sight of her nakedness stirred him. He'd lost count of the girlfriends he'd had before her. Apart from the sex, most of them had bored him rigid. Taught and trained to be analytical, he had been unable to define exactly why Jenny had such a hold over him. It certainly wasn't her mind, and it wasn't simply his loneliness or her beauty; although with her silver-blonde hair, deep blue eyes and stunning figure she put most Hollywood starlets in the shade. It wasn't even her willingness to try anything he suggested once they both had their clothes off. It was something more, something indefinable, and he, ardent Communist and one-time adherent of the doctrine of free love, who had constantly denied the existence of romantic love by arguing that it was no more than chemical attraction, had to concede that he was completely and utterly besotted.

'I'll bring you back a present. What would you like?'

'I'll leave it to you.'

'Come on, Jenny, you must want something.' He slid his hands beneath her robe and cupped her breasts, circling the delicate skin on her nipples with his thumbs. 'Why won't you allow me to introduce you to my parents as their future daughter-in-law?'

'Now is not the time.'

'Then when?'

'When things are more settled,' she answered impatiently.

'After the war?' he sneered.

'We might know where we're going then.'

'I'll be returning to London and I'd like you to come with me.'

'Be serious, Alex, I don't know what I'll be doing next week let alone years from now.'

'I love you.'

'My key?' She held out her hand.

'If I promise not to use it, can I hang on to it?'

'What's the point when you won't be using it?'

'I could leave letters for you in the stockroom.'

'You're forgetting that I won't be working here after Monday.'

'Then I'll creep in late at night. You could check for them in the morning.'

'The key, Alexander.'

He scooped the contents of his pockets from the glass tray on the dressing table. Reluctantly extracting her key from the collection of coins, wallet, cigarette case and lighter, he handed it back to her.

'If this is goodbye, you'll never find anyone who appreciates you more.'

'It might be fun to look,' she teased.

'Two can play at that game.'

'You're too fond of me to cast a roving eye.'

'Don't bank on it. Sometimes I wonder if you know the value of what we have?'

'I know, and if we had another half-hour I'd show you exactly what I think of you. As it is you'll have to wait. When I've been given my shifts, I'll call up to see Phyllis and Evan. I'll leave a note in your working jacket in the washhouse.' She stood on tiptoe and kissed his cheek.

'Don't leave it too long.'

'I need you as much as you need me,' she murmured, brushing her fingertips over his trouser fly.

'I wish I could believe that.'

'If you are really late next Sunday, and if it's safe for you to come in, I'll leave the stockroom door unlocked.'

'Sop for the stricken?'

'Pardon?'

'Nothing. Keep the bed warm and miss me?' he called back as he walked along the landing.

'I already am,' came the careless reply.

Jane stirred sleepily as Haydn left the bed. She was conscious of him moving about the room, collecting his clothes. When he lifted the latch on the bedroom door, she opened her eyes, looked around and remembered where she was. Stopping to check that Anne was sound asleep, she grabbed her borrowed slippers and ran down the stairs after him. Phyllis was alone in the back kitchen, stacking dirty breakfast dishes on the table.

'Good morning, would you like some tea?'

'Not for a minute, thank you,' Jane answered, wondering if she dared to go into the washhouse.

'Evan and Alexander left for work five minutes ago.'

Reassured that Haydn would be alone, Jane opened the door and walked in to find him stripped off in front of the stone sink.

'I heard you get up.'

'Charlie will be here in a few minutes.'

'What about breakfast?'

'No time, I'll get something in the station.' Keeping his back to her he pulled on his underpants and trousers.

'About last night.' She rested her cheek against his shoulder and wrapped her arms around his waist. 'I'm sorry you fell asleep before I settled Anne.'

'So am I.' He turned to face her as he picked up his vest and shirt.

The front door opened and closed. He lifted her chin in his hand and kissed her.

'We'll save what has to be said for the next leave, love. I've got to go.'

Bethan opened the door to Laura's house and called down the passage. Ronnie appeared in the kitchen doorway, shirt-sleeves rolled to the elbow, a tea towel in his hand.

'I know you said you'd be early, but I thought you'd give a man a chance to finish his breakfast.'

'I was hoping to get a couple of hours' sleep before going back down Alma's.'

'Her mother's worse?'

'She died early this morning. In her sleep,' she added, compounding the story she and the relief nurse had concocted.

'I'm sorry. How's Alma?'

'As well as can be expected with Charlie just gone and her mother dead. Diana is with her now.'

'I'll call in.'

'Is that wise?'

'Isn't a man allowed to visit an old friend any more?'

'You and Alma were a lot more than friends, Ronnie, and unfortunately the whole town knew it. The gossips even had her pregnant.'

'The bitches.'

'It's different in Italy?'

'Not really.' He took her bag as she walked into the kitchen. 'Tea?'

'After I've seen to your leg.' She opened her bag and removed two enamel bowls. 'You have boiling water?'

'The kettle's full, it's not long off the boil.'

'Put it back on, please.'

'You're going to scald me?'

'Of course.' She laid a white cotton cloth on the corner of the table, and set out a packet

210

of cotton wool, a roll of bandages, a bottle of antiseptic, and a pair of scissors. 'Drop your trousers.'

'Charming! What about my dignity.'

'You are wearing underpants?'

'Fortunately, yes.' He unbuckled his belt and unbuttoned his braces. 'I'm beginning to think Tina wasn't joking when she said the women in this town are starved of male company.' He unfastened his fly and kicked off his trousers.

'You've only just found that out? Sit in the chair and prop your leg on the stool.' She unwound the bandages that covered his left leg from his knee to his ankle. 'Dr Evans said you've a wound in your chest as well.'

'It's healed.'

'Not according to what he told me. Ronnie, this is an appalling mess!' she exclaimed as she surveyed the length of his shin.

'The bullet went in below the knee and came out above the ankle.'

'And both the exit and the entry wound are infected,' she said, as she inspected the weeping sores, 'and judging by the colour of the skin, probably the bullet path as well.'

'Not as badly as they were. At least the bleeding has stopped.'

'And to think you walked down the Graig hill last night.'

'I can't sit around and do nothing. Besides, I have a crutch. I don't put any weight on this leg.'

'I doubt you'd be able to. You should be in bed.'

'I'd go mad. I start in the café today. Tina's offered me a job on vegetable preparation.'

'I'll allow you to take it, only if you can sit down to do it.' She sponged off the remains of the dressings that had stuck to his wounds, and picked up the antiseptic.

'Go easy, that stuff stings.'

'If you don't keep this clean and dry, and rest the leg as much as you can, you'll have to go into hospital to have it cauterised and stitched under anaesthetic.'

'I'll rest.'

'Did you see a doctor when you did this?'

'There aren't many in the Italian Alps.'

'Did you see anyone before you saw Dr Evans here?'

'A doctor on the RAF base. I was there for a few days before I came home. I thought he performed miracles.'

'I wouldn't like to have seen it before he did.' She washed, dried and laid clean dressings on both wounds, bandaging them firmly into place.

'Can I put my trousers on now, before someone comes in and catches us?'

'It's all right, they never gossip about nurses.' She took the bowl that contained the soiled dressings, and emptied it into a strong paper bag. After going into the washhouse to wash and disinfect both bowls and scrub her hands, she returned. 'Now your chest.'

'You won't be happy until you've examined every inch of me, will you?'

'Only the damaged bits.'

He unbuttoned his shirt and pulled up his vest.

'There's no dressing on it.'

'I took it off, the wound's dry.'

'Since when?'

'This morning.'

'Take off your shirt and vest.'

'Bethan ...'

'Do as you're told or I'll have you admitted to hospital.'

'Does bullying run in the family?'

'Maud bullied you? I don't believe it.'

'Only when I wouldn't do what she wanted me to.' He stood patiently while she examined and cleaned the wound.

'You're nothing but skin and bones,' she commented as she wound bandages around him.

'I'd put some weight on if you'd allow me to eat breakfast.'

'You can eat now. I've finished.' She pinned the bandage securely.

'Tea and toast?' he asked. 'There's some brawn Diana brought up yesterday to put on it, then you don't have to bother about breakfast when you get home.'

'Sounds wonderful.' She went into the washhouse to clean up. 'Now don't go overdoing it in the café,' she warned when she returned to the kitchen.

'Me?' he asked with an innocent expression.

'Dr Evans told me yesterday he'd given you permission to go into munitions, but don't make any immediate plans. It could take weeks for that leg to heal completely, and it would be madness to go into a TNT-contaminated atmosphere with open wounds like those.'

'You don't know me. Now I have a dry place to sleep and enough food to eat, I'll heal fast.' He pushed a piece of bread on to a toasting fork and held it over the fire.

'It was that bad in Italy?'

'The last few months weren't good, but Maud died before the worst, if that's what you're thinking.'

'Diana told me she was pregnant when she died, and you blame yourself for her death.'

'I suppose I should have expected her to.'

'She only told me because she was concerned for you. As we all are. Ronnie, it's doubtful that Maud could have survived the war, what with all the food shortages and strain. It was a miracle that you managed to keep the disease at bay as long as you did.'

'No more gratitude, please.'

'The last thing Maud would have wanted is for you to spend the rest of your life mourning her.'

'If you're trying to tell me that I've been selfish in wallowing in my own grief, I know.'

'You're making me feel heartless.'

'You heartless?' He shook his head as he took the fork from the fire and turned over the bread to toast the other side. 'You couldn't be heartless if you tried. Meeting everyone last night, especially Jenny and your father, led me to do some thinking on the way home, and I made a resolution to get on with my life.'

214

'I'm glad.' She took the toast he offered her and put it on a plate. 'If ever you want anyone to talk to ...'

'I know where to come.' He laid his hand over hers. 'Thanks, Beth. You Powells have made coming home much easier than I thought it would be.'

'Don't be a stranger, Ronnie. Call in any time. With Andrew and Haydn away, my children need all the uncles they can get.'

He looked at her and remembered what Diana had said about keeping Maud's memory alive. 'You'll soon be so fed up of me, you'll throw stones when I land on your doorstep.'

Despite Bethan's warning, Ronnie limped past the café on the Tumble, and carried on hobbling through Taff Street until he reached Charlie's shop behind the fountain. The shop was open, but there were two girls he'd never seen before manning the counter, and the blackout curtains were pulled in the upstairs rooms. There was a door alongside the entrance. While he was trying to work out if it led to the living accommodation above the shop, or was part of Clayton's gramophone and radio store next door, it opened and Diana came out with a baby in her arms.

'Ronnie, what are you doing here?' she asked as she put the baby in the pram she'd parked in the shop.

'Trying to work out which is Alma's front door. I thought I'd pay my condolences.'

215

'Now isn't a good time. The undertaker's just arrived.'

'Shouldn't someone be with her?'

'My mother and my Uncle Huw are helping her with the arrangements.'

'What about Charlie, shouldn't we send a telegram?'

'Alma won't hear of it. She said he won't get any more leave no matter what.'

'Then there's nothing I can do?'

'Not until the funeral. Which way are you walking?'

'Up to the Tumble café.'

'I'll come with you. I'm meeting Wyn later to do the banking, but I've got an hour to waste before then, so I thought I'd take the baby to the park.'

'And this I take it is your baby?' He peered into the pram at the bundle swathed in layers of soft white wool. 'Do you know, I didn't even realise you were married until Gina told me yesterday afternoon. Congratulations.'

'Thank you.'

'If you can put up with my company I'll go with you. I can afford the time. There's not as much to do in the cafés as there used to be.'

'Between the canteens in the factories and the food shortages is it any wonder?'

'Not really. It's just that I'd rather be busy.'

'Me too.'

'I thought you already were, and with Wyn going into munitions you'll be run off your feet looking after the shops as well as the baby.'

'My mother helps with the baby, there's only

216

two shops and we've got a girl in each. What I'm dreading most of all is the long hours Wyn will be working. I hardly see him now, I can't say I'm looking forward to seeing even less of him.'

'You're welcome to call into the café any time.'

'I already do. Perhaps it won't be so bad now spring's finally arrived. It's certainly a beautiful day.'

He looked up at the clear blue sky. 'I suppose it is.'

'You sound as though you've only just noticed.'

'I've been so busy trying to acclimatise myself to being back in Pontypridd, I haven't had time to monitor the weather.'

'It must be totally different to what you're used to.'

'Not really. It was colder than it is here, in the mountains.'

'Maud wrote and told me so much about Bardi, I feel I know the village as well as I know Ponty. I'd love to go there.'

'Not now you wouldn't.' He limped alongside the pram as they headed up Taff Street towards Woolworth's and the turn into the park.

'Wyn said the Germans can't possibly be as bad as the papers paint them.'

'The ones I met were. But then I didn't exactly stop to chat.'

'Because they were shooting at you?'

'Guns put a damper on any conversation. But Wyn's got a point. I don't think we can believe

217

everything that's in the papers these days. You should see the things the Italian press print about the British.'

He stumbled over the bridge and looked around. After the thorough cleansing Bethan had given his leg, it was more painful than it had been in days. 'I'm sorry, I can't go much further. How about we sit over there?' He pointed to a long row of covered seating that fronted an enormous lawn studded with flowerbeds that had been patriotically turned over to vegetables.

She peered into the pram as she followed him to the bench. 'Suits me. Billy's a bit restless. Mam warned me she didn't have time to wind him properly after his morning feed before coming down to take over from me in Alma's.'

'Here let me,' Ronnie offered, holding out his arms as she took the baby from the pram.

'No really, there's no need. I can manage.'

'He certainly looks a fine, healthy little chap.'

'You're an expert on babies?' She leaned Billy against her shoulder, turning his face away from Ronnie.

'Unfortunately. Being the eldest of eleven I had little choice in the matter. Billy's at the best age. Soon he'll start teething in earnest, and dribbling with it, and once he starts sitting up and crawling he'll be into everything he shouldn't. You'll spend hours teaching him to talk and when he finally learns, all he'll do is answer back. Then when he's really on his feet he'll start playing with the kids in the street, and you'll get nothing but complaints from the neighbours about broken windows and footballs destroying gardens. He'll probably refuse to work in school, and as a result end up with a lousy job. About fifteen or sixteen years from now, he'll start courting, more than likely with the most unsuitable girl in town and ...'

'And on the other hand, he might work hard, get a scholarship to the grammar school and go to university?'

'That would be the worst outcome of all. He'd be so highly educated, you wouldn't be able to understand a word he says.'

'Some kids turn out all right,' she contended, realising he was teasing her.

'I agree. Take me for instance, I'm perfect. But just look at the rest of the Ronconi tribe, especially the girls. Papa would never have approved of their choice of husbands. Especially Tina's.'

'William adores Tina.'

'You're actually sticking up for your brother?'

'I'm fond of him.'

'Which is a lot more than any of my sisters are of me.'

'Don't you believe it. When your letters stopped coming they were all worried about you.'

'Worried and fond are two very different things. I'm always worried about them.'

'Why? They are all safe and happy.'

'Put it this way: I'd worry a lot less about them if they'd opted for life in a convent. Then I would have known exactly where they were and what they were up to.'

'You just resent them taking over the business,' she laughed.

'Probably. Here woman, you've no idea how to wind a baby.'

Before she had time to realise what he intended doing, he'd draped a clean handkerchief over the shoulder of his jacket, taken Billy from her, rested him against his arm and rubbed his back, to be rewarded with three large burps in quick succession.

'Now he'll sleep,' he said authoritatively, handing him back to her.

She pulled Billy's bonnet over his dark curly hair, and returned him to the pram.

'So tell me, what have you been doing with yourself since I went away, apart from growing up, working for Wyn Rees, marrying him and having a baby?'

'Not much.'

'You never considered returning to the Royal Infirmary? I thought you wanted to be a nurse.'

'I did. But I couldn't leave Maud after she became ill, and afterwards there never seemed a right time to go back.'

'And now you've a husband and son to look after?' He took a packet of cigarettes from his pocket and offered her one.

'I'm not sure I should smoke in public.'

'Go on, scandalise the neighbourhood. I won't say anything.'

'Do you know I used to be terrified of you.'

'Of me?' He raised his eyebrows in mock horror as he lit her cigarette.

'You were always shouting at someone in the café. Tony, Angelo, Tina ...'

'They deserved it. But I can't have done too bad a job of training them, seeing as how the cafés have survived without me.'

'I'm beginning to understand why Maud married you, and why you made her so happy. Are you ever serious about anything?'

'Only about things that don't matter.' He leaned back in the seat and blew smoke rings up at the wooden rafters. 'Tina gave me a job yesterday as a kitchen hand. Do you think she'll sack me if I don't go in for another half-hour? I noticed that the ice-cream shop by the baths is open, and as I doubt they're using sugar or cream, I'm dying to see how much worse it is than ours.'

'You want me to get them?'

'Of course. I'm an invalid, remember.' He dug his hand into his pocket and pulled out half a crown.

'My treat.'

'All right, and in return, I'll look after Billy. I can see he needs a much firmer hand than you've been giving him.'

CHAPTER 10

'I'll be leaving on the same train as Myrtle, four in the morning,' Wyn said as he watched Diana check the till takings in the High Street shop. 'I didn't realise, but apparently they put on special carriages for the munitions workers.'

'So you'll be working the same hours as Myrtle?' She removed most of the notes and half the coins, counted and bagged them.

'More or less, it's a minimum twelve-hour shift for the men. If there's a push on, it might be longer, but then you already know that. Look, as things are under control here—' he glanced at Harriet, who'd proved as quick and capable as George Collins had promised—'why don't we go down to Ronconi's restaurant for a proper lunch? We might not get another opportunity for a while. I saw some cakes in the window,' he added, hoping to entice her.

'God only knows what's in them, and Billy ...'

'Won't need feeding for another two hours.' He jiggled the handle of the pram, where the baby lay curled contently into sleep. 'Come on, Diana, lunch and cakes and five minutes' peace. There won't be many moments like this once I start in the factory.'

She looked around the shop. She could scarcely claim it was busy enough to warrant her presence. As was usual by midday the shelves were almost bare, and Harriet had already moved the few remaining pies and pasties to the bottom shelf and washed and polished the top ones. She'd also cleaned the glass in the counter, and the window, and judging by the state of the linoleum on the floor, swept and washed it. 'I have to bank this,' she held up the bag, 'before the Midland closes at twelve.'

'We'll stop off on the way.'

'I'll be back before closing to show you how to cash up, Harriet. As soon as all the stock has gone, you can lock up and clean and tidy the rest of the shop. The storeroom could do with a going over,' she added, attempting to assert her authority from the outset. She picked up her jacket, and went to the door. 'I'd rather go to the café than the restaurant. Tina may have heard from William. Mam had another dream about him last night. If she doesn't get a letter soon she'll either go mad or start looking for a ship to take her to North Africa.'

'They say no news is good news,' Wyn reminded mildly as he steered the pram out through the door.

'Knowing my brother, no news probably means he's caught up in a card game somewhere, or cornered a keg of beer or a few bottles of whisky. Now he's married to Tina I only hope it's not a belly dancer or an Arab girl.'

'Or a battle?'

'You read his last letter. Seems to me soldiers

223

spend ninety-nine per cent of their time sitting around on their rear ends waiting for something to happen.'

'And the other one per cent terrified out of their wits by bombs and bullets.'

'I'll brain him if he does anything stupid.'

Wyn didn't reply. The tension always escalated in the house when the erratic flow of William's letters ceased altogether. And even the relief when one finally arrived was short-lived as soon as Megan or Diana realised that anything could have happened in the interim between him penning the letter, weeks, if not months before, and its arrival.

They reached the bank and Diana went inside, leaving Wyn to wait with the pram. The town seemed busier than usual, even for a Saturday. There was a sprinkling of khaki uniforms amongst the black weeds of the widows and the spring dresses of the younger women, and Wyn felt a pang of envy; again regretting the accident that had prevented him from joining up.

'Sweet business so bad these days, Wyn, you're reduced to begging outside banks?'

'William!' Wyn barely recognised his brother-in-law in the fit, tanned guardsman who confronted him. 'You're the last person I expected to see. What on earth are you doing here?'

'That's a fine greeting for a serving soldier home from the war.' William held out his hand. He was all too aware of his brother-in-law's reputation and wouldn't even have risked a handshake if Wyn hadn't been married to his sister.

'Do Tina and your mother know you're home? Diana's inside, we were only just talking about you ...'

'It must be difficult to talk about anything else,' William joked. 'And the answer is no. No one knows I'm home. We hitched a ride with a lorry that dropped us off on Merthyr Road.'

'We?'

'You know, Tony Ronconi.'

The colour drained from Wyn's face when he saw the slim, dark figure standing behind William, but William, never the most sensitive of beings, carried on blithely.

'Tony this is Wyn Rees. He married Diana.'

'I didn't know Diana was married.' Tony and Wyn continued to stare at one another, neither offering the other a handshake, but William was too busy looking out for his sister to notice.

'Hi, sis!' he greeted her as she emerged from the bank. 'Have you got a kiss for the returning hero?'

Much to the amusement of several passers-by who totally misread the situation, she flung herself into his arms, making him drop his kitbag. 'Mam is going to be over the moon! She's stopped the postman every day for the last month looking for a letter from you. Why didn't you write?' she demanded indignantly, pushing him away from her and looking him over to make sure he was in one piece.

'Because I was in transit. Is Mam still with you and Wyn?'

'She moved in with us permanently after Billy was born.'

Tony stared at the pram, clearly noticing it for the first time. 'If you'll excuse me, Will, I'll push on up to the café.'

'You'll do no such thing.' Will picked up his bag and laid a restraining hand on Tony's arm. 'I don't want anyone warning my wife I'm heading her way. By the way, congratulations to the pair of you.' He peered into the pram as Diana and Wyn reluctantly accompanied them up Taff Street. 'Small, isn't he?'

'He was a lot smaller when he was born,' Diana retorted quickly, trying to fill the strained silence between Wyn and Tony.

'I'm glad to see you gave my nephew the best possible name.'

'He's Billy, not Will, and we named him after our father not you.' Diana clung to Wyn's arm, desperately trying to ignore Tony's presence beside her.

'He's got our colouring, Di.'

'He might turn fairer yet.' She was acutely aware of Tony's eyes taking in everything. Her ... Wyn ... the baby ...

'Tina in the Tumble café?' Will asked.

'Where else?'

'I'll collect her, then we'll both call on Mam. Don't suppose there's any chance of you two helping out at the café for the next week?'

'You've got a whole week's leave?'

'Why so surprised? Don't you think we deserve it after what we've been through? Well after what I've been through,' he amended with a sly glance

226

at his companion. 'Tony here sorted himself a right cushy number after he was wounded. We only met up in base camp yesterday afternoon.' Excited by the prospect of seeing his wife, William didn't notice Tony's silence as he negotiated his way through the crowds outside Rivelin's.

'Charlie's just been home for the first time in over a year, and he only got three days.'

'Charlie's home, great ...'

'He went back last week; so did Haydn. He brought Jane home, because he's going on an ENSA tour.'

William scarcely heard her as he pushed open the café door. Steam billowed towards him from the counter where Tina was heating milk for coffee. He didn't look at anyone else. Dropping his bag he moved quietly around the tables, tiptoed behind her, reached over the counter and put his hands around her waist. She dropped the coffee pot, spilling milk all over the mock marble fountain and shelf below the steamers and boilers. Whirling around with a dishcloth in her hand, her anger dissolved into confusion.

'Will!'

He pulled her across the counter and into his arms. 'Glad to see you've not become accustomed to other men handling you while I've been away.'

'Come on through.' She grabbed his hand and lifted the counter flap, pulling him towards the kitchen and the staircase that led to her rooms. 'Ronnie, you'll take over, won't you?'

'I already have,' he murmured laconically, mopping up the mess of spilt milk.

'Ronnie?' Tony noticed his brother for the first time. 'What are you doing home?'

'It's a long story,' Ronnie answered wearily, wondering how many more times he would have to relate the tragedy of Maud's death.

William held out his hand. 'Sorry, didn't see you.'

'You did seem rather engrossed in my sister.'

'She told you we got married?' he asked with a cheeky grin.

'You wouldn't have managed it if I'd been home.'

'I don't remember you asking my permission to marry Maud.'

'Come on, Will,' Tina said as a hush descended over the café.

'See you later.' Ronnie couldn't help smiling despite everyone's embarrassment. Tina and William's pleasure reminded him of the happy times with Maud, and how he'd felt seeing her again after each and every small separation.

He turned to his brother, Wyn and Diana as the kitchen door closed behind Tina. 'Tea? Coffee? I believe we have a very good line in baked beans on toast for those who don't expect many beans or butter on the toast.'

'I'll go straight home and dump my kitbag if it's all the same to you,' Tony said tersely. 'Will and I have been on the road since two this morning.'

'You're staying in Laura's house with me, and as she's away we'll have to fend for ourselves.'

'That's just what I feel like doing after twelve hours on the road.'

'If you're hungry, you'd be better off foraging down the restaurant than here. You can leave your kitbag.'

'I'll do that.' Tony pushed his bag into the corner behind the door. 'See you later.' Tipping his cap in Diana's direction and nodding to Wyn, he walked out. Diana shivered. The thought of Tony being home for a week made her blood run cold.

'That leaves you two.'

'Just tea for me please,' Diana said.

'Wyn?'

'I'll nip across and check on the New Theatre shop, make sure everything's running smoothly. I won't be long, Diana.'

Realising how much Tony's sudden appearance had shaken Wyn, Diana didn't try to detain him. She moved the pram alongside Tony's bag, and tucked the blankets around Billy. A thump echoed down from overhead, setting the lamps rocking and gales of laughter rippling around the café.

'I think I'd better try to persuade Tina and Will to swap places with Tony and me and move into Laura's for a week.' Ronnie brushed aside a lump of plaster that had fallen on to the counter. 'That way the ceiling may hold up in this place for another year or two.'

Ronconi's restaurant opposite the fountain was crowded. A patient queue of housewives vying to buy the few remaining sugarless cakes displayed in the window blocked the door. Tony pushed past them and the crowded confectionery counters into the restaurant. Almost every table was occupied by servicemen on leave and their girlfriends, but there was no sign of Gina.

'Mr Tony,' one of the older waitresses recognised and greeted him. It was the first time she had preceded his name with a 'Mr' but he was too preoccupied to notice. 'Gina's upstairs in the function room. It's the only place she can get any peace and quiet to do the books.'

'I'll find her.' He climbed the stairs. Gina was sitting on the fringe of a sea of empty tables, a pile of ledgers spread out in front of her.

'Tony, it's great to have you home.' She rose from her chair and hugged him. Closer in age to Tony than Ronnie, she knew him well, and he had a thunderous look on his face that warned her he was on the point of losing the infamous Ronconi temper.

'You're earlier than we expected.'

'You got my letter then?'

'Last week. You been to the café?'

'I saw Ronnie. He told me I'm sleeping in Laura's.'

She nodded. 'Luke and I are still living in Danycoedcae Road, but the place is full of evacuated families.'

'So I've been pushed out?'

'I hope you don't think you've been pushed anywhere. We thought you'd be more comfortable with Ronnie. And he could do with the company,' she hinted, but he was too immersed in his recent discoveries to pick up on the veiled reference to Maud. 'Tea? Are you hungry?'

'Starving.'

'They are still serving lunches downstairs, I'll get them to send one up. What do you want?'

'Whatever's going. I've learned not to be fussy in the army.'

She walked over to the dumbwaiter set in the back wall of the room. Scribbling an order on the waitresses' notepad clipped to her belt, she sent it down to the kitchen.

'Why didn't any of you write to tell me Diana Powell had got married?'

'Because you never asked after her in any of your letters,' she replied evenly, as she returned to the table.

'You knew I was seeing her before I joined up.'

'I also noticed that you'd stopped talking to her before you left.' She closed the account books and piled them on a trolley behind her, straightening the tablecloth before reaching for the cutlery tray.

'Didn't it occur to you that I still might have been interested in Diana?'

'If you'd still been interested, I assumed you would have written to tell her so. Have you seen her?'

'I came home with William. We bumped into her and Wyn on our way through town.'

'Then you've met her husband?'

'Husband?' he mocked.

'She and Wyn are very happy.'

'No girl could possibly be happy married to that queer. And don't say he's not. Everyone in town knows exactly what Wyn Rees is.'

'As I said, they seem very happy,' she reiterated quietly. Gina, like most of Diana's friends, had been suspicious of the hasty marriage to Wyn and the arrival of Billy barely six months after the wedding, but until now they had remained just that, suspicions. If anyone had asked her at the time, she would have told them in no uncertain terms that a brother of hers would be incapable of deserting a pregnant girlfriend. Now, faced with Tony's angry questioning, she wasn't so sure.

'Have you seen Mama lately?' he asked, realising that his outrage had led him to give away more than he'd intended.

'Not since just after Papa died.' The sound of the lift moving grated into the room. She went to open it.

Tony barely noticed what she was doing. All he could see, all he could think of, was the dark, Italian features of Diana's baby. His son. A child who was going to grow up calling another man—a queer—'Daddy' unless he did something about it. The question was: what?

'Feel like a walk in the park?' Diana asked, as she waylaid Wyn outside their New Theatre shop.

'You got time before Billy needs feeding?'

'Half an hour. We need to talk and we can

232

never do that at home.'

They walked down Taff Street and turned into the lane alongside Woolworth's. A few steps took them across the bridge that spanned the river, and they were instantly surrounded by green lawns and vegetable beds. Shunning the main thoroughfare and children's playground where they were more likely to meet people they knew, they headed towards the dry-stone walls of the sunken garden, the town's memorial to the men who hadn't returned from the Great War. Looking out over the heart-shaped enclosure and seeing it was deserted, Wyn pushed the pram down the stone ramp. The raised flowerbeds were resplendent with the paintbox colours of budding tulips, daffodils and violets, but neither of them wanted to linger. Instead, by tacit agreement they directed their steps towards a bench at the far end.

'It was only a matter of time before Tony came home on leave.' Diana reached across one of the armrests that divided the bench into individual seats and tucked her fingers into the crook of Wyn's elbow.

'I should have realised. I just never thought about him.'

'Why should you? Everything's been turned upside down by the war. We've had far more important things to worry about than Tony Ronconi.'

'Because he was away I allowed myself to forget him. It was a stupid thing to do.'

'It was the right thing to do. Tony is nothing to do with us.'

'Didn't you see the way he looked at Billy? He knows.'

'Suspects, maybe; there's no way he could possibly know for certain. And Tony coming back makes no difference to the way I feel about you, or our marriage.' She meant what she said, but for the first time since she had married Wyn she was unable to meet his eye. She pretended to study a trail of ivy cascading over the wall behind his head as he looked from her to the baby.

'Nothing can alter the fact that he is Billy's father.'

'Father!' She turned an indignant face to his. 'How can he be? Where was Tony when I was in labour? You, not Tony, held my hand and helped Bethan to deliver him, and he wasn't the one who got up night after night when Billy needed feeding, or comforting when he had colic. He hasn't bathed him and put him to bed every single night since he was born. No one could be more of a father to Billy than you, Wyn.'

'Do you still love Tony?'

'No,' she answered decisively. 'But I made the mistake of thinking I did. Whatever I felt for Tony ended the night he slept with me. You know, I don't think he's said a single word to me since—until today, that is, and then only because William was around.' She stared down at her fine lace gloves. She'd peeled them off her hands and knotted the fingers so tightly she'd probably ruined them. 'Wyn, you know more about me than anyone. You were the one

234

who picked up the pieces, not once but twice. You're the one I live with, the one I sleep beside every night.'

'And the one who will never be a proper husband. Not the way a woman wants.'

'I wouldn't want any other kind.' She shook the handle of the pram as Billy stirred. 'We're a family, Wyn. You're my lifeline, my security, and not only mine, Billy's too. Nothing can change that.'

'Not even Tony Ronconi?'

'Especially not Tony Ronconi.' She laid her hand over his as she left the bench. 'Come on, time we got our son home for his feed.'

He tried to return her smile, but he felt as though the first cracks had appeared in the fragile life they had built for themselves. Cracks rooted in lies that could tear the whole fabric of their marriage apart.

Saturday proved to be a long day in the Tumble café, and by the time Ronnie had closed the doors, washed the floor and furniture and locked up, it was an hour into Sunday morning. Apart from a short visit to Megan, Tina and William had scarcely emerged from the upstairs room. Their disappearance had given rise to a lot of ribald comment, but Tina had categorically refused to move out into Laura's.

Feeling more than a little sorry for himself, Ronnie hobbled up the blacked-out hill trying to ignore the pain in his leg. Turning the key in the door of Laura's house he walked down the passage without bothering to switch on the light, to find Tony sitting by firelight in the back kitchen, a bottle of whisky and a glass at his elbow.

'Drinking alone? That's a bad sign,' he commented lightly.

'I saw no point in going out. Will's shut himself away with Tina, you're working in the café ...'

'That's just two of us. There's always plenty of people in the pubs only too willing to buy returning heroes a drink.'

'I'd rather drink alone, if it's all the same to you.'

'I was hoping you'd ask me to join you,' Ronnie said as he took possession of the easy chair on the other side of the hearth.

Tony rose unsteadily to his feet, opened a cupboard and produced an extra glass. 'I'm sorry about Maud. Gina told me what happened.'

'Thank you, I've no doubt you got the full story, so can we talk about something else?'

'What do you suggest?'

'Anything other than death, religion and the war.'

'How about sex and the family?' Tony lifted the bottle and slopped a triple measure into the glass then handed it to Ronnie.

'To us?' Ronnie toasted, wondering what had caused his brother's peculiar mood.

'And victory?'

'Wow, strong stuff.'

'The best.'

'Where did you get it?'

'Ask no questions ...'

'And I'll tell you no lies, I know. You've been writing letters?' he asked, seeing an envelope on the table.

'Just one.' Tony picked it up and stuffed it into his pocket before Ronnie could take a closer look.

'It's odd to be in Pontypridd and not home, isn't it?'

'I might go up to Birmingham at the end of the week and see Mama,' Tony spoke thickly, slurring his words.

'Good idea. I'd like to go myself if I have time before I start work.'

'Gina said you were going into munitions.'

'I only wish I was fit enough to join the army and fight, but the doctor says no way.'

'Who says the army fights? I've spent most of the last year in base camp, spit, polishing and pushing useless pieces of paper from one desk to another.'

'But you'll soon be doing more?'

'How do you know?'

'A week's leave. No one gets that long unless they're on their way to the front.'

Tony neither confirmed nor denied Ronnie's suspicion. Instead he reached for the bottle and refilled both their glasses, to the brim this time.

'Last letter I had, Laura said you were courting strong.'

Tony narrowed his eyes warily. 'When was that?'

'Before the war.'

'Didn't work out. Can't see how any soldier

would want to saddle himself with a wife when he could be killed at any moment.'

'Plenty of women are prepared to take the risk.'

'You telling me I should get married?'

'God forbid I should try to tell anyone how to live. All I'm saying is that I'm glad Maud took me on. I know it wasn't quite the same thing, but when I look at Tina, Alma and Bethan none of them seem to have any regrets, or the desire to live their lives any other way.'

'Is the lecture over?'

'Sorry.' Ronnie drained his glass and left his chair. 'The last thing I want to do is intrude. I've promised to take over the café for Tina this week, and that means an early start tomorrow, so if you'll excuse me, I'll go on up to bed. You'll call down the café for breakfast?'

'Not too early.'

'I'll keep back something decent for you. If you dampen down the fire I'll see to it in the morning.'

'Don't bother. The least I can do is take over the domestic chores.'

'I'm taking my laundry to the Chinese place in Mill Street. If you sort yours out, I'll pack it together with mine. The girls are too busy to do it.'

'So I notice.'

Ronnie was tempted to say something in the girls' defence, then he noticed Tony's unsteady hand. Experience had taught him that one of the most useless exercises in life was arguing with a drunk.

Tony waited until Ronnie had stopped moving around upstairs. When he was certain all was quiet, he pulled the letter from his pocket, opened the envelope and re-read it.

All he had to do now was get it to Diana. Gina had let slip that Diana was taking over Wyn Rees's business because he was starting work in the munitions factory on Monday. If he left the note at one of the shops Diana would get it sooner or later. Hopefully sooner. While he still had some leave left.

'Put any more bleach in that water and you're going to come out like Little Nell on her deathbed,' Megan warned as she dipped a jug into the sink Myrtle had filled to rinse her hair.

'I've got to get these orange streaks out of it by tomorrow.' Myrtle lifted her head and stared at her reflection in the mirror. It was just as well she'd only met Huw in the dark since she'd started work in the factory. If he'd seen the way the TNT powder she packed into canisters had yellowed her skin and discoloured her dark hair he never would have asked her out.

'I thought you said you were going to tea with a friend from the factory?'

'I am.' Myrtle crossed her fingers behind her back as she lied. 'Moira James, she lives near Roath Park.'

'Well if she works with you, she must have the same canary tinge. So I hardly think her family are going to think you're odd.'

'She's blonde so her hair has gone green, not

239

orange. But it's not meeting her family that's bothering me, it's going to Cardiff on the train and walking through the streets afterwards. You know how people stare.'

Megan knew exactly how people stared, but most were too used to seeing munitions workers to bat an eyelid at the strange tints in their hair. She suspected that there was more behind all this bleaching and washing than Moira James's invitation to tea. Perhaps this friend had an unmarried brother around Myrtle's age? She hoped she had. Myrtle had sacrificed the best years of her life to looking after her father and brother; it was high time she began to spare a thought for her own future.

'The streaks are almost out. One more wash after your bath and you'll be as good as we can get you.'

'You really think they've gone?' Myrtle pleaded.

'So faded no one will notice. Just don't forget to put a good application of goose grease on your hands and face tonight. There's nothing worse for drying out the skin than bleach.'

'Thanks, Megan.'

Megan closed the bathroom door and walked past Wyn and Diana's room. She'd hardly seen them all day as they had elected to spend his last free Sunday for a while in the primrose fields of Creigiau with Billy. She could hear them talking, so she called out a good-night before going into her room.

She couldn't help mulling over the conversation she'd had with Bethan. She loved Diana with all the fierce protectiveness of a widowed parent, and Wyn's gentle thoughtfulness had long since endeared him to her. She hoped her fears were groundless and they really were happy and would remain so, but hoping did nothing to ease her sense of disquiet. Perhaps it was time to tackle Diana, and have that mother-daughter talk she had been postponing ever since she had been released from prison.

Jenny stumbled out of the shop into the blackout and Judy Crofter.

'Steady,' Judy warned, 'it doesn't take much to knock me off my pins at this time in the morning.'

'I would have given anything for another ten minutes in bed.'

'You'll get used to the hours.'

'When? I've been doing this for a week now.'

'Wait until you've been at it for six months. Here—' Judy linked her arm into Jenny's—'four legs are steadier than two, or so the sailor said to the prostitute.'

'Judy!'

'That's nothing compared to some of the things you'll be hearing on the factory floor now you've finished your training. There's no room for prissiness in munitions. Come on, that's our train whistling.'

Jenny clung to Judy's arm as they pushed and shoved their way through the crowded confusion of the blacked-out station yard. Charging up to the platform, hemmed in on all sides by talking,

241

shouting and laughing girls, she was beset by a sudden pang of terror. What was she doing? She'd led such a sheltered life. When she hadn't liked school her parents had allowed her to leave early. The only work she had ever done had been in the shop, and that was easy enough. She'd managed her training, but what if she couldn't cope with the actual work? What if she caused an accident? After all, she'd be dealing with shells, bombs and explosives. It wasn't like messing up someone's order, or leaving out a ration of butter.

'Let's try and sit together, so we can have a natter.' Judy pushed Jenny down the platform away from the first carriages, which the men had commandeered and the women never entered unless shortage of standing room forced them to.

'I'd prefer a nap.'

'What time did you get to bed?'

'Judging by the way I feel, too late.'

Once the doors were shut and the blinds checked by the guard the whistle blew again and the train chugged out of the station.

'Who's your friend, Judy?' a voice echoed from the facing seats. Jenny was astounded that anyone could see enough to notice that she was new.

'Jenny Griffiths, meet the gang. I would introduce you, but you'll never sort one from another in this light.'

'First day?' the harsh voice enquired.

'After training,' Jenny qualified.

'It's always the worst.'

'It's not that bad,' Judy asserted.

'What do you think? Erik's got his friend Wyn the queer into the factory.'

'Wyn's married.' Jenny felt duty bound to stick up for her friend's husband.

'From what I hear that doesn't mean anything.'

'They have a baby.'

'Doesn't look much like Wyn Rees.'

'You'd better not let him hear you say that, Maggie,' Judy warned.

'Why not? What can he do to me?'

'Sue you,' Jenny countered.

'He wouldn't dare. And I tell you something for nothing now. The foreman will be keeping an eye on him and Erik. If there's one thing the men can't stand, it's pansies on the shop floor.'

'Maggie ...'

'I'm serious, Judy. Mark my words. He'll be lucky to get home in one piece tonight.'

CHAPTER 11

'A letter came for you, Mrs Rees.' Harriet handed Diana an envelope. 'I found it under the door when I opened the shop this morning.'

Diana glanced at the handwriting, and failed to recognise it, but a queasy feeling of foreboding stole into her stomach. She tore it open, took one look at the signature at the bottom of the page and pushed it into the pocket of her jacket. 'Just a bill from a wholesaler. Now, if you open the till I'll show you how to subtract the takings from the float for the midday banking.'

'Sorry I'm late.'

'You are five minutes early.' Huw Davies lifted his cap and ran his fingers over his bald crown, smoothing back the tufts of ginger hair at the sides of his head. He felt as clumsy and awkward as when he'd first taken a girl out, nearly thirty years before. He'd been sixteen, she fifteen, and he had bought her an ice cream from a cart in the park. Afterwards neither of them had known what to do, so they had hung around foolishly until the park keeper had evicted them when he'd closed the gates. He only hoped this outing was going to end on a more promising note. 'Would you like something to eat or drink before we go? The buffet's open.'

Myrtle shook her head as she stole a sideways glance at him. He looked different out of uniform: shorter without the added height of his helmet, and broader dressed in tweeds. 'No, thank you. Megan let me sleep in this morning. I only finished breakfast a couple of hours ago.' She followed him out of the booking hall and up the steps that led to the platforms.

She stood alongside him as they waited for the train, not quite sure what to do with her hands. He hadn't offered her his arm. Did that mean he regarded her as nothing more than a distant relation through marriage?

'I bought a *South Wales Echo* to see what's showing in the pictures in Cardiff. If you're not in a hurry to get back tonight we could have lunch, spend the afternoon looking at the shops, and finish up with a film. Jesse James is on in the Capitol. But then perhaps you don't like Westerns?' he suggested diffidently.

'I like all kinds of films. Well, almost all kinds,' she amended, blushing at her eagerness to please. 'And I'll watch anything that has Tyrone Power in it.'

The train drew in. Huw walked along the platform ahead of her, and held the carriage door open.

'That's first class,' she said, preparing to walk back to third.

'I thought I'd splash out. Special occasion, first outing and all that.'

He helped her up the steps and through the door. She sat back in her seat trying not to look overwhelmed at the unaccustomed extravagance, hoping that his gesture meant that he intended to ask her out again. If only she could think of something witty and amusing to say, something that would make him laugh and at ease with her. The way the men in the factory were with Judy Crofter and the other young girls who never seemed to be nervous and tongue-tied when they were in male company.

Diana forced herself to leave the letter in her pocket until she reached the park. Halting at the first seat, she looked around before removing it. Impatient, she accidentally tore the single sheet of paper. Jigsawing it together she read,

> *I have to see you. I will be at the bandstand in the park at one o'clock on Monday and Tuesday afternoons. If you don't come, I will visit you on Wednesday in Wyn's house. I know where it is.*
> *Tony*

She looked at her watch, it was twelve-thirty. She had promised Wyn that Tony wouldn't make any difference to their marriage, but if she didn't meet Tony, and he did visit the house there was no predicting what he might say or do, and probably within earshot of Wyn's father.

She sank her face into her hands. Why did life have to be so complicated? It had all seemed so simple when Wyn had asked her to marry him. They had set up home, created a haven for themselves and Billy outside of the world,

246

but between Erik and Tony it now looked as though the world was beating a path to their door. Why wouldn't people allow them to live in peace?

'That wasn't exactly what I had in mind when I invited you for lunch.' Huw surveyed the remnants of their meal. He'd wanted to buy Myrtle something special, but the Ministry of Food directive that protein was to be included in only one course of a restaurant meal, and the limited menus outside most places that no amount of imaginative labelling could conceal consisted of variations on vegetable stews, had led them to a small coffee shop in the Royal Arcade. The blackboard in the window had promised beef fritters, mashed potatoes and carrots, but the description had proved more impressive than the reality. There was more batter, mashed potatoes and carrot in the fritters than the occasional greyish strand that might have been meat or—as one of their neighbouring diners had suggested—gun-cotton.

'It was fine,' Myrtle lied valiantly.

'Do you have any pudding?' he asked the waitress as she approached to clear their plates.

'Danish Apple or prune flan,' she answered briskly.

'Custard?' Huw ventured hopefully.

The waitress shook her head. 'But we do have mock cream, sir. It's sixpence extra.

'Just the Danish Apple pudding, please,' Myrtle said shyly, hoping the apples would take away the cloying, greasy taste of the fritters.

247

'You sure you don't want the mock cream?' Huw urged, wanting to spare no expense.

'No disrespect intended, but if it's anything like the mock cream I've eaten in the canteen at work I'd rather not.'

'Can't say I blame you, madam.' The waitress poised her pencil over her pad. 'Just the one Danish Apple?'

'Make that two,' Huw looked to Myrtle. 'And coffee?'

'That would be nice.'

'Let's hope the pudding is better than the meal,' he said, as soon as the waitress was out of earshot.

'It wasn't that bad.'

'No?'

'I've eaten worse in the canteen.'

'This isn't a canteen.'

'It's just good to be outside the factory.' She looked at her watch. 'On a normal working day I'd still have three hours of my shift to go. But instead of being tied to a bench, straining my eyes and cramping my fingers, here I am being waited on hand and foot, with window shopping and a film to look forward to, and nothing to do until tomorrow morning. So,' she smiled, 'this is absolute bliss.'

'It is good not to be working,' he agreed.

'What would you be doing now?'

'Depends on what shift I was on. If it was nights, I'd be thinking of getting up.'

'You live alone, don't you?' she asked, knowing full well he did from her conversations with Megan.

248

'Have done for the last twenty years, ever since my father died.'

'Aren't you ever lonely?' She flushed as she realised the implications of her casual remark.

'Sometimes,' he admitted. 'But then, I've always tried to help Megan out with William and Diana. Diana never knew her father, and William can only just about remember him going off to war, but then Megan's probably told you that. Megan was the only girl in our family, and the baby,' he smiled, 'although there's only two years between us. When our brothers left for London, I felt it was up to me to look after her. I spent a lot of my free time with her and the children when they were growing up. Well, as much as she and the force would let me,' he amended. 'So in a way they've been my family. And, being a policeman I spend most of my working hours with people, but not always the kind I like. After a particularly hectic day a bit of peace and quiet doesn't go amiss.'

'I suppose not,' she murmured, disappointed at his response.

'Mind you, peace and quiet can't compare with the right kind of company, like now.' He leaned back as the waitress put two small portions of pudding in front of them. 'There's more breadcrumbs than apple,' he complained.

'At least what there is looks like real apple.' Myrtle cut into the mess with a spoon. 'And it is,' she declared after she'd tasted it.

'What were you expecting?'

'Carrots. All we get for pudding in the canteen is carrots in disguise. Yesterday it was mock apricot flan, which meant they mixed them with plum jam, the day before almond flan, which turned out to be carrots soaked in almond flavouring. But then with what it's costing in merchant seamen's lives to bring food into the country, it's unpatriotic to complain.'

'I quite agree, so let's toast victory.' He lifted his coffee cup to hers. 'Are there any shops you'd particularly like to visit?'

'I wouldn't mind taking a look at anything that's on offer.'

'Clothes?' he asked apprehensively, cringing at the thought of trailing behind Myrtle in a lingerie department.

'Food. Megan does a wonderful job with our ration cards, but if there's anything extra or different to be had here I'd like to take a treat back.'

'We'll see what we can do.' He took out his pocket watch and opened it. 'The film doesn't start for another two hours, so we'll have plenty of time to sniff out a surprise.' He slipped his hand into his inside pocket and pulled out his wallet before signalling to the waitress.

'I'll go and powder my nose.' Myrtle went into the tiny toilet cubicle, opened her handbag and reached for her last bottle of pre-war eau-de-Cologne. Splashing it on to her hanky and wrists, she studied her face in the mirror then dabbed on an extra layer of powder. She had no illusions about her looks. The last twenty years had added a stone to her figure and unmistakable lines around her mouth and her eyes. Even as a young girl she had never been pretty. Before Huw, only two men had asked her out. Twenty years before, when she'd been eighteen and her mother had still been alive, she'd gone to a chapel concert with a young minister, and when she was twenty a lay preacher had taken her to a lecture on the Holy Land. Her father had insisted on meeting and interrogating both men, and neither had wanted to repeat the experience after facing him.

At least she and Huw were talking without too many embarrassing silences, and perhaps, if she kept their friendship from her father, there would be more outings. It made no difference that her father knew and liked Huw. He liked him because he was Megan's older brother and a policeman. The moment he found out that she had been seeing Huw alone, he'd order her to stop behaving like a lovesick schoolgirl and attend to her duties in the house. The notion of her having an independent life away from her family and home had always upset him, and it had taken all of Megan and Diana's powers of persuasion to induce him to give his consent to her working in the factory.

Pushing her compact and scent back into her bag, she checked the seams on her only pair of stockings and returned to the café.

'Ready?'

She followed Huw to the door, debating the best way to let him know just how much she was enjoying herself. Would it be so forward of her to tell him?

Diana sat on the park bench, watching the

seconds tick by on the gold wristwatch Wyn had presented to her to mark Billy's birth. If Tony hadn't offered her the option of meeting him today or tomorrow, she would have felt compelled to walk across the park to the bandstand. As it was, she couldn't bear the thought of confronting him. Not now. Tomorrow, perhaps? After she had spoken to Wyn. But would it be better to keep Tony's letter from her husband? After all, she had told Wyn that Tony was nothing to do with them, or their marriage.

Her mind a turmoil of doubt and indecision she left the bench and retraced her steps over the bridge and into the town. She hesitated at the entrance to Taff Street. Where could she go? Home? Her mother would take one look at her and realise something was wrong, and the last thing she wanted was an inquisition with Wyn's father sitting in the kitchen. Besides, her mother's health hadn't been strong since she had been released from prison. It wouldn't be right to risk upsetting her by telling her the sordid truth about Billy's real father, not when she and Wyn had worked so hard to convince both their families that everything was settled and happy between them. But she needed to talk to someone.

Bethan was the obvious choice, but these days her cousin was either working or sleeping. She barely had time for herself, let alone anyone else. Jane—they had been close when they had both lodged in her uncle's house before they had married, but after being bombed out, Jane had enough troubles of her own. Phyllis? She'd be busy with Brian and with Bethan's children, and Alma would be trying to get back into the routine of running the business after her mother's funeral.

She had always been close to William, but she hadn't dared tell him the real reason why she had stopped seeing Tony, for fear of what he might do to him. And he was married to Tina, Tony's sister. There was no telling how the Ronconi girls might react if they found out they were related by blood as well as marriage to Billy.

Hardly knowing where she was going, she turned left, heading for the Tumble and the junction of Taff and High Street. She could call into the shops, but it was too early for the banking, and she felt too restless to serve behind a counter, especially on a Monday, traditionally one of the slowest days of the week.

She stopped outside the Tumble café. Perhaps she should call in on Will and Tina, not to tell them about her troubles, but just to talk, about something—anything—that would help take her mind off her problems. Pushing open the door she went inside. Two tram crews, both with conductresses wearing trousers, still considered a shocking sight in Pontypridd, were sitting in the back room. The front room was empty.

'Diana, good to see you. Tea?' Ronnie reached for a cup.

She looked around: there was no sign of William or Tina but she could hardly walk out just after she'd come in. 'Yes please.'

'You look as though you've lost a shilling and found sixpence.'

'Just at a bit of a loose end. Monday's always slow. It's too early to do the banking, and too late to walk home to see Billy because as soon as I got there, I'd have to turn round and come back into town.'

'Things have been so slow here, I'm glad of someone to talk to.' He poured the tea and put it on the counter. 'Sugar?'

'Two please, if you can spare them. Seen any sign of my brother?'

'Your brother, no. But Tina appeared about an hour ago, piled a tray with food and disappeared upstairs. I think they're making the most of his leave,' he added superfluously. 'So tell me,' he asked, as she stared down into her tea and stirred it. 'How's business?'

'The shops? Not too bad. Of course the sweet shop in the New Theatre is barely ticking over, with sugar so heavily rationed.'

'But you are selling something?'

' "Something" being the operative word. "Don't ask what's in it, just eat it" seems to be the motto in the food trade these days. The toffee and boiled sweets we stock would have been thrown in the bin before the war. It's amazing what people will eat when there's nothing else on offer.'

'You run a pie shop as well, don't you?'

'Wyn and I have gone half-shares with Alma. She supplies us with cooked meat, brawn and pies, we own and run the shop and we're generally sold out by midday.'

'We're so short of things to put on the menu I was wondering if she could supply us. I've been meaning to talk to Tina about it, but it's pointless trying to discuss anything with her until William goes back.'

'You'll also have to check with Alma. I think she's hard pressed to supply two shops at the moment, although she was thinking of expanding.'

'The kitchen in our High Street café isn't being used at the moment. She's welcome to take it over if she wants to. I'll talk to her about it when she's had a chance to get over the funeral. She seems to be having a rough time lately.'

'She's had worse.' Diana coloured as she recalled that the most difficult time for Alma was just before she'd married Charlie, right after Ronnie had deserted her to marry Maud. 'Her mother had been ill for a long time, so it was expected. But to go back to the shops, Alma and I were hoping to open more places that could be run along the lines of the High Street shop, which is supply only, so your idea of utilising your kitchen in the High Street café could be a good one. But that will be up to Alma. It all depends on what stock she can get from the slaughterhouse.'

'The figures will need going into. We haven't much capital set aside. This café's takings are down on what I remember, but like your sweet shop we're ticking over. Seems to me that's all any legitimate business can expect to do in wartime. More tea?' As he turned the tap on the urn, the door opened. Diana looked up and saw Tony standing in the doorway, a thunderous expression clouding his clean-cut Italian features.

'I see you're very busy,' he mumbled, swaying on his feet.

'As busy as trade warrants,' Ronnie answered, assuming Tony had spoken to him. 'Can I get you anything? Black coffee, for instance?'

'All I want is five minutes alone with her.' Grabbing Diana's wrist with one hand, he lifted the flap in the counter with the other. Too stunned to protest, Diana didn't make a sound as he dragged her off the stool.

'What the hell do you think you're doing?' Ronnie remonstrated, as one of the tram drivers walked out of the back room to pay his bill.

'Stay out of things that don't concern you,' Tony snarled.

'Your brother's in the kitchen, Diana,' Ronnie said in a loud voice for the customers' benefit as Tony pushed her through the swing door. Smiling at the driver, he muttered, 'Sorry, must go. Family reunion. I'll send someone out to take your money.'

Jane was sitting in the back kitchen with Phyllis. Between them they'd cleaned the house, finished the washing, hung it on the line and done what little baking they could with the stores on the pantry shelves. Although they had Bethan's two children as well as Brian and Anne, both babies were sleeping and Brian and Rachel were playing happily on the floor with a collection of old wooden trucks that had once belonged to Haydn and Eddie.

'Is the mending basket still in the same place?' Jane asked.

'I haven't found anywhere new to hide it. But you don't have to work all the time. You're supposed to be taking it easy so your ribs will heal.'

'If I don't do something, I'll start screaming.'

'It will be easier, once you get used to living here again.'

'If you really are serious about looking after Anne for me, perhaps I ought to take up Jenny's suggestion of working in munitions.'

'And what would Haydn say about that?'

'Not a lot, seeing how he isn't here. And then again, he didn't exactly ask me what I thought about him touring the front. In fact he didn't even tell me he was going until the night before we came here.'

'So you want to get your own back on him by working in munitions when you know he wouldn't approve?' Phyllis suggested gently.

'I want to do something more than just sit around, cooking, cleaning and looking after Anne. Being trapped in that cellar was horrible. Everything was so dark and quiet after the bomb fell that for a long time I wasn't sure whether I'd been deafened by the blast or killed. It was only when Anne started crying that I realised we'd been buried alive. And even then it seemed to take an eternity for them to dig us out.'

'I can't even begin to imagine what it was

like,' Phyllis said, dropping her knitting on to her lap.

'I would like to help build a bomb that would do to Berlin what the Germans did to our house.'

'That's only natural, but you have to consider Haydn's feelings. Some men hate the idea of their wives working.'

'You know Haydn isn't like that.'

'I'm not so sure.'

'I've been reading the paper,' Jane continued, glossing over Phyllis's suggestion of Haydn's disapproval. 'They say it takes seven factory workers to keep one front-line soldier supplied with arms. If we are going to win this war thousands more women are going to have to volunteer.'

'Perhaps you could talk to someone at the Labour Exchange. I know, from what Myrtle Rees has said, there's three shifts a day in the factory. They might take into account that you're a mother and let you work part time. But I still think you ought to write to Haydn and let him know what you're thinking of doing.'

'Only if you really wouldn't mind looking after Anne.' Jane neatly evaded giving a direct answer. 'Now that I can't feed her any more, it won't matter who gives her a bottle.'

'Get well first.' Phyllis patted her arm as she picked up the kettle and went out to the washhouse to fill it. 'You may feel differently about the idea a few weeks from now.'

'Not after losing my home and everything we owned in London.'

'All I'm saying is don't make any decisions in a hurry. It will take you a while to recover.'

'And helping to put together a bomb might be just the medicine I need to get better.'

'Watch the counter.'

'Mr Ronconi ...'

'The counter,' Ronnie repeated to the cook, 'and take off that apron. It's spattered with grease. Here,' he slipped off the khaki jacket he was wearing and handed it over as the man walked past.

'What do I do if anyone wants anything from the kitchen?'

'Knock on the hatch.' Ronnie closed the swing doors as soon as he left, pushing the bolt across so no one could get in. 'You all right, Diana?' he asked, as she sank, white-faced and dark-eyed on to a stool.

She nodded unconvincingly. He turned to his brother who was leaning against the wall, looking as though he'd collapse without its support.

'What the hell do you think you're doing, coming into the café drunk in the middle of the day and pushing Diana around? The customers will be talking for months.'

'What I do, or don't do, is no concern of yours, *big* brother,' Tony retorted belligerently, as he reached into his pocket for his hip flask.

'No? You create a scene in a business that's owned by the family. Harass a customer who happens to be Tina's sister-in-law and a friend of all your sisters, and you think it's none of my business?'

'Friend?' Tony mocked. 'She's no one's bloody friend.' He took a step towards Diana. As Ronnie moved between them Tony shoved him aside. Ronnie tottered unsteadily, forced to put all his weight on his crutch.

'You'd better go and sleep it off in Laura's before you make even more of a fool of yourself than you already have.'

'Not until I've talked to her.'

'You're in no fit state to talk to anyone, let alone a lady.'

'Now she's a lady?' Tony sniggered, then upended the flask into his mouth.

'You've insulted her and me enough. Go now, before I make you.'

'Make me! All you can make me do is laugh. You look like a bloody scarecrow and you haven't even got the strength of one.' He sidestepped as Ronnie reached out to take his flask. The crutch slipped and Ronnie went crashing to the floor, hitting his shoulder on the cooker on the way down.

'Look what you've done now, you fool!' Angrier with Tony for causing Ronnie pain than for manhandling her, Diana was on her knees in an instant.

'He's all right.'

'You don't know that.'

'I'm fine,' Ronnie protested as he struggled to his feet looking anything but.

'I want ... no, I *demand* to see my son. It's my right—'

'Get out of here, Tony, before William comes down.' Diana helped Ronnie on to the stool she'd been sitting on. Picking up his crutch she handed it to him.

'What son?' Ronnie asked in bewilderment, as he rubbed his shoulder.

'Ask the slut. That baby of hers is mine.'

'Don't be ridiculous,' Diana countered forcefully as she helped Ronnie unbutton his shirt.

'I can count as well as any other man. Why the hell didn't you tell me?'

'There was nothing to tell, even if you'd been in a mood to listen.'

'You were my girlfriend.'

'You were the one who stopped talking to me, remember?' She peeled back Ronnie's shirt. White shreds of skin hung from a rapidly swelling, reddened area that covered his upper arm and shoulderblade. She threw a tea towel into the stone sink and turned on the tap.

'And whose fault was that?' Tony grabbed her, pushing his face close to hers. His warm, whisky-soaked breath wafted over her. She recoiled swiftly in disgust.

'It didn't work out between us, Tony. Leave it at that.' She wrung out the cloth and pressed it against Ronnie's shoulder. Tony caught her arm and spun her round.

'I'm not leaving anything, not until I've seen my son. I know my rights,' he added vehemently.

'What exactly do you want, Tony?' she charged angrily. 'Billy? You intend to take care of him in an army camp? You have

261

a woman waiting in your barracks who can change his nappies and feed him?'

'You can keep him,' he muttered. 'But I've a right to see him. To tell him who is father is.'

'Rights! Even if he was yours—which he's not—you have no rights: not over me, and certainly not over Billy.'

'I'll go to court.'

'That will be a new one for Ponty magistrates and the *Observer*. A man wanting to acknowledge a legitimately born child as his bastard! Are you that eager to see Wyn put me out on the streets? Do you want to make me destitute enough to go to the courts to sue for whatever the magistrate will order you to pay in maintenance? Because if you do, I'm telling you now, five bob a week will be nowhere near enough to keep us. We'll take all your guardsman's pay and more.'

'I ... I ...' He dropped his flask to the floor. The whisky trickled out on to the red tiles, forming a puddle in a dip beneath the butcher's block. He stood there watching it grow, while his drink-fuddled mind groped for words to explain what he wanted. It was impossible. The more he tried to think, the less certain he was of what he expected from Diana.

'Is that what you want?' she reiterated. 'Because you've made a fine start by pushing me in here. Ronnie's right, you've created a scene that's going to keep the gossips going in this town for years. God alone knows what Wyn's going to say about this.'

'Bloody queer,' Tony mumbled, regaining some of his belligerence.

'He's *my* husband and the father of *my* son.' She stood her ground for a moment, then tackled the bolt on the door.

'Where are you going?'

'To get help for Ronnie.'

'Oh no you don't. You're not walking away from me, not a second time.' He clamped his hand over her neck and forced her into the corner of the room. Fighting for breath, she backed into the gas cooker and hit her arm on a pan of hot fat. She cried out in pain, knocking over a stack of clean saucepans piled on a shelf behind the stove as she struggled to free herself from his grip. Ronnie hauled himself to his feet as someone hammered on the other side of the door. He lifted his crutch and brought it down on Tony's head just as the door finally gave way.

Eyes blurred by tears of pain and humiliation, Diana watched William step through the doorway into the kitchen. He took in the situation at a glance. Leaving Ronnie to Tina who followed him in, he stepped over Tony who was half sitting, half lying in a dazed stupor and went to Diana. Leading her to the sink, he slid back the scorched sleeve of her jacket, exposed the skin on her forearm and ran the cold tap over it.

Tina peeled back more of Ronnie's shirt, tutting at the red marks that were already bruising purple-black. 'I told you when you came home that you looked dreadful. A breath of fresh air would have been enough to flatten you, but what do you do? Take it easy? Oh no, not you. You have a go at Tony who's done nothing but live off the fat of the land for the last year.'

'Great—my shoulder hurts and I get a lecture from my sister.'

'What happened?' William asked, as he examined Diana's arm.

'Tony came in drunk and looking for trouble, so I laid him out. Diana was at the counter when he arrived and very foolishly tried to help.'

'Sis?' William asked sceptically.

'I thought I could calm him down.'

'Stupid girl. Especially considering you two had a bust-up before he joined up. This arm is a right mess. I think we should call the doctor.'

'I'm shivering from shock, not the burn.'

Ronnie looked across at her, then reached out to the fat-fryer with his fingertips to check the temperature at the bottom of the pan. 'We haven't had any orders for chips for over an hour so it couldn't have been that hot. Her arm is red now, but I doubt it will blister. Slice a raw potato over it, bind it with a tea towel soaked in cold water and it should be right as rain in a few hours.'

'Thank you, Dr Ronconi. I didn't know you'd studied medicine in Italy.'

'Ronnie's right, I've done worse than this at home.' Diana took another clean towel from the pile on the work surface and threw it into the sink.

'Do you think Tony needs a doctor?' Tina asked.

'He took a lot more punishment than this in

training camp.' William crouched beside him and lifted his eyelid.

'You mean he's done this before?'

'Get drunk? We all do from time to time,' William confessed.

'And pick fights?'

'I never do, especially after I've had a few drinks. It's difficult to gauge the other man's strength. Some of the small blokes can be surprisingly strong, especially the Scots ...'

'I wasn't talking about you, I was asking about Tony. Has he picked fights before?' Tina demanded furiously.

'Now and again.'

'And got knocked out cold?'

'This isn't the first time I've seen him like this.'

'With a lump this size on his head?' Tina enquired caustically.

'I doubt he even feels it. It will soon go down. People in his state usually develop rubber skulls. But boy is he going to have a hangover tomorrow.'

'William's right,' Ronnie confirmed. 'Once he sleeps off the whisky he'll be fine. I'll give you a hand to get him upstairs, Will. He can sleep it off there.'

'Not in my rooms he can't.'

'Be reasonable, Tina, he's in no condition to go anywhere else.'

'William and I had a ten-hour honeymoon when we got married, and I haven't seen him between then and now. The last thing I need is a drunken brother cluttering up the place while

I'm getting to know my husband.'

'We'll put him in the living room, he'll be out of the way there,' William proposed.

'I'll keep an eye on him. As soon as he comes round I'll send him on his way.'

'And you really look as though you should be running up and down stairs looking after a drunk as well as a café, Ronnie,' Tina snapped.

'My shoulder's bruised, not broken,' he said as he pulled on his shirt and buttoned it.

'If you ask me, this is a bloody mess all round.' William looked from Ronnie to Tony, the spilt whisky, fat and scattered saucepans.

'I'll clear it,' Tina announced in a martyred voice as she picked up a bucket of sawdust and sprinkled a couple of handfuls over the rapidly congealing lard on the floor.

'Come on, sis.' William held out his arm. 'The sooner I get you home, the sooner I can come back and help Tina to sort this out.'

Diana leaned against the sink, shaking her head. 'I still have the banking to do.' She couldn't bear the thought of walking out into the café and facing the cook and the customers.

'The banking can wait until tomorrow.'

'No it can't. You've no idea how much thieving goes on under cover of the blackout. I daren't leave the takings in the shop tills overnight.'

'Then I'll do it.'

'You wouldn't know how.'

'So tell me.'

'Take her out the back way,' Ronnie

suggested, sensing why Diana was so reluctant to move. 'There's two doors in the yard: left-hand one connects to the slaughterhouse the other to the yard at the back of the White Hart. Take your pick.'

William put his arm around Diana. This time she didn't protest. He looked back at Tina as he led her to the door.

'You take care of Diana, I'll see to these two fools,' she said briskly. 'And you don't have to worry about me coping, I've been coping for years. Italian women are brought up to it, but Gina, not me, nursemaids that one.' She pointed to Tony. 'I'm not giving up our time together for anyone, especially a drunk.'

CHAPTER 12

'Want to tell me about it?' William asked Diana as he escorted her through the side entrance into the yard of the White Hart.

'Didn't you hear?'

'Shouting, and crashing, that's why Tina and I came downstairs. Whatever it is, Di, I'd rather hear it from you than someone else.'

'As you saw, Tony was drunk. He said a lot of stupid things.'

'Is there any truth in them?'

'What do you think?'

He led her across the road past the New Theatre. Compared to Saturday afternoon, the town was deserted. 'So, is Tony Billy's father?' he asked bluntly.

'Then you did hear what he said?'

'I think the whole street did, and you haven't answered my question.'

'You're my brother. I shouldn't have to defend myself to you.'

'Whether Tony is or isn't Billy's father, he obviously has reason to think he might be.'

'You saw him, he was drunk. He didn't know what he was saying.'

'You're avoiding the issue, Di.'

'I don't think he was happy about the way we stopped seeing one another.'

'If I remember rightly, neither were you.'

'Things are different now, I'm married.'

'For how long, after Wyn hears about what just happened?' William asked.

'He's stood by me through worse.'

'I'm trying to help, sis, but I can't unless you tell me what's going on.'

'You heard Ronnie. Tony came into the café fighting mad and half out of his mind with drink.'

'And that's what you're going to tell Wyn?'

'Wyn and I have no secrets. He already knows all there is to know about me.'

'More than me?'

'More than anyone. And we've lived through gossip before, and survived.'

'Don't you think this has more serious implications? Not just for you and Wyn, but Billy. Bastard is an ugly word, and allegations like the one Tony's just made have a habit of sticking. How are you going to feel when Billy has to face the taunts of the other kids when he starts school?'

'Billy's not a bastard,' she contradicted forcefully, 'and Tony will soon be gone. Then this whole thing will be forgotten.'

'I hope you're right, for all your sakes, especially Billy's,' he said fervently as they turned the corner into Market Square.

'It will be all right. You'll see.' It wasn't a pronouncement, more a prayer, but she didn't succeed in convincing herself, much less William.

'Thank you for a lovely day.'

'It's not quite over yet.' Huw helped Myrtle from the train and reached into his sports coat for their train tickets.

She followed him, trying to read her watch in the pool of light from the collector's torch.

'It's only just half-past nine,' Huw informed her as they walked down the steps into station yard. 'How about a coffee in the New Inn?' he hazarded bravely, deciding that if she wasn't ashamed to be seen with him in the lounge of the best hotel in Pontypridd, he'd risk his pride by asking her to go out with him again.

'I really should be getting home. I feel guilty leaving Megan to look after my father on my day off.'

He knew Mr Rees was invariably in bed by eight every evening. What he didn't know was that the old man rarely fell asleep before midnight, and the front parlour that had been converted into his bedroom was ideally placed to monitor all the comings and goings in the household.

'It doesn't matter.' He failed to keep the disappointment from his voice.

'Perhaps just a quick one,' she relented, daring to put her own wishes above her father's for the first time in her life.

'It will be as quick as they can serve us. Did you really enjoy the film?' He reached the bottom of the steps and held out his arm. Secure in the knowledge that they couldn't be seen in the blackout, she took it.

'It was lovely. Do you think that's what Jesse

James was really like?'

'Most crooks I've met looked more like Boris Karloff than Tyrone Power.'

'That's because the only ones you've met are from Pontypridd.'

'You think they breed a better-looking lawbreaker in America?'

She laughed, and his step lightened at the sound. He felt as though he'd caught a glimpse of the real Myrtle behind the façade of polite, dutiful deference her father had instilled into her. 'Do you have a day off next week?' he asked impetuously.

'Tuesday.'

'Two days before mine. By the look of it we could wait months for our days off to coincide again, but I'm on days all this week, so my evenings are free.'

'So are mine.'

'I'll be finished by six, but I'd have to go home to wash and change afterwards, which means I wouldn't be able to meet you much before seven. Is that too late for you?'

'I never go to bed before half-past nine.'

'Although you have to be up at four?'

'I try to catch an hour's sleep when I come home.'

'Well if we only have two and a half hours, that rules out Cardiff, but we could go to the pictures. If we time it carefully we might be able to see the main feature, or I could book tickets for the second house in the Town Hall if you prefer.'

'There's a new variety there this week.'

'Shall we risk it?'

'Yes please.'

He closed his hand around the fingers nestling in the crook of his arm. 'I'll get the tickets, then. Is tomorrow night too soon?'

She threw all ladylike hesitation and caution to the wind. 'Not a bit. I'll really look forward to it.'

Diana woke with a start, and looked around at the familiar furniture in the bedroom. The light was burning on the bedside table, illuminating the alarm clock. She read the time, ten o'clock, and sat up abruptly.

'Where do you think you're going?' Wyn pressed her back on to the pillows.

'Billy ...'

'Your mother gave me a hand to bath him and put him to bed. If you make any more noise you're likely to wake him.'

'I didn't mean to sleep so long,' she whispered, looking over to the cot where her son was sleeping peacefully.

'How's your arm?'

She tried to move her forearm. It felt stiff and strange. She looked down at the bandages and it all came flooding back to her. Tony—the awful scene in the café—William walking her home. Her mother sending for Bethan, who had dressed her burn, given her a pill and sent her to bed.

'Oh God, Wyn ...'

'It's all right. I heard what happened.'

'From William?'

'He told your mother, and he met me off the train.'

'What are we going to do?'

'Nothing.' He sat alongside her on the bed and put his arm around her shoulders.

'You weren't there. You didn't hear what Tony said, but Ronnie did. He knows everything ...'

'Whatever he knows, he's kept to himself so far. And seeing as how it involves his brother I think it will stay that way. All William told me was that Tony came in drunk and looking for a fight and you stepped in between him and Ronnie.'

'He didn't tell you that Tony said Billy was his child?'

'No, but Tony shouting out allegations in a drunken stupor doesn't prove anything.'

'It proves that I slept with him.'

'If anyone says that to William's or my face they'll get the same treatment Ronnie meted out to Tony.'

She peered up at him in the soft glow of the lamplight, seeing the cuts and bruises on his jaw and his swollen black eye for the first time.

'It's already started, hasn't it?' She reached out, touching his battered face tenderly with her fingertips.

'No. I got these in work. And before you go taking all the credit, some of my colleagues don't like new men coming in, especially friends of Erik's. The factory nurse cleaned me up. It's nowhere near as bad as it looks.'

'I don't believe you.' She wrapped her arms

around his chest as tears welled up in her eyes. 'None of this would have happened if you hadn't married me.'

'Of course it would have.'

'I don't mean the factory, I mean Tony.'

'It will soon blow over. Ronnie told William that he intends to put Tony on the first train to Birmingham tomorrow morning. If we stick together, sit it out, the gossip will die down, it always has before.'

'There's still my mother and William.'

'If you want to tell them the truth, go ahead. I doubt that it will come as a shock. I think your mother has suspected it for a long time, and if William had been around when we'd got married, we would have had to face a lot more questions than we did.'

She clung to his arm, burying her head in his shoulder. 'I'm sorry Wyn, so sorry ...'

'Come on now, love. This isn't like you.'

'More gossip and scandal is the last thing we need right now.'

'I don't think anyone needs it at any time. I'll see the boss tomorrow, ask him to put me on the night shift. That way I can help out with the shops and the banking. I don't want you walking around town by yourself until we're sure Tony's gone.'

'That's silly.'

'No it isn't. Promise me you'll stay in the house tomorrow?'

'But the shops—'

'Alice is capable enough, she can look after things until I can change my shifts.' The front door opened and closed. 'That's Myrtle coming home.' He left the bed.

'Are you going to tell her?'

'Only that Tony got drunk and said some stupid things. Would you like some supper?'

She shook her head.

'Your mother said you haven't eaten since breakfast.'

'I couldn't eat, not now, Wyn.'

He tucked the counterpane around her as though she were a child. 'Nothing's going to change,' he said firmly. 'You're my wife, and you were right in the park. That is my son sleeping over there. No one else's.'

She looked up at him. 'I love you.'

He dropped a kiss on to her forehead. 'And I love you too. You sure I can't get you anything?'

'Nothing.'

'Then try to sleep. I'll be up in a while.'

He walked down the stairs and into the living room, glancing at the parlour door as he passed through the hall. He couldn't hear his father, but that didn't mean the old man was sleeping. If he ever discovered what had happened in the café, they'd never hear the end of it. Billy was his pride and joy, his link with the future, his immortality. He couldn't even begin to imagine how his father would react if he suspected the child wasn't bonded to him by blood.

He pushed open the door. Myrtle was sitting in one of the easy chairs, a faraway, dreamy expression in her eyes.

'Good day out?' he asked, picking up the kettle.

'Yes thanks,' she replied blushing at the lies she'd told Wyn and Megan about Moira James and Roath Park. 'Megan's gone to bed. I'll make us some tea if you like.'

'You sit there, I'll make it. I'd like to talk to you if you're not too tired.'

'Is something wrong?' she asked, panic-stricken at the thought that one of the neighbours had seen her and Huw together and told her father. His temper had always been unpredictable, more so since he'd been ill. 'If it's about what happened today ...'

'You've heard?'

'I suppose I should have told you, but I was afraid of what Dad would say. You know what he can be like?'

'Only too well.' Wyn went out into the kitchen and filled the kettle.

'But honestly, Wyn, he behaved like a perfect gentleman the whole time we were out. You don't think it was wrong of me to accept his invitation, do you?'

'Wrong of you to accept what invitation?' he asked, mystified by the question.

'Huw's of course.'

'You've been out with Huw Davies?'

'Wasn't that what we were talking about?'

'No.' He laughed softly at the thought of his sister and Huw Davies courting.

'What's so funny?' she demanded indignantly.

'You. Huw asks you out and you think you've got to keep it quiet.'

'Dad wouldn't like it.'

'To hell with what he'd like, and I hope the old bugger has got that empty glass he keeps next to his bed pinned against the wall to hear me say so.'

'Wyn!'

'Myrtle, go out with Huw. Have a wonderful time, marry him if you want to.' He returned to the living room and picked up the teapot.

'Don't be ridiculous. Women like me don't get married.'

'Like you? What makes you so different from everyone else?'

'I'm thirty-eight.'

'And thirty-eight-year-olds aren't allowed to get married?'

'This is the first time Huw's asked me to go anywhere with him, it was a day out, that's all. I hardly think he has marriage on his mind.'

'You seeing him again?'

'Tomorrow.'

'Then he has marriage on his mind.'

'Do you really think so?' she questioned eagerly, surprising herself as much as Wyn.

'Huw's old enough to know a good thing when he sees it. He wouldn't be chasing if he didn't mean to catch you.'

'Still, you won't breathe a word of it, will you? Dad ...'

'You've got to learn to stand up to him, Myrtle. He's going to find out sooner or later, and better from you than the chapel minister.'

'I'd just rather he didn't find out yet. I really like Huw, and Dad can be so intimidating.'

'Intimidating! That's a new way of putting it. Myrtle, Huw's a policeman, he meets people ten times more terrifying than Dad every day of the week. And as he obviously likes you, he won't be put off by Dad's or anyone else's nonsense. I wish you well, both of you.' He returned to the kitchen to warm the teapot. 'But it wasn't that I wanted to talk to you about,' he said as he walked back into the living room. 'Tony Ronconi got drunk this afternoon. He went to the café on the Tumble. Diana was there and he attacked her.'

'Tony? But why on earth would he do that?'

'Because he thinks Billy is his son.'

'His! Wyn, I don't understand.'

'Yes you do,' he contradicted softly, taking the chair opposite hers. 'Even you can't be that naive.'

She stared at her knees as he lifted down the tin tea caddy embossed with a portrait of Edward VII that had been a wedding present of their mother's.

'Did he hurt Diana?'

'Her arm was splashed by hot fat, but it's not serious. I've just talked to her. She's upset of course, but she'll soon get over it.' He returned to the kitchen, wet the tea and brought in the pot.

'Your face!' she exclaimed, looking up and seeing it for the first time.

'I walked into a door in the factory.'

'A likely story.'

'Initiation ceremony.'

'I was hoping they'd leave you alone.'

'They will tomorrow; you should see the other fellow. All those training sessions and boxing lessons with Joey Rees in the gym paid off.'

'I'll be back in tomorrow ...'

'And you'll ignore me and get on with your own work. I can take care of myself. You don't have to play the big sister to your sissy little brother all your life.'

'I'd like to help.'

'You can by ignoring the gossips. But then you've been doing that for years, haven't you, Myrtle?'

'You and Diana seem so happy.'

'We are, but it's not exactly a normal marriage.'

'You won't leave her?' she asked anxiously. Diana wasn't only her sister-in-law, but her closest friend. Diana and Megan had blown the only breath of fresh air that had been allowed into the house since her mother had died.

'No, Myrtle, I won't leave her.'

'And she won't leave you?'

'She says not.'

'Does she know?' she asked hesitantly.

'That I'm a homosexual?' He looked her in the eye. 'It's all right. Using the word isn't going to change anything. Yes, she knows. In fact she probably knows more about me than I do. I'm lucky to have her for a wife. And you for a sister.' He poured out the tea and handed her a cup. She reached out and touched his hand.

'I'm sorry, Wyn.'

'For what?'

'Everything you've had to go through. When

279

you were little I tried to protect you from the other boys but they tormented you no matter what I did.'

'You can't change human nature. As the saying goes, "we're all born different" and I accepted a long time ago that I was born more different than most.'

'Be careful.'

'I've no intention of getting myself thrown into prison,' he reassured her. 'And with the present manpower shortage and surge in blackout crime the police have better things to do than chase the likes of me. But that's enough about Diana and me. Tell me, where did Huw take you?'

While she talked about the Cardiff shops and Tyrone Power, he allowed his mind to wander. How much longer could he go on living a lie? Was it simply coincidence that he and Diana had both been attacked today? Or could it be one more sign that the cracks were widening and the vultures gathering? How much longer before they swallowed him, Diana and Billy?

Gina walked into the café on the Tumble at midnight. There weren't many customers. A couple of railway workers waiting for their late-night shift to begin, three usherettes from the New Theatre, and a uniformed constable talking to an uneasy-looking black-marketeer.

Ronnie was behind the counter, keeping half an eye on the tables as he polished the metal ice-cream goblets.

'I thought you'd be packing up by now,' she complained.

'Not until the last tram has gone and the train from the afternoon shift of munitions workers has come in.'

'Tina and William upstairs?'

'After what happened this afternoon, I've had orders not to disturb them unless the place burns down. Has Tony come round?'

'Not since you and William dumped him on Luke and me. I got fed up with sitting in Laura's, so I thought I'd come down and see what's happening.'

'Not a lot.'

'What exactly did Tony do this afternoon?'

'Go berserk. From what I could see, little brother just wanted to let off steam.'

'You expect me to believe that, after you disturbed Luke and me in the middle of our tea and dragged us down to Laura's to look after him?'

'Tina wanted him out of her rooms. You can hardly blame her. William's only got a week.'

'So Luke and I had to give up our evening and sit up half the night to accommodate Tina?'

Ronnie glanced at the back room. No one looked as though they were about to move, or order food. 'I need to sit down and rest this leg. Come on through, I'll send the cook out here.'

She followed him into the kitchen. Pulling up a stool he slumped next to a workbench littered with bowls of ready peeled potatoes and chips. 'That's better.' He grimaced as he rested his leg on a sack of vegetables.

'Did you really knock Tony out like William said?'

'It was him or me.'

'In that case I hope he doesn't feel like hitting someone when he wakes up. Luke's developed a lot of muscles in the pit, but he's still a Quaker at heart. They don't believe in thumping people the way we Catholics do.'

'I only did it because Tony left me with no other option.'

'Is Tony the father of Diana's baby?'

'And where did you hear that?'

'Luke heard it in Griffiths' shop when he bought his cigarettes.'

'So that's why you came down?'

'Well is he?' she reiterated.

'I'm the one who has just returned after a five-year absence. You tell me.'

'There was something odd about her marrying Wyn Rees in such a hurry.'

'But she is married to him, and he has accepted the baby as his. Which is why I'm putting Tony on the first train to Birmingham tomorrow morning.'

'Rather you than me.'

'He'll do as he's told.'

'I'm not so sure, Ronnie. A lot of things have changed in five years.'

He winked at her. 'Not that many.'

'But what if the baby *is* Tony's?' she persisted.

'What if he is?'

'He's our nephew.'

'His name is Billy Rees. I think we should

remember that for his sake, whoever his father is, don't you?'

Ronnie had packed Gina off to Luke, closed the café and was just finishing washing the floor when there was a knock at the door. Switching off half the lights, he pulled the blackout and saw Wyn's large, stocky figure standing outside. He turned the key and opened the door.

'I know you're closed. I was hoping for a word.'

'Come in.'

'I wanted to thank you for stepping between Diana and your brother this afternoon.'

'Anyone would have done the same.' Ronnie closed the curtain and pulled two chairs down from one of the tables.

'I doubt it. From what William told me, Tony was drunk and looking for trouble. A fit man in that condition is no joke to tackle, especially for someone in your state of health. He is also your brother.'

'Which was why I did it. I'd offer you a coffee or tea, but I've switched everything off. However, I do have a bottle of brandy tucked away.'

'I only came round to thank you. I won't keep you any longer.'

'Wyn—' Ronnie detained him as he walked to the door. 'Tony was drunk, he really didn't know what he was saying, or doing. I'm sorry he insulted your wife. But it's obvious after today where Diana's loyalties and affections lie.'

'Thank you.'

'What I'm trying to say ...'

'I know what you're trying to say.' Wyn held out his hand and Ronnie took it.

'I'll see that Tony is on the first train out of here in the morning.'

'I'd appreciate it if you let Will know so he can tell us. I was going to change shifts so Diana wouldn't have to go out by herself while he's in town.'

'There's no need.' Ronnie opened the curtain and pulled back the bolt.

Wyn stood on the pavement outside, listening to Ronnie relocking the door. He had never felt more alone in his life. He had a sympathetic wife and a loving sister, but neither of them really understood how he felt. It wasn't their fault. The fear of exposure, the sense of futility that came with living a lie, the isolation and loneliness that was with him every day of his life could only be understood by someone in the same position as himself. There was someone, and a place he could go. If he dared.

Torn between his conscience and a need for sympathy, he walked back through the town towards Tyfica Road.

Huw stood in the centre of his kitchen that also did duty as his living room and tried to imagine he was a stranger seeing it for the first time. It was clean, but not as clean as it had been before Megan had moved in with Wyn and Diana, because since then she had only managed to 'do' for him once a fortnight, as opposed to the weekly visits she had made before Billy's birth.

Megan was always going on at him to replace the ancient dogskin hearth-rug that was more burnt hole than rug, the age-grimed, dingy wallpaper, moth-eaten chair covers and curtains and generally make an effort to dispel the air of dilapidation that no amount of cleaning could brighten. He had money put away, but what use would that be when so many things were rationed?

He left the room and went into the parlour. He had trouble opening the door. Swollen with damp it juddered noisily over the bare floorboards that his father had stained a deep mahogany to match his mother's heirloom furniture. The surface of the ornate Victorian table and chairs was marred with large white spots, and the doors on the mahogany dresser had warped since he had last looked at them. He ran his fingers over the damage. He should have lit a fire in here in winter. Once a week would have been enough to keep the worst ravages of cold and damp at bay. Even the carpet, a genuine Persian that had been his grandmother's pride and joy, was stained with mould. Megan had thrown out the curtains when she had replaced them with blackout. They had fallen to bits when she had taken them down.

Closing the door, he walked upstairs to the bedrooms. The one he used was clean and spartan. His clothes hung in the wardrobe, the bed was made, an alarm clock stood on the tallboy, the carpet had been recently swept, the furniture dusted, but even he could see it was not the sort of room a woman would feel comfortable in.

Much to Megan's disgust the other two bedrooms had become dumping grounds for things no longer in daily use, but deemed by him to be too good to throw out. There was a radio he'd meant to get around to fixing some time, just to prove Frank Clayton's diagnosis of 'broken beyond repair' wrong. There were half a dozen holed pots and pans that needed patching. Considering the present national emergency it might be better to donate them to the scrap metal collections. There were five boxes of 'best' china that his father had put away after his mother had died, because if there were more than two place settings of crockery in the cupboard, they allowed the dishes to pile up in the sink without washing them. Bits of wood, nails, tools, odd collections of things that might prove useful but never had, and if he were realistic, probably never would.

There was no getting away from the fact that he had allowed the house to get into a state. Hardly the sort of place a man could ask a woman like Myrtle to live in. When he got to know her a little better he could ask her how she'd change it, if it was hers. She couldn't possibly object if he invited Diana or Megan to chaperon her. Was he being too hasty? One outing, and he was already thinking of marriage and moving her into his house. Best not to say anything. Bide his time. The last thing he wanted to do was frighten her off.

Wyn walked along Gelliwastad Grove towards home, but instead of turning right into Tyfica Road he kept on walking until he reached Graigwen Place. At the end of the street stood the substantial Victorian villa of Jacobsdal, a rambling house that the Council had requisitioned and turned into accommodation for the motley collection of refugees who had fled Europe and drifted into the town.

He checked the street as carefully as the blackout allowed, before stepping through the twin posts that had once sported gates, and on to the gravel drive. His feet crunched alarmingly on the small stones, so he moved on to the soft earth of a flowerbed. Trees cast strange, elongated shadows in the faint glow of moonlight. Shrubs and bushes loomed, an impenetrable jungle on his left. A rustle stopped him in his tracks. He turned swiftly, to see a shadow darting past. A cat, or a rat? It was too dark to see.

Ahead gleamed faint lines of white paintwork, chequer-boarding shining black squares. Alongside the window he could just make out the door. He hit his hand against an ancient bell-push as he raised his knuckles to knock. He had to rap twice before there was a shuffling inside.

'Who is it?' called a guttural voice.

'Wyn Rees to see Erik,' he murmured.

The door opened a crack; a light shone dimly at the end of a long passage. 'He's playing cards in the hall. Carry on until you reach the double doors.'

Wyn walked down the stone-flagged corridor. The house was freezing, the temperature several degrees lower than the air outside. Pushing open the doors that faced him, he found himself in a huge room. He could see why the inmates had christened it the 'hall'. A pot-bellied metal stove stood on a stone plinth at the far end of what had probably once been a ballroom. All the parquet flooring in the immediate vicinity had been ripped up, presumably to feed it.

Four men sat around a rickety card table as close to the stove as safety would allow. Erik had his back to him. He recognised him by his blond hair and worn flannel work shirt. Erik had been a history professor in his native country, but now he wore only labourer's clothes, almost as though they were the insignia of his refugee status.

Alerted by the silence of his companions, Erik turned round. He was a short, slim man with startlingly blue eyes who looked younger than his thirty-six years. 'Wyn?' he smiled. 'What are you doing here so late? Nothing wrong, is there?'

Wyn looked from Erik to the faces of the men sitting with him, and wished he hadn't come.

'You want to talk to me?' Erik suggested, sensing his friend's unease.

'Only if you're not too busy.'

'I'll get Jan to take over my hand. It's all right, we're staking our sugar ration, not serious money.' Laying his cards on the table he shouted through the open door. The man who had let in Wyn appeared.

'Come on through to the kitchen. I'll make you some tea. You look as though you could use it.'

Wyn followed him down a maze of narrow corridors into what had been the servants' quarters. They finished up in a small black and white tiled scullery.

'The house looks big from the outside, but I had no idea it was this big.'

'You've never been in here before?'

'Only the gardens as a kid, because I wasn't supposed to.'

'The pull of the forbidden has always been stronger than duty. Do you want China tea, or some of Jan's herbal? It is very good, helps the digestion, and is guaranteed to aid a good night's rest.'

'I shouldn't have come.'

'Nonsense, it's open house here day and night. It has to be with so many of us living under one roof, and friends are always welcome.' Erik reached down a wooden box and spooned some dried leaves into a jug. 'I can guess why you're here.'

'You've heard about what happened to Diana?'

'It's all over town. I told you marriage is no answer for people like us.'

'Diana's a nice girl.'

'So was my wife.' Erik lit the gas, and took two cigarettes from his pocket. Lighting them both on the flame before putting the kettle on to boil, he handed one to Wyn.

'I didn't know you were married?'

'I was young. My father insisted on it. He saw it as a cure for my "disease". He picked the prettiest and most well-endowed girl in town. She was also experienced, but he saw that as an advantage. As he couldn't trust me to do my marital duty, he hoped she would seduce me.'

'And this girl didn't mind marrying you?'

'It was a matter of economics. Her father was poor, mine was rich. Poor father,' he shook his head fondly, 'he would have been better off keeping his money. The honeymoon was a disaster. She went off with a lifeguard, I consoled myself with a waiter.'

'Are you serious?'

'But of course. Wyn, take the word of someone who has tried and failed. No matter what you do, your marriage to Diana is doomed. You're like a fish trying to live with a bird. In their own environs birds and fish are perfectly nice creatures; but no matter how fond they are of one another, one needs air to survive, the other water.' He strained the tea, and handed Wyn a cup. 'I'm sorry, you came here looking for sympathy and reassurance, and I am not being very helpful.'

'I just don't know which way to turn!' Wyn raged, allowing his anger to surface for the first time since William had met him at the station.

'Look at it logically. What can you do, except go on the way you are?'

'And carry on putting up with the taunts, the gossip, the insults to Diana? She deserves better.'

290

'And maybe one day she'll find it. You aren't the only one who is unhappy, Wyn. I'd rather be fighting in my own country than here. As it is, on a more personal level, I'd like to see more of you, talk to you the way we are now, get to know you better.'

'So would I. But ...'

'... you made a promise to Diana. So in the meantime you live with your wife, and spend all your free time with her.'

'At least we can see one another in the factory.'

'After today I think we should keep it to seeing, not talking. Those bruises do nothing to enhance your appearance.'

'I'd like to make plans, look ahead, but I can't see a future for myself, and I'm not just talking about the war. This tea is foul.' Wyn abandoned his cup. 'I'm sorry, you have your own problems without listening to mine.'

'Stop apologising, I'd like to help.'

'I have to go.'

'It's late. Everyone will be asleep in your house. Stay a while. Come into the hall with the others. We could play cards, or chess. You do play chess?'

'I'm not very good.'

'Neither am I.'

'Why don't I believe you?'

'You're right, this is disgusting. Perhaps I made it the wrong way.' Erik emptied both cups down the sink. 'Come on, I'll introduce you to my fellow lodgers. You'll find that we Europeans are a little more tolerant than most of your countrymen.'

'Some other time.' Wyn hesitated at the door. 'I shouldn't have disturbed you. I don't even know why I came.'

'Loneliness?'

'That's all the more reason to stay away.' He walked out of the room knowing, without looking back, that Erik was watching him leave.

CHAPTER 13

Ronnie had deliberately placed the alarm clock out of reach on the tallboy opposite the bed. It was the only way he could guarantee that he would get up in the morning. When it rang, he reluctantly forced himself into consciousness, folded back the bedcovers and fumbled his way through the blackout. Silencing the bell, he hitched up the cord on his pyjama trousers, pushed the curtains aside and stared out at the murky silhouette of the mountain that flowed down to the back wall of Laura's house.

Dawn was still two hours away. He wondered how he'd managed to run the Tumble café nineteen hours a day for all those years before he had married Maud. This was only the second morning he'd had to open up for the early morning tram and train crews, and he felt as though he were sleepwalking.

Allowing the curtain to fall, he switched on the light. The sight of Tony still lying in one half of the double bed irritated him. Pulling back the bedclothes, he folded them over the footboard before picking up his crutch and the dressing gown that had been Eddie's.

Tony creased his eyes against the light. He began to protest, but as the symptoms of hangover penetrated his awareness, his mumblings turned into a moan.

'It's morning,' Ronnie announced in a deliberately loud voice. Scooping his clothes from the chair next to the bed, he limped to the door.

'My head hurts like hell.' Unable to face moving to the bottom of the bed to retrieve the sheet and blankets, Tony curled into the foetal position and pulled the pillow over his head.

'And so it should after what you drank.'

'It's worse than it's ever been before.'

'Probably because I hit you.'

Tony lifted the pillow fractionally higher. 'You hit me?'

'You needed curbing.'

'What was I doing?' Tony sat up and reached across to the washstand. Lifting the huge water jug to his lips he drank deeply.

'You can't remember?'

'Not much. Bloody hell, I thought I was parched enough to drink anything but this water is foul.'

'It's been standing there since I arrived.'

'You haven't refilled it with fresh?'

'I prefer to wash downstairs.' Ronnie opened the door and padded down the stairs on bare feet, wincing as his soles came into contact with the flagstones in the passage. Only the soft glow from the fire illuminated the kitchen. Switching on the light, he picked up the kettle, filled it in the washhouse and put it on the hob to boil.

Leaving his clothes on one of the easy chairs he walked outside to the ty bach. There was a smell of daffodils and bluebells in the air. Summer was following close on the heels of spring, and it occurred to him that it would be the second summer since Maud had died. When he had returned to Wales he had thought everything would remind him of her, but if anything it had been easier to carry on with his life here, than it had in Italy. The longer he stayed in the town the more he realised that most of his good memories of Maud were rooted in Bardi, not Pontypridd.

Back in the washhouse he stripped off his dressing gown and pyjamas, filled the huge Belfast sink with cold water and plunged his head into it. The shock cleared the last vestiges of sleep from his brain.

'I've wet the tea.' Tony wandered in and sank down on to Laura's upturned wooden washtub behind him.

'Do you want a medal?'

'Did I make a total fool of myself yesterday?'

'Yes.'

'There was still no need to thump me,' Tony complained ruefully, rubbing the crown of his head.

'Yes there was.' Ronnie doused a coarse flannel in the water, soaped it and rubbed his chest. 'At the time you were pushing Diana Powell around.'

'Did I hit her?'

'No, but only because I was there to stop you. You also demanded that she hand over Billy to you.' He rinsed out the flannel and wiped the lather from his skin.

'Oh hell!'

'You really don't remember?'

'I remember sitting in the park waiting for her, getting angrier and angrier ...'

'And drunk.'

Tony ignored Ronnie's jibe.

'You really don't remember what happened in the café?'

'Nothing.'

'Go and pour that tea. We have to talk.'

'I'll find Diana this morning and apologise.'

'Wyn Rees might kill you if you try. You've set the whole town talking. What on earth possessed you to say those things?'

'I was angry because she'd married Wyn. Angry because she didn't even tell me she was pregnant. So I got plastered.' Tony went into the kitchen, took two cups down from the dresser and poured out the tea.

'Sensible men crawl into a corner to get drunk, do it quietly, and then sleep it off,' Ronnie shouted through the open doorway.

'I wish I had.'

'I bet you do.' Ronnie finished washing, let the water out of the sink, sluiced it down, and walked into the kitchen. He climbed into his underwear, picked up his trousers and put them on, slipping his braces over his vest to keep them from falling down. Sitting on a chair, he glanced at Tony as he rolled on his socks. His brother was hunched over the table, his head in his hands, his pyjama buttons undone. 'Are you the father of her baby?'

'I'm a more likely father than Wyn Rees.'

'Then why didn't you marry her?'

Tony shrugged his shoulders.

'For pity's sake Tony, you're not a child and I'm not asking you who stole the last biscuit out of the barrel. If you thought enough of Diana to climb into bed with her, why didn't you marry her?'

'You thought enough of Alma to sleep with her all the time she worked for us, yet you never married her.'

'For which I'm heartily ashamed of myself.'

'Just as well you didn't though, isn't it? Because if you had, you wouldn't have been able to marry Maud and take her to Italy.'

'Are you trying to tell me that you were only using Diana until something better came along?'

'Wasn't that what you did with Alma?'

Ronnie's hands closed into fists. Tony backed out of his chair. Slowly, deliberately, Ronnie unclenched his fingers.

'If you set out to seduce Diana to emulate me, you've turned out a sorry mess of a man, Tony. It's bad enough I made a mistake, without you following in my footsteps.' Picking up his tea he put it on the mantelpiece. Prising the top from a Vaseline tin he smeared a thin layer on to his fingers, rubbed it through his hair, marked a parting and combed it until it lay flat.

'I didn't set out to do anything,' Tony confessed miserably as he settled into one of the easy chairs. 'I loved her.'

'Funny way you had of showing it.'

'I wanted to marry her. I asked her. We were on the point of buying the rings when she decided to stay behind in the café one night after closing. That's when I found out I wasn't the first.'

'Then you're not the father ...'

'I'm the father, all right. The first was Ben Springer, and it happened years ago.'

'Didn't she work for him in his shoe shop?'

'For a while, after she and Maud came back from the Infirmary. He raped her.'

'And that's why you wouldn't marry her? Because she had been raped?'

'A girl can do something besides open her legs. She can fight back.'

'Did she?'

'I don't know. All I know is that after we ... afterwards she was sick. I thought ... I didn't know what to think. Before I could ask her about it, she left.'

'And you didn't go after her?'

'You can't blame me for not wanting another man's leavings. I'd already joined the army. A few days later I began training.'

'And you never wrote to her?'

'What was the point?'

'You abandoned her. Left her carrying your child?'

Tony had never seen his brother like this before. Grim-faced, darkly serious.

'I didn't know about the baby,' he protested. 'How could I? She never told me.'

'All I can say is, thank God she met Wyn Rees.'

'A queer?'

'He gave her a name and a roof over her head. What would you rather, your son born in Tyfica Road or the workhouse?'

'That's exactly it. Billy is my son. I never thought I'd feel this way about him.'

'You've made a right pig's ear of your life and hers.'

'You could have done the same thing. For all you knew Alma might have been carrying your baby. In fact half of Pontypridd thought she was in the family way after you'd gone. She went through hell until Charlie offered her a job and married her, so don't come the lily-white hero to me, dear brother.'

'I wasn't the one who got drunk and screamed that a married woman's child was mine in the café.'

'I told you, I'll go round to Tyfica Road and apologise.'

'And start another rumour. Like hell you will. You're out of here on the first train to Birmingham. You're going to spend the rest of your leave helping Mama with the little ones.'

'If I apologise ...'

'If you even try, Wyn Rees will knock your block off and justifiably so. And all the sympathy would be on his side. Diana is his wife.'

'And the kid he thinks is his?'

'He doesn't think anything, Tony. He knows. Diana isn't the kind of girl who'd trick a man into marrying her. Wyn Rees married her because he wanted to.'

'A man like that wouldn't know what to do with a wife.'

'He knows how to take care of one, which is more than you do. This may surprise you, little brother, but there's a hell of a lot more to marriage than what goes on between the sheets.' He tipped hot water into his shaving mug. 'Get dressed, and packed. We're going down the station to buy that ticket.'

Tony looked at him sideways. 'This couldn't have anything to do with you by any chance? Diana's a pretty girl. Apart from the colouring, she even looks a little like Maud. They were as close as sisters. You're not thinking of replacing Maud with—'

Tony didn't say another word. Ronnie dropped his shaving brush, grabbed the collar of his brother's pyjama jacket, hoisted him out of the chair and slammed him against the wall.

'I don't know what's got into you, but it's time someone did some straight talking and as Papa's dead it falls on me. I picked up the pieces of your mess yesterday, not because of you, but because of Diana. Whatever's happened to her, she's a good girl, and they're rarer than five-bob notes. You had your chance to marry her and lost it. If you have a single shred of decency left, you'll never set foot in Pontypridd again.'

'She was used goods.'

'She was a victim.'

'You couldn't expect me to marry a girl who'd been with another man?'

'Seems to me she didn't have much choice in the matter. Grow up, Tony. It's not a woman's past that's important but her future. You've picked up your morality from the Middle Ages.'

'If by that you mean I expect my wife to be

a virgin on my wedding night, you're damned right.'

'After what you did to Diana, she wouldn't have been that anyway.'

'I was in the army. I could have been killed. A lot were. Eddie ...'

'Men have been using that excuse since the Trojans fought the Spartans. Have you thought what would have happened to her if you had been killed?'

'She had her family.'

'You left her with a baby and the choice of going into the workhouse, or finding a man not quite as picky as you. One who'd settle for "used goods" as you put it, and the responsibility of keeping another man's child. As I said, thank God for Wyn Rees. He'll do a better job of bringing up that boy than you would have. Go and pack, Tony, and while you're at it, stop thinking about yourself, and spare a thought for Billy. He won't always be a baby. How do you think he'll feel if he ever finds out that his father abandoned his mother after seducing her?' Releasing his hold, Ronnie turned aside and retrieved his shaving brush. He was vaguely aware of Tony leaving the room. He didn't trust himself to go after him.

Diana had made an even bigger mistake than Tony. She'd been naive enough to believe herself in love with a shallow idiot who'd put no more value on her than he would have a whore in station yard. Less in fact, because he would have had to pay for a whore.

After last night, he'd sympathised with Wyn.

Now he felt even sorrier for Diana. Trapped in a marriage of convenience with a baby to bring up, what could she possibly know of love and happiness?

'We're there.' Judy Crofter rose to her feet as the train pulled into the sidings of the factory. 'Come on, lazybones.' She shook Jenny, who was sitting in the corner of the carriage.

'I'm not used to getting up in the middle of the night, and I'm not at all sure I want to get used to it,' Jenny griped as she hoisted herself out of her seat to join the queue of girls jamming the train aisles.

'It gets better,' Myrtle said kindly as she moved in behind her.

'How long have you been working here?'

'Six months.'

'I'll never last that long.'

The train doors opened and cool air blew in. After the close, fetid stuffiness of the carriages it had the bracing effect of an Arctic breeze. They moved forward slowly, shuffling off the train, along the platform and into the huge sheds that housed the changing rooms. Men through one entrance, women another. Jenny had been amazed by the size of the women's cloakroom which was divided into two sides by a high barrier: a 'dirty side' to house their streetwear, and a 'clean side' where their work clothes were kept.

The girls ranged up in front of rails of coat-hangers and started undressing. Coats, jackets, skirts, blouses, dresses, shoes and jewellery were hung away in lockers. Jenny let down her waist-length hair, meticulously careful, after heavy warnings about the catastrophic damage just one stray spark from a metal object could cause, to pull out every hairpin. Crossing the barrier to the 'clean' side, she took down the trousered, sludge-coloured overalls she'd been issued with on her arrival, pulled them on and fastened the row of rubber buttons. Even the belt had a rubber buckle. The cloth was thick, heavy and itchy like Welsh flannel, and about as glamorous in her eyes. Tying her hair back with ribbons, she tucked it into her equally drab dust hat. The last thing she did was lace up the rubber-soled shoes that looked even more cumbersome than army boots.

'Stunning,' Judy mocked.

'All I can say is I'm glad there aren't many men around to see me.'

'We're here to work, and meet production targets,' a forewoman's voice barked from the back of the cloakroom, 'not attract men.'

'Not that there's any around here worth attracting,' Judy retorted.

'You say something, Crofter?'

'Not me, Miss.'

Walking into the factory area, Jenny was struck by the same low level of noise she'd noticed on the introductory tour the day before. The only sounds were the radio playing softly in the background, and the small clicks as shells were picked up and put down. Going into the work cubicle designated as hers, she sat behind the screen designed to protect her face and body from the worst effects of possible explosion, picked up a pair of tongs and began the slow, laborious process of pouring powder into caps. It was tedious and repetitive with none of the aura of excitement she'd associated with the manufacture of munitions when she'd volunteered for the work.

Long before the bell signalled tea-break she longed to tear down the screen, abandon the tongs, bring the caps closer and use her hands to pour the powder. Her supervisor, Myrtle Rees, recognised the danger signs of impatience and walked up behind her.

'You're doing great, Jenny. Slow and steady does it. It's the careful ones like you who are best for this work.'

'Thanks, Myrtle, I needed that.' She pushed back a stray hair that had escaped the confines of her cap.

Myrtle walked on down the line. She hadn't looked for or wanted promotion, preferring to be at the cutting edge of the job actually making shells. But now, when she was actively involved in the training of so many raw recruits, she could see how her experience could help others, and in the long run increase production.

She reached the end of the line and glanced across the factory floor. Through a glass partition she could see Wyn standing with a group of men, taking instruction from Erik who was showing them how to operate the machine that pressed out the metal casings for the largest shells. The one thing all the workers, men and women, had in common was the desire to turn out as many top-quality bullets, bombs and shells as they could to aid the war effort.

She knew Wyn: he would make a careful and conscientious machine operator. She only hoped the other men would realise that and respect him for wanting to contribute despite his disability.

But even her concern for her brother couldn't entirely spoil her delicious sense of anticipation at the evening that lay ahead. It sparkled like a magical fairy on top of a Christmas tree, only this fairy was actually within reach. She'd never been happier. There were just three more things she wished for: her father to mellow, Wyn to be left alone, and for Huw to ask her to be his wife.

'Drink after work?' Judy asked Jenny and Myrtle as they sank into seats in the train carriage at the end of their shift.

'Drink? You mean a coffee in Ronconi's?' Myrtle asked.

'No, I mean a beer in the White Hart. My throat is drier than a sandbag in a chapel.'

Myrtle was visibly shocked by the suggestion.

'Don't give me that look: a load of us are going.'

'Girls?' Jenny asked doubtfully.

'You don't think women should go into pubs?'

'My mother would spin in her grave at the thought.'

'Your mother never slaved all day in a factory doing a man's job. Come on, we work bloody hard and we've earned a break. Our money is as good as the men's any day. In fact it's a damned sight better than the miners', because there's more of it.'

'I can't go, I'm meeting someone.' Myrtle was glad she had an excuse.

'Ooh, don't tell me it's the copper ...'

'And I have to check on the shop,' Jenny broke in, seeing Myrtle flinch.

'I thought Freda was looking after it for you.'

'She is.'

'Well then, she's done it before. You haven't got a secret man tucked away waiting for you to come home, have you?'

'No,' Jenny snapped.

'Don't you think it's time you looked for one?'

'I've only just lost Eddie.'

'Can't live in the past.' Judy cut her short, not wanting to talk about the dead or Dunkirk. Four families in Leyshon Street had lost sons, and there'd been a sort of understanding between her and one of the boys that she'd rather not think about. 'Come on, just one drink. Sally and the others will be going, won't you, Sal?'

'Who's taking my name in vain?' Sally shouted from the corridor.

'Drink? White Hart?'

'You bet. We've persuaded a couple of the boys to go, including that really nice young one with the Liverpool accent. He sends shivers down my spine every time he says hello.'

Judy dug Jenny in the ribs. 'First round's on you. Mine's a pint of bitter.'

'A pint?' Jenny echoed, shocked but also excited by the sheer outrageousness of exploring the forbidden, male territory of a pub.

'I had no idea things had changed so much in Pontypridd,' Ronnie commented to Tina as she brought her and William's tea tray into the café. 'I just saw Judy Crofter, Jenny Powell and a crowd of women walk into the White Hart.'

'Some of the munitions workers drink there after work.'

'Women in pubs?' He raised his eyebrows.

'Why not? Women work at least as hard as the men these days, and in some cases harder. They're making their own money, why shouldn't they spend it where they want?'

'Do you go into pubs?' he asked, stunned by the idea of his sisters drinking in a bar.

'I have done once or twice,' she confessed breezily, 'when Gina's taken over here for me.'

'And William approves?'

'William hasn't got a say in the matter.'

'What haven't I got a say in?' William walked down the stairs behind her.

'Whether or not I drink in the White Hart.'

'You go into pubs by yourself!'

'Not by myself. With Jenny, Judy and that lot.'

'Women in pubs?' He crossed his arms and looked at her. 'The sooner the war's over and I put you back in the kitchen where you belong, the better.'

'I'd like to see you try,' Tina retorted fiercely.

'Unusual to see you two out and about,'

307

Ronnie commented in an attempt to deflect the argument.

'Don't get your hopes up, we're going to the pictures,' Tina informed him crisply.

'And there's me thinking that you were going to relieve me so I could have an early night. What are you going to see?'

'Robert Taylor in *Flight Command*, although why I have to go and watch the RAF ...'

'You'll go because I want you to take me,' Tina said hotly, still burning with indignation.

'I suppose that's a good enough reason.' William offered her his arm.

'Enjoy yourselves,' Ronnie called after them. 'Do you want me to keep you anything back for supper?'

'After what he's just said, we're going the whole hog,' Tina answered as William opened the door for her. 'Drink in the New Inn afterwards and fish and chips on the way home.'

Ronnie looked around the deserted café. Too early for the people coming out of the theatres, pictures and pubs, and too late for shoppers, it was a dull and dreary time of day. He wiped down the counter, swept the floor, then sat in a chair with an old copy of the *Observer* he'd found in the kitchen. Just as he'd begun to scan an editorial threatening all manner of vague punishments for people who persisted in spreading pessimistic and groundless, anti-patriotic rumours, the door opened and Jenny Powell walked in. She took her coat off, and meandered unsteadily to his table.

'Enjoy your drink?'

'Not really. Two sherries on an empty stomach is as much as I can take.'

'I thought you got free meals in the factory canteen?'

'Not free, tenpence for three courses, and they all tasted like greasy rubber today.' She took the chair opposite his. 'So I thought I'd treat myself to tea here instead of going home to cook it.'

'Look like you're finding it hard work.' Giving up on the article, he folded the paper away.

'It's more monotonous than I thought it would be. What are you serving?'

'Baked beans on toast without butter, Welsh rarebit without much cheese or egg, beans and chips, sausage and chips, dried egg and chips ...'

'What are the sausages like?'

'Great as long as you don't want to know what's in them. If you do, I suggest pastie and chips. The pasties aren't up to Alma's standard, but I guarantee there is some meat in them.'

'What part of the animal?'

'Ears, hooves and tail. That's all that's left after the army has taken its cut.'

'Lambs' or cows' ears?'

'Donkeys', they're larger.'

'You've persuaded me: pastie and chips. I don't suppose you could add beans to that as well?'

'Only if you promise to hide them under your bread and butter. You know the rules.'

'I'll eat them so quickly no one will know they were there.'

He went behind the counter, opened the hatch and shouted through the order. 'I miss not having a waitress to boss around but trade just doesn't warrant employing one any more.'

'I doubt you'd find one. I was lucky to get Freda to take over the shop for me.'

'Do you still want her to?'

'After all I said about wanting to help the war effort, my pride wouldn't let me walk out of the factory.'

'You really do look as though you're sleeping on your feet.'

'That's because I'm not used to the hours. I made the mistake of staying up to listen to *It's That Man Again* last night, and there was a request show afterwards. I didn't get to bed until ten, which was fine when I could lie in until six. Four o'clock is positively uncivilised. Are you working here every night now?'

'Only until William goes back, then Tina will want to take over again.'

'I had hoped to invite you for tea one day this week.'

'Not this week, I'm afraid.'

'William goes back on Saturday, doesn't he?'

'Unless Tina refuses to let him go.'

'I drew the long straw in work when it came to days off. My first one is next Sunday. I never bother to cook for myself, but I would if I had company. How about dinner then? You'd be doing me a favour.'

He hesitated. She broadened her smile.

'Sunday will be fine,' he agreed, wishing he could think of an excuse not to go, but with

Tina working, and Gina busy with housework, evacuees and her husband, Sunday was no different to any other day.

'One o'clock.' She watched him as he opened the hatch and shouted at the cook to hurry her order. A week without Alexander nagging her to go out with him, or get engaged or married, had been lonely, but there'd also been a wonderful feeling of relief. Knowing he no longer had her key and couldn't walk into her house unannounced again had brought a sense of freedom.

She should never have become embroiled with a man who wanted so much from her. Ronnie was still mourning Maud, and he had made it perfectly clear in Bethan's that he didn't want to get involved with another woman again, but like her, he must miss the physical side of marriage. Probably more—weren't men supposed to set greater store by it than women?

Thin and wounded, he was still handsome and he was already looking a lot better than when he had arrived. He also knew how to conduct an affair. Hadn't he proved that by carrying on with Alma all those years and not marrying her? Alexander didn't know it yet, and neither did Ronnie but she had made up her mind. Soon Ronnie would be visiting her for more than just a meal.

'You look smart,' Diana complimented Myrtle as she walked into the living room.

'Do you think so?' Myrtle surveyed her image anxiously in the mirror. Her skirt and blouse were neatly pressed but old, her lightweight, summer coat pre-war. She'd done her best with the parazone and Miner's liquid make-up that the advertisement recommended for munitions workers, and had used up more of her precious cologne, but she still didn't feel as well turned out as she would have liked.

'Meeting anyone?'

'A couple of the girls. We're going to the theatre.'

'Gadding about again?' her father complained from his sofa. 'You were out all day yesterday.'

'It was my day off.'

'Your mother would shake her head at the way you've turned out, my girl. If only she knew how you were neglecting your duty. I'm beginning to wonder why I even bothered to have a daughter. All that suffering to bring you into the world, only for you to farm me out to strangers.'

'Hardly strangers, Mr Rees,' Megan intervened briskly.

'Going out twice in one week indeed,' he continued as though Megan hadn't spoken. 'And to a theatre! When was the last time you set foot in chapel, that's what I'd like to know? The minister was here today. He's disgusted with the way people are ignoring their spiritual lives, turning aside from worship, just when their prayers are needed most.'

'I told you, Dad, we hold services in the factory.'

'The sabbath is a day of rest.'

'Not for Hitler and his Nazis.' Megan pointed

at the door behind the old man's back. 'Have a good time, love.'

'Mind if I walk part of the way with you?' Diana asked. 'I told Wyn I'd meet him in the New Theatre shop.'

'I'm only going as far as the Town Hall,' Myrtle said quickly not sure how much, if anything, her brother had told Diana about her and Huw.

'It's better to have company part of the way than none. I'll get my coat.'

'Goodnight, Dad.' Myrtle kissed his withered cheek.

'I'm not feeling well,' he snivelled peevishly.

'Then I'll give you one of those special pills the doctor left for you,' Megan offered.

'It's not that I need. I'm cold.'

'Then have some hot soup. 'Bye, Myrtle.' Leaving her knitting, Megan opened the door for her.

'You don't have to keep it from us.' Diana linked her arm into Myrtle's as they walked down the road.

'Wyn told you?'

'Wyn's said nothing, but I was talking to my mother earlier. And don't worry, it was out of your father's earshot. All this parazoning, make-up, scent and care with your clothes. There has to be a man.'

'You sure Wyn hasn't said anything?'

'No, but if you've told him, you can tell me. I promise not to whisper a word, except to my mother.' Diana was glad to have something other than her own problems to think about.

'You won't say anything to my father? You saw how he was tonight when he thought I was going out with the girls. I don't know what he'd do if he knew I was seeing a man.'

'What could he do?' Diana asked practically.

'Make life very difficult.'

'Myrtle you're over thirty.'

'Thirty-eight.'

'Whatever, you're a grown woman. You hold down a responsible well-paid job.'

'Which he hates because he thinks I should be looking after him.'

'My mother's glad to do it. It makes her feel she's doing her bit. She's nowhere near strong enough to work the hours you do in munitions, so freeing you makes her feel that she's contributing to the war effort too. But going back to your father, don't you think it's time to tell him that you're old enough to run your own life?'

'He'd only get upset. He could even have a relapse.'

'Haven't you noticed he only has those when he doesn't get his own way.'

'I hate rows, and he wouldn't approve.'

'Of the man? Is it someone you've met in the factory?'

'No.'

'Who is it? I'm dying of curiosity, and if Wyn knows he'll tell me if I ask.'

'This is only the second time he's asked me out. It's probably nothing. Just friendship.'

'But you like him and hope it's more?'

'Yes,' Myrtle conceded.

'Then tell.'

'Promise not to laugh?' Myrtle finally realised Diana wouldn't give her any peace until she told her.

'It's someone funny?'

'Your Uncle Huw.'

Diana stopped and stared at her in astonishment.

'I knew you'd think it was funny.'

'No I don't. I think it's wonderful for both of you. You're absolutely perfect for one another. Uncle Huw is quiet, but persistent when it comes to getting his own way. He always used to get William and me to do what he wanted when we were children without us even realising it, and being a policeman he deals with troublesome people all the time, so your father would present no problem to him. The only surprise is why my mother or I didn't think of matchmaking you two before.'

'Then you're not shocked?'

'Shocked, of course not. Can I be matron of honour?'

'I told you, this is only the second time he's asked me out.'

'Then have a good time, and insist he takes you to a café afterwards. He's always in a good mood after he's eaten. That's when you can turn the conversation around to weddings.'

'I'll do no such thing. Can I ask you something?' Myrtle began hesitantly.

'That sounds ominous.'

'Is it considered all right to kiss a man when

you're not married these days?'

'You've never been out with anyone before?'

'Not in a long time, and then only to a chapel social. I don't know what to do. All the girls in the factory ever talk about is men, and they seem to think anything goes. But I'd hate for Huw to think I was fast.'

Diana remembered what Tina had said in Bethan's, and could imagine exactly the sort of thing the girls in the factory were saying. 'They're probably just missing their husbands if they're overseas.'

'Most of the girls I work with aren't married.'

'I'm not at all sure I'm the one to advise you about this.'

'I couldn't ask anyone else.'

Diana thought back to her experience with Tony—and Ben Springer. 'If it seems right to you, do whatever you want. But don't let a man force you into anything, Myrtle. No matter how much you think you like him.'

CHAPTER 14

Anne started whimpering at the exact moment the hands on the alarm clock reached six o'clock. Jane didn't need to switch on the light to check. The baby had established her routine and since arriving in Graig Avenue, she hadn't deviated from it by one minute. Jane reached across to the cot and stroked Anne through the bars, but she knew she had only a moment's grace. If Anne wasn't picked up in the next five minutes she would start screaming, and if she didn't get her downstairs and feed her, the noise would wake the entire household, which wouldn't be fair on her father-in-law. It was the first free Sunday he had been given in months.

Stepping out of bed, she pulled on her dressing gown, tightened the belt, and carried Anne down to the back kitchen. Still half asleep, she made a fresh bottle, washed and changed Anne while it was cooling, then sat in the easy chair in front of the window that looked out on the tiny back yard. The house was quiet, peaceful. The rising sun created golden spots of light that played across the dark wood furniture and danced across the blackleaded grate, but all she could think about was how much longer it was going to be before Anne slept in. It didn't have to be much longer: the way she felt at the moment, another hour would have been blissful.

The day ahead loomed full of people she liked, but would rather not be with, and things she didn't want to do. Phyllis and Evan were kind to her, but it was becoming increasingly difficult to accept their company and hospitality graciously, when her every waking thought and most of her dreaming ones were centred around Haydn. She missed her husband so much, she physically ached for his presence and his touch. And since he had left she had been tormented with guilt over her resentment at his insistence on leaving her in his father's house. She knew he had only been thinking of her and Anne, and their safety. She should have told him so, instead of arguing with him.

Had he forgiven her? He'd been gone over a week and all she'd received from him were two scribbled postcards to let her know that he'd moved in temporarily with one of the engineers until the tour began, *'which will be any day now.'*

The postcards were pre-war. Nothing was produced these days as glossy and extravagantly coloured as the prints of Broadcasting House he had sent her. She'd imagined him perched on the edge of a desk occupied by a glamorous secretary, brushing against her as he'd leaned over to filch them from her stationery tray. Perhaps he'd even scrawled them while the girl flirted with him.

She burned with resentment at the image she'd created. Jealousy was eating away at her peace of mind, and now it was threatening to spoil the small pleasures Phyllis had organised for the day. The vegetables for the dinner were already prepared, the apple pie for 'afters' made, Diana and Alma were eating with them, and Megan was coming for the afternoon as the minister and his wife had offered to sit with Wyn's father. It had already been decided that if it was fine they would walk over the mountain after they'd eaten, perhaps coming back via the old reservoir tanks at the back of Graig Street. Evan had even sorted out a couple of old jam jars the night before, tying string around the necks so Brian could fish for tadpoles in their murky depths.

She sat back in the chair as Anne grew heavy in her arms, watching the baby's eyelids flicker and her mouth relax. As soon as the bottle was empty she tucked her into her day cot. Moments before, she'd heard the plop of the Sunday newspaper falling through the letterbox.

Putting the kettle back on to boil, she went to fetch the paper. After making a pot of tea, and pouring herself a cup, she curled into Evan's chair again, and unfolded the wartime thinned pages of the *News of the World*.

She started with a jolt and dropped her cup. It fell on to the tiled hearth and shattered, spraying tea over the rug and scattering shards of china on the tiles. Oblivious to the mess she continued to stare, mesmerized by the photograph on the front page. A beaming, happy Haydn, flanked by two girls, his arms around their shoulders, their lips glued to his cheeks. She recognised his companions. Ruth and Marilyn Simmonds, their blonde hair cascading in a perfect sweep of curls to their shoulders, their eyes turned to the camera, trim figures nestled as close to Haydn's as they could possibly get without actually crawling into his clothes.

She glared at the caption.

HAYDN POWELL LEADS A BBC CONCERT PARTY ON A MORALE BOOSTING TOUR OF THE FRONT. AND JUST LOOK AT THE MORALE HE'S TAKING WITH HIM TO CHEER OUR BOYS.

She scanned the rest of the page and thumbed through the paper. There was nothing else, not even a paragraph.

'Jane? Are you all right? I heard a crash.' Phyllis walked in, already washed and dressed, Brian following her, dragging his teddy bear by the ear.

'My tea! I'm sorry. And china's so difficult to replace these days.' Jane leaped to her feet.

'It's nothing, as long as you haven't hurt yourself.' Phyllis rolled up the rug and carried it through the washhouse into the back yard. She shook the china fragments into the ashbin, then dumped the rug under the cold tap. Before she returned, Jane had fetched the bucket and floorcloth and was on her knees picking up the remains of the cup.

'Has something happened?' Phyllis asked, seeing tears in Jane's eyes.

'Nothing.' Jane wrung the floorcloth out in

320

the bucket before attacking a stubborn spot on a tile. 'I'm sorry about the mess.'

'It's easily cleaned.'

Jane threw the cloth over the remaining puddle of spilt tea in the hearth and mopped it up. 'I'll wash out the rug and put it on the line.'

'Now it's soaking, it can be left until tomorrow.' Phyllis went to the cupboard in the washhouse. 'I've seven others. When I was expecting Brian I had nothing else to do except make them. It's all right, I'll empty the bucket.' Phyllis took it from her. 'I'd love a cup of tea if there's any more in the pot.'

Jane took down two fresh cups. She laid out the paper on the table and stared at the photograph as she poured the tea. All she could think of was the swift way Haydn had dumped her in Pontypridd so he could go on this tour. Well, two could play at that game. He had a life of his own. Now, thanks to his desertion, so did she.

She went to the pantry and brought out the jug of milk. Filling Brian's cup she handed it to him.

'There's a good photograph of Haydn on the front page of the paper,' she announced as Phyllis returned.

Phyllis walked to the table and looked. 'Are they twins?'

'Sisters. Pretty, aren't they? I've met them.' What Jane didn't say was that she'd met them at a BBC party when she'd been seven months pregnant and felt as graceful as an elephant, and both girls had flirted with Haydn for all they were worth.

'Don't the reporters know he's married?' Phyllis eyed Jane cautiously.

'Haydn would tell them if they asked, but kisses don't mean anything in the circles he moves in. You know showbusiness people. It's always "darling" and hugs and kisses all round.'

'Are you really all right, love? I'm not sure how I'd react if I saw a picture of Evan being kissed by two girls like these on the front page of the Sunday paper.'

'Perfectly.' Jane gave her a cold, brittle smile. 'I've been thinking, my ribs feel so much better, I'd like to go down the Labour Exchange tomorrow. It will take them at least a week or two to process my application to work in munitions, and by then I'll be perfectly fit.'

'You want to go because of this?' Phyllis folded the paper away, clearing the table for breakfast.

'Of course not. But as Haydn's doing his bit, I feel I have to do mine.'

Diana walked slowly along the track that led to Shoni's pond. She had to watch her step because the pram wheels kept sinking to the hubs in the black silt that had blown from the colliery trams and slag heaps on to the path, but the inconvenience was amply compensated by the solitude and the weather. It was a beautiful, clear day. The trees had unfurled their leaves, the only clouds in the sky were as delicate and flimsy as lace, the birds were singing, and, best of all, she had nothing to do until midday when she'd promised to visit her uncle's house.

Wanting some time to herself after the upset of Tony's return, she'd called in Alma's on her way through town, and, under the pretext of taking Billy for an airing, had made arrangements to meet her in Graig Avenue instead of walking up the hill with her as they'd agreed earlier in the week.

After Alma's she had gone to the park, but it had been crowded with women in summer dresses and men in Sunday suits and uniforms, most of them neighbours and acquaintances. They had stopped, looked into the pram and made the usual bland, customary remarks, but after the scene in the café she couldn't help feeling that as soon as she left them they'd begun whispering about her. So after ten increasingly uncomfortable minutes, she had headed up Graig hill, and deciding it was too early to go and sit in her uncle's house, had turned into the lane opposite the Graig Hotel that led to Shoni's pond.

It was hot, heavy work pushing the coach pram along the unmade road, and by the time the lake came into view, she was ready for a rest. Checking Billy, who slept through practically anything in the morning, she pulled the insect netting over the pram and moved into the shade of a beech tree. Spreading her cardigan over last year's leaves, she sat down. She had come prepared. Two ready-made bottles and a couple of clean nappies were tucked into the foot of the pram. No one was going to want anything from her for at least two hours. Feeling guilty at having left her mother with all the work of her father-in-law's Sunday dinner, she delved under the pram covers and removed the copy of *Rebecca* that had taken six weeks of waiting to get from the central lending library.

Leaning back against the tree, she opened the book, folded the slip of newspaper she had been using as a marker into the front cover and lost herself in the Cinderella world of a bystander who could only look on, never participate, in the wealth and riches of Monte Carlo society.

That was when Ronnie saw her. On his way from the top end of the lake he paused on the bank, and looked down to see a girl in a flowered blue and white dress with a straw hat on her head, totally engrossed in the book on her lap.

Smiling to himself at the peaceful scene in a world at war, he continued to limp along the path that bordered the bank. When he reached the half-way point he saw the pram. The girl lifted her head to turn a page and he realised it was Diana. He waved and she waved back.

'Enjoying the weather?' he asked as he drew alongside her.

'It's glorious. Tina thrown you out of the café already?'

'She shooed me out when she came back from seeing Will off at the station yesterday. I think she wanted something to take her mind off him.'

'That's hard on you when you built up the business.'

'Not really. To be honest I was just as happy to get out of there as Tina seemed to be to get back. I'd forgotten how tedious café work can be, especially after spending the last five years working on a farm, albeit a poverty-stricken one.'

'Won't you go back to running the cafés after the war?'

'I don't know what I'm going to do tomorrow, let alone that far ahead.'

'I'm sorry, that was thoughtless of me, it must be hard to plan for the future without Maud.'

'No harder than it is for anyone else in these unsettled times. At least Maud and I had five uninterrupted years. Tina and William will be lucky to spend the odd week together until the war is over.'

'But on the bright side, there's not much danger of them quarrelling.'

'I wouldn't say that. They came pretty close to it once or twice that I could hear.'

He took off his jacket, cleared an area of sticks and the worst of the leaves and spread it out. 'Mind if I sit with you for a while? I keep making the mistake of thinking this leg of mine is better than it is, and I walked much further than I intended. It was the pond bringing back so many childhood memories. Fishing for tiddlers and tadpoles ...'

'... picnics of jam sandwiches and lighting bonfires to roast potatoes.'

'Not when I was around.'

'No, not with you,' she agreed. 'You were so much older than the rest of us, you seemed like a grown-up. And an angry one at that. As I said before, we were all terrified of you.'

'I'm not that much older than you,' he protested.

'Ten years was an enormous gap when we were kids. Somehow it doesn't seem so big now.'

'Another twenty years and you'll catch up with me, thirty and you'll be older,' he teased.

'Apple?' She reached into the pram and brought out a couple.

'Can you spare it?'

'Wyn's cousin has a farm in Ynysybwl. These are the last of his winter store. They're wrinkled, but still good. If we don't eat them now they'll start going off.'

'Thank you.' He bit down into it, savouring the sweetness. It had been a long time since he had eaten fresh fruit.

'What you did with Tony the other day—'

'Was what any older brother would have done to keep a younger one in check. I'm only sorry you were around when he got ugly drunk.'

'I dread to think what would have happened if you hadn't been there.'

'You would have knocked him out. A push of the little finger would have been enough. He wanted to apologise to you the following morning, but I wouldn't let him. I thought it better that he leave town. Tony can be thoughtless and quick-tempered, but he's not

326

all bad when he's sober ... but then you'd know that.'

'I should never have gone out with him.'

'He should never have treated you the way he did.'

'He told you about it?'

He nodded. 'But don't worry, I won't tell anyone else.'

'Half the town suspects the truth. Wyn and I knew it would be that way when we married.'

'Didn't you ever think of letting Tony know about the baby?'

'I had no reason to. He didn't seduce me, I wanted to make love to him,' she said flatly. 'I ... I had my reasons.'

'Tony told me you'd been raped before you started courting him.'

'He did?' She turned aside and stared down at a clump of bluebells at her feet. The blue petals had withered, giving way to the green seed pods. 'It's not easy to explain, but after what happened I wanted to find out if I could be married. It sounds stupid now, but it never occurred to me that I could get pregnant. But I'm not sorry I had Billy.' She raised her head defiantly. 'He's the best thing that ever happened to me, and Wyn and I intend to do all we can to give him a good start in life.'

'I know you will. But I can't help thinking that if Tony had married you ...'

'No,' she shook her head vehemently as she recalled the disastrous, embarrassing scene played out between her and Tony in the upstairs

327

room of the café. 'I could never have married Tony.'

'So you married Wyn Rees instead?'

'I told him about the baby, and he asked me to marry him. We know everything there is to know about each other. I wouldn't have it any other way. There are enough secrets in my life. I'm sorry, I don't know why I'm telling you all this.'

'Probably because if you don't tell someone, you'll go mad with the strain of trying to bottle it all up?' he suggested. 'Tony's outburst must have been quite a shock.'

'I promised Wyn that Tony's return wouldn't make any difference to us, but it did. And not only to us, to Tony. I can see now how much I hurt him.'

'You hurt Tony! I would have thought it was the other way round.'

'Look at Billy,' she smiled fondly as she glanced at the pram. 'He's absolutely perfect. It must be hard on Tony knowing he has a son and can never acknowledge him. If it was me, I wouldn't be able to stand it. All I had to do was imagine someone taking Billy from me, handing him over to another woman to bring up, and telling me I couldn't even see him. After that, it wasn't so hard to understand why Tony got drunk and said the things he did.'

'You do realise that is exactly what would have happened to you and Billy if Wyn hadn't married you, and you'd had to go into the workhouse.'

'My mother couldn't have supported me, but

328

my cousin Bethan would have taken me in. Tony knew that.'

'Whichever way I look at it, he left you in a mess.'

'Which Wyn got me out of.'

He threw his apple core into the centre of the pond. It sent ripples out in ever increasing circles to the shore, lapping in little wavelets against the watery crust of last winter's debris.

'And now you have a family, and a business?'

'I've got it made,' she concurred with a touch of bitterness.

'Seems to me you've made the best of what you've got, and isn't that all any of us can do?'

'I suppose so. I've never talked to anyone about this except Wyn. It's most peculiar, I feel as though I've known you all my life.'

'You have.'

'Not like this. I was only sixteen when Ben Springer raped me. Laura and Trevor were kind to me when I went to them for help, but I couldn't talk to them about it, not really talk, the way we are now. Wyn knows because he found me wandering in Taff Street the night it happened. I was in too much of a state to go home. So he took me to his house, bandaged me up, gave me some of his sister's clothes, and generally looked after me. That was over five years ago, and he's carried on taking care of me ever since.'

'Tony was a fool to let you walk away from him.'

'He didn't want me after I told him he wasn't

the first, and I couldn't undo the past.'

'It wasn't your fault that you were raped.'

'Try telling that to some of the men in this town.'

'I think a lot of them are going to have their eyes opened by this war, particularly when the Germans invade.'

'It's hard to explain, but it's something you can't forget, or put behind you. I feel common, dirty ...'

'There's no reason to. You're still the same person you were before. And just because you've had two bad experiences it doesn't mean your whole life is blighted. I knew a girl in Italy who was raped by a platoon of German soldiers. She joined the Resistance and at first all she wanted to do was kill every German she could get in her gun sights. But she changed.'

'How?'

'The usual story,' he smiled. 'She met a man and fell in love. They married.'

'He married her after that?'

'Why not? You of all people should know it wasn't her fault.'

'If they were married, he'd want to touch her. She'd have to sleep with him, let him ...' she shuddered and he wrapped his arm around her shoulders. She rested her head against his chest. He bent his head and kissed her forehead. A light, gentle touch that sent shivers down her spine. His lips moved to hers, brushing against her mouth with a tenderness as delicate as it was fleeting. She leaned back weakly on her elbows. Ronnie was looking intently into her eyes.

'Was that by nature of an experiment?' she asked.

'It felt more like the first thaw after a long winter to me.'

'Ronnie ...'

'I know.' He turned away from her, picked up a stone and skimmed it across the surface of the lake. They watched it bounce, once—twice—three times before it finally sank. 'You're married, my brother is the father of your son and ...'

'I wasn't going to say that.'

He turned and gazed into her eyes. Deep brown eyes, as unlike Maud's as it was possible to get, but they evoked the same passion. He knew exactly how he felt about her, because he had felt this way once before. And Tony had recognised it before he had.

Without thinking of the consequences he gathered Diana into his arms and kissed her again. Less tenderly and more passionately than before. She broke free, scrambled to her feet and ran down to the bank. He could hear her breath coming in quick short gasps as he stumbled awkwardly after her. Her eyes closed and she slipped, almost fainting as he rushed to catch her. Sliding his hand beneath her forehead, he held her until she stopped retching.

'I'm sorry, I should have realised.'

'It doesn't matter,' she gasped.

'The last thing I want is to hurt you.'

She tried to back away.

'I promise I won't touch you again. Not that way. Here, you're shivering.' He went over to the tree, picked up his jacket and slipped it over her shoulders. 'Did you ever think of talking this over with Trevor or Andrew John?' he asked as they returned to the pram.

'I couldn't have.'

'Diana, it's no different to any other injury, like my leg. It won't heal unless you treat it. I'm sure old Dr John or Dr Evans ...'

'Wouldn't understand?'

'You're probably right,' he acknowledged reluctantly.

'And you're forgetting one thing. There's no point in healing this particular injury.'

'Isn't there?' he asked quietly.

She picked up her cardigan. 'I have to go. My uncle is expecting me for dinner.'

'I'll walk you up there.'

'There's no need.'

'But I'd like to.' He took the pram. 'Come on, I'll push it.'

'On a crutch?'

'I'll invent a new step to accommodate it.' He led the way, leaving her to collect the library book. She followed him over the grassy bank on to the track.

'It's been such a long winter I'd forgotten how much I love spring.' He deliberately steered the conversation on to the impersonal.

'It must be beautiful in Italy.' She made a conscious effort to fall in with his mood.

'Very.' As he wove a tale for her about the Italian countryside, and the warm springs, hot summers, dry cool autumns and winters, she began to smile again. Once or twice she even laughed at his poor jokes. But all he could think of was her reaction when he had kissed her that second time, and he felt a murderous rage for the man who had raped her, for his brother who had used and abandoned her, and even for the man she had married. A man who for all his good intentions could never hope to give her anything like the life she deserved.

Jenny had laid the table with her mother's best white linen tablecloth, wedding present silverware, and porcelain that had lain untouched apart from yearly cleanings in the sideboard for over twenty years. She had pulled back all the curtains, opened the windows wide in the rooms she used, and had even walked up to Shoni's early that morning to pick flowers to put on the table. Too late for the best of the bluebells, so she had settled on primroses. She was determined to give Ronnie the best meal he'd had since he had come home.

A little judicious black-market trading with half a dozen tins of fruit from the secret store her father had set aside for emergencies when war had been declared had procured a chicken from one of the farmers in Penycoedcae. She'd made roast as well as boiled potatoes, and stuffing from breadcrumbs and a spoonful of dried herbs. Because vegetables were only just coming into season she had settled on a bunch of early spring greens and carrots which were rubbery from winter storage. For afters she had made a trifle with stale sponge cake, tinned fruit, custard made of eggs and real milk and even a dollop of cream that she had coaxed out of George Collins in exchange for two more tins of her precious fruit.

She straightened the silver knives and forks that she had polished until she could see her face in them, glanced at the clock and went into her bedroom to check her hair and make-up. The lipstick was her last. Tomorrow she'd have to resort to beetroot juice unless Alexander could come up with something through his black-market contacts. Perhaps she shouldn't close him out of her life altogether. There were so many things he managed to get that no one else could. Not just make-up, but stockings and, last Christmas, four dress lengths of material, two of good wool and two summer cottons. He'd insisted they had been pre-war, bankruptcy draper's stock, but from her black-market dealings in the shop she knew just how much goods like that could fetch.

She stood back and checked her reflection in the mirror. Her powder was almost at an end, her stockings were her last pair of silk, the dress, a red crêpe-de-Chine had been Eddie's favourite, not that he'd ever actually said so, but she'd known he'd liked it from the way his eyes had lit up whenever she put it on, and underneath she was wearing the silk underclothes he had brought back on his last leave from France. Hopefully there would be an opportunity for Ronnie to admire them before he left.

The stage was set, the meal was ready, she looked as good as she could make herself, all she needed was her guest. She walked from the back bedroom to the front window. It was ten minutes past one. If he didn't come soon the meal would be spoiled.

The street outside was crowded with people making their way home from chapel, but none resembled Ronnie. She stepped back just in case Alexander was around. She knew he'd called into the shop every evening on his way home from work last week, because he'd opened a 'tab' for the first time, presumably in the hope that Freda would clear all new credit accounts with her. But if he'd expected her to climb the hill to Graig Avenue to put a note in his jacket as she'd promised, he had another think coming.

She had a momentary panic. What if Ronnie had knocked the shop door and she hadn't heard him—what if he didn't come at all? Patting her hair to make sure it was still in the roll she had copied from a series of diagrams in *Woman's Weekly,* she walked down the stairs and into the shop. She brought out the account books from under the counter. Sitting on the stool she provided for old ladies to rest themselves, she took a pencil from one of the card displays hanging behind the door and pretended to tot up figures. It was hopeless, the numbers danced before her eyes. If Ronnie didn't arrive in the next few minutes the chicken would be burnt, or she'd have to take it out, and then it would grow cold and greasy. Where could he be? If there hadn't been so many people on the hill she would have gone out and stood on the pavement to look for him.

She'd just decided to go upstairs and check the oven when a tap on the window startled her.

'Sorry I'm late,' Ronnie apologised as she opened the door. 'I met Diana over in Shoni's and gave her a hand to push the pram up to Graig Avenue.'

'You went to Shoni's?'

'I fancied a walk.'

'Come in.' She noticed Mrs Richards and Mrs Evans staring at her from across the road as she opened the door wider.

'That's a delicious smell. I hope you haven't gone to too much trouble?'

'Just a normal Sunday dinner.'

'It's a long time since I've had one of those. Tina warned me when I came back that even if the meat ration could be stretched once in a while, women are too busy to cook them any more.'

'It will be some time before I'll be able to do one again. I won't get another free Sunday for seven weeks.'

Conscious of his difficulty climbing stairs, he hung back. She ran on ahead of him, swinging her hips, making her dress flare to her thighs just as she'd done before. Wondering if she was doing it deliberately, he struggled to ignore the effect the naked skin above her stocking tops was having on him, and followed her into the living room.

'This looks very nice,' he said, admiring the table.

'I'll just go and dish up the meal. There's a bottle of sherry in the cupboard, perhaps you could pour us a drink.'

'You'd like one?'

'Please.'

He looked around the room, wondering again why he hadn't made his excuses when she had invited him. If Jenny had asked him to dinner so she could talk about Eddie, he wasn't at all sure he was prepared to listen. Particularly after seeing the effects a few drinks had on her earlier in the week.

'Chicken?' She proudly carried in the bird on an enormous platter, surrounded by roast potatoes and stuffing balls.

'We could do wonders with a couple of chickens a week in the restaurant. Wherever did you get it?'

'Ask no questions and I'll tell you no lies.'

'That seems to be everyone's watchword these days.'

'Will you carve?' She handed him a newly sharpened knife. 'I'll bring in the vegetables and gravy, then we can start.'

He cut the legs off the bird and sliced the meat thinly, putting a selection of both white and dark meat on to their plates, less on his own than hers, realising that she'd probably have to live off the chicken for the rest of the week.

When she finally finished ferrying dishes, she sat opposite him at the table. Although her conversation was innocuous enough, all through the meal her foot found its way to his no matter which way he stretched his legs. He could smell her perfume, warm, heady, sensuous, more suited to evening than day wear, and he was overcome by a wave of nostalgia for the light, flowery cologne Maud had used. A fragrance similar to Diana's.

'I can't remember the last time I had a meal like that.' He sat back, deliberately moving his chair away from the table, and out of the reach of her legs.

'There's plenty more. You've eaten hardly any meat.' She picked up a forkful and tried to put it on his plate.

'I couldn't.'

'I hope you've left room for dessert.'

'You've got to be joking.'

'It's fresh trifle. Made with tinned peaches, real egg custard and real cream.'

'I didn't think it was possible to make a trifle in wartime.'

'George Collins was feeling in a generous mood, so I took advantage.'

'I'll help you clear the dishes. By the time we've washed up I may have room for some.'

'Men don't wash up.'

'Try telling that to my sisters. Come on, the sooner we start the sooner we'll finish.' And the sooner I can go, he thought to himself as he picked up his plate.

CHAPTER 15

'Did Ronnie tell you that he called into the shop to see me yesterday?' Alma asked Diana as they sat on the mountain with Phyllis, Megan and Jane, watching Evan play football with Brian.

'He mentioned that he wanted to talk to you about supplying the cafés.'

'I thought you were working flat out,' Megan commented.

'I am, but I've been thinking of expansion for some time. Ronnie said the High Street café isn't doing so well. He could keep on the tea, coffee and snacks side which are all prepared up front, and turn the kitchen over to us if we can find someone to run it.'

'Like?'

'Ronnie would do it, but as his leg is almost healed he hopes to go into munitions in the next week or two. He suggested you might take it on, Diana.'

'He didn't say anything about it to me today.'

'It was only a suggestion, nothing's definite yet. I said I'd talk to you.'

'I've already got the shops and Billy.'

'The shops don't take up much time now you've got a girl in each of them, and I can look after Billy,' Megan broke in. 'I think it's a good idea. The more you expand now, the more there'll be for the boys to come home to at the end of the war,' she enthused, thinking of William and hoping to see him as a fully fledged partner in one of Charlie and Wyn's shops.

'How would Charlie take to going into partnership with Ronnie as well as Wyn?' Diana reached out to catch the ball that Brian had kicked, before it hit the pram Billy and Anne were sleeping in.

'He left the business in my hands. If it gives us another kitchen to work out of, I can't see him objecting, can you?'

'Not when he's away and unable to make decisions himself,' Jane chipped in brightly. 'It seems to me that with the men gone we've just got to get on and make the best of our lives. We could waste years just sitting around waiting for them to come back.'

'Any more?' Ronnie asked as he plunged his arms to the elbows in soapy water and felt around the bottom of the sink for stray knives and forks.

'You're a glutton for punishment.' Jenny wiped the last saucepan and stacked it on a shelf.

'I like things neat and tidy.'

'So I see. Tea with your trifle?'

He glanced at the magnificent bowl laid out in solitary splendour on the marble cooling stab in the pantry. Jenny had even found a sprinkling of coconut to dust the cream whirls that decorated the top. 'It looks too good to eat.'

'Does it now?' She brushed against him as

she walked past and untied the apron from her waist. 'Damn!'

'Something the matter?'

'The bow's knotted.'

'Here, turn around, and I'll have a go.' As he fiddled with the ribbons, she backed into him.

'Give me some room, woman.'

'You're the first man who's ever asked me to do that.' She slipped off her shoe and ran her foot up the inside of his leg.

'Don't, I'm likely to fall over. I've only got one good leg, remember.'

She turned around to face him. 'Then it might be an idea to rest it. My bedroom's next door.'

He took a deep breath as he realised this was why he'd been wary of accepting her invitation. Even through all the table-talk about being brother and sister-in-law, the signals had been there. He'd just been too out of touch with courting practice, and too stupid to pick up on them. He debated whether to remind her he was Italian, and they liked sweet, modest girls who allowed them to do the chasing, but he had a feeling that under the circumstances she might not appreciate the joke, so he settled for a mild, 'I'm not at all sure that's a good idea.'

'Why?'

'Because I'd rather remain friends.' He gave her the standard cliché as he succeeded in pulling the ribbons apart. After handing her the apron, he removed the tea towel he'd tucked into the waistband of his trousers before he'd washed the dishes.

'What would be the harm in it? It's not as though we'd be hurting anyone. I'm lonely, you're lonely ...'

'And not at all eager to get my face rearranged by Alexander Forbes. The man has muscles. I can't compete with a miner in my present state of ill-health.'

'I told you, Alexander is only a friend.'

'And what would I be?'

'A lover,' she whispered seductively, 'and a strong one at that.' She locked her arms around his neck. 'Rumour has it, you put your brother in his place.'

'Only because he was drunk. If he'd been sober I wouldn't have stood a chance.'

'You expect me to believe that?' She ran her fingers over the front panel of his trousers. A touch that had always aroused Eddie and never failed to excite Alexander. 'You can't tell me you don't miss married life?'

He reached down and caught her hands in his. 'It wouldn't work Jenny. You'd be thinking of Eddie and ...'

'I can't spend the rest of my life thinking about the dead, and neither can you.'

'Isn't that what we're doing now?'

'No. When I said lover, I meant just that. A lover. I wouldn't want anything more. Not a husband, not a fiancé, just a man I could make love to without worrying about ties, or emotion. Someone who would call in now and again for a good time. You do want a good time don't you, Ronnie?' She stepped away from him and unbuttoned the imitation pearls at the neck of her dress. He watched, mesmerised, as her hand travelled down the line to her waist. Pushing the frock over her shoulders, she allowed it to slide to the floor.

The breath caught in Ronnie's throat. The only time he'd seen underwear like hers before was on pin-ups in men-only magazines. Her silk stockings were fastened by blue-ribboned garters, her lace-trimmed, silk camisole and French knickers were so fine they were almost transparent. Reaching out, she unfastened the collar studs on his shirt. When she'd succeeded in loosening them, she stood on tiptoe and kissed him.

Despite his earlier protests, his hands seemed to develop a will of their own. Encircling her waist, he pulled her to him as he returned her kiss. Beneath the thin layer of silk her body was firm, yet soft. Her perfume no longer heavy and oppressive but sensual, intoxicating.

She caught at his hand. Walking backwards she led him out of the kitchen on to the landing, pulling him towards her bedroom.

'It's all right,' she reassured him as he hesitated on the threshold. 'It overlooks the back, no one will see.'

The whole scene had taken on the surreal atmosphere of a dream. The porcelain quality of her beauty, the provocative lingerie, her offer of sexual favours was the substance of male fantasy not reality. As he struggled to regain his senses he forced himself to remember the crude lath and plaster walls, and rough, clumsy furniture of the attic bedroom he and Maud had shared in his grandfather's farmhouse.

He felt her fingers tugging at his fly and said the first thing that came into his head. 'Mrs Evans has her binoculars trained on the front of the house.'

'She'll think we took a long time to do the washing up.'

'Jenny, I like you ...'

'That's all I want.'

He hadn't been a saint before his marriage, but lovemaking with Maud had been so very different from the meaningless acrobatics he had indulged in with various girlfriends before she had come into his life, that what they had shared had spoiled him for anything less. And then there was Diana. He had kissed her only a few hours ago. A sweet, gentle, tender kiss that for all its disastrous consequences, still meant more to him than these cold-blooded advances.

'I'm sorry, but I can't do this.' He moved back, disentangling his hand from Jenny's. 'I'm really sorry. It's nothing to do with you, it's me.'

'Why? I've told you I don't want anything more from you.'

'The problem is, I might.' He returned to the kitchen, checked his fly, pulled down his shirt-sleeves, buttoned his collar and reached for his jacket. She walked in behind him, blocking the doorway.

'All you men are the same. You're supposed to be the "love them and leave them" sex but when it comes down to it you can't wait to fasten a ball and chain around a woman's ankle. Every man I meet wants to put a ring on my finger to show the world he owns me.'

'Like Alexander?'

'Yes, damn you! Like Alexander.' She picked up her dress from the floor. He turned to help her with the buttons. 'And stop being so bloody nice.'

'Thank you for allowing me to catch a glimpse of the new emancipated woman who can swear as well as any man.' He smiled, hoping to diffuse the situation with humour.

'Don't you dare patronise me.'

'I'm sorry, Jenny.'

'And stop apologising. I've shocked you. Go on say it. You think I'm a slut? It's all right for a man to chase a woman and drag her into bed, but not for a woman to do it to a man.'

'I'm all for equality between the sexes, just too old and tired for affairs. Marriage gave me a taste for domesticity.'

'If I was a man I might agree with you. It must be convenient and comforting to have a wife slaving away for you in the background.'

'I was happy once,' he murmured, refusing to be riled. 'I'd like to think I could be again.'

'Be honest, all you want is someone to cook your meals, wash your socks, and drudge for you.'

'If I wanted that, I'd get a servant. Sorry, Jenny.' He fastened the last button at the neck of her dress, bent his head and kissed her cheek. 'I really am. Thanks for the meal.'

'I wish I could say we'd do it again.'

345

'So do I. You're quite a girl. I hope you find what you're looking for.' He slipped past her, knocking his leg painfully on the door frame as he picked up the crutch he'd left outside the kitchen.

She watched as he limped awkwardly down the stairs. The shop bell rang as he unlocked and opened the door. It closed and she was left alone with the silence.

She went into her bedroom and sat on the bed. Tears of rage and frustration scorched, hot and humiliating on her cheeks as she snatched a pillow and flung it at the door. How dare he reject her! How dare he! Wasn't she prettier than most girls? She'd show him! She'd sleep with Alexander and every eligible bachelor in town. Make Ronnie Ronconi and all the Victorian-minded men in Pontypridd realise that the new age was here to stay. That women could work like men, earn the same money as men, and behave like men if they chose to. That the days when girls sat at home learning to cook, clean and sew until boys came courting were finally over. That they no longer had to flutter their eyelids in gratitude and delight at the prospect of a ring, as restricting and binding as any slave chain.

And she'd begin today. By sleeping with Alex. And tomorrow? She'd look around the factory. She'd find someone to sleep with tomorrow. And then both Ronnie Ronconi and Alexander Forbes could look out.

'No.'

'Wyn ...'

'Absolutely not, Diana, and that's final.' Wyn's voice echoed down the stairs into the front parlour where Megan was settling his father for the night.

'That's the first time I've heard those two behave like a normal married couple.' Mr Rees rubbed his hands gleefully as Megan stirred his nightcap of cocoa with just a touch of brandy.

'Perhaps they've had their rows in the shops before now, out of our earshot,' Megan said calmly as she set the cup on the table next to his bed.

'What's it about?'

'I've absolutely no idea.'

'She hasn't got another man, has she?' the old man squinted sideways.

'I'll pretend I didn't hear that.'

'Mothers always stick up for their daughters.'

'And fathers should stick up for their sons. If there's nothing else, I'll go and listen to the radio. Goodnight, Mr Rees.' She left the room, closed the door and climbed the stairs. The bathroom door was open, which meant Wyn and Diana had finished preparing Billy for bed, but their bedroom door was closed.

'Diana?' she called softly.

'What is it, Mam?' Diana opened the door, looking as cool and unflustered as usual.

'Once you've got Billy down, I'd be happy to babysit if you and Wyn want to go out for an hour.'

'Billy's almost sleeping. I'll have a word with Wyn.' Diana saw her mother's frown. 'It's not

347

a serious quarrel, Mam,' she reassured her.

'Every young couple should have their own space. I wish you and Wyn did.'

'See you in a minute.' Diana closed the door and looked at her husband. He was standing next to the cot nursing Billy in his arms.

'Did you hear that?'

'I had no idea I was shouting so loud.'

'And I had no idea you could be so stubborn.'

'I just don't think it's a good idea.'

'But it is. Taking Ronnie into our partnership with Alma could double our turnover.'

'You don't know that for certain.'

'It will, if Alma can get the stock. She's keen on the idea, and building up the business will give her something to do while Charlie's away, and keep me out of mischief while you're in the factory.'

'You have enough to do with Billy.' He laid him in the cot, tenderly stroked the down on his head and pulled the blanket over his tiny shoulders.

'No I don't. Mam looks after him better than I do.'

'Can't you find anyone other than Ronnie?'

'Who?'

'I don't know. Someone—anyone?'

'Everyone's working in the pits or munitions these days. Ronnie's got the kitchen, the business know-how and the drive. He proved that when he built those cafés up from practically nothing.'

'I thought his father did that.'

'His father opened the High Street café. He

wouldn't have even thought of expanding if Ronnie hadn't pushed him into buying the other two places, and look at them now. They're more successful than the original café.'

'Have you thought what will happen after the war when Tony comes home and wants to work in a business we own a third of?'

'We're talking about Ronnie, not Tony. And we're only taking over the kitchen in one of the cafés. If we can increase production it might be nice to open three new shops, one each. That way we can divide them up, and end the partnership whenever we want to.'

'You've got a lot to learn about business, Diana. Things are never that simple. If you, Alma and Ronnie do succeed in opening three new shops they're not going to have the same turnover. Then you'll be arguing over who gets the best one after the war.'

'Then we'll sell them, rent them out ... who knows what's going to happen after the war. I'm sick of that phrase. It's as if everything's been put on hold until then. Well I ...'

'And I had no idea you could be such a spitfire.' He sat on the bed. 'Come here?' He held out his arms. She glared at him. He smiled.

'I hate you, Wyn Rees. It's impossible to have a really good row with a grinning fool who brings logic into an argument.'

'Are you going to tell me what happened today?'

'Nothing.'

'I know you, what is it?'

She went to him, wrapped her arms around his chest and leaned against his shoulder. 'I went for a walk up Shoni's this morning before I went to Uncle Evan's, and I met Ronnie. I talked to him, Wyn, really talked, the way I talk to you. After all, when you think about it, it isn't that surprising. Maud was like a sister to me, we're practically related.'

She felt his muscles tense beneath her fingers. 'You like him?'

'In the same way I like William, and there wouldn't be any more to it than business if that's what you're worried about. Alma and I won't even see him once he's working in munitions. I just happen to think we could double our turnover and profits, if we took over the kitchen of his café.'

'But you're attracted to him?'

'If I was normal, I might be,' she replied honestly. 'But I'm not normal, and I'm not likely to change.'

'Not married to me, you're not.'

'It's like you say it is with Erik. You've admitted that you want to spend time with him.'

'I told you I walked away from Jacobsdal the other night.'

'I didn't ask you to.'

'I made you a promise.'

'I didn't ask you to make that either. Wyn, being married doesn't mean we can't have other friends. If we try to live in each other's pocket, we'll drive one another mad.'

And if we don't, we'll risk growing apart

and closer to someone else. He recognised the danger but the thought remained unspoken in his mind. It occurred to him it was the first time they'd been less than honest with one another.

'Your mother's right.' He rose from the bed and pulled her to her feet. 'We need a break. We've both been working too hard this past week. Put on your glad rags, I'll take you out.'

'To the chapel social? I'd sooner stay in and do the mending.'

'I was thinking more along the lines of the New Inn for a drink. They serve travellers on Sundays. We'll be travellers.'

'I'll get my comb and lipstick.'

'Diana?'

She turned to look at him.

'You're right, I was letting my anger with Tony get in the way of common sense. If Ronnie and Alma can work out something, by all means expand the business with them.'

'Thank you.' She kissed him on the cheek. 'I'm not going to run off with Ronnie, you know.'

'It's not that I'm afraid of.' He opened his wardrobe and flicked through his ties.

'Then what?'

'Myself. Sometimes I feel as though I'm hurtling through life on a rollercoaster just like the figure of eight in Barry. I'm speeding out of control and I can't stop. I don't have a clue where I'm going, and I'm afraid of dragging you down with me.'

'Wyn ...'

'And then again, maybe I just need a break. Come on, woman, if we're going, it's time we went.'

'Well, fancy meeting you here.' Judy Crofter accosted Alexander Forbes as he waited on the Cardiff platform for the Pontypridd train to come in.

He glanced at her. She seemed vaguely familiar, but he couldn't imagine how he'd met her. She wouldn't have looked out of place in station yard. Peroxide blonde hair, brassy and tawdry after Jenny's long silver tresses, blue eyed, brazen and forward.

'I'm Judy Crofter,' she introduced herself. 'I live in Leyshon Street. You lodge with the Powells in Graig Avenue.'

'That's right.' He raised his hat politely.

'You probably don't remember me. The last time we met there were loads of people around. It was the farewell party for William and Eddie Powell and the Ronconi boys.'

'Of course,' he answered politely, still unable to place her.

'It's been a lovely day, hasn't it?'

'So people have been telling me. I was indoors most of the afternoon, listening to an illustrated talk on the origins of the Celts in St John's church hall.'

'Poor you. I was in Roath Park, rowing on the lake with friends—lady friends,' she added to emphasise that she was unattached. 'Oh good, here comes the train. I do hope we get a seat, but with all these people trying to get on it looks as though we're going to have to fight for one.'

He stepped forward and opened a carriage door, standing back so she could go ahead of him.

'That's first class, my ticket's third.' She looked down the platform at the mob outside the third-class carriages. 'But I doubt I'll worm my way through that lot and keep my coat on my back, so I suppose I'd better upgrade my ticket.'

'In that case, after you.'

Judy needed no second bidding. She climbed the step and he followed.

'First is so much nicer.' She settled back into the cushioned upholstery and rested her head on the snowy-white antimacassar, trying to look as though she was used to travelling that way. 'I'm lucky to have a Sunday off,' she chattered. 'Working in munitions we only get one off in seven.'

'You're in munitions? Then you know my landlord's daughter-in-law, Jenny Griffiths? She started a couple of weeks ago.'

'I showed her the ropes. The hours fagged her out. I think she found it tough going.'

'It's the same everywhere. The war goes badly, the government sets impossible production targets.'

'Not that impossible. We do well on our section.'

'I don't doubt you do.'

'Mind you, we've had to take on a couple of useless ones. The crache are the worst. Don't know what graft is. But then by the look of you, you didn't know what a pit was before the war?'

'I was a curator in a museum.'

'A museum. I've never been in one.'

'Really?'

'I know there's one in Cardiff but I never had the urge to go. Until now, that is.' After Jenny's cool indifference, Judy's crude flirtatiousness held a bizarre attraction. Alexander realised he'd always know exactly where he was with a girl like her. Whether he wanted to be there or not was another thing. She dug him in the ribs. 'Here, you wouldn't think of taking me to one, would you? I could probably do with educating.'

'I'd be delighted,' he murmured blandly, hoping she wouldn't press him to a date.

'You've got a really funny accent, where do you come from?'

'The Home Counties. Near London,' he added, seeing she didn't have a clue where the Home Counties were.

'Now London is one place I would like to go. You been there?'

'Often.'

'Tell me about it?'

'The museums, the sights ...'

'The nightclubs. Is it true a girl can earn four times what they pay in munitions just serving cocktails?'

Alexander was glad when the familiar scenery of Pontypridd came into view. After helping Judy down from the train, he followed her to the ticket booth.

'You going up to Graig Avenue?'

'Yes,' he answered reluctantly, unable to think of anywhere else he could call in on a Sunday night in Pontypridd.

'I'm meeting someone,' she answered, regretting the arrangement she had made to have supper with Dai Richards in Ronconi's café. Alexander Forbes was not only crache, but good looking. She'd heard the rumour that he was supposed to be carrying on with Jenny Powell, but if Jenny was stupid enough to keep him a secret from her friends, she couldn't blame those same friends for treating him as fair game. 'But I'm free tomorrow night. I always go for a drink in the White Hart after work, why don't you join me?'

'I won't finish my shift until six.'

'We'll say seven, then?'

'They don't allow miners in working clothes in any of the pubs.'

'In that case we'll make it eight. That gives you plenty of time to go home and wash and change.' She caught hold of his buttonhole, and gave him a sloppy wet kiss. 'I believe in us war workers having fun. Don't you?'

Despite her resolve to cool the situation between herself and Alexander, Jenny had sliced the cold chicken and made sandwiches. The trifle still stood untouched and tempting on the marble shelf in the pantry. She looked up at the clock. Apart from her brief outing earlier that morning to pick primroses for the table, she had been inside all day. Waiting. First for Ronnie, and

355

now—hopefully—for Alexander.

She wasn't at all sure that he'd try the stockroom door tonight, a whole week later than she'd suggested. He usually made a point of going out on his day off, and he had told Freda that he was going to be free today. Suspicious, or just tittle-tattling, Freda had passed the message on. The question was, would he bother to call in on her, even if he walked up the hill after blackout? After the way she had treated him the last time she'd seen him, she oscillated between doubt and certainty. She'd unlocked the door to the stockroom and sat at the window all afternoon, scanning old magazines, hoping to see him every time she looked up from a page.

Dusk was falling. Soon it would be time to close the blackout and then she'd have no way of knowing if Alexander had passed the shop without calling in, and with Mrs Evans across the road watching her every move she could hardly go out and accost him in the street.

She crossed her fingers, and tried to concentrate on a beauty problem page specifically aimed at munitions workers. There was nothing in it about hair. All week she had struggled to keep every single strand under the unbecoming dust cap. She pulled a lock forward and examined it closely. Was it her imagination, or was it already turning green? What if it did? Not even Alexander would want her then. Perhaps after the way she'd treated him, he wouldn't want her at all. And then how would she feel? With hardly any men in the town, it would be too bad to be rejected by the two most eligible bachelors on the Graig.

People came and went. Chapelgoers on their way to Temple, churchgoers on their way to evensong in St John's, a few salvationists to the citadel. Dai Richards swaggered past in his conscripted brother's best suit and a red and green striped tie, most unsuitable for chapel. She wouldn't even have noticed Dai before the war. He was only seventeen. Four years younger than her, practically a baby. But with most of the young men gone, there were plenty of women who would settle for an evening with him. Had she stooped that low?

When she could no longer see the pavement, she drew the blackout and switched on the radio. There was a concert from the troops. The first song was 'Somewhere in France with you'. Tears began to fall from her eyes again. Tears for Eddie, for the miserable mess they had made of their marriage, a mess she entirely blamed on herself. More tears at the injustice of being widowed at twenty-one ... of self-pity ... of loneliness ...

She heard a step on the stair. She turned to the door just as Alexander opened it. He leaned against the post.

'I was passing so I tried the stockroom door. It was open. I hoped you'd left it open for me.'

'I did.' Heart thumping, she left the sofa and went to him.

He put his arms around her. 'I've been wanting to do that for two weeks. God how I've missed you!' Tossing his hat on to a chair he swung her off her feet, running his hand up her skirt.

'You've only just walked in.' She laughed out of sheer joy and the relief of knowing she was still wanted.

'It's all right, I locked the door behind me. No one can get in to disturb us.' Picking her up, he carried her into the bedroom, threw her down on to the mattress and sat beside her, setting to work on the row of pearls on the front of her dress.

'You saw your parents?' she asked incongruously as he eased her dress back from her shoulders.

'I'll tell you about them later. You wore these, just on the off-chance I'd call in?' He fingered her silk underwear and gartered stockings.

'Of course,' she lied.

'After the way you tried to shut me out I wasn't sure you wanted to see me again.'

'Of course I want to see you,' she breathed headily as he slid his hands beneath the legs of the knickers. 'But please be careful, this is my last pair of stockings.'

'Not any more.'

'You brought me stockings?'

'And a few other things.' He sat up and took off his jacket. 'I didn't know if I was going to see you, so I left them in Graig Avenue.'

'I've a few surprises for you too,' she murmured, as he bent over her again.

'Like?'

'A special meal.'

'Jenny ...'

'Later, Alex ... later.'

'This is brilliant.' Alexander scooped the last spoonful of trifle into his mouth, settled back on the pillows and beamed at her.

'You've no idea of the trouble I went to make it.'

'I can guess. How about giving me the key back?'

'I can't, I had to give it to Freda.' It was tucked away in the top drawer of the sideboard. Incensed by Ronnie's rejection, she still wasn't sure what she wanted, but she knew what she didn't; and that was a return to the straitjacket of marriage she had found herself trapped in with Eddie.

'You'll get another one cut?'

'When I get the chance.'

'If you're busy I can do it.'

'I'll get around to it.'

'When?'

'Please, Alex, don't push me.'

'I need to know where I am with you. I did some thinking when I was away. I'm not getting any younger. It's time I settled down.'

'How can we in wartime?'

'It's quite simple. In view of my atheism, and your widowhood, we go to a registry office, take out a marriage licence, sign it in the presence of witnesses and set up home together.'

'Not yet.'

'I'm beginning to feel like something you keep on the side to amuse yourself with. Like a man with a mistress, only you're the man and I'm the mistress. We don't share anything except sex.'

'And that is wonderful.' She crept closer to him and took the bowl from his fingers. 'Or don't you think so?'

'Yes I think so, but there has to be more to life. A home, children ...'

'Children! How can anyone even think of bringing a child into a world at war?'

'People are doing it all the time.'

'Not me. It's downright irresponsible. Besides, I have a job, an important job.'

'How is it going in the factory?'

'Fine.'

'Really?' He raised his eyebrows, debating whether to let her know he'd met Judy on the train. And even without Judy's testimony, he'd heard enough stories about the munitions factories to know that the working conditions in them were only marginally better than underground.

'Yes, really,' she asserted defiantly, ignoring his scepticism.

'That offer of a ring still stands.'

'An engagement ring?'

'Only if you set the date for the wedding when I slip it on to your finger.'

'How can I? You're forgetting I haven't been widowed a year. I need time, Alexander, please?' She widened her eyes, giving him her most appealing look.

'A week?'

'Longer.'

'How much longer?'

'Must we talk about this now?'

'Yes.'

'At least six months.'

'Fine, six months it is. Then I take you out, and I mean out, and tell Evan Powell and the world that we're getting married.'

'Alex ...'

'I'm serious, Jenny, you put me off again, and I'll start looking elsewhere. I've had enough of being kept dangling on a string.'

CHAPTER 16

'This won't do at all. I warned you, Ronnie.'

'It was almost healed, Bethan,' he protested as she examined his leg. 'It's just that I banged it yesterday, knocked off the scab ...'

'And set yourself right back where you were when you came home.'

'I'm not going into hospital,' he insisted.

'No?' She stood back, hands on hips and stared at him.

'No,' he repeated firmly.

'All right.' She threw the old bandages into a box and wrung out a pad of cotton wool in antiseptic. 'Last chance. You stay in bed and rest. If it heals over in the next couple of days I won't call the doctor in.'

'I can't, I promised to help Tina with the café.'

'Then I'll telephone Dr John right now.'

'There's no one to look after me. The girls are busy with the business.'

'Move in with Luke and Gina. There's an evacuee family there with a young mother who stays home: she can take care of you.'

'There isn't a spare bed, much less a spare room in Danycoedcae Road.'

'Compromise. I take you up to my house, and Maisie and I will see to you.'

'You've got enough to do without taking in patients.'

362

'My house or a hospital? What's it to be?'

'Your house is full of kids and noise. I'd never have a moment's peace. Suppose I stay here and take it easy, *very* easy,' he emphasised, 'for a few days. Then, if it doesn't improve, you can cart me off.'

'I know your idea of taking it easy.'

'I swear, I won't put my leg down except to go to the ty bach or cook.'

'Cooking's out, it involves standing. I'll get the girls to send food up.'

'Then I can stay here?'

She hesitated for a moment. 'Only if I have your solemn promise not to put a foot to the floor more than twice a day for the next four days.'

'You have it.'

'I should never have allowed you to work in the café,' she declared as she laid fresh dressings over the reopened wound.

'There wasn't anyone else to do it.'

'Tina would have had to manage if you hadn't been home.' She cleared up the mess of dirty bandages and bowls and took them out to the washhouse.

'Tea?'

'I'll make it. And after you've drunk it, I'm putting you to bed.'

'No one's done that since I was a baby.'

'You're behaving like one.'

'You heard from Andrew lately?' he asked in an attempt to coax her out of her starched-nurse mood.

'Not since last week, and then the letter

was months old. There must be an enormous mountain of undelivered Red Cross mail stacked somewhere between here and Germany.'

'It must be hard on him, sitting around in a POW camp with nothing to do except worry about you.'

'And get angry with me for not telling him things that I know will trouble him.'

'Surely not angry, Beth?'

'Yes, angry. Why are men so stupid, and why am I pouring out my problems to a patient?'

'Try brother-in-law.'

'You've enough troubles of your own.'

'Seems to me problems are the only things people have too much of these days. Perhaps an effort should be made to share them around on a more equitable basis. Like rationing. Can't you just see it? New Ministry of War directive, "No one is allowed to have more than one worry at a time. All problems must be part-exchanged for another. Hoarders will be prosecuted." '

'Nice idea.' She picked up the kettle. 'Pity it wouldn't work. Take no notice of me, it's just a bad day. Andrew's birthday.'

'At least he'll be back, Beth.'

'I wonder if I'll know him when he walks through the door. A lot can happen in a year. I've changed, and from his letters I suspect he has.'

'But not in ways that matter, surely?'

'I wish I could agree with you. Alma said Charlie seemed like a stranger when he came home, but at least they were able to spend a few days with one another. Heaven only knows when, if ever, I'll see Andrew again.' Lifting down the teapot she set about making the tea.

'You still love him, don't you?'

'All I have are memories and photographs. To be honest, when I compare them to his letters, I'm not sure any more.'

'Have you tried writing to tell him how you feel?'

'So I can depress him even more than he is already?'

'Hasn't it occurred to you that he might be feeling the same way, which is why his letters seem angry?'

She looked at him and smiled. 'Perhaps you should write a column in the *Observer*. "Problem page from the male point of view, from one of the few members of the species left in the town".'

'At least it would keep me off my feet and occupied. I'm not sure I know how to rest.'

'I'll get Diana to bring you up some books from the library.'

'There's no need to trouble her.'

'She comes this way every day to check on the High Street shop, it wouldn't be taking her out of her way.'

He fell silent, wary of protesting too much.

'You two haven't had a quarrel after that nonsense about Tony, have you?'

'No, of course not. Look, if you really think she wouldn't mind, ask her to look out for a couple of Agatha Christies, will you, please? I read one in the RAF camp and liked it.'

Bethan found Diana in the kitchen of Alma's shop. She and Alma were sitting at one end of the enormous preparation table, drinking tea and eating tongue rolls.

'Elevenses, because there's never any time for dinner,' Alma explained. 'Want one?' She pushed the bag of rolls across the table, and reached for the teapot.

'Just a peaceful sit down would be bliss.' Bethan took the vacant chair next to Alma's.

'Busy morning?' Diana glanced at her cousin over the top of her cup.

'The usual. I'm looking for help. Ronnie's hit his leg and opened his wound.'

'How did he manage that?' Alma asked.

'He didn't say.'

'He could have done it in Shoni's yesterday, I met him there.'

'Then he's an even bigger idiot than I thought he was. What was he doing walking through the woods? I warned him if he didn't rest, he'd end up in hospital.'

'You know Ronnie: telling him to take it easy is like ordering a mongrel to stay away from a butcher's stall. He probably saw it as an invitation to go on a route march.' Alma picked up another roll and reached for the butter.

'Well, he'll have to stay put now. I've put him on bed rest for a week and I tucked him up myself.'

'You're not naive enough to think he'll stay there, are you?'

'No, which is why I was hoping you'd help.'

Bethan looked to Diana. 'He needs something to do and he said he might read if you got him some Agatha Christie books.'

'I'll call in the library.'

'That's what I was hoping. You wouldn't mind dropping them off as well, would you?'

'I've got a better idea than books,' Alma broke in before Diana could answer. 'I saw the manager of the slaughterhouse this morning. I've got some definite figures on what we can have in the way of unrationed offal and meat. Perhaps Ronnie could work out the overheads and production figures on the basis of us taking over the kitchen of his High Street café.'

'I don't care what he does, as long as he keeps off that leg,' Bethan said decisively. 'If he doesn't, he'll end up in hospital, and then he can forget all about going into munitions for months.'

Diana walked into Laura's house loaded down with three bags. One of library books, one of food, and one with paper, pencils and lists of costings that Alma had sent up. She called through, 'It's only me' before heading down the passage and into the kitchen. She found Ronnie on his feet in the washhouse, filling the kettle.

'I heard you coming in and thought you'd like tea.'

'Bethan would kill you if she knew you were up.'

'I've just been to the ty bach.'

'Liar. It's no joke, Ronnie, Bethan told me how bad it is.'

'I'll rest now.' He carried the kettle into the kitchen and set it on the hob before lowering himself into an easy chair. She saw him grimace as he lifted his leg to prop his foot on a stool.

'According to Bethan you should be in bed.'

'Then I'd have to walk up and down stairs every time I wanted to go out the back.'

'There is such a thing as a chamber pot.'

'Which I haven't used since I was three, and before you say another word, I've no intention of starting again now.'

'I could get Wyn and Uncle Huw to come round and carry a bed down into the parlour.'

'You'll do no such thing. I promise to be a good boy, Miss.' She glared at him and he dissolved into laughter. 'Was that supposed to make me afraid?'

'Yes.'

'Don't be cross. What have you brought me?'

'Tongue rolls for your dinner, all the Agatha Christie books they had in the library, and some accounts that Alma thought might keep you busy. She talked the slaughterhouse into giving her extra supplies, and wants to go ahead with the expansion.'

'Good.'

'Do you think you'll be well enough to start it off?'

'Give me two or three days.'

'That's not what Bethan said.'

'I'm a quick healer. You in a hurry?'

She looked at the clock. If she wasn't back to give Billy his midday feed, her mother would do it. And it was far too early to start the banking. 'Not especially, why?'

'I thought we could go through the figures together, seeing as how we're going to be business partners.' His heart beat faster as he looked at her. It was no use reminding himself that she was married and the mother of his brother's child. He wanted to be with her. It was as simple and as dangerous as that.

'All right.' She pulled a chair to the table and opened the bag Alma had given her. 'At least if I stay, I can stop you bobbing up and down every five minutes.'

Alexander walked down the hill with mixed feelings. He would much rather have spent the evening with Jenny than in a pub, but despite the warm welcome, marvellous supper and ecstatic reception, last night had ended on a sour note. Sheer frustration had driven him to give her the ultimatum that they make their relationship public or end it, but he had no regrets. Even six months was too long. He was tired of all the subterfuge. He respected his landlord, Evan Powell, and he would have liked to be able to look him in the eye every time his daughter-in-law's name cropped up in conversation. Something he certainly couldn't do at the moment.

He hadn't even intended going out, but after coming home from the pit, bathing in the tin bath in the draughty and uncomfortable washhouse, changing, and eating supper he had felt restless, and as he had no place else to go, he'd decided to give the White Hart a try.

Crossing the road, he slowed his step as he walked past Griffiths' shop. Freda was behind the counter. On impulse he called in and bought a packet of cigarettes. She didn't mention Jenny's name, and he didn't dare ask, but no sound echoed down from upstairs, and when Jenny was home she usually had the radio on.

Did that mean she was working late? Or had she gone out with another man—Ronnie Ronconi again?

He carried on down the hill. Skirting station yard he resisted the temptation to eye the girls touting for trade, crossed the road and entered the Hart. Blinking against a fug of tobacco smoke, he peered into the bar. It was crowded with men playing darts and eking out their rationed pints. He walked on down the passage into the back room. An enormous crowd of women had commandeered the central tables, glasses of beer, shandy and sherry lined up in front of them. Cigarettes in mouths, they were laughing, drinking and chattering, making more noise than the men in the bar.

'Gets you a bit, doesn't it?' the barman remarked as he walked past him with a tray of clean glasses. 'But as the boss says, "Business is business." Their money is as good as everyone else's and seeing as how they earn it, why not?'

'Why not indeed?' Alexander echoed following him to the bar. As a fully paid up member of the Communist party he'd always advocated equality between the sexes, he'd just never assumed it would take such blatant proportions. Now he was faced with it, he was disturbed to discover that it shocked him to the core.

'Alexander! Over here!'

Judy Crofter waved to him, her peroxide curls bobbing against her rouged cheeks, her lips stained a deep vermilion that blenched the colour from the rest of her face. But her pale skin was nothing compared to his when he noticed the woman sitting beside her. If looks could kill, the one Jenny was sending his way would have been enough for the barman to have reached for the sawdust bucket to cover his corpse.

'That's enough figures for one day. I can't look at another number.'

'I know what you mean, they won't stand still on the page.' Ronnie closed the child's exercise book he'd been working in.

'Do you want a hand to get up the stairs?' Diana asked.

He looked at the clock. 'The restaurant will have closed by now so Gina will be along soon with my tea. I'd rather eat it down here.' He bundled the sheets of paper together. 'Can you spare some time tomorrow?'

'If you like.'

'I'd like, very much indeed.' He looked into her eyes. 'I wasn't sure you'd want to come near me again after yesterday.'

'Yesterday was just one of those things. No harm done.'

'No?'

'Ronnie, I don't want you to get the wrong impression. I'm happy as I am.'

'Are you?' His eyes were dark, serious in the gathering twilight.

'There's no reason why we shouldn't be friends.'

'Friends?' he repeated slowly. 'Is that what you think we are?'

'How can we be anything else?'

'That's what I'd like to find out.'

'Ronnie, I'm married. I have a family. I can't offer any more than friendship.'

'Then it will have to do.' The 'for the moment' hovered unspoken between them.

The front door crashed open. 'Ronnie, are you upstairs or down?' Gina strode down the passage, slammed back the door and burst in carrying a hay box made out of a wooden ammunition crate. 'I didn't know you'd be here, Di. I brought your tea, Ronnie.' She dumped the box on the table, and turned to her brother. 'What are you doing out of bed?'

'Going through accounts with Diana. She's been here all afternoon and can verify that I've behaved myself.'

'Has he?'

'I took out an hour to do the banking, so he could have danced the highland fling then, but while I've been here he didn't put a foot to the floor.'

'And don't even think of doing so for at least a week,' Gina ordered.

'You sound like Bethan John.'

'She called in to see me and Tina. You'd

372

better follow her orders to the letter. If you don't, you'll find yourself in the Graig Hospital because neither Tina nor I can spare the time to look after you.'

'Grown up bossy, haven't we?'

'I've no time for your sarcasm, Ronnie. Can you stay another ten minutes, Di, to dish this out and clear up after his lordship? I'd like to be home to wash Luke's back before tea. He can't reach all of it himself, and what he misses ends up on the bedclothes.'

'In that case you'd better hurry.'

'Thanks.' She kissed Ronnie absently on the cheek and dashed out through the door.

Diana took the box into the pantry, lifted the lid and the straw that covered the saucepan hidden in its depths, and ladled half the stew it contained on to a shallow soup plate. Cutting four slices off a rather grey national loaf she found in the bread bin, she piled the plate and the bread on to a tray and carried it in to Ronnie.

'You eating there or at the table?'

'Here.' He lifted the books and papers from his lap and dropped them to the floor. 'Knowing Gina, she will have brought enough to feed an army. Why don't you join me?'

'I'll have supper at home with Wyn.'

'What time does he get in from the factory?'

'Today, around six. I'm meeting him in the New Theatre shop.'

'Then you've half an hour to spare.'

'Just enough time to tidy up the pantry.'

'It doesn't need doing.'

'That's what you think.'

'Sit and talk to me.'

'We've talked all day.'

'Only about business.' He stuck a spoon into the stew. 'You know, this has been the first good day I've had in a long time.'

She stacked the exercise books, papers and pencils neatly on the table. 'I've enjoyed it too. Perhaps it's because we've had something worthwhile to do.'

'You don't think it's the company more than the work?'

'Stop fishing for compliments.' She went into the pantry, rearranged the hay around the saucepan, and replaced the lid on the box. He was right, the pantry didn't need tidying, but she waited until his spoon stopped clinking in the bowl before emerging. He was sitting back in the chair, ashen with pain and exhaustion.

'I'll help you up the stairs.'

'It's all right. I promise to go as soon as you leave,' he added in response to her sceptical look. 'My leg aches too much to do otherwise. I thought nurses were kind women who soothed pain. Bethan's brutal.'

'Only with patients who don't do as they're told. You want tea?'

'No thanks. I've drunk enough to float the navy today.' He watched while she carried the tray into the washhouse. After soaking the dirty dishes in the sink, she returned to the kitchen and gathered her coat and bag from the chair. 'You'll be back tomorrow?'

'If we work at the same pace as today we

should have the final figures to show Alma. Is there anything you want me to bring?'

'Just yourself.'

'Ronnie ...'

'I know, friends.' His face creased in pain as he moved his leg slightly. 'But we're friends who are playing with fire, Diana, admit it.'

'So, Mrs Powell, do you come here every night after work?' Alexander was acting the disinterested acquaintance for all he was worth. As Judy had reserved him a seat next to her, he had been forced to sit between her and Jenny; but although Judy was doing most of the talking, his attention had been riveted on Jenny, who persisted in ignoring him despite all the sly glances he sent her way.

'I've only been working in the factory a week,' she replied tersely.

'But she's getting really good at her job,' Sally interrupted from across the table. She had no idea who Alexander was, other than the best-looking man she'd seen since the call-up had decimated the male population of the town, and that in itself was enough for her to want to get to know him better.

'Is that right?' He picked up his pint of beer and raised it to his lips.

Jenny didn't answer him. Turning ostentatiously to the girl sitting behind her who was recounting the birth of her last child in colourful, graphic and, as far as Alexander was concerned, embarrassing detail, she appeared to develop a sudden and intense interest in maternity ward procedures.

'I think I've had enough of sitting round here.' Judy clutched Alexander's arm. Brushing her face against the rough tweed of his jacket she deposited a thick smear of pink powder on his sleeve. 'Do you feel like going to a café?'

'I've already had my tea.'

'Well none of us have eaten, have we, Jenny?' She tapped Jenny on the shoulder to gain her attention.

'I'd be quite happy to watch you eat.' Alexander gave Jenny a hopeful smile as she turned her head.

Judy giggled as though he'd cracked an amusing joke. 'Let's go.' She leaned over and scrabbled beneath the table for her handbag.

'Mrs Powell?' Alexander stood back and offered Jenny his arm.

'No thank you.' Ignoring him, she smiled as Judy surfaced, red-faced, and jealous eyed. 'Two's company, three's a crowd.'

'If you say so.' Judy gloated visibly as she linked her arm into Alexander's and shouted goodbye to her workmates.

Feeling as though he'd finally had his public slap in the face, Alexander was left with no choice other than to leave Jenny and escort Judy to the door.

Diana made her way down the hill, neither seeing nor acknowledging the greetings of her neighbours. Preoccupied with the expression on Ronnie's face when he had told her they were playing with fire, she attempted to analyse her feelings for him. Used to Wyn's quiet diffidence, and during their brief courtship, Tony's somewhat erratic ardour, Ronnie's soft-spoken, self-confidence unnerved her. Despite all that she had told him about herself, he seemed neither shocked nor disgusted. He hadn't even unduly pitied her. Only persisted in trying to get to know her better.

She realised that the sensible thing for her own, Wyn's and Billy's sake was to avoid Ronnie as much as possible, given that they moved in the same confined circle of family and friends. But no matter how much she tried to justify her visits to him as duty calls on a sick friend, she knew Ronnie was right. They were playing with fire. A flame that could easily consume what was left of the unorthodox marriage she and Wyn had so naively and optimistically embarked on.

Before she reached the shop she resolved to tell Wyn exactly how she felt about Ronnie. But even as she walked through the door of the theatre she suspected that once she came face to face with her husband she would break the resolution, take the coward's way out and say nothing.

If only Wyn would lose his temper and order her to stop seeing Ronnie, the decision would be taken out of her hands. But Wyn was not a man who lost his temper easily. He always looked at difficult situations reasonably and logically, seeing them from every perspective, and generally setting his own feelings aside in favour of others. But it wasn't just Wyn. She didn't want to stop seeing Ronnie. Not while he remained in Pontypridd. No matter that she had a husband and a son to consider, she could no more resist the lure of his company than a moth could resist the deadly attraction of the flame. Even though it meant, at the very least, a painful singeing of its wings.

'Has Mr Rees been in yet?' Diana asked Alice as she walked into the foyer of the New Theatre.

'Been and gone, Mrs Rees. He said you weren't to worry about putting the takings in the night safe, but to go straight home. He'd see to the banking and meet you back at the house later on.'

'Did he say where he was going?' Diana had to make an effort to keep her voice steady.

'No, but he had a man with him. One of the foreigners from Jacobsdal. From the way they were talking I think they intended to go for a drink.' Unable to look her employer in the eye, Alice began straightening the row of sweet boxes on the counter. Diana turned away, sensing a well-meant sympathy she could not take. 'Do you want me to give him a message when he comes back, Mrs Rees?'

'No, Alice. I'll catch up with him later.'

Confused and inexplicably angry, Diana left the shop, but she didn't walk on through town towards Tyfica Road. Instead she turned back up the Graig hill. If Wyn wanted to spend time with Erik in Jacobsdal, then there was nothing to stop her from spending time with Ronnie. She would clear his tea dishes, soak his washing and

378

prepare his breakfast for the morning. The more she did for him, the less he'd have to do, the quicker he'd mend and the sooner they could make a start in the kitchen of his High Street shop. It made good sense—and it would have made even better if she'd believed that was her only motive for returning to Graig Street.

Alexander sat opposite Judy in Ronconi's café watching her shovel sausage and chips into her mouth in between high-pitched, noisy outbursts of hysterical laughter that he suspected were designed to draw attention to her—and to them as a couple. He couldn't help wondering how on earth he'd ended up with the woman. All he'd wanted was some company, preferably Jenny's, and here he was with a girl he had absolutely nothing in common with, and who didn't remotely interest him, listening to stories of how difficult it was to buy make-up, and how impossible it was to get perfume and how hard it was to sit still on a factory line filling powder caps all day.

'So what about it?'

The sharp question intruded into his reflections.

'What about it?' Judy repeated, her mouth opening wide enough for him to see half-chewed lumps of sausage and chips wedged between her tongue and teeth.

'Sorry, I was miles away.' He pushed his chair as far from the table as the wall behind him would allow.

'What we going to do now?' she demanded

impatiently. 'We could go back to my place if you like?'

'To meet your family?' he asked warily.

'My father's worked nights for years. He lost a leg in an accident in the colliery, so they gave him a cushy job as a night watchman. My mother ran off before he even left the hospital. Can't say I blame her, really. Watching a man take his leg off every night to go to bed must be a bit like living in a horror film. Don't know how Diana Rees stands it ... where was I?'

'Your house,' he reminded her.

'Oh yes. All my brothers are in the army. So,' she leaned over her plate to get closer to him, 'we would be all alone.'

'Apart from the neighbours and the twitching curtains.'

'I don't give a fig what the neighbours say.'

'I've heard there's a good film on in the White Palace.'

'You want to go to the pictures?'

'Why not?'

'All right.' She used her fingers to scoop the last few chips from the grainy soup of vinegar and salt on her plate, speared them on her fork and crammed them into her mouth. 'If we hurry we might get all of the short and the first feature.'

He paid the bill while she took her hat and coat from the rack. As he handed the money over to Tina he wondered whether or not he dare try Jenny's door again that night. This was one evening he really wished was over before it had begun.

'I thought I heard someone down here.' Ronnie limped down the stairs and stood in the doorway of the kitchen watching as Diana raked the ashes from the grate.

'Thought I'd come back and clear up.'

'There was nothing that couldn't wait until morning.'

'I know. It's just that I had a spare couple of hours.'

'I thought you were going home to have supper with your husband?'

'He's gone out with friends.' Her lips closed into a serious line that warned Ronnie not to trespass further. He hobbled forward, crying out as his crutch slipped into a crack between the flagstones and his foot hit the floor.

'You really should be in bed.' She turned around, impatience giving way to concern as he sank on to the bottom step of the staircase.

'I'm going.'

'I'll help you.'

'Not for a minute you won't.'

'It's really hurting, isn't it?'

'I have to admit. It's burning like hell.' He watched as she reached for her coat. 'Where are you going?'

'To telephone Bethan.'

'You're in a doctor's house.'

'So?'

'The telephone's behind you.'

She turned around sheepishly, staring in horror as she saw the blood-soaked cuff on his pyjama trouser leg. He looked down.

381

'I guess that's why it hurt.'

'Stay there. I'll phone, then I'll help you up the stairs.'

'This is one hell of a way to get a woman into my bedroom,' he grinned through pain and gritted teeth. 'But remind me to remember it. At least it works.'

CHAPTER 17

When Britain declared war on Germany, Alexander had sincerely believed that it had taken more courage to stand back and proclaim himself a conscientious objector, than it would have to join the foolhardy idiots who had rushed to the nearest recruiting office. But as he sat next to Judy in the closeted darkness of the White Palace, he began to wonder how much longer his pacifist views could survive the war news.

Wavering film of exhausted British and Commonwealth troops retreating from Greece filled the screen, followed by blurred, hazy shots of Balkan forests and villages being overrun by German divisions. Carefully selected photographic images of the devastation wrought by the Luftwaffe's blitz on London came next. Magnificent and historic buildings reduced to rubble provided a backdrop to cinematic portraits of ordinary men and women going about their daily tasks.

The stock caricature was of the white-coated, indomitable, cheery, cockney milkman who refused to allow Hitler to disrupt his routine, even when he was reduced to leaving milk on doorsteps that had no house behind them. Shops without windows, roofs or doors, that bore hastily chalked signs: 'More open than usual.'

'They always save the good news until last,' Judy whispered as the face of Hitler's deputy, Rudolf Hess, filled the screen followed by pictures of what was left of the aircraft that had carried him from Germany to Scotland, ostensibly to bring an important message to the Duke of Hamilton. Whatever the contents of the secret missive, they obviously weren't significant enough to bring the war to an end, Alexander reflected grimly, as Hess faded from view.

A rousing cheer rocked the hall as the German battleship, *Bismarck,* smoke pouring from her decks, slowly sank beneath turbulent waves. The commentary filled the silence that followed. 'The Nazis labelled her unsinkable ...'

Alexander scarcely heard a word. The expression in the eyes of the defeated troops retreating from Greece haunted him. He was educated, intelligent, yet he had fooled himself into thinking that he could contribute to the war effort by mining coal. What was the point, when Britain might not even exist as Great Britain a few months from now?

How much longer before the coal he dug was shipped to the Greater Reich? What would the Germans call the country after they invaded? The province of Britain? The British territories of Greater Germany?

'You can always come back to my house afterwards,' Judy whispered, bending her head close to his. He could smell the sharp acid tang of her perspiration and the unappealing scent of her vinegary breath. It was easier to pretend he hadn't heard her than formulate an answer.

The crowing cockerel signalled the end of the news, and he settled back to watch the main feature. Half-way through the film he realised he hadn't heard any of the dialogue or taken in a single frame. All he could see was his own face in the queue of defeated men patiently shuffling towards the coast of Greece. Perhaps it was time to bury principles forged in a time when people could afford to think for themselves, and join in the defence of his country while something still remained to defend.

'Actually you may have done yourself a favour.' Bethan lifted the final layer of dressings from Ronnie's leg, and cleaned away the mass of clots and pus. 'Looks like the bang you gave it brought the infection to a head. This blood is fresh.' She held up a pad of cotton wool stained bright red, as proof. 'Clean and uncontaminated.'

'Now you tell me bleeding is good,' he complained.

'And here we have the reason why it took so long to heal.' Using a pair of tweezers she pulled a crumpled piece of blackened linen from the mess on the bandages. 'Who cleaned this for you after you were shot?'

'The fellows with me.'

'And what did they use?'

'Torn-up handkerchiefs.'

'First rule of nursing: count the instruments and dressings you push into a wound. They left one in your leg. Doesn't it feel any easier?'

'To be honest, at the moment I would prefer

you to amputate it than clean it.'

'That's a bit drastic. Stay there.' She scooped the soiled dressings into one of her bowls. 'Exactly there,' she warned as she went to the door, 'and I'll prepare a poultice to put on it.'

'Damn, and I was hoping to go dancing.' He lay back on the pillows, his pyjamas rolled above his knee, his leg exposed in all its torn and bloody glory on a thick wedge composed of newspaper and four of Laura's oldest towels.

'Good job you came back and found him when you did,' Bethan said to Diana as she joined her in the kitchen.

'He's going to be all right?'

'Now. There was a piece of dressing in the wound. From the mess, I think an abscess formed around it. Now it's finally broken, his leg will probably heal, and not before time. I've cleaned the worst away. Once I've sterilised and packed the wound he should begin to recover. But if he'd been left in those bandages overnight, there's no telling what might have happened. If blood poisoning had set in he'd have been in a pretty pickle.' She scrubbed her hands in the washhouse before going into the pantry and fetching a bag of oatmeal and a small saucepan.

'You're making porridge?'

'Poultice for his leg. The doctors don't agree with half the nurses' practices, but with the shortage of medical supplies, beggars can't be choosers, and it works as well as mercury salts without the expense, not to mention the risks of skin irritation. Once I've packed and dressed the wound, I'll give him something to make him sleep. You can go home if you like.'

'Thanks.' Unable to think of a single reason why she should stay, Diana reached for her coat.

'Ronnie said you've been here most of the day?'

'Going over books and figures.'

'Then you, Wyn and Alma are making him a partner in your business?' The telephone rang. 'You or Ronnie expecting a call?'

'Not as far as I know.'

'Then watch this for me will you.' Bethan handed the oatmeal and water over to Diana. 'I left this number at home. Looks like I might be needed elsewhere.'

Bethan returned just as Diana took the simmering oatmeal from the stove.

'There's been an accident in the Albion. A miner's had his arm torn off, and he's still trapped in machinery.'

'You go, Beth, I'll see to Ronnie.'

'You sure? I could be gone for hours.'

'I just pack the wound with this?'

'Irrigate it first with iodine. I left a bottle on the dresser upstairs. Dilute it twenty parts to boiled water. And don't forget to cool the poultice before you use it. A burn on that leg would just about finish off Ronnie.' Bethan put on her cape.

'Won't you need the things upstairs?'

'They've always got first-aid kits in the

collieries. It's more important I get there quickly. If you get stuck, call the relief nurse.'

'I'll manage.' Diana only just succeeded in suppressing a small smile as she walked up the stairs.

'You sure you won't come in?'

'Quite sure, thank you.' Alexander laid his hands over Judy's and lifted them from his shoulders. Tipping his hat he turned and walked back up Leyshon Street towards the Graig Hotel. He hesitated on the corner. Once he was certain the streets were empty he turned back down the hill. He could have found his way to the back stockroom door of Griffiths' shop blindfolded, let alone on a moonless, blackout night. Five minutes later he was trying the door. It was locked. He knocked softly, but there was no answering sound from upstairs.

Cursing under his breath, he lobbed a stone at the window. He needed to know exactly why Jenny had pushed him into leaving the Hart with Judy. If she wanted to use Judy as a blind to fool other people, he wouldn't be happy about it, but at least he would understand her behaviour. If she'd made up her mind to have nothing more to do with him, he wanted to know about it. Now!

The stone rattled against the glass and fell back into the yard without provoking a response. He looked up at her bedroom window. He had two options. He could either walk around to the front of the shop and bang on her door until she answered, waking the entire neighbourhood in the process, or he could climb the drainpipe in the hope that he'd be able to raise the sash on her window high enough for him to crawl inside.

Testing the drainpipe to see if it would bear his weight, he began to climb.

'Comfortable?'

'Let's say you're less experienced but gentler than Bethan.'

'That's a backhanded compliment if ever I heard one.' Diana opened a safety pin and pushed the point carefully through the surface layers of the bandage. Fastening it, she stood back and surveyed her handiwork. 'The pill Bethan left is next to the glass of water.'

'What is it?' Ronnie questioned suspiciously, picking it up and holding it between thumb and forefinger.

'Bethan said it will kill the pain.'

'And me probably for the next twenty-four hours.'

'We have to make you rest somehow.' She gathered the bowls, spare gauze and iodine.

'You're going?'

'I have to. Wyn and my mother will be wondering if I've eloped.'

'That could be arranged.'

She saw the look in his eyes and the quip she had been about to toss back at him remained unspoken.

'Good God, what's that!' he exclaimed at the hammering on the door.

'At a guess I'd say someone trying to get in.' Diana ran down the stairs and opened it to find the landlord of the Morning Star on the doorstep.

'You're not Nurse John,' he complained looking past her.

'She had to go up to the Albion. Is something wrong?'

'Alexander Forbes has fallen from the roof of Griffiths' shop. We tried telephoning the doctor from the pub, but he's out on a call, then someone said they'd seen Nurse John's car outside here.'

'She left half an hour ago. Is Alexander badly hurt?'

'I don't know. I left the women fussing over him. You'd better come,' he said, adopting the premise that a nurse's cousin was better than nothing.

'I'll just tell Mr Ronconi where I'm going, then I'll be with you.'

She ran back up the stairs to Ronnie's room, leaving the landlord to ponder on the events of the night. He decided that the Powells were quite a family. Between their lodger falling off the roof of their daughter-in-law's house—and there was only one thing a man would climb on a widow's roof for—and Diana Rees, Powell that was, in the bedroom of the recently widowed Ronnie Ronconi, the gossips' tongues would be wagging for years. This was one night that was going to go down in Graig history.

'Where on earth have you been?' Wyn opened

the kitchen door as Diana walked through the porch into the hall.

'If you let me in, I'll tell you.'

'Here, you're shivering. You're not hurt, are you?'

'I'm not, but everyone else is.'

Megan was sitting, tense and poised on the edge of her seat in front of the fire.

'You all right, Diana?' she asked anxiously.

'I'm fine, Mam.'

'Then I'll go to bed.'

'No don't, at least not until I've told you what happened.'

'We were worried sick,' Wyn said. 'Alice said you came down the shop, and she gave you my message ...'

'Yes, and I decided to go back up and spend an hour clearing Ronnie's kitchen. Bethan ordered him to rest because his leg wasn't healing, so we worked on figures for the shop all day.' She took the tea Megan handed her and recounted in as few words as possible the trauma of Ronnie's leg and Alexander falling from the back of Jenny's shop: '... the landlord of the Morning Star said it was the roof, but it wasn't. Alexander only got as far as Jenny's bedroom windowsill.'

'It would have been better if it had been the roof,' Megan observed cuttingly. 'That way he might have saved her reputation by pleading cat burglary as a defence.'

'Did you see Jenny?' Wyn asked.

'She came out to see what all the commotion was about. Once she realised Alexander had only bruised his back, she was furious. He pulled the drainpipe from her wall. It looked a right mess even in torchlight.'

'Poor Jenny.'

'Poor Alexander,' Diana responded. 'He got no sympathy at all.'

'Nor should he,' Megan said harshly. 'What did he think he was doing bothering a young widow?'

'Rumour has it he's been getting some encouragement,' Wyn commented quietly.

'If he had, she would have opened the door to him.'

'They could have had a row,' Diana suggested.

'No doubt the gossips will have the whole story sorted by tomorrow.' Megan left her chair. 'You sure Ronnie is going to be all right?'

'Bethan seemed to think so, but I'd better go back up there tomorrow to check if he needs any more help.'

'Well I'm for bed.' Megan went to the door.

'I'm sorry I worried you, but I thought I should stay with Jenny until they took Alexander away in the ambulance.'

'As long as you know this husband of yours was half out of his mind. He was just about to go down the police station to post you missing. Good night, both.'

'Good night, Mam. You wouldn't really have gone to the police station, would you?' Diana turned to Wyn as her mother closed the door behind her.

'Not without trying Ronnie's first.'

'Me being in Ronnie's is no different to you being in Jacobsdal.'

'I know.' He picked up her empty cup. 'Well, I suppose I'd better get to bed too. Early start tomorrow.'

She took the cup from him and carried it into the kitchen. 'Did you have a good evening with Erik?'

'He beat me at chess, and I lost ten shillings at cards.'

'Expensive night.'

'You know me and cards, I'll get my revenge. What about you?'

'As you heard, I had a busy evening.'

'The afternoon you spent with Ronnie must have been quiet.'

'It was.' She looked at him. 'What are we going to do, Wyn?'

'Go to bed before we both fall asleep on our feet.'

'And afterwards?'

'Go on as we are. What else can we do?'

'Don't you think next week is a bit soon, Jane?' Evan asked, as he picked up his snap box from the table.

'No. The doctor says my ribs are as strong as they've ever been.'

'Working in munitions is hard,' Phyllis said doubtfully. 'All the girls say so.'

'That's the letterbox.' Evan went to the door and returned with the mail. 'You sure you're fit for work, Alexander?' he asked as Alexander left the washhouse where he'd been cleaning his teeth.

'I'm sure; just a bit bruised and stiff, that's all.'

'You didn't get much sleep.'

'I'll catch up tonight.'

'Then we'd better get a move on, or we're going to miss the cage.'

'I'm ready.' Alexander took his snap box from the table and stowed it in his haversack before pulling his cap down low over his face. Both he and Evan knew the poor attempt at disguise wouldn't stop him from being ribbed unmercifully by the other miners. Neither doubted for an instant that the story of his fall would have spread overnight from one end of the Graig to the other.

'Here you are Jane, letter for you—' Evan handed it over—'and a card for us, love, from Haydn.' He handed it to Phyllis as he pecked her on the cheek before leading the way to the front door.

'You sit and read your letter, Jane. I'll see to the dishes,' Phyllis offered, piling a tray with breakfast crockery and carrying it out to the washhouse.

Jane sat in Evan's easy chair. Taking a knife from the drawer in the table, she opened the blue and white, airmail letter-envelope carefully, spread out the single sheet that did double duty and began to read.

Dear Jane, this is the first chance I've had to put pen to paper. We've been incredibly busy.

You simply wouldn't believe the hours of work we put in. Between travelling and showtimes, we're sometimes on the go for twenty hours a day. It's a nightmare just trying to make sure that we don't lose anyone, or the staging, on the road. We don't have scenery, it's considered a luxury in a war zone. You'd be amazed by some of the places we've performed and slept in. But everyone is pulling together ...

Jane's imagination worked overtime imagining just what Haydn meant by 'pulling together'.

... and we're surviving well. Some of the reporters and cameramen following the news from the front have taken a few shots of us entertaining the boys to send back home, but I don't need to tell you the sort of pictures that are getting published, you must have seen them in the papers. But I do want you to know that I am missing and loving you and Anne more and more with every passing day. When I talk to the soldiers I realise how much we have to be grateful for. At least when this tour is over we'll be together again, in Pontypridd, for a while. Some of the boys I've met haven't been home since the war broke out. I hate these sheets, I'm running out of room ...

Then you shouldn't have written so big, she thought, angry with him for considering it necessary to stress that they would only be together in Pontypridd.

I hope you and Anne are well. I can't wait to

get back and see you both. Remember me to Dad, Phyllis and Brian. All my love as ever,
Your husband,
Haydn

'Did he say anything about you working in munitions?' Phyllis asked as she carried a tray of newly washed crockery and cutlery into the pantry.

'He didn't object to the idea.' Jane omitted to tell Phyllis he didn't object because she hadn't told him.

'I'm glad.'

'And he asked to be remembered to you, Dad and Brian.' Jane tucked the letter into her pinafore pocket. 'I'll go and strip the beds if you like, while you put the boiler on to start the washing.'

'Coo-ee, Phyllis, Jane.' The front door opened.

'Not Mrs Richards,' Jane groaned.

'You didn't expect her to stay away after last night's happenings with Alexander, did you?'

'Phyllis, have you heard the news? Isn't it wonderful?' Mrs Richards walked into the kitchen, and stood there, beaming as though she'd just won the Irish sweepstake.

'What news?' Jane asked, mystified.

'About Russia. It's just been on the wireless. Hitler's invaded them, not us. My Viv says we'll be all right now. The Germans will be too busy fighting the Communists to spare any troops to cross the Channel. Don't you understand? Now Russia's on our side we're not on our own any more. We're going to win the war, and it won't be all that much longer before our Glan and your Dr John are home.'

'I hope so,' Phyllis breathed headily, thinking of Eddie and all the other boys who would never hear the news. 'I really hope so.'

'Well, you're a dark horse, I must say,' Maggie addressed Jenny as they walked down the platform to the cloakroom.

'I can hardly help it if a man falls off my drainpipe,' Jenny bit back acidly.

'If I'd known you had your eye on him, I would have left him alone.' Judy paused, hoping Jenny would say more.

'There's nothing between Alexander Forbes and me.'

'No?' Sally enquired sceptically as she opened her locker.

'No,' Jenny said vehemently.

'My brother was there when it happened. He said Alexander was lucky to get away with bruising, the height he fell. Rumour has it he won't even have to take a day off work.'

'I wouldn't know.'

'Didn't you talk to him after it happened, Jenny?' Judy enquired artfully.

'I had no reason to.' Jenny bent her head forward and ran her fingers through her hair, looking for stray hair-clips.

'Not even to present him with a bill for your drainpipe?'

Maggie and Sally laughed, glancing from

Jenny to Judy as they walked through to the side of the cloakroom where their overalls were stored.

'Diana, it's good of you to take over here,' Bethan greeted her cousin as she walked into Laura's house.

'Just thought I'd see how Ronnie is after last night.'

'Much better. I think that rag in his leg must have been the reason why it didn't heal. Scar tissue is forming already, and it looks as though he really is on the mend now. Want a cup of tea?'

'Please.' Diana took off her coat and hung it on the back of the door. 'How was the man in the Albion?'

'He died on the operating table in the Cottage.'

'I'm sorry.'

'So am I. It was such a senseless, stupid thing to happen. All the collieries are under such pressure to up production, safety measures are being thrown out of the window.'

'You sound just like your father.'

'With good reason. I worry about him working in the Maritime.' Bethan poured out two cups of tea.

'Want me to take one up to Ronnie?'

'No.' Bethan sat at the table. 'He was sleeping when I left him.'

'You gave him another pill?'

'It's the only way to keep him quiet. I saw Alexander in the Cottage last night. He was lucky to get away with just a few bruises. They didn't keep him in.'

'I went to the Morning Star after the landlord came here looking for you.'

'So I gather. I called in Graig Avenue early this morning on the way down here.'

'How did Uncle Evan take it?'

'Much as I expected. He wasn't shocked. Eddie's dead, Jenny's only twenty-one, she can't spend the rest of her life mourning him.'

'But it hasn't been a year yet.'

'I know, but my sympathies lie with her. Time seems to lose all meaning in a war. A day—a week—a year—what's the difference when the Germans could invade tomorrow, or a bomb could drop on the factories and blow us all to kingdom come? The only thing that seems important is what's happening right this minute.'

'There has to be more to life than that, even in wartime.'

'Does there?' Bethan asked seriously. 'I'm not so sure. Think about it, all we have is the here and now. The past is gone, we can't be sure there's going to be a tomorrow, so why shouldn't people live each moment as though it's going to be their last?'

'Because if there's a tomorrow we'll all be racked with guilt.'

'So, if it comes, we'll worry about it then.'

'How does this live for today and hang tomorrow philosophy fit in with Andrew being stuck in a camp?'

'It doesn't. I had a letter from him this

morning.' Bethan pulled a crumpled piece of paper from her uniform pocket. 'He finally got the letter in which I'd told him that I had taken on the job of district nurse, and he's raging mad. I didn't think he could get any angrier than when he found out I'd kept my pregnancy from him. I was wrong.'

Not knowing what to say, Diana remained silent.

'I've been telling myself that I have to make allowances for him because he feels left out. That he's having a worse war than any of us because he's been forced into a corner where he can't even fight back, or defend himself, but ...' Her voice tailed away as she reached for her cigarettes.

'He's angry with you, so you're angry with him?' Diana suggested.

'I can't forgive him for being his usual selfish self and refusing to see life from any point of view other than his own. Even he should realise that winning this war takes precedence over everything else. That ending this mess so boys no longer have to die, and he and all the other POWs can come home, has to be more important than whether Maisie or I give Eddie his bottle. Damn, I didn't mean to cry on your shoulder.'

'You're not crying.'

'No, but I feel like screaming. Why did I have to marry a short-sighted, selfish, crache officer?'

'That's a bit hard on Andrew, but if it will make you feel better, go ahead and scream. I don't mind.'

'I'd only succeed in waking Ronnie.' Bethan opened her handbag and rummaged fruitlessly in its depths. 'You got a light?'

'Here.' Diana found the silver lighter Wyn had given her for Christmas and lit Bethan's cigarette.

'Truth be told,' Bethan continued ruefully as she inhaled deeply, 'my marriage was never made in heaven.'

'You and Andrew were happy,' Diana protested.

'Before he went away, we were happier than we'd ever been, but I can't help wondering if it was because we knew we'd soon part.'

'That's an awful thing to say.'

'Is it? I've thought of nothing else since he left, especially when I was pregnant. I wouldn't be without the children, or him, not now, but I can't help wondering what it will be like for us when he eventually does come home. He'll want me to give up work, stop driving his car, running the house the way I want to ...'

'Sounds to me as though you're more worried about giving up your independence than your marriage.'

'It's the same thing. Andrew will want to put me back into an apron and turn me into a housewife again.'

'Not once you explain you want to carry on working.'

'You think he'll listen? Believe me, Diana you have no idea how lucky you are to be married to a man like Wyn who genuinely doesn't feel threatened by his wife working.'

'He's not the only one. Charlie ...'

'Charlie didn't mind Alma working alongside him in the shop. But he was annoyed when he found out that she had expanded the business without telling him, and he and Alma are closer than any other married couple I know.'

'He got over it.'

'Did he? When he came home on that last leave Alma told me he seemed like a stranger.'

'And you feel you don't know Andrew any more?' Diana asked astutely.

'Sometimes I wonder if I ever did. I realised when I married him that his mother had spoiled him. That we were from different worlds. That he'd always had exactly what he wanted without ever having to work or fight for it. It must have been hard for him to lose his freedom and the luxuries he'd always taken for granted at the same time.'

'Are you saying that because you're more used to hardship, it would have been better if the Germans had put you, not Andrew, into that camp?'

'I'd probably cope better than he seems to be doing from his letters,' she said caustically. 'What really concerns me, is that when I call in on most soldiers' wives all they can talk about is the good times they shared with their husbands. Their wedding day, or this trip or that trip. All I remember are the arguments. Like when Andrew ran out on me before we were married, leaving me pregnant, not that he knew I was having his baby because I was too proud and stubborn to tell him. And afterwards, when we were married in London, trying and failing to live with him and running back here.'

'But he came after you. He bought you the house.'

'And perhaps that's when the trouble really started. I look back on those days, and all I can recall is both of us trying too hard. Too afraid to say what we really meant or felt in case it upset or hurt the other. Please, shut me up. I'm not making any sense.'

Diana considered what was happening in her own marriage. The strained politeness that was developing between her and Wyn at the expense of honesty.

'You're making sense,' she acknowledged ruefully.

'You really think so? I've been wondering if I'm going mad.'

'Only as mad as the rest of us.'

Bethan took Andrew's letter from her pocket, screwed it into a ball and threw it on the fire. 'It will be a good few weeks before I write to him again.'

'Beth ...'

'What's worse—no letters at all, or angry ones? After today I know which I'd prefer.'

Evan stood outside Griffiths' shop and looked up. The blackout blinds were drawn at least an hour before it was strictly necessary. The shop door was locked. He rapped his knuckles hard on the door. Twice more brought a 'We're closed.'

'It's Evan, Jenny,' he shouted back.

There was no reply but he heard her footsteps on the stairs. The door opened and he walked inside.

'Come up,' she invited politely. 'Would you like some tea?'

'Not for me thanks, love. I've just eaten. I thought you'd like to know that Alexander is fine, he went to work today.'

'It's good of you to call and let me know.'

'If you'd like to see him you could come up the house with me now.'

'I don't think that would be a good idea.'

'Look, love,' he faced her as she stood with her back to the counter. 'I know it's none of my business, but Alexander must think a lot of you to risk his neck the way he did.'

'I never asked him to fall in love with me,' she blurted out uneasily. Ashamed and embarrassed she averted her head as the tears began to fall from her eyes.

He put his arms around her. 'I know you didn't, but it's only natural. You're a young, attractive girl, and you're single. We all knew it would only be a matter of time before some man would start paying attention to you.'

'All I want is to be left alone.'

'You can't stay alone for ever. You and Eddie—' he took a deep breath after saying his son's name—'well it wasn't all roses between you, I know that. Don't try to live in the past, Jenny. If you do you'll have a miserable life.'

'You don't mind?'

'About you and Alexander? No, love. Why should I?'

'But Eddie ...'

'If Eddie had been the one who'd survived, I would be giving him the same advice. You loved him while he was alive.'

'I ... I ...'

'Let's say the best way you could,' he interrupted tactfully, 'and now it's time to move on.' He glanced at the clock. 'I'd better be going. You sure you've got no message for Alexander?'

She shook her head.

'Your mother is dead, your father is in hospital and not likely to come out for some time. Please, you're as much my daughter as Eddie was my son. Don't stay in every evening when you've a family to visit. Come and see us?'

She nodded.

'You sure I can't give Alexander a message?'

'Just that I'm trying to make a life for myself, and between work and the shop there's not much time left.'

'You have to have some fun.'

'I need time.'

'You'll talk to Alexander soon?'

'Perhaps.' It wasn't much of a concession, but it was all Evan could get. 'Mr Powell?' He stopped and turned around. 'Thank you for what you said about Eddie.'

'I was his father. I know exactly how difficult it was to get on with him.'

'But I didn't help matters.'

'It wasn't you who killed him, love. A German bullet did. And don't you ever forget it.'

CHAPTER 18

'You sure you should be doing that?' Diana asked as she walked into the kitchen of the Ronconis' High Street café to find Ronnie pushing a huge, old-fashioned, scrub-down table against the wall.

'Dr Evans gave me a clean bill of health this morning. Where are the baking tins?'

'There were so many, Alma talked George Collins into dropping them off for us later in his van.'

He leaned against the table and surveyed the kitchen, which was as clean as three days of scrubbing could make it. 'How many is "so many"?'

'About fifty, all that Alma could spare.'

'And if they're not enough?'

'They'll have to be. Haven't you heard ...'

'... there's a war on?' he chanted. 'I've picked up on the rumour.'

'You can't get tins, saucepans or metal kitchen utensils for love or money these days. They're all being melted down into Spitfires.' She looked around at the sacks of flour, Alma's spare meat cutter, the mixing bowls and the implements that had been part of the café kitchen's original equipment. 'Alma's taken on a fourteen-year-old boy to help in her shop and sending her chief cook up here.'

'Good, because along with the all-clear this morning, I had a starting date.'

'For munitions?'

'Monday.'

Diana pretended to study the dismal view out of the high, narrow window in the hope that he wouldn't read the expression on her face. Ronnie had become far too adept at sensing her moods during the weeks she had helped Bethan to nurse him and taken over the running of Laura's house. And while she had grown closer to Ronnie, she had drifted further and further from Wyn, scarcely seeing her husband for more than a few minutes late at night when he came home from Jacobsdal, or horribly early in the morning before he left for the factory.

Ronnie stepped behind her and closed the communicating door between the café and the kitchen.

'I'm going to miss seeing you every day.'

'And I'm going to miss you.' She forced a smile.

'I've done about as much as I can here. What say you we mitch off and spend the afternoon in Shoni's?'

'I can't afford the time.'

'Come on, I bet you don't get many invitations like that?'

'The last one was when I was in junior school.'

'We'll celebrate me being able to walk without a stick by paddling in the lake. We could even take some food and a bottle of pop, and have a picnic.'

'And pretend we're six years old?'

'No.' He lifted her hand, unfolded her fingers and kissed her palm. 'If you were six years old I wouldn't be asking you.'

'It's certainly a glorious day.'

'And I bet it's the last one we'll see this summer. Autumn is around the corner.'

'You're a pessimist; there'll be a few more sunny days before winter sets in.'

'For you perhaps, but not for me. I'll be locked inside the factory six days a week, that's why I was hoping to get some fresh air now.'

'All right, you can stop nagging, I'll go,' she capitulated.

'I'll get my jacket.'

'I'm not walking there with you. I'll meet you later by the pond.'

'That's ridiculous.'

'No it's not. Can you imagine what Mrs Evans will say if she sees us walking down Pit Road together in broad daylight? And once she spreads the news, Mrs Richards will have us in the middle of a torrid affair that will relegate Tony's outburst to the shade.'

'Every cloud has a silver lining.'

'Not that particular one.'

'I still don't see why you can't walk up the hill with me after you sat with me in Laura's house, day after day.'

'You needed nursing, you were ill.'

'Not that ill.'

'That's debatable.'

'If we don't stop arguing we'll never get there. When and where do you want to meet?'

'The top end of the lake in an hour.'

'Make it an hour and a half?'

She knew he wanted her to ask why he needed the extra half an hour, so she didn't. 'Fine, that will give me time to check the shops.'

The deafening clatter of picks and shovels dwindled to a few ragged tappings as the whistle sounded. A hush descended over the close, fetid darkness of the coal face, as men downed their tools, stretched their aching muscles and reached for the snap boxes that held their cold dinners.

On his first day underground Alexander hadn't believed that he could ever become accustomed to the foul air, filth, darkness and waterlogged atmosphere of the pit; now he peeled back the dust-encrusted flap of his haversack and extracted his tin without giving a thought to the unhygienic conditions.

Moving down the line he sat alongside Evan. He'd been Evan's 'butty', or helper, for his first six months underground, and it had taken a great deal of negotiating with management by Evan on his behalf to promote him to the position of fully fledged miner. Leaning against the coal seam, he prised open his tin with fingers. swollen by scabs and dirt and took out one of the dripping and salt sandwiches Phyllis had packed for him.

'You seem to be a bit stiff. Your back still giving you trouble?' Evan asked.

'I saw the doctor on my last day off. He said it will take time for the bruises to work out.'

What he didn't tell Evan was he'd seen an army doctor when he'd tried to join up, but as soon as the recruiting office had discovered he was a miner, they had given him his marching orders. The attacks on Britain's merchant shipping fleet had given home-produced food and fuel a prized status they'd never enjoyed before the war. And much to Alexander's chagrin, he discovered that mining had been designated a protected occupation by the War Office.

'I would have thought three months was enough time to heal any injury.'

'Apparently not this one. But then, I've no one to blame but myself.' Alexander unscrewed the top on his metal flask and took a swig of cold tea. As with working in the pit, he had become accustomed to the strangely unappetising, metallic taste. 'I never did explain why I was trying to crawl through Jenny's bedroom window.'

'Don't feel you have to on my account. It's your and Jenny's business, not mine.'

'Jenny's your daughter-in-law.'

'As I told her at the time, she's a young widow; she can't grieve for ever.'

'She seems to be doing her damnedest.'

'You haven't spoken to her?'

'Not since that night. I've seen her a couple of times, but she walked away from me. I tried writing, but she didn't answer my letters.'

'She told me she needed time to sort herself out.'

'By the look of it, as much as my back needs to heal.'

Evan bit down on his sandwich, spitting out what might have been a piece of coal, or even a husk of grain. The national loaves were renowned for having peculiar objects in them.

'We had been seeing one another before that night,' Alexander admitted suddenly.

'Half the Graig gathered that much.'

'I didn't want it to be a hole in the corner relationship, but she wouldn't be seen in public with me. I tried to push her, but she kept on saying she needed time to mourn.'

'Perhaps she did.'

'That night, the night I fell, I went to the White Hart. She was there with a crowd of girls from the munitions factory, including Judy Crofter.'

'Alf Crofter's daughter from Leyshon Street?'

'She certainly lives in Leyshon Street. I'd talked to her once on the train from Cardiff to Pontypridd. I don't even like the girl, but that evening Judy latched on to me and wouldn't let go. She more or less insisted I take her to a café. I tried to get Jenny to go with us but she wouldn't. I even thought of telling Judy I was going out with Jenny, but Jenny was so obsessed with keeping our relationship secret, I knew she'd be furious if I as much as mentioned her name. By ignoring me, she practically pushed me into taking Judy to the café. So, I spent the evening with Judy, walked her home and left her there. Then I decided to visit Jenny to sort out exactly where I was with her.'

'After spending the evening with Judy?'

'I told you I didn't want to. Only the night before I had asked Jenny to marry me.'

'And what did she say to that?'

'What do you expect? That she needed time to think about it. I gave her six months.'

'And now?'

'I thought you might have some idea of Jenny's feelings towards me.'

'You think because Phyllis and I call in on her she talks to us about you?'

'I hoped she'd mentioned my name.'

'Not that I've heard.'

Alexander pushed half of his uneaten sandwich back into the box. 'I can't stop thinking about her.'

'Then do something about it.'

Alexander recognised the irritation in Evan's voice. 'I'd like to,' he said quietly.

'As I said, it's between you and her,' Evan said as he unscrewed the top on his metal bottle.

'I'd welcome some advice.'

'Talk to her.'

'I told you, I've tried.'

'Obviously not hard enough.'

The whistle blew signalling two minutes to the end of the break. Evan opened his haversack and pushed his empty tin and metal flask into it.

'You don't think I'd be wasting my time?' Alexander hauled himself to his feet.

'Only she can answer that.'

'If she'll meet me.' Alexander resolved to make one last effort to see her. After all, the worst that could happen was she'd tell him to leave her alone, which was precisely what he'd been forced to do since he'd fallen from her window.

'Why is the water always so cold here?' Diana asked as she sat on the bank of Shoni's, slipped off her sandals and dangled her feet in the lake.

'Because it has a stream flowing in at one end and out of the other.' Ronnie sat alongside her, his jacket slung over his shoulder, the basket he'd brought on the grass behind them.

'But it looks calm enough in the middle.'

'You ever swum out there?'

'Not since William told me it has no bottom.'

'And you believed him?'

'He and Eddie were horrible when they were boys. I remember coming here once with Maud, and Eddie jumping in from the diving rock and dredging up a disgusting black thing that he told us was a rotting dead dog. He and Will chased us with it, and Maud and I ran screaming all the way home.'

'And was it a dead dog?'

'Five years later Eddie told me it was a log.'

'Girls are so gullible. I remember playing the same trick on Laura and Bethan with a bag of dead kittens.'

'And it was a log?'

'No, a bag of dead kittens.'

'That's revolting.'

'Children are revolting.'

413

'Are you going to tell me what's in the basket?'

'Surprises.'

'I hate surprises.'

'A blanket for us to sit on, pasties from your shop, a bottle of Vimto, and—' he delved into the bottom and produced a Mars bar.

'Chocolate! Wherever did you get it?'

'Ask no questions ...'

'I'm sick of that phrase.'

'Isn't everyone?' He rolled up his shirt-sleeves and pushed his hat to the back of his head. 'It's hot here. Shall we follow the stream up the valley, find ourselves a shady spot and have a picnic?'

She was about to protest that she'd rather stay by the lake, when she saw a procession of small boys with home-made fishing rods cobbled together from sticks, twine and bent pins walking in Indian file along the opposite bank. On fine days, there were generally as many children around Shoni's as there were in the park. It was closer for everyone who lived in Penycoedcae and on the Graig, no one had to dress up in their best clothes to walk down Pit Road, the lake was cool for swimming in, and less crowded than the paddling pool in the park, not to mention free, which was more than could be said for the baths. The only drawback was Shoni's reputation for being the drowning pool for every unwanted cat and dog in the district and, so rumour had it, the occasional bastard baby or difficult granny or grandfather.

Picking up the basket, Ronnie held out his

hand and helped her to her feet. They walked slowly up to the top end of the pond, where the water was fringed by thick, close-growing woods; one of the few surviving remnants of the primeval forest that had once covered the whole of Wales. Entering them was like penetrating a dark tunnel that led to an altogether cooler, different, more mysterious world.

As a child Diana had equated these woods with the mystical, savage world of the ancient Druids. Wandering beneath the tall trees in the half-light that filtered down through the close-growing leaves and branches, she found it easy to believe in the old pagan gods she had heard about in school. Her teacher would have been horrified if she'd known that her class had been more enthralled with the stories of Druidic brutality and human sacrifice, than her educational tales of the Christian good that had superseded the old Celtic ways.

'It never ceases to amaze me that flowers bloom in this gloom.'

Diana looked around, seeing the deep pink of campions and the purple glow of violets peeking out of the long grass that covered the roots of the centuries-old oaks. Buttercups spread across their path, their brilliant, yellow petals reflecting the few rays of sun that penetrated the dense mantle of greenery. The stream bubbled alongside them, its cool, clear water frothing over smooth brown pebbles that children had banked up in the shallows to create stepping stones.

'I never used to appreciate nature,' Ronnie

continued as they penetrated deeper into the woods, 'until I worked on the farm.'

'I can't imagine you on a farm.'

'I'll have you know I made an excellent farmer.'

'I think it's probably the clothes. I can't picture you in dungarees and a straw hat.'

'I can wear dungarees covered in cow muck, and chew straw with the best of labourers.'

'To me you'll always look at home in a suit, shirt and tie, leaning against the counter of the café, shouting orders to the cook or the waitress.'

'That was the old me before I learned to plough a straight furrow, clean out pigs and milk cows.' He stepped off the narrow path and pushed his way through a copse of may into a small clearing hemmed in by flowering brambles and beech trees. Stamping down a patch of nettles, he opened the basket and spread the blanket. 'Your picnic spot, madam?'

She sat beside him.

'Quiet times?' he asked as he lifted the bags from the basket and laid them between them.

'Thinking about the new kitchen. I'm not at all sure that I'm up to running it without you.'

'If you make a complete hash of it, we'll just have to sack you.' He handed her a pastie.

'That's what I'm afraid of.'

'On the other hand, with the labour shortage the way it is, we're unlikely to find anyone better. You never know your luck, you might end up coping, but I think it's only fair to warn you: if you do succeed in producing more than the two shops and the cafés can sell, you'll only end up making more work for yourself. You and Alma will have to get a bus down to Treforest and look around for another shop for you to supervise.'

'While you're slaving away in the factory.'

'Wyn's surviving the experience.'

'He doesn't say much about it. In fact, he doesn't say very much at all these days. But then I hardly see him. He spends all day in the factory, every evening in Jacobsdal and his days off sleeping and going over account books.'

'You resent it?'

'No, but I miss him. When we married we were close, and now ...' she glanced at him, looking away quickly when she saw a disconcertingly intense expression in his eyes.

'And now?' he prompted.

'Other people have come between us.'

'Erik?'

'You know about Wyn's friendship with him?'

'There's talk in the town. And it's not only Erik, is it?' he questioned softly.

'I suppose it's only natural,' she continued hastily, not wanting to discuss what was happening between them, 'considering we spend most of our time with other people. We've grown apart, but things will change after the war.'

'If you think the end of the war will make a difference to you and Wyn, you are deluding yourself.'

'I want to make a success of our marriage,' she protested.

'Don't you think that's an impossible task, given Wyn's nature?'

'No. You may not think so now, but we were ideally suited.'

'I can't see how.'

'Wyn married me because he wanted a wife and family to stop the gossip, and his father from belittling him every chance he got. I needed a father for my baby, and I was terrified of the thought of a conventional marriage. We were happy those first few months, Ronnie. We really were.'

'Happy, or relieved because you thought you'd solved your problems?' He took a tin mug and the bottle of Vimto from the basket. After pouring her a drink, he screwed the top back on the bottle, went to the stream, jammed it between two rocks and left it there to cool. 'Do you know you hardly ever mention Billy?'

'Billy's wonderful.' There was a sparkle and animation in her eyes that hadn't been there when she'd talked about Wyn. 'He's happy, thriving, and doesn't seem to care who looks after him as long as he's fed, changed and played with. He's just as content in my mother's or Myrtle's arms as mine. But that doesn't stop Wyn's father from predicting all sorts of dire consequences for the death of family life after the war.'

'Why, because grandmothers, grandfathers and aunts are taking over childcare from the women who are needed to do the work the men did before they were called up?'

'He thinks a woman's place is in the kitchen.'

'If he lives long enough to see the end of the war, he'll be in for a shock. Some women will never go back to being housewives.'

'Bethan certainly doesn't want to.'

'What about you?'

'I like looking after the business.'

'You and Bethan aren't the only women who actually want to work, and believe me, working mothers don't do kids any harm provided there's someone to look after them. There were so many of us at home, the younger ones never knew who was going to feed or bath them, just that they would be fed and bathed, and it didn't make any difference to the way they turned out. At least I don't think it did,' he qualified with mock gravity. 'Tina and Gina would have probably been just as difficult if they'd had my mother's undivided attention.'

'There's nothing wrong with them.'

'You've never lived with them.'

Diana wedged the mug in the long grass and leaned back against a tree. 'I know it's silly to allow Wyn's father to bother me, but I can't help worrying. It's easier when I'm busy. There's no time to think when I'm caught up in the daily chores. When I'm doing the banking, tidying, cleaning, or looking after one of the shops, I don't have to consider anything beyond what needs to be done. Then, when I get some time like now, I imagine what it's like in North Africa and Europe for the tens of thousands of soldiers who are fighting and getting killed, and I start worrying about William, Haydn, Andrew and Charlie, and the Nazis across the Channel.

Now that they've almost conquered Russia, they might decide to turn around and invade us, and then heaven only knows what's going to happen to us, and Billy ...'

'Or this planet once it blows up.'

'It's not going to, is it?' she asked anxiously.

'It might, but there's no point in worrying about things we have no control over, Diana. It's hard enough just trying to live out the day we have. Another pastie?'

'No. How can you make jokes about serious things?'

'Because you're a solemn little goose, and I think I've fallen in love with you.'

She stared at him, wondering if she'd misheard what he'd said.

'I warned you months ago that we were playing with fire, yet you still kept coming to see me.'

'You were ill, your sisters were too busy to look after you.'

'And now?'

'There's the business.'

'Hang the business. I only allowed you and Alma to use the kitchen in the High Street café because it gave me an excuse to see you.'

'You know the way I am.'

'Because you're that way now, it doesn't mean you'll always be the same.'

If he'd kissed her, tried to make love to her, she could have run from him, but by simply talking to her he gave her no excuse to leave. The old, sick feeling of fear crawled over her skin. She shivered uncontrollably.

He bent forward and kissed her the way he
had that first time: tenderly, lightly, so lightly
she couldn't be certain his lips had actually
touched hers. He leaned back on his hands
and looked into her eyes. 'Any more than that
will have to come from you.'

'It won't.'

'Perhaps not yet, but it will.' Children's voices
echoed towards them from the direction of the
pond. 'Come back with me?'

'To Laura's house?'

'Please.'

She thought of Wyn, of Billy, of her life:
a lonely, arid one for all of her husband's
kindness. Was it so wrong of her to want to
be loved just this once? She rose to her feet.

'I have to do the banking.'

'Then come this evening?'

'No.'

'You could sneak in the back way, over the
mountain if you don't want to be seen. I'll leave
the kitchen door open for you.'

'I said no, Ronnie.'

'I heard you, I just didn't choose to believe
it.'

'I like you ...'

'You love me. Almost as much as I love
you.'

The silence between them was almost un-
bearable.

'Come on, woman,' he went to the stream
and picked up the bottle, 'are you going to
leave me to do all the clearing up?'

Jane sat, one of an assembly line of girls strung out in front of a canvas conveyor belt that turned out fuses for shells. The first girl put a spoonful of powder into the fuse, the next pressed down the powder before passing it on to the girl who layered cordite over the powder. A detonator was slotted over the cordite before another worker pressed everything firmly together. The girl who sat beside her put the cap on; she slipped in the plunger.

It was slow, dangerous work, and although Jane had only been working in the factory eight weeks, she'd already seen five small accidents on her line alone. What the management called 'minor incidents', although they were anything but minor to the girls whose fingers had been blown off, split or burnt.

Pushing yet another completed fuse towards the girl who took them to the X-ray machine to check they'd been assembled correctly, she heard the tinny clatter of the bell signalling the end of their shift. The belt slowed as the next shift walked on to the floor.

Glad to relinquish her seat to her relief, she stretched her aching fingers and walked towards the door to the cloakroom. Peeling off the thick woolly overall and dust cap she bundled them together with her shoes, stowed them away and crossed to the 'dirty' side. Opening her locker, the first thing she took out were her cigarettes and matches, although she'd have to wait until she was on the train before she could light up.

'More women pick up bad habits in this place

than on the streets,' Maggie observed, as Jane climbed into her own clothes.

'I need something to buck me up,' Jane complained as she finished dressing.

'You and me both,' Judy echoed. 'Coming to the White Hart with us?'

'I don't know.'

'You need to think about it?'

'The way I feel I'll fall asleep in my beer. It's so hot.'

'It won't be once we hit Ponty. Autumn's on its way, can't you feel it in the air?'

Pulling on her cotton summer dress and brushing out her short hair, Jane picked up her bag and followed Maggie and Jenny down the ramp to the platform. Judy was close behind them. It was difficult travelling to and from work with both Jenny and Judy. The two women rarely said a word to one another. Maggie had hinted that the strained atmosphere had something to do with Alexander falling off Jenny's roof, although Jane had failed to see the connection between Judy and Alexander.

She couldn't help feeling guilty every time she was with Jenny, because no matter how hard she tried, she wasn't comfortable in her company. Jenny was her sister-in-law—a member of Haydn's family—the only family she'd ever had, but Jenny behaved no differently towards her than she did to any of the other girls in the factory.

'Are you going for a drink, Jenny?' Jane asked, offering her a cigarette as the train pulled in.

'Of course.' She climbed on to the train and

grabbed a seat opposite Myrtle. 'You going to the Hart, Myrtle?'

'Perhaps,' Myrtle answered absently. Leaving her seat for the window she looked down the platform for her brother. Wyn and Erik had been called into the manager's office just before the end of the shift, and there was no sign of either of them. If they didn't get to the platform soon the train would leave without them, and because only the munition specials pulled into the factory station they would have to make their way into the main station in Bridgend to get home; a detour that could put as much as two hours on to their travelling time.

The whistle blew and doors slammed up and down the train.

'You waiting for Christmas to take your seat?' Judy asked.

'Just checking ...' the train lurched forward as Wyn, grim-faced and serious, ran down the platform alongside Erik. Someone opened a door for them and she saw them climb into a carriage lower down the train as it moved out. Turning round, she finally took her seat.

'You seeing the law tonight, Myrtle?' Judy enquired snidely.

'Not tonight, he's on evening shift,' she divulged as colour flooded her cheeks.

'You want to pinch a grenade to put under that one. It will take an explosion to spur him into proposing.'

'Judy's right,' Maggie advised. 'You're not getting any younger, and the rate he's going,

424

you'll still be courting when you're ninety. Tell him you want an engagement ring.'

'Not everyone's as pushy as you, Maggie,' Jenny observed frostily.

'You seen this, Jane?' Sally handed her a magazine as Myrtle pulled a library book from her bag.

'What is it?' Jane asked warily. The *News of the World* photograph had preceded a whole string of articles and interviews with Haydn. She had barely recognised her husband in the description of the popular singer and male pin-up the journalists portrayed, but with a five-month absence between them punctuated by few letters, and the ever-present guilt of the last day and night they had shared, she was no longer sure she knew what Haydn thought.

'Go on, read it,' Sally urged.

Jane glanced at the page. In the top right-hand corner was a pre-war photograph of Haydn. The impossibly handsome man she had fallen in love with, a warm smile curving his lips, eyes slightly misty as though he were focusing on something just out of camera shot, blond hair gleaming, impeccably dressed in a black evening suit and bow tie. The headline HAYDN POWELL WOWS THE TROOPS appeared above another photograph, this time with the Simmonds girls. They were wearing short skirts that showed off their legs and low-cut summer blouses that left little to the imagination.

'I'm glad my Paul is fighting, not looking down on a view like that.' Sally took her cigarettes from her bag.

'The photographer wouldn't have dared take that if they'd been leaning forward,' Judy commented, looking over Jane's shoulder.

'Haydn's tour seems to be a roaring success,' Sally said as she offered her cigarettes round.

'It would be, wouldn't it?' ˜Jenny said as she took one. 'The troops don't exactly have a choice of theatres they can visit.'

Jane was too busy scanning the article beneath the photograph to contribute to the conversation. After the usual flattering paragraph about the morale-boosting programme Haydn and the girls were presenting, there were a couple of sentences that unleashed the jealousy she was finding more and more difficult to keep in check.

... troupers to the last, the performers who normally sleep in the best suites and eat the finest French cuisine West End hotels have to offer, bunk down in slit trenches, wash in canvas buckets, dress and make up in the backs of lorries, and stage their shows without curtains or props, wherever and whenever they can find an audience.

A little bird told me that even in these primitive conditions, or perhaps because of them, romance has flourished. The question on everyone's lips at the front is, 'Which one of the Simmonds girls has caught handsome Haydn Powell's roving eye? Is it Ruth or is it Marilyn?'

'We both adore him,' cooed Ruth to our on-the-spot reporter. 'He's the tops, not only with

426

the WAACs and nurses, but with the men.'

'Every woman wants him for a boyfriend and every man for a friend,' echoed beautiful Marilyn. Watch this space for more.

CHAPTER 19

The staff had closed up. After cleaning the shop and kitchen and scrubbing down the tiled floors they had all left for the day. Alma's footsteps echoed hollowly as she walked from the shop to the back rooms and food storage areas, checking for dirt or anything left undone. She knew even before she ran her finger over the shelves and peered into the meat safes that all the surfaces would be spotless. They were.

Diana was right: she did have good staff, but then they should be. She paid them enough.

Closing the kitchen door she walked out from behind the counter into the handkerchief-sized hallway that opened on to the stairs that led to her flat. The evening stretched ahead of her, yawning and empty. For so many months before Charlie had come home there hadn't been enough hours in the day. She had spent every minute frantically rushing around the shop, dashing up and down stairs, stealing as much time from the business as she could to sit with her mother.

The few days she had spent with Charlie had already taken on a distant, dream-like quality. And now—there was nothing. All the hours of care, all the nights she had sat up with her mother, and suddenly she was left with no claims on her time except those of work and tending the grave in Glyntaff that now held both her parents.

She walked slowly up the stairs into her mother's room. The bed had been stripped. The mattress lay on its side, the furniture shrouded in dustsheets. She opened the wardrobe door. Her mother's clothes still hung on the rail: her underclothes, stockings and blouses were neatly folded on the shelves at the side. She knew she should pack them up and take them down to the WVS for distribution to the victims of the Blitz. Her motives weren't entirely charitable. The room had to be cleared because it would soon be needed for another.

Closing the door, she went into the living room and switched on the radio. Strains of Bach filled the air, the mellow tones harmonising with the sunshine that streamed through the window, but neither the music nor the sun could lighten her dark mood. Perhaps she should go for a walk, but even as the thought occurred to her, she sank down on to the padded window-seat. She felt restless, yet too mentally and physically exhausted to make the effort required to do anything. She hadn't even eaten since the elevenses of tongue rolls she had shared with Diana. And because it was easier to do nothing than make a decision, she continued to do just that; sitting, staring out over the rooftops of the row of shops across the road to the topmost branches of the trees that grew along the bank of the river behind the town.

If only Charlie would come home now, when her time was entirely her own. They could go away together, steal a few days out of the war. Stay in a hotel somewhere by the sea like Swansea, or Porthcawl. The shops would run smoothly whether she was there or not. Her friends were kind, but they didn't *need* her, not in the way her mother had, or Charlie.

She thought back to what he had said about Masha. Had Charlie ever really loved her or had she simply been a substitute for the wife he had been forced to leave in Russia? Where was he now? Did he ever think about her the way she thought about him? She hadn't heard from him in months, and sometimes she wondered if there was any point in continuing to write to him when she never received an answer.

A boy cycled down Taff Street. He was wearing the flat cap of the telegraph service, and in the same instant she recognised the badge on the front, she knew. Before he even stopped outside the shop she knew. He straightened his uniform jacket, pushed the cap forward to cover his eyes, pulled the small yellow envelope from his bag and walked towards her door.

And she knew.

The sun was sinking over the mountains as Diana left her Uncle Evan's house. Wyn's farming cousins had given them a bag of peas and beans, and her mother and Myrtle had insisted on passing half on to Phyllis. It hadn't been easy to refuse Evan's pressing invitation to stay to tea, but using the excuse of the theatre shop she had managed to get away.

It was close to teatime and the Avenue was

quiet. She hesitated for a moment on the steps outside before deciding that no one would think it odd if they saw her walking over the mountain on a lovely evening like this. As Ronnie had said, no one knew how many more good days there'd be before winter set in.

Children skipped towards her as she passed the last houses and left the unmade road for the rough track that curved above the high garden walls of Phillip Street. They smiled shy hellos, their hands full with pails and bowls that contained what remained of the small, round whinberries that had stained their mouths, teeth and hands dark purple. The berries would make good pies and tarts—if any remained uneaten by the time they reached home.

She walked slowly, passing the last of the whinberry pickers as she climbed higher. Sitting on a clump of heather she looked over the rooftops of the rows of terraces that clung to the hillside below her, and gazed down on the green lawns of the park. Four of the crache, dressed in white, a most unserviceable colour for a mining town, were playing tennis on the club courts. The pool in the public baths shone a deep cerulean blue that looked more inviting from a distance than it ever had close up. Turning her head she studied the Graig again, picking out the back of Laura's house behind the massive twin, water-storage tanks.

Was Ronnie waiting for her behind the lace curtains that screened the kitchen window? Would he have left the washhouse door open? She didn't have to turn back towards Graig

Street. She could carry on walking down the hill to Graig Terrace and join High Street from there, but as she rose to her feet and dusted the beads of heather from the skirt of her dress she knew she wouldn't.

She considered the enormity of what she was about to do. Unlike other women in the town, she didn't even have the excuse of her husband's absence, or the war. Apart from rationing, shortages and increased workloads, it hadn't affected her own or Wyn's life, and unless the Germans invaded it wasn't likely to. Neither she nor Ronnie was in danger, not like William or Charlie. And Ronnie wasn't likely to get called up, not after it had taken his leg so long to heal.

She was terrified of what was going to happen in the next few hours, afraid that if she did go to Ronnie it might turn out as disastrous an experience as the dreadful night she had stayed in the café with Tony. Yet she was more frightened of staying away. Ronnie loved her, and she knew that she could live her whole life without experiencing the feelings she had for him, ever again. If she ignored them and walked away now, she might end up regretting it for the rest of her life.

If she allowed him to be, Ronnie would not only be her lover, but remain her friend. And more than anything, she wanted to be loved the way Charlie loved Alma and the way William loved Tina: with consideration and respect for who she was, as well as her body. And perhaps, if she experienced physical love just once in her

432

life, she would be able to settle for what Wyn had to offer.

Or would she? Ronnie's cool determination and blunt conviction that they were destined to become lovers, unnerved her. He didn't so much live life as evaluate it, seizing what he wanted, no matter the cost.

He had been right to warn her that they were playing with fire. Common sense dictated that she should never see him alone again. It wasn't as though it would be difficult. Once he started in munitions, he'd be working long hours. The same as Wyn's—only unlike Wyn he wouldn't be walking up to Jacobsdal every evening.

Was she going to Ronnie because she had lost Wyn? She looked around. She hadn't reached Graig Street yet. It wasn't too late to turn back. Bewildered and confused she continued to stumble over the rough tussocks of grass past the tanks to the back of Laura's house.

She looked over the low dry-stone wall down the narrow garden to the lean-to washhouse. How would Tony react if he could see her now, or if he ever found out how she and his brother felt about one another? But then there was no reason why he should; not while she remained married to Wyn, and with Billy to consider there was no way she could do anything else.

What possible harm could there be in seeing Ronnie this one last time? Afterwards she'd leave, go home to her son and her husband and do her best to forget Ronnie and get on with her life.

She climbed over the wall and ran down the

433

path to the back door. Opening it quickly, she slipped inside the washhouse, muffling the latch with her fingers as she closed the door behind her. The air was so still she could hear the clock ticking in the back kitchen. Her heart thundered erratically against her ribcage. What if Ronnie wasn't alone? What if Tina had walked up from the café to keep him company, or Gina and Luke had called in to see him? How could she possibly explain her presence in the washhouse to them, when Ronnie's leg had healed weeks ago?

'I hoped, but I didn't really believe you'd come.' He stood in the doorway, a dark silhouette in the dying light.

'I had to call in on Uncle Evan and Phyllis.'

'You walked down over the mountain?'

'It's a fine evening.'

'It was a pretty wonderful afternoon.' He opened the door wider, and stood back. 'It's more comfortable in the kitchen than the washhouse.' He stepped behind her as she moved forward, turning the key in the back door. The click sounded so final, so irrevocable, she shivered uncontrollably as she entered the room.

'Can I get you tea?'

She shook her head mutely.

He left the room. She heard him walking along the passage, the rasp of the front door bolt as he rammed it home.

'Precaution against anyone walking in on us.'

She couldn't stop shaking. He took a step

434

towards her and she moved back. Dropping her handbag to the floor she tore at the neck of her blouse, ripping the buttons from their loops as she pulled the neck wide. His hand closed over both of hers, immobilising them, before fastening the collar she had opened.

'No,' he whispered, 'not that way.' Wrapping his arms around her he held her very close and very still. Afterwards she had no recollection of how long they had stood there, only that when he finally released her she was no longer trembling.

His lips brushed the top of her head as he moved away. Taking her by the hand he led her out of the room and up the stairs into the back bedroom that he had occupied since he'd come home. It was bathed in soft, golden rays of light that highlighted the tiny dust particles in the air. The sun shone through the window, a huge, fiery ball already half hidden behind the mountain. He sat on the patchwork quilt and held out his arms.

She moved towards him, her limbs strangely heavy, as though she were walking over dry sand. He reached out and drew her down beside him. She sat, tense, quivering, her breath coming in shallow, nervous gasps as he shrugged off his jacket, unbuttoned his waistcoat and lay back, hands beneath his head.

'You sure about this?'

'Yes.' She lay beside him. He made no attempt to kiss or undress her, simply moved towards her, embracing her body with the length of his. The rough cloth of his trousers rubbed against her bare legs. The clips on his braces pressed through the thin cotton of her dress. She steeled herself to receive his touch without flinching, but there was no rush, no haste, only a quiet, unhurried caress that encompassed every part of their bodies. A gentle coming together of hands, palm to palm; his face resting against hers, the smell of his shaving lotion mingling with her perfume, the warmth of his skin radiating through layers of clothing to her own. She moved slightly, tracing the outline of his lips with her fingers.

'We have all the time in the world,' he smiled, after she'd kissed him.

'I have to be home ...'

'Not for hours, or you wouldn't have come.'

'You know me too well.'

'And I intend to get to know you better.' Cupping her face in his hands, he gazed intently into her eyes. 'Do you remember what I said this afternoon?'

'You said a lot of things.'

'Among them, if you wanted more than just a kiss, you would have to make the first move.'

'I thought I'd just made it.'

'A start,' he whispered.

She reached up to the buttons on her collar, and this time, he made no move to stop her.

'Wyn keeps saying we shouldn't believe everything that's printed in the papers these days,' Myrtle consoled Jane, as Jenny and Sally went to the bar to buy more drinks. 'And I should think that especially goes for articles like that one about Haydn. They deliberately make them sensational to take people's minds off the war.'

'On the other hand Haydn always did have a roving eye, even when he was in school.' Judy still blamed Jenny for what she considered to be Alexander's defection, and as a result she felt vindictive towards all the Powell women, including Jane. 'He was going out with Jenny at an age when most boys were content to play marbles.'

'Who was going out with Jenny?' Sally asked, returning with a tray of beers and sherries.

'Haydn Powell.'

'Going out! We were playmates,' Jenny protested, glancing at Jane.

'I don't remember kissing any of my playmates, and the whole school knew what went on between you and Haydn over the patch next to the playground.'

'What's the matter, Judy? Jealous because no one wanted to kiss you when you were twelve years old!' Jenny mocked, turning the tables on her, sensing that Judy was only taunting Jane because she couldn't get at her.

'The pair of you were at it for years.'

'I married Eddie, not Haydn,' Jenny stated firmly, hoping to put an end to the conversation.

'Well, it will be interesting to see if Haydn does come back from his North African tour with another wife. Perhaps he'll set up a harem like an Arab sheikh. I wonder if he'll keep you on as number one, Jane?'

'And I wonder how you can spout such a lot of nonsense, Judy.' Jenny lifted her drink from the tray on to the table.

'I'd better go.' Jane finished her sherry and picked up her handbag.

'If you're walking up the hill I'll come with you.' Jenny left her seat.

'But you've just bought another drink.'

'Here,' Jenny handed it to Judy. 'Call it a consolation prize,' she called back as she followed Jane out through the door and on to the Tumble. She caught up with her as she walked under the railway bridge.

'Take no notice of them, Jane. We're all under a lot of strain, working the hours we do, and single girls like Judy most of all. They've never been married and now there's not enough men to go round they're afraid of being left on the shelf. It's all too easy for them to become jealous of the ones with husbands as good looking as Haydn.'

'I know.' Jane remained tight lipped as she forced back the tears gathering at the corner of her eyes.

'I remember how proud Haydn was when he stopped me in town to show me your engagement ring. He'd just bought it. All he could talk about was you ...'

'Was that before or after Eddie hit him through the shop window?'

'Jane.' Jenny took a deep breath as she caught hold of her arm. 'Don't let Judy and the other girls spoil what you have with Haydn. You have a beautiful daughter, and a strong marriage. You only have to see the way he looks at you to realise how strong.'

'Especially during the last five months.'

'He writes, doesn't he?'

'When he can.'

'Which is more than Eddie did when he first went away. Please, don't get angry with Haydn when he isn't here to defend himself. I was a stupid, foolish girl when I married. I had no idea what being a wife really meant, and I certainly didn't realise how much hard work goes into making a marriage. Then, I made the mistake of allowing my pride to rule my heart and my head, and let things slide until it was almost too late. It wasn't easy to start again with Eddie. By the time he came home on that last leave we'd drifted so far apart I thought we'd never get together again, and just when I thought we had a chance, he was killed.'

Jane turned and looked at her sister-in-law. For the first time she saw grief and pain beneath the outward veneer of self-confident independence. 'I'm sorry, I didn't realise. Everyone's always saying how well you've coped with Eddie's death.'

'Coped? I cry myself to sleep every night thinking about the sad mess I made of our marriage.'

'I'm beginning to wonder if there is such a thing as an entirely happy marriage.'

'I like to think so, but then I always loved fairy tales that ended "happily ever after". Look, why don't we give the pub a miss tomorrow night, and go to the early showing in the Park cinema. It's *Wuthering Heights* with Laurence Olivier and

Merle Oberon. I've seen it twice, but I feel like a good cry.'

'I'd like that, if Phyllis doesn't mind putting Anne to bed.'

'Good, and ask her if you can stay for supper at my place afterwards. I never cook for myself, it will give me the excuse I need to eat properly for once.'

'I'll let you know what Phyllis says tomorrow morning.'

Jenny stood in the shop doorway and watched Jane walk on up the hill, wondering if there *was* such a thing as a truly happy marriage. Perhaps the relationship she had forged with Alexander had been perfect after all. More passion than talk. Pity he hadn't wanted to keep it that way.

Diana opened her eyes and looked around the unfamiliar bedroom. The moon shone through the uncurtained window casting shadows over the dressing table and on to the bed. She stretched out, realised she was naked beneath the bedclothes—and remembered. Turning her head she saw Ronnie lying beside her, his eyes open, his mouth curved into a smile.

'You must have been exhausted.'

'I fell asleep?'

'Two hours ago.'

She struggled to sit up, but he pulled her down beside him. 'Don't go.' He leaned over, pressing her back on to the pillows.

'I have to.' She was very conscious of his naked body next to hers, and for the first time she realised she wasn't trembling or afraid. It had taken months of sleepless nights before she had become accustomed to lying beside Wyn, yet here she had lain, naked and asleep in Ronnie's arms the very first time she had shared a bed with him.

The memory of what had happened between them brought a soft flush of colour to her cheeks. 'Now I know what it is supposed to be like. Thank you.'

'I think it's the gentleman who should thank the lady in this situation.' He closed his hands around her waist. 'You do realise that I'll never let you go now.'

'But you have to. I have a family, a son ...'

'And a man who loves you very much and won't rest until you marry him.'

'I have a husband.'

'You'll have to divorce him.'

'Ronnie, I decided that if this was ever going to happen between us, it could only happen once. There's Tony's feelings to consider, as well as Wyn. I owe my husband everything. I can't ever leave him.'

'No?' He moved his hands to her breasts, stroking her nipples lightly with his thumbs. She burned where his skin touched hers, not from fear, but passion. She moved closer, entwining her legs into his, wrapping her arms tightly around his neck as she kissed him again, and again.

'You think you can walk away from this?' He threw back the bedclothes as he caressed her. 'Forget me, and carry on living with a man who can never love you the way a woman should be loved?'

'It won't be easy.'

'I'll make it impossible.' He kissed her eyes, her throat, and as his lips travelled down over her body, evoking responses she'd never dreamed of, she realised he was right. She'd never be able to give him up. Not now.

'Do you really think there has been talk about us in the factory?' Wyn asked Erik as they walked down the passage to the door of Jacobsdal.

'What difference does it make if there has or hasn't? I've already been transferred to the North Wales factory. Management isn't going to change its mind about that now the decision's been made.'

'I suppose not.'

'You could come with me.'

'How?' Wyn asked. 'I have a wife, a son, a sick father ...'

'And you think they need you?'

'They're my family.'

'And you'd be happier living with them than coming with me?'

'It isn't an option.'

'It could be if you change your name. With people moving all over the country it's impossible for the authorities to track down who anyone really is.'

'I have an identity card.'

'Lose it, get another. You wouldn't be the first. Hasn't it occurred to you that you could become anyone you want with that injury? All you'd have to do is say that you lost your leg in the blitz, inform the authorities that you've also lost all your papers in the bombing, pick an area where the church and the records office went up in flames, and no one will be any the wiser.'

'It's so simple for you, isn't it? You have no one to think about but yourself.'

'It wasn't always like that for me.'

'I'm sorry,' Wyn said contritely, recalling the time Erik had told him about his father and his wife. He had heard enough stories of the Nazi invasion of Eastern Europe from the other refugees in Jacobsdal to have some idea of the murder and brutality they had inflicted on the civilian population as well as the opposing armies.

'Diana's an attractive girl; she'll find another husband to be a father to her son.'

'Even if she did, there's still my father. He's ill. He needs looking after.'

'Which your mother-in-law is doing. I'm not suggesting that you come with me tomorrow. As soon as I'm settled I'll send you my address. You can follow on when everything's been resolved.'

'Nothing ever will be resolved, not in my life.' Wyn held out his hand. 'I can't believe that you're leaving tomorrow and I'll never see you again.'

'You'll see me again.' Erik shook his hand. 'Our friendship isn't destined to be abandoned like this.'

'How can you be so sure?'

443

'Second sight. My grandmother was psychic,' Erik joked. He hugged Wyn. 'Take care, my friend, and write. And don't let those machines in the factory go to rack and ruin. I've nursed them too long for you to turn them into scrap iron.'

Diana sat up in bed with a start. 'Why didn't you wake me? It's nearly twelve o'clock.'

'You're about to turn into a pumpkin?'

'I should have been home hours ago.' Throwing back the bedclothes she stepped out of bed.

'Did I tell you, you're very beautiful?' He gazed at her body, silvered by moonlight.

'I'm also very late. Wyn will have called into the police station by now.'

'He'll guess where you are.'

'So might my mother and his father.' Pulling on her French knickers and bust shaper she threw on her dress, ran a brush through her hair, grabbed her bag and sandals and rushed down the stairs.

'Wait!' He followed her out on to the landing. 'You can't walk through town this time of night by yourself.'

'I can't walk with you.'

'You can. Wait, Diana, please.' He stood naked on the top stair, watching as she ran out of the front door. Diving back into the bedroom he pulled on his trousers and shirt, picked up his jacket and raced after her.

'Not thinking of throwing yourself in, are you,

lad?' Huw Davies climbed the steps of the old bridge to the flattened summit of the high arch where Wyn was standing, looking down on the swirling black river below. 'This wall is very low for someone of your height.'

'I was miles away.'

'So I gather.' Huw sat on the wall and looked down. 'There's been a few drowned along this stretch, and not all of them wanted to go. A father and son disappeared in a whirlpool just down there a few years back.' He pointed to where the cellars of the Bridge Hotel protruded beyond the new bridge that had been built adjoining the old. 'Swept away when they were trying to reinforce the bank against flooding. The bodies were washed up down Treforest way.'

'That must have been hard on the wife and mother.'

'It was. I was the one who had to tell her. I don't think she ever got over the shock. You know something—' he pulled out his cigarettes and offered Wyn one—'I don't think I've ever broken the news of a suicide to a family where it hasn't hit just as hard as an accidental death or a murder. Not even in the families of the unmarried mothers who did away with themselves before the baby was born. In my experience there's nothing so bad that it can't be sorted.'

'You don't really believe that?'

'I think that if people stopped to consider what they were doing, we wouldn't have any suicides, or any attempted ones to prosecute.

445

Between me and you, that's one law that's always struck me as being a bit daft. Some poor bugger at the end of his tether tries to top himself, fails, and we arrest him and send him to jail to compound his misery. It's like rubbing salt into the wound.'

'I suppose it must be. I've never really thought about it.'

'And then again, if he does succeed, it cancels all his insurance policies and pension. Leaves his family destitute.' Huw turned his back on the river and looked down the steps. 'And even supposing he doesn't give a damn about his family or his insurance policies and is really determined, he'd need to pick out the right place. The river runs deep and shallow around here. A man could jump in the wrong spot and end up a cripple and a burden to be nursed.'

'I came here to think, not pick out a place to jump.'

'I believe you, boy. After all, you've got a fine wife and son to live for. Want some company to walk back through the town?'

'I wouldn't say no.' Leaning on the parapet instead of his stick Wyn negotiated the steps back to street level. 'I've been meaning to have a talk with you. I believe the saying goes "I have a bone to pick with you." '

'I've done something to upset you?'

'Taken my sister out.'

'She's old enough to make up her own mind who she sees.'

'Both of you are, but do you know she's

446

been bending over backwards to keep it from my father?'

'I thought she was trying to keep it from all of you.'

'The rest of us are a little cleverer than Dad.'

'I know she's ashamed of me ...'

'Ashamed,' Wyn laughed softly. 'She's been waiting for a proposal. Anything less isn't worth quarrelling with my father.'

'You mean ...'

'She likes you, Huw. You seem to like her, but I must admit I have been wondering what you were waiting for.'

'I'm only a policeman. She's—'

'Working in munitions.'

'She's a lady,' Huw contradicted.

'Then I can tell Megan to set aside rations for a party?'

'As soon as I can get a ring on Myrtle's finger.'

'It won't be difficult.' Wyn paused outside the cattle market. 'And I really wasn't thinking of jumping off the bridge. If you must know, I was wondering how difficult it would be for a man to disappear.'

'From his family, or himself?'

'Just his responsibilities. You've convinced me it's impossible.'

'You and Diana ...'

'Are fine. It's my father who gets me down,' Wyn said, not entirely untruthfully.

'You weren't thinking of throwing him over the bridge?'

'Can I tell the judge it was your idea?'

'Once I put a ring on Myrtle's finger he'll have something other than you to moan about.'

'If you have any sense you'll get Myrtle away from him.'

'Just as soon as I can do up my house.'

'That might take too long. Good-night, Huw.'

Wyn walked up the hill and along Gelliwastad Road. Despite his dismissal of Erik's suggestion, he couldn't stop mulling it over. It would be wonderful to start again with a clean slate. If it wasn't for Diana and Billy, and the responsibility he felt towards his father, he would be sorely tempted. Without Erik's friendship and support, life in Pontypridd and the factory loomed grim and unbelievably lonely.

Turning into Tyfica Road he climbed the steps of his house and opened the front door. Kicking his shoes off in the porch he picked them up and stepped into the hall. The hands on the grandfather clock stood at midnight. Another four hours and he'd have to get up. He was just about to go up the stairs when the kitchen door opened. Megan stood in the passage, her long nightgown and knitted shawl gleaming ghostly white in the darkness.

'Is something wrong?'

She beckoned him into the kitchen. 'Diana hasn't come home. I thought she'd be with you.'

'No,' he shook his head. 'What time did she leave?'

'Four o'clock this afternoon. She was going

up to Evan's. Didn't you see her at the theatre shop?'

'I didn't go to the shop tonight.' He hoped she wouldn't ask him where he'd been.

'The theatre would have closed an hour ago. Even if she'd been held up or stopped to talk, she should have been home by eleven. You don't think something could have happened to her?'

'Like Alexander falling off another roof, or Ronnie's leg getting worse?'

'I'm sorry, I know I'm foolish to worry. It's just that ...'

'She's been walking around town with a night's takings from the shop in her handbag. You've every right to be concerned.' He bent down to lace on his shoes.

'You can't go out now, you have to be in work in a couple of hours.'

'Someone has to find her.'

'What's going on?' Wyn's father tottered unsteadily out of the parlour into the hall.

'Nothing,' Wyn said sharply. 'Go back to bed.'

'That wife of yours run off,' he gloated in a grating voice.

'Diana hasn't run off anywhere with anyone,' he snapped. 'I'll be back shortly.' He walked briskly down the passage, slamming the door behind him.

CHAPTER 20

Diana's footfalls echoed loudly; resounding into the darkness as she tore through the deserted streets of the town. Frantic to reach home, she missed the entrance to Market Square. Too agitated to retrace her steps, she carried on running down to the Penuel Lane turn to Gelliwastad Road. Turning the corner by Penuel chapel, she stopped, stunned by a sight she hadn't seen in over two years. Ahead of her the Gothic fountain gleamed white and ghostly, shimmering in a pool of bright light that spilled out of the window above Alma's shop. As she drew closer she heard a hammering. Her Uncle Huw was banging on the shop door.

'You seen Alma tonight?' he asked, as though it wasn't in any way remarkable for her to be in Taff Street in the middle of the night.

'No, but it's not like her to ignore the blackout.'

'I know, and she's not answering. If I don't break a window one of the ARP's wardens soon will. It's a wonder they're not already here.'

'Smash one of the panes in the kitchen door,' she suggested. 'They're small squares, easier to board over and replace.'

'Good idea. You wait here. If something's wrong I may need you.' He went around the back. Seconds later she heard the breaking of

450

glass and his slow steady tread as he moved through the shop. A torch flashed briefly as he wrestled with the bolts on the front door. As soon as he opened it, Diana ran past him and up the stairs.

Alma was sitting in her darkened bedroom holding one of Charlie's thick, woollen jumpers to her chest. Diana called her name, she looked up, and Diana froze as Alma's eyes, cold, dead, looked straight through her.

'You haven't drawn the blackout in the living room and you've left a light burning.'

'I'm sorry.' Alma's voice was faint, remote. 'I've only just left there. I must have turned it on instead of off.'

Diana walked to the window, pulled the blind and switched on the lamp next to the bed.

'Is something wrong?'

'I have this pain. It keeps coming and going.' Alma uncurled her fingers and Diana saw the yellow telegram in her hand.

'I've turned off the light in the living room and pulled the blackout.' Huw read the situation before Diana, but he was more accustomed to dealing with tragedy and grief. Pushing his big clumsy hand into his pocket he pulled out a clean, inexpertly ironed handkerchief and handed it to Alma.

'Is it Charlie?' Diana asked.

'Missing.'

Diana had to bend her head to catch what Alma was saying.

'That means there's still hope, love,' Huw said awkwardly. Alma's face contorted in pain.

'You really are in trouble.' Diana lifted Alma's feet and laid her back on the bedcover.

'I'm afraid it's the baby.'

'You're pregnant?'

'Five months.'

'Does anyone know?'

'I wanted Charlie to be the first.' She stuffed a corner of the pillow into her mouth to stop herself from crying out.

'I'll go to the station and telephone Bethan.' Diana laid her hand on Alma's forehead.

'Please hurry, Uncle Huw.'

'Just as quick as I can, love.'

Wyn passed Ronnie in Market Square. He doubled back, addressing him by his name to make certain it was him, before grabbing his arm.

'You seen Diana?'

'She left my house about twenty minutes ago. I followed her, because I didn't want her going through town alone at this time of night.'

'I must have missed her in the blackout.' Wyn relaxed his hold as he peered into the gloom. 'What was she doing in your house so late?'

'We fell asleep.'

'In your bed?'

'I'm sorry you were worried,' Ronnie apologised, grateful for the shadows that shrouded both their faces, 'but I'm not sorry for falling in love with ...' he choked on the rest of the sentence as Wyn knocked him flat on his back. He lifted his hands to protect his head as his shoulderblade cracked painfully on the

452

cobblestones. As he struggled to rise, his fingers curled instinctively into fists.

'Get up and fight, you bastard so I can kill you, right here and now. You'll be worth swinging for.'

Ronnie relaxed his hands as he realised he couldn't punch Wyn, not even in self-defence. He'd taken too much from him already.

'And how happy do you think killing me will make you, or Diana?'

The calm mention of Diana's name confirmed Wyn's worst suspicions. He turned his back as Ronnie scrambled up from the ground.

'She must have walked up Penuel Lane way, for me to miss her,' he mumbled. 'I'd better go and see.'

'She should be home by now,' Ronnie agreed. 'Do you mind if I walk with you to check she's all right?'

'Yes, damn you! She's my wife. I've been looking after her for the past year and I think I can be trusted to carry on doing so.'

'Of course. But ...'

Wyn caught hold of his shoulder and pushed his face very close to Ronnie's. 'I may have to accept what's happened between you, but I don't have to like it. And I warn you now, you ever hurt her the way your brother or that bastard Ben Springer did, and I *will* kill you. And that's not an idle threat.'

'I know. I heard what happened to Springer.'

'I made sure he'll never do what he did to Diana to another girl.'

'There's a difference between me and them,

453

Wyn. I love her. And I'll do anything in my power to make her happy.'

'Including leaving her alone?'

'No.'

'She'll never leave me.'

'She will if you ask her to.'

'I'll see you in hell before I do that.' Wyn turned on his heel.

'Do you think she's happy now?' Ronnie called after him. 'As happy as I could make her?'

'Uncle Huw's right, Alma: missing doesn't mean dead. No more than killed in action does.' Diana wrung a damp cloth and laid it on Alma's forehead. The pains were coming alarmingly close together, and she was gabbling, saying anything—everything she could think of—to take both her and Alma's minds off what was happening. 'Look at the telegram Mam got after Dunkirk telling us that William was dead, and he turned up just fine ...'

'I'm going to lose Charlie's baby, aren't I?' Alma stared at her, and Diana wished that she would cry, break down, anything other than suffer in this wretched, dry-eyed misery.

'Not if Bethan and I have anything to do with it.'

'I want him so much. Now more than ever. No one really understands about Charlie—' She doubled up as another pain took hold.

'That Charlie isn't an ordinary soldier? We all know that. Would you like some tea ... no ... I'd better not give you anything. Oh why doesn't Bethan come?'

'I'm here.' Bethan walked in and dropped her bag on the floor. She went to the bed, laid her hand on Alma's stomach and pulled out her watch to time the contractions.

'I want this baby.'

'I know, and I'll do all I can to make sure you keep it.' She looked to Diana. 'Tea, strong with plenty of sugar.'

Huw was already in Alma's kitchen, boiling a kettle. 'Wyn was in the station looking for you. They were about to send out a search party. I told him where you were and that I'd bring you home as soon as you weren't needed.'

'Thanks, Uncle Huw.'

'It's none of my business, but—'

'That's right,' she said quickly. 'It is none of your business.'

'I saw Wyn standing on the old bridge tonight. He was looking down into the water. He said he was thinking.'

Always anxious to play down a potential drama, Diana knew her uncle wouldn't have mentioned seeing Wyn if he didn't think it was important. 'You talked to him?'

'For a while. He's not happy, Diana.'

'I know.'

'He's a strong man, a good man. He's put up with a lot over the years.'

'What are you trying to tell me?'

'Like most men he's too proud to ask for help when he needs it. Take care of him, love, because if you don't I could be knocking on your door one night.'

'I'll look after him.'

'I knew you would. Now, how many sugars do I put in Alma's tea?'

'The contractions have stopped and the baby's heart is beating strongly. You're a lucky lady, but you really should have gone to the doctor's months ago.' Bethan pulled the bedclothes to Alma's chin and tucked her in.

'I know. I'm sorry. I feel awful.'

'That's the drug I've given you: if you don't fight it, you'll soon be asleep.'

'You'll stay?'

'I'm not going anywhere.'

Alma raised her hand and handed Bethan the telegram. She lifted it to the lamp. The word MISSING stared up at her in thick, black letters.

'It's missing presumed dead.' Alma tightened her grip on Charlie's sweater.

'They've been wrong before.' Bethan refused to believe that Charlie—big blond, larger than life Charlie—could be dead. First Eddie, then Maud ... not Charlie ...

'I have to see his commanding officer.'

'He won't know any more than what's in the telegram.'

'I have to go.'

'You're not going anywhere until you're well again. And then it would be better to write first. If you turn up at Charlie's home base without an appointment, you probably won't even be seen.'

Alma turned a white anguished face to

Bethan's. 'You don't understand. He might not be dead.'

'That's what I've been trying to tell you.'

'But he still won't be coming back.' All Alma could think of was the conversation she'd had with Charlie on his last leave: *If by some miracle I do find Masha, I think that after twelve years, she, like me, will have a new life.*

Her own voice echoed back from that other, happier time: *And if there's room in it for you?*

How do you expect me to answer that? I don't know what Masha and I will think of each other after twelve years. Yesterday you felt like a stranger after only a year's separation.

Perhaps he had found Masha and she hadn't felt like a stranger. She hoped so. She would still lose him, but far better to another woman than to the war.

'You haven't left Alma alone?' Wyn lifted the boiling kettle from the hob as Diana walked into the kitchen a little after half-past three in the morning.

'Uncle Huw sent for Bethan. She's staying with her. Alma's pregnant.'

'I didn't know.'

'None of us did until tonight. She went into premature labour after she got a telegram telling her that Charlie was missing. Bethan's hoping it's just the shock and things will quieten down. Alma desperately wants the baby. Now more than ever.' She looked at the clock. 'You don't have to leave for the station for another half-hour. Would you like some breakfast?'

'I was just about to make tea. Want me to pour you a cup?'

'Please. I'm exhausted. But then you must be too. How much sleep have you had?'

'Not a lot.'

'Do you realise this is the first time we've had breakfast together since you went into munitions?'

'It feels more like supper to me.'

'Want some porridge or toast?' she asked as he tipped shaving water into his mug and stood it on the mantelpiece.

'Toast would be good, thanks.'

'I don't know what Uncle Huw told you, but I wasn't with Alma all evening.'

'I know. I met Ronnie in Market Square.' He tried, unsuccessfully, to hide the bruises on his knuckles.

'You hit him?'

'I didn't go looking for him,' he asserted defensively. 'I wanted to make sure you were all right. I came in around midnight, you weren't here, your mother was worried, so I went out again hoping to find you. I ran into Ronnie instead.'

'I'm sorry, Wyn.'

'I've been expecting it. Are you going to take Billy and leave?'

'No.'

'He told me he loved you.'

'I married you. I made some vows; I don't want to break them any more than I already have.'

'Erik's leaving town tomorrow. He's been

458

transferred to another factory.'

'Close by?'

'North Wales. I won't be seeing him again.'

'I'm sorry, Wyn.'

'It's a mess all round, isn't it?' He stared into the mirror as he wet his brush and lathered his face with shaving soap. 'Sometimes I think it would be a lot easier if I was able to join up and never come back, like Eddie.'

'Don't ever say that. I couldn't bear to lose you.'

'You wouldn't lose me, because we've never really belonged to one another, Diana. We just pretended, and hoped everything would work out. That's a terrible basis for a marriage.'

A claw of cold fear knotted in her stomach as she remembered her uncle's warning. 'Promise me you won't do anything stupid?'

'Like what?'

She couldn't even say the word. 'Eddie left such a mess behind him. Look at what's happened to Jenny if you don't believe me. And if you need any more proof, you should see Alma. She's distraught.'

'You really want us to soldier on?'

'We're lucky, we have Billy. I've always known we were fortunate to have him, but seeing Alma fight to keep her baby tonight made me extra grateful for him ... and you.'

'I suppose we get on most of the time and we like one another.' There was an odd, detached tone in his voice that terrified her.

'It's more than most married couples.'

'But it's not enough for you, is it?'

'It will be from now on.'

'Ronnie told me tonight that he won't give up seeing you.'

'I'd already decided, and told him that tonight was the first and last night we'd spend together,' she said, stretching the truth.

'You don't have to on my account.'

'But I want to. I'm not cut out for sneaking, hole in the corner affairs. I'm hopeless at lying.'

He ran the razor over his chin and rinsed it in the mug. 'Whatever you do, Diana, it still won't work between us.'

'Please, Wyn. We have to try.'

He looked at her reflection in the mirror. 'You're sure that's what you want?'

'I'm sure,' she answered resolutely.

'Diana said you've had post. Have you heard from Charlie's commanding officer?' Bethan asked Alma as she walked into her bedroom.

'Nothing since the letter saying they would let me know if they heard anything more. It's been two weeks since I had the telegram. You'd think they would know something by now.'

'I suppose it depends how and where he disappeared.'

'It has to be Russia. If they sent him there when the Germans invaded, the timing would be about right. Sergeant Lewis was home on leave last week, and he told your Auntie Megan that they don't usually send out telegrams until six or seven weeks after they've lost contact with someone, in case they have to apologise when

460

they turn up. You know how the army hates to be proved wrong.'

'If he has been taken prisoner it could be months before you get any definite news. It was two months before I heard Andrew had been captured and another four before I had a card with his address on.'

'If Charlie has been mistaken for a Russian soldier I may not hear anything until the war's over.' She looked down at the pair of bootees she was knitting. 'You know the Russians haven't signed the Geneva convention. The Germans can treat the Russian POW's any way they want. They don't even have to allow the Red Cross access to them.'

'Charlie's a British soldier. He wouldn't be put with the Russians.'

'He wouldn't have been in uniform if he was behind enemy lines.'

'And we could go on speculating about this for days.' Bethan studied Alma critically as she plumped up the pillows behind her head. Alma's appetite was non-existent, she had lost a significant amount of weight since she had heard the news, and enforced bed rest had made her pale and weak. 'Dr Evans told me the baby's heartbeat was strong this morning when he looked in on you.'

'Did he?' Alma asked eagerly.

'Although he, along with the rest of us, is still furious that you kept the pregnancy from everyone for five months. And I'm just as angry with myself for not spotting the signs.'

'A white shop assistant's coat is marvellous for concealing a bulging waistline.'

'I'll remember that when I get fat.'

'You never sit still long enough to get fat.'

'I'm not going to nag you, because I know how tedious that can be, but you really will have to take better care of yourself from now on. If Charlie walked through that door right this minute, how do you think he'd react to seeing you like this?'

'I'm doing everything you tell me to.'

'Except resting. Diana told me you insist on the girls bringing up the takings for you to count every night.'

'I have to do something.'

'How about moving in with me for a week or two? You'd have Maisie and the children for company, and me for part of the day. And although most of the leaves have fallen off the trees, the view from my window is still country rather than town.'

'I thought I wasn't supposed to move?'

'I spoke to Dr Evans this morning and he agreed a short car ride to Penycoedcae wouldn't do any harm, and a change of air might do you good. I could take you up now. What do you say, just a week or two?'

'Charlie's commanding officer might write.'

'You're forgetting I have a telephone and there's one downstairs. The girls in the shop could check your mail, and I'll call in when the shop's closed. I'll notify the post office that you're moving in with me, so they can redirect any telegrams that come in.

'Maisie and Liza have enough to do without waiting on me.'

'As if you're such a bother. And I admit I have an ulterior motive. I won't have to go so far to keep an eye on you, and I'll be able to monitor exactly what you're eating. Dr Evans's biggest complaint is that you should be gaining, not losing weight.'

'I eat plenty, I just can't keep anything down.'

'Because you're not resting. Tell you what, final bribe, you come and stay with me, and I'll write to Charlie's CO and tell him that you're ill, and any news would be better than none.'

'Would you, Beth?'

'If you let me pack your bags.'

'They're on top of the wardrobe.'

Bethan lifted them down.

'Dr Evans meant what he said about the baby's heartbeat?' Alma asked, looking for reassurance.

'Doctors never lie. If they're not sure of something they hum and ha, and try to look as though they're weighing up the options, when all the time it's just a cover-up to fool their patients into thinking they know more than they do. And that's coming from a doctor's wife. I promise you, if you follow my advice you'll have a bouncing baby by Christmas.'

'It's just that since the night I had the telegram, I've hardly dared hope. I do so want a boy. One with white-blond hair and deep blue eyes just like Charlie.'

'It could be a girl with red hair and green eyes.'

'No,' Alma shook her head. 'It's a boy, and he's going to look exactly like his father. I just know it.'

'Aren't you going to read your letter from Haydn?' Phyllis asked as Jane left the table and picked up her own and Alexander's plates.

'Later.' She carried the dishes out to the washhouse as Phyllis and Evan exchanged glances. She returned to the kitchen and drew a pitcher of boiling water from the copper set into the kitchen stove.

'Game of chess, Alexander?' Evan asked.

'Yes, thanks.' Although Alexander had made the decision to confront Jenny weeks ago, he still hadn't managed to see her. By the time he washed and changed and went down the White Hart, she had invariably left, and although he kept a lookout on the hill and in the town on his days off, he hadn't as much as seen her, let alone been able to corner her.

'I'll do the dishes if you'd like to give Anne her last feed and put her to bed, Jane,' Phyllis offered as she folded the tablecloth ready to shake outside.

'Thank you.' Jane picked up Anne from the day cot, and the bottle warming in a bowl of hot water. She went upstairs and fed the baby, sitting on the edge of the bed so she could look out of the window. The weather had broken. Autumn had given way to winter and that morning she had seen a frosting of ice on the inside of the window pane. Everyone was hoping that the weather would be mild, with fuel rationed so heavily, but for all the hardships of war, superficially her life wasn't all that dreadful.

She was earning more money than she'd ever thought she would, over three pounds a week, and she had saved quite a bit already. She hadn't needed to touch a penny of the money Haydn had arranged to have paid into the bank in Pontypridd, and at the rate she was going she'd soon have enough to put a down payment on a house. So if Haydn did go off with one of the Simmonds girls, she'd be able to carry on working and supporting herself and Anne, always provided Phyllis was willing to carry on caring for the baby.

As soon as Anne finished the bottle, she tucked her into her cot, curled up on the bed and opened the letter. Haydn had never written in such small, close-packed writing before.

Dear Jane,
I've only just seen some of the rubbish the press have been printing about me and the Simmonds girls. I hope it hasn't reached Britain, but if it has, I know you're sensible enough to ignore it. Believe me I'm missing you and Anne more and more every day ...

The words danced before her eyes, just as trite, absurd and unbelievable as those in the articles. Loath to read any more, she tossed the letter aside in disgust, remembering Haydn as he had been when she had first seen him: singing on stage, flowers in hand as he'd danced from one chorus girl to another, smiling, flirting, gazing at them with adoring eyes. Haydn at the parties in London, kissing women right left and centre, addressing every female between the ages of sixteen and fifty as 'Darling'.

She shivered as she remembered the last time they had made love in their London home. Her protest ...

'You'll find someone else to do this with.'

She couldn't allow herself to think about him. It was too destructive. She had to concentrate all her energy into building a life for herself and Anne. A good life, with friends around her.

For all his letters professing that he missed her, Haydn seemed to be managing very well on his own. It was up to her to prove that she could be just as self-sufficient. Then, if he ever did decide to visit Pontypridd, she'd show him that neither she nor Anne needed him, and he could do what he liked with one or the other, or both Simmonds girls, for all she cared.

'Letters, Nurse John,' the postman called to Bethan as she ran around the garden with Rachel, catching snowflakes on her dark woollen gloves so she could show her daughter the eight-sided patterns. Wrapping Rachel's scarf around her neck, she carried her to the wall and took the bundle from him.

'You heard the news?' he asked.

'No,' she answered in trepidation. 'I haven't had the radio on all morning.'

'It's not good. That bi ... blimmin, silly ... sausage—' he substituted the innocuous words for his first choices, which he only just remembered shouldn't be used in front of ladies—'Hitler is at the gates of Moscow. Looks like we'll soon be in this war on our own again.'

'At the gates of Moscow isn't in control of Russia.'

'I wish I had your optimism, Nurse John.'

'It's easy: try to look on the bright side.'

'What bright side? The "know it alls" who predicted it would all be over by Christmas 1939 are now saying it will all be over by Christmas 1941, but not the way we want.'

'I'm sure the editor of the *Pontypridd Observer* would appreciate a list of these "know it alls". He's always campaigning against seditious talk that could lose us the war.'

The postman touched his cap, pulling it down over his eyes. 'Well, if I'm going to deliver this lot to the Queen's Hotel, I'd best be on my way.' Pulling up his muffler and tugging his fingerless mittens over his hands, he climbed on his bicycle and continued up the lane.

Bethan set Rachel on the path where she carried on trying to catch snowflakes. Maisie knocked the window, waving a garland of newspaper streamers that the children had painted red and yellow. Bethan managed a smile as she waved back.

'Time to go in, Rachel. Grandad and all the aunts will be here soon for your party.'

'And Uncle Ronnie?'

'He promised you he'd try to come, didn't he?' Bethan climbed the steps and pushed open one of the double doors. Maisie closed the dining-room door quickly as they walked into the hall, but not quickly enough.

'My party table?' Rachel jumped up and down in excitement.

'You'll see when it's teatime.'

'Now ... please.' Rachel appealed to her through dark brown eyes that reminded her so much of Andrew's she couldn't resist her.

'A peek,' she compromised. She pushed the door open a few inches and picked Rachel up so she could look over the huge oak table. Rachel's eyes rounded in wonder as she stared at the dishes set out on the pristine white cloth. Bethan's best damask because Andrew's parents were coming. It wasn't the 'make-do' jam and paste sandwiches, or jellies and custards that Jenny had acquired from heaven only knows where, that caught Rachel's eye. Maisie had baked her a cake and covered it with icing. Made from milk powder and half of Bethan's monthly sugar ration, it wasn't up to pre-war standard, but it was still icing, and it didn't matter to Rachel that the candle was the standard utility issue, or that the 2 on the top was cut from cardboard.

'There's your age.' Bethan pointed to the figure Liza's sister had painted with tiny pink and blue flowers.

'Two,' Rachel chanted.

'Can we dress Rachel in her party frock, Nurse John?' Liza's sisters asked.

468

'In the kitchen, it's too cold in the bedroom.' Bethan handed her daughter over. As they ran down the passage giggling and laughing, it suddenly struck Bethan that the first real loss Rachel would experience in her young life was the evacuees when the war was over. Hopefully Maisie and her daughter would stay, but the others would undoubtedly be claimed by their families. All nine children fought, squabbled and played as though they were one big family. Not always happily, but then, Bethan reflected, thinking of her own childhood, that wasn't the way with real brothers and sisters either.

She went into the dining room where Liza, Maisie and Alma, whose visit had stretched to a month, were putting the finishing touches to the room.

'Letters. One for you, Liza. Looks like it's from your father. One for you, Maisie.'

'That will be the pattern I sent for from *Woman's Weekly.*'

Bethan flicked through the rest. Amongst the bills, and directives from the Health Authority detailing her next series of shifts, was one from Andrew.

'Sorry, Alma, nothing for you.'

'I've given up hope of hearing anything.' Alma wiped her hands on her apron before moving a plate of cheese straws that were too close to the edge of the table.

Bethan looked over the table. Food supplies were getting tighter and tighter, the girls had worked miracles, but the only way they had been able to organise the party was by asking everyone to contribute something from their own rations.

'We can't do any more until everyone arrives,' Maisie said, as she opened her envelope.

'I'll be in the study.' Bethan left her coat on. It was as cold in the unheated rooms in the house as it was outside, and she couldn't spare the coal or the wood to heat any more than the kitchen, and on this one special occasion, the dining room.

Slipping her thumbnail under the glued down section at the side, she slit the letter open and unfolded it. True to form it had taken four months to reach her.

My Dear Bethan,
Time goes on, and still nothing happens. Sometimes I think I'll go insane for lack of news. You have no idea how cut off we feel from the war here. Thank you for the photograph you sent of the children. I couldn't believe the one of Rachel, she has grown so much, short frocks and holding Eddie on her lap as though she is a little mother. I really am missing out on their childhoods. You say that my father and old Dr Evans are coping well. Sometimes I wonder if there'll be jobs for Trevor and me when we finally return. Everyone seems to be managing without us. From what the boys are saying in camp, you are not the only superwoman. All the wives are working in the ATS, WAAFS, WRNS or munitions, as well as running a home, bringing up children and taking in evacuees. And we continue to sit and do nothing ...

Bethan heard the children scampering and calling to one another in the bedrooms above her. She felt sorry for Andrew but she found herself wishing that he'd find something more positive to write about in his letters. Did he really think she enjoyed working gruelling hours as well as coping with shortages, the children, and the added responsibility of a houseful of evacuees?

The boys who planted gardens in the spring are harvesting vegetables, salad and tomatoes between the barracks. Some of them ran a sweepstake as to whether or not we'd be here to eat them; unfortunately I lost a cigarette and chocolate ration on the result. There are so many rumours—that the war will finish soon—that it won't—that it will go on for years—I couldn't bear the thought of that. Imagine me a wizened, grey-haired old man climbing the hill to Penycoedcae and seeing you, a little, grey-haired old lady sitting in the drawing room with the blinds closed against the glare of the sun, knitting and listening to the wireless.

I'm trying to be funny. The problem is when you don't know what's in front of you, it ceases to be funny. I'm sorry I'm whining more than usual, but I have a reason. The RAF bombing raids over here don't just kill Germans. But you're not to worry about me, I learned the art of cowardice and staying out of bomb and bullet range a long time ago. Besides, everyone looks after doctors, because they never know when they might need one.

I gave the photograph you sent me to an artist in the camp, and he sketched the children for me. It's not much, but it's the only present I can send you. With luck you may get this somewhere around Rachel's birthday. Give her my love, as there's nothing else I can send her from here, and tell her and Eddie that they do have a daddy and be loves them very much. One day I hope to show all of you just how much. All my love, Andrew

Bethan looked up to see her father standing over her.

'From Andrew?'

'Yes.' She wiped a tear from her eye. 'He sent a sketch of Eddie and Rachel.'

'It's well drawn. You do realise that now Hitler's been stupid enough to extend his Russian campaign into winter, his eastern army will soon be wiped out.'

'What do you mean?'

'You've never read *War and Peace*?'

She shook her head.

'If the Russians don't get him, their winter will, just as it destroyed Napoleon's army in 1812.'

'Dad, if you're only saying that to make me feel better ...'

'Remember what I'm telling you next spring.'

'If you're right, you'll remind me.' She smiled at Rachel, who charged down the stairs and into her grandfather's arms. 'Are Phyllis and Brian with you?'

472

'And Megan, Diana, Billy, Jane and Anne. Wyn's working, but Tina, Ronnie and Jenny will be up soon.'

She took his arm as they walked into the dining room. Hidden behind the door was the birthday table the older children had set up for Rachel. Parcels wrapped in painted newspaper and brown paper lay heaped on a green cloth embroidered with daisies. The practice strains of 'Happy birthday to you' wafted out of the kitchen where Maisie and Liza were unwrapping Phyllis and Megan's gifts of food.

'It's hard being without Andrew on a day like today.'

'At least I know he's safe.'

'And he'll be home soon.' He patted her hand.

'I know, Dad, the Russian winter.'

'It's true,' he protested at her sceptical smile. 'I'll talk to you this time next year.'

'When we'll be on our way to winning this war. You'll see.'

CHAPTER 21

'Why haven't you been to see me?' Ronnie cornered Diana in the kitchen, where she'd gone to heat the babies' bottles.

'Because I told you that night would be the first and last.' She couldn't even bring herself to look at him. If she did, she knew she'd break her promise to Wyn.

'And I thought we agreed that was impossible.'

'Hush!' She went to the door, closing it after making sure everyone else was in the dining room serving the children tea. 'Please, Ronnie, don't make this any harder for me than it already is.'

'I can't go on without seeing you.'

'I've Wyn and Billy to consider.'

'And us?' He grabbed her hand and forced her to look at him. 'You love me, Diana, I know you do.'

'Find another girl, Ronnie. One who isn't married.'

'Your husband can't ever love you. Not the way I do.'

'But he *is* my husband, and that's why I can't see you again. Not alone like this.' Blinded by tears she pushed the bottles into a jug. He took it from her, put it on the table and held her gently in his arms. 'If you love me, Ronnie, please, help me,' she begged.

The front doorbell rang.

'The others will wonder what we're doing if I don't answer it.'

He looked into her eyes. Seeing her determination—and her anguish—he finally released her.

'This is only for now,' he warned, holding on to her hand as she slipped away from him. 'Don't think I'm giving up on us, because I'm not. And I won't.'

She gripped his fingers tightly, clinging to them for an instant before walking into the hall.

A man huddled into an army greatcoat, collar up to protect against the snow, stood on the doorstep. 'Is this where Mrs Raschenko lives?'

Alma recognised the guttural accent even through the closed door of the dining room. Wrenching it open she ran into the passage; she stopped when she saw a small dark man with a Polish officer's insignia on his shoulder standing in the porch.

'Mrs Raschenko?' He removed his cap. 'I knew your husband. He didn't do you justice.' He took her hand and lifted it to his lips. 'He said you were beautiful; he didn't tell me you looked like an angel. I'm Captain Melerski, Edmund Melerski, of the Polish Air Force, now seconded to the British Army, at your service.' He bowed and clicked his heels.

Bethan came out into the hall, with Eddie in one arm and Billy on the other.

'I'm a friend of Feodor's,' he explained.

'Please come in, Captain.' Bethan kicked open

the kitchen door. 'If you wouldn't mind sitting in here, it's the warmest room in the house.'

'I'd be grateful.' He stepped inside.

'Would you like company?' Bethan asked Alma tactfully.

'Please.'

'Here let me.' Diana took Billy, starting as though she'd had an electric shock as Ronnie brushed against her and lifted Eddie from Bethan's arms.

'We'll keep everyone out of the way, Beth.' He walked ahead of Diana into the dining room.

'Tea, Captain? If you're hungry we can offer you some eggs and fried potatoes.'

'Real eggs?'

'We keep chickens, not that they lay well in this cold weather, but we have some to spare.'

'I can't remember the last time I ate a real egg.'

Bethan went to the pantry, took one out of the bowl, thought of Charlie, hoped the captain had brought good news and took two more.

'I couldn't possibly. You have children.'

'And you fight to protect them.'

'It's good of you to say so, but I haven't done much fighting for a while.' He unbuttoned his greatcoat, folded it neatly and laid it on the end of the bench set before the table. Bethan pulled out the chair closest to the stove for him.

'But you did fight alongside Feodor?' Alma ventured.

'We occasionally worked together. Are you ill?' he asked tactfully, glancing at her smock.

476

'Expecting a baby.'

'Feodor didn't tell me.'

'I wrote to him, I don't think he got my letter. Have you heard anything?' she asked nervously.

'Nothing since he went missing. I can tell you very little about his last known movements or location.'

'I understand. All I want to know is if he's alive or dead.'

'The truth is, Mrs Raschenko, we simply don't know. This isn't an official visit. I had to go to Cardiff on business and I asked the CO if I could stop off here.' He opened his briefcase and removed a brown paper parcel. 'This is everything Feo left behind on the base.'

Alma's hands shook as she untied the string and tipped the contents on to the table. It didn't seem very much to show for a life. A silver cigarette lighter and case. His gold wristwatch. Her photograph in a pocket-sized leather wallet. 'He didn't have another one,' she murmured as she opened it.

'We have a rule, Mrs Raschenko. Nothing personal can be taken on a mission.'

She put it down and picked up a bundle of letters, including every one she'd written to Charlie since he'd left. All of them were unopened. The topmost envelope was addressed to her in Charlie's writing.

'Was he in a battle?'

'Not exactly.'

'He was captured by the Germans?'

'He worked undercover, but then I think you guessed that much.'

She nodded.

'He along with several others were betrayed.'

'Then he was captured by the Germans?'

'That's all I can tell you, Mrs Raschenko.'

'Couldn't you contact the Red Cross and get confirmation?' Bethan asked.

'The last thing we want to do is draw attention to him. He wasn't in uniform.'

'Then he would have been shot as a spy?' Alma's eyes were liquid with misery.

'We simply don't know, and to be honest I doubt that we will until after the war is over.'

'If you don't mind, I'd like to go upstairs and read the letter.'

Bethan nodded. 'Put your coat on, it's cold up there.'

'I will.'

Bethan sliced the potatoes and tipped them into the fat she'd heated in the frying pan.

'I wouldn't have come if I'd known about the baby.'

'Believe me, anything that will alleviate the suspense Alma's been living in since she got the telegram that Charlie was missing, will help.'

'Charlie?'

'It's what people called him around here.'

'I didn't know.' The captain left his chair, picked up a fork, and turned the potatoes as Bethan beat the eggs. 'When will the baby be born?'

'Christmas.'

'Will you let me know?'

'If you wish.'

'I'd like to write to the child, send him something to keep for the future.'

'Then you do think Charlie is dead?'

'Like everyone else, I hope, but I've worked in the area where he disappeared. I know the circumstances and what he was up against.'

'Then ...'

'Please, I can't say any more than I already have. Feodor was a strong man, a clever man. If it's possible for anyone to survive, he will.' He picked up the leather photograph frame. 'He had a lot to live for,' he added, almost as an afterthought, unconsciously using the past tense.

Alma sat huddled into a blanket in a chair in Bethan's small sitting room. Steeling herself, she opened the letter.

My darling wife, Alma,
I am writing this at two in the morning while waiting for my transport out. If you are reading this, something has happened to me, and you will probably not even know what. I have seen horrors in this war that someone as kind, gentle and loving as you, couldn't even imagine. Savage, inhuman brutality I hope you will never hear about, let alone experience. If I am dead, I will be at peace, remember that, and if I survive I may be forced to return to Russia. If I do, I will never be allowed to return, but I will try to contact you, as I promised, at the end of the war.

Remember me and our life together from time to time, but only the joy we shared, that way you will be able to find happiness with someone else, just as I found happiness with you after Masha. Please, my darling, try to live every day without sorrow or sadness. I only wish it could have been with me. I want you to think of me as dead from this day on. No plans, no destructive false hope. Above all, I beg you to get on with your own life. Be happy, with Ronnie, if you think he deserves you. If you need help, turn to Evan. Thank you for your love, and the last two days in April that I will treasure for as long as I draw breath. I love you with all my heart and soul, goodbye. Feodor

'Alma?' Bethan had to call Alma's name twice before she looked up. 'Are you all right?'

'Yes.'

'The captain is leaving. Would you like to say goodbye?'

'Will you say it for me?'

'Of course.'

'And apologise to the others. I think I'd like some time on my own.'

'Of course.' Bethan closed the door quietly as she left. Alma hadn't even noticed she'd switched on the electric fire.

Ronnie was waiting in the hall.

'How is she?'

'She wants to be alone for a while.'

'I can understand that, but if there is anything I can do you'll let me know?'

'Of course.'

'Jenny, Tina and I are going with the captain. The snow's getting thicker and he's offered us a lift down the hill.'

'See you soon?'

'Christmas Day if not before.' Ronnie kissed Bethan on the cheek. 'And before I forget here's something for my niece.'

'You spoil her. You've already given her a doll.'

'You'll have to put these away for when she's older.'

He pushed the parcel into Bethan's apron pocket as the others filed into the hall to get their coats.

She didn't remember the parcel until bedtime. When she unwrapped it, she had to bite her lip to stop herself from crying. Maud's wedding and engagement rings lay together in a small box, and she could only guess at the pain it had cost Ronnie to part with them.

'What time did you say Jane came in?' Haydn glanced impatiently at the clock. He had taken an early train from London to be sure of arriving in Pontypridd by three o'clock, and had been absolutely furious to discover, not only that his wife wasn't in his father's house, but that she was working in munitions, and had taken her one day off a week, three days before, to go to Bethan's daughter's birthday party.

'About five,' Phyllis answered, 'but the girls sometimes go for a drink afterwards.'

'In the café?' Haydn asked suspiciously.

'The White Hart.'

481

'My wife in a pub!'

'All the girls go there, there's nothing wrong with it.'

'No? She promised to love, honour and obey me—now I find out that she's taken a job and hasn't told me a thing about it. Then you tell me that she goes out drinking with ...'

'Workmates?' Phyllis suggested mildly.

Haydn looked down at his daughter, who was sitting on his lap cuddling the teddy bear he'd brought her. 'What I can't understand is why she didn't say anything?'

'Perhaps she was afraid you'd disapprove.'

'Too royal. I earn enough to keep her and Anne.'

'Her job isn't about money, Haydn,' Phyllis protested. 'It's about doing her bit.'

'Isn't it enough that I toured the front?'

'Not for her. After you left she didn't know which way to turn. There wasn't enough to do in the house to keep us both occupied, and then ...' She fell silent, concentrating all her energies on chopping up the lump of tough stewing steak she'd bought.

'What?'

'What I was about to say to you would be overstepping the mark.' Phyllis was sensitive about the position she occupied in the household. As Evan's mistress she had no rights, especially when it came to criticising his children.

'You've gone this far, you may as well go the whole hog.'

She took a deep breath and came out with

what was on her mind. 'It's not easy for a wife not knowing where her husband is, or what he's doing, but it must be a lot harder seeing his face plastered over the newspaper with two beautiful girls.'

'Jane knew what I did for a living when she married me.'

'If she knew it involved kissing girls for the photographers, she's a lot more tolerant and understanding than most wives I know.'

'It's five o'clock. I'll go down the hill to meet her.'

'You may miss her.'

'How? It's a straight up and down hill. If I don't see her on the way, I'll call into the Hart.' He picked up his daughter, gave her a kiss and lifted her into her wooden playpen.

'There's no need to hurry back. I'm making a stew and it can be easily warmed up if you're not here on time to eat it.'

'We'll be here.' Buttoning on his greatcoat he walked out.

'When we started doing this, I thought it was dreadfully daring; now it's just one more part of the day,' Jenny said as she walked into the White Hart with Jane, Ronnie and Judy.

'The most welcome part,' Judy said gleefully.

'Are you girls telling me that I'm going to have to get used to the decadent life?' Ronnie asked.

'Stick with me and you'll do all right,' Judy flirted. She smiled when she saw Alexander talking to the barman. He was dressed in a suit, so she guessed that he'd had the day off. He really had kept to himself since he had fallen from Jenny's window. As far as she knew, he hadn't gone out with, or even talked to, any of the other girls. 'I'll get them in,' she offered, eager to reach the bar before anyone else beat her to it. Opening her handbag she stood alongside Alex and dug him in the ribs. 'Guess who?' she grinned.

'I was sure it was my turn,' Jane said as she sat down.

'Never refuse a free drink.' Maggie took a powder compact and lipstick from her bag, and checked her reflection before adding another coat of bright red vermilion.

'Face powder and lipstick? Wherever did you get it?' Jenny begged.

'Ask no ...'

'Come on. I'd give anything—well, almost anything—for a lipstick.'

'Six tins of fruit?' Maggie came back sharply.

'Two.'

'Three?'

'Done.'

'Here you are.' Maggie screwed down the lipstick and handed it over. 'I'll pick up the tins on the way up.'

'Seen this one, Jane?' Sally handed over a newspaper with yet another photograph of Haydn and the Simmonds girls, this time against a London backdrop. The caption read, THEY'RE BACK. 'You didn't say he'd finished his tour.'

'Didn't I?' Jane answered carelessly, feigning

484

nonchalance to conceal her shock.

'He looks cold, but then he would, wouldn't he, after living in all those hot countries?'

'I don't know about cold, Sally, but I wouldn't mind a pair of gold earrings like the ones those girls are wearing, or one of those fur coats, now that brass monkey weather's arrived.'

'They look extremely unpatriotic,' Jenny dismissed. 'No one should make such a display of themselves when clothes are rationed and there's barely enough food to put on the table.'

'They could be pre-war,' Sally suggested.

'And I could be a flying pig.'

Jane didn't hear a word they said. She'd had another letter from Haydn yesterday, but like the last time, she'd only read the first paragraph in which he'd complained that he'd received hardly any of her letters. Little did he know that she hadn't written any for the last two months, for him to receive.

'Here you are, four sherries and two beers.' Judy dumped them on the table. 'I'll just go back and get mine.'

Jane picked up her sherry and drank it down in one.

'Steady ...' Jenny warned.

'I'm thirsty. Anyone else want another one?'

'I'll get them,' Ronnie offered, giving her a sideways look as he walked to the bar.

'I could buy you a new one.'

'I want this one.'

'The lady's got taste, if you don't mind me

saying so, sir. That's a fine diamond and it's cleaned up beautifully. You won't find quality like that in a new one, not in wartime.'

'You see,' Myrtle smiled as Huw slipped his mother's engagement ring on to her finger.

'What do I owe you ...'

'It was pleasure to renovate such an outstanding piece,' the jeweller fawned.

'You expect us to buy the wedding ring from you?' Huw asked shrewdly.

'Well it just so happens I have one tray left of non-utility, high carat rings.' He glanced over his shoulder. 'Twenty-two carat, not nine. Although government regulations force me to stock the utility range, take my word for it, they're rubbish. But these will last until your golden wedding.' Like a conjuror producing a rabbit from a hat, he reached under the counter and lifted a velvet stand on to the glass counter.

'They're beautiful,' Myrtle gasped.

'Aren't they?' The jeweller gloated visibly at his success in hooking and landing his catch.

'Pick whichever you like,' Huw offered generously.

'You choose.' Myrtle demurred.

'You know me by now: I'll go for the most expensive because I've been a cheapskate over the engagement ring.'

'If I may suggest—' the jeweller took the widest band, and incidentally the most expensive, from its bed. 'It will be a perfect fit, madam.'

Huw looked down and saw the sparkle in

Myrtle's eyes. It was enough for him. 'We'll take it.'

'Huw! You haven't even asked how much it is.'

'You like it?'

'I love it.'

'Then it's yours. This was the easy part. Now we have to face your father,' he whispered as the jeweller went to look for boxes.

'You know something? For the first time in my life I'm not afraid of him.'

He smiled at her as he pocketed the ring box. 'Good, because from now on I'll allow no one, not even him to upset you.'

'Jane, let's go up to my house.' Jenny tried to stop her from opening her handbag to look for her purse. 'I'll make us some coffee.'

'I don't want coffee,' Jane protested noisily.

'What you don't want is any more to drink.'

'Leave the girl alone,' Judy interposed, peeved because she'd got absolutely nowhere with Alexander. 'She's worked hard and she's entitled to a bit of fun.'

'She has to work tomorrow, and she can't do that with a hangover.' Jenny looked over to the bar, trying to catch Ronnie or Alexander's eye, but it was hopeless, they were too engrossed in conversation.

'If I want another drink, I'll have one,' Jane declared, swaying precariously over the table as she tried to leave her chair.

'I'll get them.' Jenny picked up her handbag.

'It's my round,' Maggie objected.

'You can catch up tomorrow.' Making her way to the bar, Jenny reached out to touch Ronnie's arm just as Alexander moved between them. He turned and stared at her in surprise.

'Jane's drunk,' she muttered, but not too low for Ronnie to hear. 'I think she should go home.'

'Jane?' Ronnie repeated in astonishment. 'Quiet, mousy Jane?'

'If you think that, you don't know her.'

'She's normally so responsible. What on earth possessed her?' Alexander asked.

'One of the girls has been plaguing her with photographs of Haydn and his other women.'

'And there's certainly been enough of those in the papers lately. He's a dull bugger to pose for them,' Ronnie flatly condemned his brother-in-law.

'That isn't going to help me get her home.' Alexander looked across to where Jane was holding forth, eyes feverish, hands gesticulating wildly.

'I'll slip across to station yard and get a taxi.'

'Would you? I'll never manage her on my own, and as she's working tomorrow, she really ought to sleep it off.'

'I'll give you a hand to get her outside.' Ronnie returned with her to the table.

'Look girls, a man.' Maggie grabbed Ronnie's arm. 'I was beginning to think you were an extinct breed like the dodos they told us about in school.'

'You're looking at one of the last who's brave enough to hazard female company. Sorry, ladies, but I'm going to have to break up this happy gathering. I'm here to escort Mrs Powell to a party.'

'There's a party?' Jane tried and failed to focus on Ronnie.

'Family party, tonight. Don't tell me you'd forgotten?'

'Just one more drink ...'

'We'll be late, and then Bethan will be mad with us. Tell you what, I'll bring some bottles. Alex has gone to get a taxi, Jenny's coming.' He took her arm and helped her to her feet. 'This your coat and handbag?'

She nodded, fighting back the tide of nausea that threatened to engulf her as the room swayed.

'Then let's go.'

Alexander had asked the taxi driver to drive the gas-powered vehicle across the Tumble and park it in front of the Hart. It was just as well. Jane's legs were going out from under her before Jenny and Ronnie even got her to the door. Jenny breathed a sigh of relief when she saw the enormous gas balloon, looking for all the world like an enormous carbuncle on the roof of the waiting car. Even with Ronnie's help she felt she couldn't have hauled Jane another yard.

Alexander climbed in first, dragging Jane behind him. After a moment's hesitation ˜Jenny sat beside her.

'You coming, Ronnie?'

'With all that crumpet sitting neglected and lonely in there? No chance,' he winked. 'See you later, Jane. Hope you're soon feeling better.'

Concerned in case Jane passed out, Jenny and Alexander watched her anxiously. They had no time to look out of the window, and that's how they missed Haydn walking down the hill.

Indignant and furious at what he'd already decided was his wife's blatant neglect of their child, and him, Haydn walked through the bars of the White Hart, until he finally ended up in the back room. He stared at the crowd of women sitting around the centre table in amazement, then he heard someone call his name.

'Don't you recognise me?'

'Ronnie, you look a damned sight better than when I last saw you.' Haydn turned away and continued to scan the room. 'I was hoping to find Jane here.'

'She left a couple of minutes ago.'

'But I walked down the hill. I couldn't have missed her.'

'She took a taxi with Jenny and Alex. Look, as you're here have a drink with me.'

'Who's Alex?'

'Your father's lodger. Between me and you, I think he's sweet on Jenny,' he added, seeing a jealous light in Haydn's eye.

'Eddie's only just been killed.'

'A year and a half ago,' Ronnie reminded him as tactfully as he knew how. 'What are you having?'

'Some other time. I've only got a seventy-two-hour pass and I was hoping to spend some of it with my wife.'

'It is ... it's Haydn ... Haydn Powell!'

Haydn screwed his face into a pained expression before turning to face the women. Ronnie had never seen such a change in a man within the space of a few seconds. Haydn beamed, as though he'd only come home to see his fans.

A crowd of girls pushed their way through the bar towards him, as they groped in their handbags for pencils and paper.

'Visiting your wife?' Judy asked snidely as he backed towards their table, signing autographs.

'That's right.'

'We weren't sure you'd want to.' She folded over the newspaper she'd shown Jane.

Haydn recognised the *Daily Mirror*. He'd already seen the latest photograph of himself and the Simmonds girls splashed over the front page. It had been lying on an empty chair, and that was when he began to wonder.

'Oh boy, have you had a skinful,' Bethan said as Alexander and Jenny carried Jane through the door. 'Here Alex, I'll take over and get her upstairs.'

'I'll help,' Phyllis offered.

'Can I do anything?' Jenny hovered in the passage hoping Phyllis would say no, so she could leave. She hadn't been alone with Alexander since he'd fallen from her window, and she had no intention of talking to him now if she could help it.

'You can start by telling us how much she's had,' Bethan called down the stairs.

491

'About six sherries. Unfortunately she drank them in about half an hour.'

'Could be worse.'

'Put the kettle on and make some coffee, will you please, Jenny?' Phyllis asked as she ran up after Bethan.

'She'll soon sleep off six sherries,' Bethan declared as Phyllis slipped off Jane's shoes. 'It's probably worse because she drank them quickly on an empty stomach.'

'It's worse than you think. Haydn arrived a couple of hours ago,' said Phyllis.

'Where is he?'

'He went down the Hart to find her. He was none too pleased when he discovered Jane was working, and even less pleased when I told him she was probably in the Hart. I dread to think how he'll react when he sees her in this state.'

'Oh well, there's nothing like hitting a man right between the eyes.'

'That's what I'm afraid of.'

'Don't worry. If you can put up with me a bit longer, I'll talk him out of his mood. Here, give me a hand to undress her and get her into bed.'

Ignoring Alexander, Jenny lifted the kettle from the stove and went into the washhouse.

'You're looking well,' he ventured when she returned.

'I am, thank you,' she replied stiffly.

'I've been wanting to talk to you.'

'Not enough to climb up to my bedroom window again, I hope?'

'I'm sorry about that.'

'Not as sorry as I am. Have you any idea how much it cost to repair that down-pipe?'

'Send me the bill and I'll pay it.'

'If you're feeling generous I'd like the gossips silenced as well.'

'One good thing came out of it. I talked to Evan. He doesn't mind us going out together.'

'And because my father-in-law has no objections, you've already decided we can carry on where we left off?'

'Jenny, I'm sorry I embarrassed you. Please, couldn't we at least talk?'

She hesitated.

'Perhaps we could go to the cinema one night this week, or the theatre, or the New Inn? Anywhere you want. I promise I won't mention engagements or marriage, not unless you bring up the subject.'

'No,' she answered slowly. 'Between work and supervising the shop I really don't have time for much else.'

'Just an outing ...' The front door opened and Evan walked in, black and grimy from the pit, in sharp contrast to the immaculately uniformed Haydn who followed close behind him.

'Jenny?' Evan greeted her in surprise. 'How nice to see you. I hope you're staying for tea.'

'I'm afraid I can't. Some of the girls are coming round, but thank you for asking. I only called in with Jane. Haydn, you're looking well. It's good to see you home.'

'Is Jane here?' Haydn asked as she picked up her coat.

'Upstairs. But I wouldn't go up right now if I were you. Phyllis and Bethan are with her.'

'What's the matter with her?' He walked down the passage to see Jenny out. 'Is she ill?'

'Not exactly.'

'What do you mean, not exactly?' he demanded angrily.

'She's had a bit too much to drink.'

'Are you telling me my wife is drunk!'

'It's hard on all the women in munitions. Having to work long hours in foul conditions, and it's worse for Jane. Every break-time at least one girl taunts her with photographs of you and those two blonde floozies ...'

'Thank you for bringing her home.' Haydn opened the door.

Jenny would have liked to say more, but the ghost of their old courtship and Eddie stood between them. She looked up, and saw Alexander standing in the passageway behind Haydn. 'Goodbye, Haydn. If I don't see you again, have a good leave.'

'Wait!' Alexander called out. Grabbing his coat he ran after her. Haydn watched them go, then closed the door as Phyllis walked down the stairs.

'How drunk is she?' he enquired acidly.

'She only had a couple of sherries; the trouble is they were on an empty stomach.'

'And how often has this happened before?'

'This is the first time,' Phyllis countered indignantly.

He waited until she reached the bottom of the stairs before running up them and along the landing to his old bedroom. Bethan was pulling the eiderdown over Jane. She smiled and put her finger to her lips.

'If she's plastered she's not going to hear anything,' he asserted.

'She's only had a couple, Haydn.'

'I get my first leave for nine months, and I come home to find my baby with Phyllis, my wife not only working but drunk—'

'You sound like a pompous, self-righteous schoolmarm.'

'I have a right to.'

'Right? What about Jane's rights? She's worked hard since you left her here. She's often stopped off for a drink on the way home with the girls, and this is the first time I've seen her like this. There has to be a reason for it. Do you know what it is?'

He thought back to the photograph in the *Mirror,* but he wasn't in the mood to excuse Jane's behaviour.

'You've no idea of the strain the women who've been left behind are under.'

'That's all I've been hearing since I've got home. Do you think it's so damned easy at the front?'

'At least you know what's going on. We have to rely on censored letters, what little news the War Office deigns to release, and rumour. And believe you me, the rumours fly thick and fast from one end of town to the other. They've had every man who's ever left Pontypridd killed ten times over. And while we're coping with that, we still have to fight the war here. Contend with severe rationing of just about every essential, bring up children on our own, look after evacuees as well as answering the call for women workers to fill the places of the men.'

'Jane had no business working. I can support her and the baby and support them a lot better than—'

'It's not a question of money or support,' Bethan said carefully, realising that his anger was bordering on the irrational.

'Don't tell me: you women "want to do your bit",' he sneered.

'Without munitions the soldiers can't fight. If they don't fight, we'll end up being invaded like France.'

'There's plenty of single girls who can work. Jane has a baby. They wouldn't have taken her if she hadn't volunteered. And you can't tell me she didn't volunteer to spite me.'

'We're all working. Diana's running Wyn's businesses and helping Alma out until the baby's born. And as soon as Alma's baby is born she'll go back to work. With Charlie posted missing, she has no option but to provide for her child.'

'That's different, Charlie could be dead.'

'Just as a stray bullet could have got you while you were travelling round the front. Do you think Jane never worried about that happening? For pity's sake, Haydn, get down off your high horse. Andrew's in a prison camp, he has enough money to provide for me and the children and he'll be coming back when all this is over, but that hasn't stopped me from taking on a full-time job as district nurse and opening my house to evacuees.'

'That's different, you're needed.'

'So is Jane in munitions.'

'After farming my baby out?'

'Megan and Phyllis are looking after my own and Diana's children as well as yours. That's their way of fighting this war. You make me mad, turning up here without any warning after nine months away, and expecting to find Jane sitting around waiting for you.'

'I certainly didn't expect to find her drunk.'

'And you never got drunk on tour?'

'That was different.'

'Why—because you're a man? Grow up,' she snapped irritably as she folded Jane's dress on to a chair. 'You said you've only got a few days' leave. If you don't use the next couple of hours to calm down and get to know your daughter, you'll mess up whatever's left of it. I've seen enough marriages go to pieces already in this war, without wanting to watch yours disintegrate as well.'

CHAPTER 22

'There's a letter for you, Wyn.' Diana handed it to him as he walked through the door.

'Thank you.' He looked at it, knowing it was from Erik even before he turned it over.

'Hungry?'

'Starving. Where's Megan and Dad?'

'She's helping him shave. Don't you remember? Tonight's the night Myrtle's bringing Uncle Huw to tea. I wonder if he'll still want me to call him uncle when he's my brother-in-law?'

'Have either you or Megan had the courage to tell Dad what he's in for?'

'We thought we'd leave it to you men.'

'Cowards.'

'That's us. Do you want a sandwich or can you wait another half-hour?'

'I can wait.'

'Is it from Erik?' she asked as he opened the envelope.

'Yes.'

'You must miss him.'

'Do you miss Ronnie?' he asked, watching her carefully.

'I saw him on Saturday at Rachel's birthday party,' she said, refusing to meet his steady gaze.

'Alone?'

'For a few minutes in the kitchen. I was

heating the babies' bottles.'

'I don't need to know every little detail, Diana.'

'But I need to tell you. I haven't changed my mind since we talked about him, Wyn. I made you a promise and I intend to keep it.'

'But being in the same town as Ronnie, and not being able to see him is quietly killing you?' he asked, crediting her with what he'd feel if the situation were reversed.

'Of course not.'

He might have believed her if she'd been able to look him in the eye.

'I'll wash and change, then I'll see if I can help Megan smarten up my father. After all, it's not every day a daughter gets engaged.'

'Why can't I stay alone with you in the same room for more than five minutes without tearing my clothes off?'

'And mine.' Jenny snuggled under the bedclothes, wrapping her arms and legs around Alexander so she could siphon some of his warmth into her body.

'I think I actually prefer winter to summer.' He clamped his hands over hers to stop her from tugging at the hairs on his chest. 'We can spend longer together without anyone suspecting a thing, now the nights have drawn in.'

'I let you into my flat and my bed for the first time in months, and you're making plans for the entire winter? This puts us right back to where we were when I had to ask you to hand over my key.'

'Sorry, I didn't mean to push.'

'No? You want to own me, body and soul, Alex, and I'm not prepared to give any more than I just have.'

'It's enough,' he assured her swiftly.

'If it isn't, you'd better leave now.'

'You know I don't want to.'

'And I don't want to be plagued by a man who won't be content until he's changed my life. I like it exactly the way it is.'

'I understand. What you're saying is you'll see me on your terms, not mine?'

'You do understand?'

'That I have to learn to ignore you until such time as you decide you would like to spend an hour or so in my company?'

'You make it sound as though you are a toy that has to stay in the cupboard until I want to play with you.'

'Isn't that exactly how you're treating me?'

'No, Alex. I'm trying to put our friendship on an even footing where we both keep our independence and run our own lives without interference from the other. I don't want to control you, only make the decisions as to how often, where and when we meet. What you have for your dinner, or who you see when you're not with me, is your own affair.'

'And if I choose to spend my time with other women?'

'If you have the energy—' her hand slipped down between his thighs—'go ahead.'

'And you?'

'If I have the energy, I'll look around for

another man. But before you start throwing tantrums and playing the jealous lover, I'll play fair and give you the opportunity to tire me out.'

'I'm not used to women behaving like this.'

'Like men behave towards women, you mean?'

He leaned over and picked up his cigarette case from the bedside cabinet. He would have liked to contradict her, but he knew she was right. She was treating him no differently to the way he'd treated his casual girlfriends before he'd met her, and he hated the way it made him feel. Like a vulnerable pawn totally dependent on the whim of a Grand Master.

'I'm going to have trouble adapting.' He opened his case.

'You know where the door is. Perhaps you'd better go now, before we start quarrelling again.'

'That was a plea for patience and under-standing, not a cue for you to throw me out.'

Taking the cigarette case from his hands she closed it and slipped it under the pillow. Caressing his back lightly, her fingers moved downwards, teasingly, tantalisingly to the soft skin on the inside of his thighs. As he tugged the sheets and blankets over both their heads, he realised that although he had lost control for the present, there were compensations.

And even Jenny would want to settle down—eventually. Possibly with him, if he managed to make her fall in love with him.

'I still think we should have waited until Megan

or Diana could have come with us.' Huw opened the door of his house in Bonvilston Road, and stood back to allow Myrtle to walk in ahead of him.

'You need a chaperon?' Wearing Huw's ring on her finger had given her a confidence she would never have believed herself capable of possessing.

'It's your reputation I'm thinking of.' He helped her off with her coat and hung it together with his own on the old-fashioned, Victorian hallstand that was far too large for the narrow passageway. 'Kitchen's straight ahead of you, second door on the right. I did warn you the house is in a bit of a state.'

'It just needs decorating.' The warmth of the stove blasted welcomingly towards her as she walked into the room and looked around at the massive, age-stained oak furniture and dingy wallpaper.

'It needs a woman's touch. You can do whatever you like. I've quite a bit of money put away.'

'There's no sense in buying furniture now. There'll be more choice after the war.'

'Would you like tea?'

'I'd like to thank you for my rings,' she said boldly.

'You did in the shop.'

'I meant properly, with a kiss.'

His face turned crimson. He ran his finger around the inside of his collar in a futile attempt to loosen it as she reached up, wrapped her arms around his neck, stood on tiptoe and kissed him, hard and inexpertly, on the mouth.

'Thank you,' she murmured, her face as scarlet as his when she finally stepped away.

'Being married is going to take a lot of getting used to.'

'Don't tell me you're nervous too?' she blurted out.

'I've lived alone for so long with no one to please except myself, I'm afraid I've grown selfish and sloppy in my ways. But I don't understand why you should be worried. You kept house for years for your father and brother.'

'It's not housekeeping I'm nervous about.' She pretended to study a religious picture of Moses parting the Red Sea that hung above the mantelpiece. 'But of sleeping in the same bed with you.'

'You don't have to. There's three bedrooms upstairs.'

'I want to.' She could feel her cheeks burning, but working with girls like Judy had taught her, if not to overcome embarrassment, at least to ignore it. 'I have a confession to make. I'm very inexperienced about these things. You see, that's the first time I've ever kissed a man. I mean really kissed—'

'I know what you mean,' he interrupted.

'I feel strange. Apprehensive and excited all at once. The women in the factory talk about men and lovemaking all the time, the single girls as well as the married ones. Does that shock you?'

He thought back to some of the things he'd seen and heard the women do in station yard.

'After more than twenty years on the beat in this town I think I'm shock-proof.'

'It's just that I thought if we could spend some time alone together, getting used to one another, it would make it easier for me on our wedding night.'

'We could start with another kiss?' he suggested, putting his arms around her. For all his high-minded opinion of Myrtle, it was as much as he could do to keep his hands clasped around her waist as her lips brushed against his. 'Time we went to see your father.'

'Can I come back here with you tomorrow night?'

'You do, and you might find yourself honeymooning early.'

'I wouldn't mind.'

If he'd known what it had cost her to make that remark he might not have been quite so dismissive. 'But I would.' He went into the hall to fetch her coat. 'There's a time and place for everything. I may be old-fashioned, but in my book, bed definitely comes after the wedding service.'

'I need a hand in the kitchen,' Megan said as Myrtle and Huw walked into the living room.

'I'll help,' Diana followed her mother.

'Me too,' Myrtle offered.

'Glad to see you've finally decided to come home,' her father grumbled. 'And before you start on the food, you can make me a cup of tea.'

'Not before we all sit down, Dad.'

504

'That's all you know! You may as well move out and live in that factory of yours for all the attention you give your own father these days. I haven't been strong enough to sit at the table for weeks. I'll have mine on a tray over here.'

'Then I'll get your tray ready.'

'And I'm supposed to talk to myself while you lock yourself up in the kitchen with Megan and Diana?'

'Here, Mr Rees, I'll keep you company.'

'It's kind of you to spare a sick, old man the time, Constable Davies,' he griped in a martyred tone. 'You got everything under control in the town?'

'We're trying, Mr Rees.'

'Not hard enough, judging from all the reports of blackout crime in the *Observer.*'

Wyn retreated to the corner of the room, leaving Huw no option but to take the chair opposite the sofa his father was lying on.

'I haven't come here to talk about blackout crime, sir.'

'No, you've come for tea. A bachelor is always looking for a free meal, and your sister's not a bad cook. I'll give her that. Better than Myrtle,' he carped, hoping his daughter was listening.

'I've come to tell you that Myrtle has agreed to be my wife.' Huw had been practising the announcement all day. At their age, he felt that neither he nor Myrtle needed to ask anyone's permission, and it was the most tactful way he could think of emphasising that fact to the old man.

It was as much as Wyn could do to keep

a straight face. Paralysed by shock, his father stared open-mouthed at Huw.

'You want to marry, Myrtle?' he spluttered when he eventually found his voice. 'Whatever for?'

'Because I love her, she loves me, and we believe we can make one another happy.'

'That's ridiculous. You're both far too old to get married.'

'There's an age limit?' Huw smiled to lessen the sting in his words.

'What do you think people are going to say? Myrtle's a spinster. Always has been. The minister's wife said she was born that way.'

'So is every woman,' Huw pointed out wryly.

Silence reigned, so strained, so dense, Wyn could hear his own pulse throbbing below his ear. All three men focused on the door to the kitchen where there was precious little rattling of cutlery and crockery, considering the women were supposed to be preparing tea.

'We've fixed a date four weeks from now. I'm going to see the minister tomorrow. If the chapel can't accommodate us, it will be a Register Office do.'

'No daughter of mine is getting married in a Register Office.'

'It was good enough for your son,' Huw reminded mildly.

'Had to be, didn't it? That was a shotgun job. You should have heard what the minister and his wife had to say about my grandson appearing six months after they tied the knot.'

'Nothing unchristian I hope,' Huw commented gravely. 'I'd like to set your mind at rest and tell you that I can provide for Myrtle. She'll want for nothing, I promise you. I have my own house in Bonvilston Road. It's not as good as this one, and it needs a bit doing to it, but it's all mine. There's no mortgage on it, and I've enough put away for Myrtle to do anything she wants, even exchange it for a bigger one elsewhere in the town if that's what she decides. So, as you can see, we've nothing to wait for.'

'Nothing! What about me?' the old man demanded petulantly. 'Who's going to look after me in my old age if my own daughter abandons me? That's what I'd like to know!'

'Me, Mr Rees.' Megan bustled in with a full tray, which she set on the table. 'You'll be pleased to know I made a cake in honour of the occasion.'

'You knew about this?'

'Hoped, more than knew. Isn't it marvellous to have something worth celebrating in these dark days?'

For once the old man was completely at a loss for words.

Haydn was sitting listening to the radio, nursing his grievances and his daughter, who'd grown from a contented baby into a plump contented toddler during the nine months he'd been away, when the kitchen door opened and Jane walked in, pasty-faced and shivering.

'I saw the suitcase in the bedroom. I had no

idea you were coming home.'

'I wanted to surprise you. I think I succeeded in surprising myself more,' he replied coldly.

'It's bedtime, love,' Evan nodded to Phyllis.

Phyllis leaped to her feet. 'You'll dampen down the stove, Jane?' she asked as she followed Evan out.

'I didn't even know the tour was coming to an end.' Tightening the belt on her dressing gown, Jane sank down into the chair Evan had vacated.

'Evidently,' Haydn said drily.

'I didn't mean to drink so much ...'

'But you did.'

'I was angry.'

He remembered the photographs, but he didn't ask her to elaborate.

'How long have you got?'

'Seventy-two hours, and I've lost twelve of those already. It's all I could wangle, and I doubt there'll be any Christmas leave this year. We've too many shows to get out.'

'I'll ask my supervisor if I can have tomorrow afternoon and the day after off.'

'You're not going into work tomorrow!'

'I have to.'

'Don't be ridiculous. The war effort won't grind to a halt if you're not there to polish the gun barrels, or whatever it is you do.'

'I work on an assembly line. If I don't turn up there's no one to take my place.'

'So?'

'The fuse output will go down. They need every bomb they can get, and they're no good without fuses. I put the detonators into them.'

'I get three days and you tell me you can't spare the same?'

'What I do is important, Haydn.'

'You're being ridiculous.'

'Am I?' She rose to her feet and went to the stove. 'Would you like some tea?'

'I'd like to know what's going on. I come home to find you working and frequenting pubs ...'

'Frequenting! I call in now and again with the girls after work.'

'The same girls I saw Ronnie, Alexander and God only knows how many other men sniffing around.'

'Ronnie's my brother-in-law. I happen to work with him, and Alexander is—'

'I know who Alexander is after. Ronnie told me. Jenny led Eddie a merry dance when he was alive, and nothing seems to have changed now he's dead.'

'She is a widow, Haydn.'

'Is that what you'd like to be?'

'Seems to me from what I read in the papers, I'm the abandoned wife.'

'I didn't abandon you, I brought you to my father's house so you and our child would be safe, and out of the blitz. You were the one who abandoned Anne so you could work. You leave her with Phyllis, get drunk—' he stabbed his finger towards her—'and you accuse *me* of abandoning you? I really thought, really believed all this time that you were looking after our daughter ...'

'Phyllis cares for her beautifully.'

'Is this your way of telling me that after the war is over you'd like to leave her with Phyllis?'

'Don't be absurd.'

'If you have anything like a conscience left, you can start exercising it right now. I'm your husband, the one you promised to obey, remember? And I expressly forbid you to go to work tomorrow.'

'I'm going.'

'I won't allow it.'

'How are you going to stop me, Haydn? Lock me in the bedroom?'

She walked over and looked down on the sleeping child in his arms. 'It's time she was in bed.'

'How do you know? You're not the one who usually puts her there.'

'I'm tired, Haydn. I have a hangover, and I have to get up early in the morning. I've done all the arguing I'm going to for one day.' Closing the flue on the stove and raking out the ashes, she carried them through to the metal ashbin in the back yard then washed her hands in the washhouse. Standing in front of him, she held out her arms. 'Can I have Anne, please?'

'How can I trust you to look after her?'

'I think I've done a better job than you for the last nine months, don't you?'

He glared at her for a moment. She stooped down, and he reluctantly handed Anne over.

'Good-night Haydn.'

He heard her walking up the stairs, but he

continued to sit and seethe, until sleep finally overcame him, and that's where Jane found him in the morning. Stretched out in an easy chair, his feet propped up on a stool. She covered him with one of Phyllis's knitted blankets, before cleaning her teeth and brushing her hair. Forgoing her usual morning tea, she closed the door quietly behind her and left the house.

'Morning. Myrtle's behind me,' Wyn said, as he bumped into Huw in the black shadows that shrouded Tyfica Road.

'I had to go to the station early, so I thought I'd walk round this way,' Huw lied as he retreated to the foot of the steps to their house.

'Bit of a detour, isn't it? Still, I believe you, thousands wouldn't. And in case you're interested, my father's still in shock. Forgive me for not hanging round but I'll freeze to death if I don't keep moving.'

'It is nippy.'

'Was that Wyn?' Myrtle asked as she closed the door behind her.

'He's gone on ahead.' Huw reached out, fumbled for her gloved hand and tucked it into the crook of his arm.

'What are you doing here? I know you're not on nights this week.'

'I thought we could make some plans. I have the day off so I could meet your train tonight, and take you to Ronconi's for tea.'

'I'd prefer to buy fish and chips and go back

to your house. You didn't have time to show me anything except the kitchen yesterday.'

'In that case I'll ask Megan along.'

'She'll think you're afraid of me.' Stopping on the corner of Tyfica Road and Gelliwastad Grove, she clamped her mittened hands on his shoulders, and pressed her mouth against his. He tasted of cold and tea. 'There, I've finally done what I wanted to do all last night. That's a thank-you for dealing so cleverly with my father. Now what about tonight?'

'We'll get fish and chips.'

'Good. I'll bring a tape measure. I bet the bedrooms could do with new curtains.'

'They probably could.'

'And new wallpaper and eiderdowns?'

'Whatever you want.'

'I can't wait to move in.' She clung even more tightly to his arm. 'We are going to be so happy.'

'I don't see how I could be any happier than I am now, love,' he declared as he patted her hand, feeling the outline of his mother's ring through the thick woollen cloth.

'Girls, what do you think? Myrtle's not only got an engagement ring, she's actually getting married,' Judy announced to the packed carriage as the train drew out of Pontypridd.

'You lucky thing,' Maggie congratulated her enviously. Huw Davies might be ginger and balding, but he was a policeman with a respectable job and a steady wage that wasn't dependent on war production. In two years she'd

512

be thirty-eight, the same age as Myrtle, and she'd give her eye teeth for a man ten years older than Huw, with half of his assets. Almost any man had to be a better prospect than being left on the shelf.

'Can we all come to the wedding?' Sally asked.

'You expect them to close down the factory for the occasion?' Jenny offered her cigarettes around.

'We've got to do something, we can't just ignore an occasion like this.'

'How about a bachelor party in the White Hart?' Jane suggested coolly, still smarting from Haydn's outrage.

'Women don't have bachelor parties,' Judy informed her tartly.

'I don't see why not,' Jenny broke in. 'If men can take their mates down to the pub the night before they get married, I see no reason why women can't do the same.'

'I'm not sure I want a party ...' Myrtle began tentatively, imagining her father and the minister's reaction to the idea.

'Nonsense,' Jenny retorted. 'We can't all come to the wedding, so when would we give you your presents, if not at a bachelor party?'

'I suppose we could rent one of the upstairs rooms in the Hart,' Sally said doubtfully.

'Rent an upstairs room and hide away. Whatever for?' Jenny rejected the idea scornfully. 'We'll take over the back bar like we always do. Just give us the date, Myrtle and I'll arrange everything.'

'We haven't fixed it yet.'

'When you do, let me know and we'll give you a send-off to remember.'

'Sounds to me as though it's likely to be one the whole town will remember,' Maggie murmured, wishing that this particular party could be hers.

Ronnie swung the circular sheet of metal over the mould. Centring it on the press, he nodded to Wyn, who pulled a lever down sharply.

'One more perfect bomb casing,' Ronnie announced as Wyn released the clamp. 'We make a good team.' He lifted the shell, giving it a cursory inspection before depositing it carefully in a large wire basket that had been emptied three times already since they had come on shift.

'I've really tried to hate you, do you know that?'

'The same goes for you. Let's face it, Wyn, basically we're good blokes, and neither of us particularly enjoys fighting.' The whistle blew for break and he looked across the factory floor through the small window that overlooked the assembly area where the conveyor belts were grinding to a halt.

He followed Wyn from the shop floor into the corridor that led to the canteen. Caught in the flow of women, they found themselves behind Judy Crofter, Sally and Jane.

'He said he'd be in the Hart again tonight,' Judy insisted, oblivious to everyone around her except Sally.

'If Alexander Forbes is in the Hart tonight, it won't be to look at you,' Sally dismissed coolly. 'If eyes were teeth, he'd have crunched Jenny Powell into little pieces last night. I've never seen a man with such a bad case of lust as him.'

'Everyone knows Jenny's so bloody hoity-toity, she won't have him. What he needs is another evening with me.'

'You'd have to tie him down first,' Sally sniggered.

'You'll be laughing on the other side of your face tomorrow. I'll catch him and get him to the altar before Myrtle lands Huw Davies, you'll see.'

'Get a move on,' a voice shouted from the back of the queue. 'At this rate, the whistle will blow for the next section's tea before we're served.'

The girls moved on, and Ronnie caught up with Wyn. 'Is your sister marrying Huw Davies?'

'Next month.'

'Good for Huw. I've always liked him, he's a fair policeman and a nice bloke. Are you pleased?'

'For Myrtle, yes. Both of them really, they seem very happy,' he added with a touch of bitterness.

'Diana thinks a lot of Myrtle.' Ronnie fell silent as he realised who he was talking to. He picked up his tea and carried it over to the table Wyn was sitting at. The canteen was so crowded and time so short, he couldn't have sat at another one, even if he'd wanted to.

'I never really knew Maud,' Wyn said, as he stirred the grey-brown mess in his cup. 'I saw her, of course. In fact I picked her up off the floor once when she fainted, but that's not really knowing someone. Was she like Diana?'

'In some ways,' Ronnie agreed. 'She was incredibly gentle, kind and considerate, but once she'd made up her mind to do something, nothing would shift her: argument, logic, bribery and I suspect, though I wouldn't know, blows.'

'A bit like Diana. Once she makes a promise, she never breaks it.'

'No matter how much it costs her?' Ronnie raised his eyes to Wyn's to let him know he understood exactly what he was telling him.

'It's not the cost to her, but the cost to other people she's concerned about.'

'That's what I was afraid of.' Ronnie pushed his cup aside. The tea suddenly tasted even worse than usual.

The whistle blew again, and they began filing out. Ronnie wondered if it was worth the effort of moving. He decided he'd probably feel more refreshed if he lay down on the floor next to the machine and did without the tea. Perhaps he should try it next time.

He glanced at the clock. They were heading into the final three-hour stint of the shift. The assembly lines had already started up. Three hours and he'd be leaving, four and he'd be in the White Hart, six and he'd be home. Drink, eat, sleep, get up and repeat the day again ... and again ... and again.

Nothing to look forward to except chance meetings with Diana like the one in Bethan's house. Meetings that caused more pain than pleasure.

Jane picked up a fuse, and a detonator. Just before slotting it in she called out for a supervisor.

'This doesn't look right.'

Myrtle took it from her. 'Well spotted. I'll put it to one side.' Holding it out at arm's length she walked down towards the X-ray machine at the end of the line.

Jane picked up the next fuse and another detonator from her box. As she slotted the detonator into the fuse, the world burst before her eyes, erupting in a cascade of fire, smoke and blinding white light.

Everything fell quiet, too quiet, just as it had when the bomb had fallen on their house in London. A merciful darkness blacked out everything as she was flung headlong into nothingness.

CHAPTER 23

One minute Ronnie was lifting the finished casing from the machine, the next he was thrown against the press as an explosion rocked the ground under him. Landing flat on his face he cowered as a ball of flame roared overhead, scorching the air and singeing the back of his overall. He closed his eyes tightly, waiting for it to either recede or roast him. He didn't have to wait long. A gust of freezing air followed. Opening his eyes he saw that half the outside wall of the factory was engulfed in flames; the other half was no longer standing.

'What the hell happened?' He looked to Wyn, but he couldn't even hear the sound of his own voice above the crashes, bangs and sirens screeching into action.

'A minor incident.' Wyn had lip-read the question. He had been in the factory longer than Ronnie, and had become accustomed to the management's euphemisms.

'Mother of God! The whole damn place is coming down on top of us!' Ronnie rolled on to his back and pushed himself under the inadequate shelter of the press he and Wyn had been operating. The whole roof was swaying, rocking from side to side like a cradle. Kicking Wyn further beneath the machine, he covered his head with his hands as shards of sheet metal

518

splintered apart and hurtled downwards.

They remained there, huddled together while all around pieces of what had been the factory hailed down, blanketing the fires.

After an eternity Ronnie gradually became aware of people screaming. He looked out from under the machine. The wall that had separated their section from the assembly lines had gone. In its place was a vast dome of bent and twisted metal. A man stood next to it, shouting for help to get the bins of ammunition and shells out of the flame path.

As he rose hesitantly, a second explosion knocked him to his knees. He couldn't hear himself think. He had a sudden, overwhelming craving for peace and quiet without even being aware of the continuous, ear-shattering wail of the alarms. Everywhere he looked he saw bodies, flung into untidy heaps of lolling arms, legs and heads, like broken mannequins.

Wyn crawled out behind him and hauled him to his feet. They looked at one another. It was useless to even try to talk, but they both knew what needed to be done. Slowly, carefully, they picked their way across the floor, stamping out sparks with their boots until the rubber melted and burnt the soles of their feet. They headed in the same direction. Towards the bins of gunpowder and cordite that stood miraculously intact next to the roof that had caved in on the assembly lines.

Someone grabbed his arm and pointed to the right, where the ramp to the canteen stood unscathed.

'Go out and tell them to shut off those bloody sirens,' Ronnie shouted illogically into the man's ear, before continuing resolutely towards the bins.

He stumbled, looked down and saw a girl lying at his feet. Picking her up, he carried her past the bins and handed her to a fireman who was standing at the head of a line of water bucket carriers. Flames licked at his feet and around a bin of finished fuses. He kicked the bin, rolling it out of the fire path as he stumbled into the loading bay.

Bodies and people were everywhere. Girls sat, slumped with their backs to the wall, their overalls covered in smoke smuts and powder burns, nursing scorched fingers and faces while the factory nurse and emergency first-aiders concentrated on the more serious cases laid out on blankets hastily thrown on to the tarmac.

Wyn was ahead of him, handing over a girl he'd helped outside to a first-aider. The yard was awash with battered, blackened corpse-like figures. He didn't know where to start. Another team of factory firemen ran past with a hose.

'Either of you hurt?' the deputy manager asked. 'No? Good, over there with the others.' He pointed to the wall.

'I'm going back in to see if anyone's alive beneath that roof.' Wyn turned round.

'Don't be a fool man. Leave it to the professionals.'

'My sister worked there.'

'I forbid you. You are not allowed—'

'The hell we aren't!' Ronnie bellowed. 'You can't just leave them.'

'Help is coming ...'

Ronnie didn't waste any time pointing out that it might come too late. As Wyn headed back towards the smoking ruins of the factory, he followed.

Maggie recognised Wyn and Ronnie as she sat leaning against the wall, nursing her bloody and battered hands and shivering with cold. She watched as they worked steadily, side by side, picking up the injured, handing them out to the firemen behind them, pushing aside twisted girders and bins of explosive material.

'I never took those two to be heroes.' Sally slumped beside her.

'You all right?' Maggie moved her head carefully. Her neck hurt and she was too shocked to explore the pain.

'Do I look it?'

'You've lost your eyelashes, but they'll grow back. You seen any of the others?'

Sally shook her head and looked at the mess around her. 'I'd give anything for a fag and a beer.'

'Have to wait until the end of the shift.' Maggie tried to smile but it hurt her face. 'The way it's looking now, we'll be doing overtime.'

Dr John called Bethan minutes after he received the message that all the medical personnel and able-bodied men who could be spared from the town were to go to the munitions factory immediately.

She threw on her uniform, kissed her children goodbye, said a hurried farewell to Maisie and Liza, warned Alma not to have her baby before she got back, jumped in Andrew's car and raced down the hill. Turning right up Graig Avenue she did an emergency stop outside her father's house. Leaving the engine running, she dashed up the steps and opened the door, shouting for Haydn.

'Sis?' He appeared in the kitchen doorway with Anne in his arms.

'Is Phyllis in?'

'Here, Beth. What's wrong?'

'There's been an explosion in the factory.'

'Jane!'

'I don't know any details, but they're asking for all the help they can get.'

She turned and ran down the steps. Haydn handed Anne over to Phyllis, grabbed his coat and dashed out after her.

He had no time to shut the passenger door before she pressed the accelerator to the floor. Slamming the car into reverse, she careered backwards, turning into Iltyd Street before driving out of the Avenue on to Llantrisant Road.

'What happened?'

'Explosion, dead and injured. That's all Dr John told me.'

'No numbers?'

'No nothing. And even when they know, they won't be broadcasting them. Accidents like this

522

don't happen. They're bad for morale.'

'I thought that maxim only applied to military disasters.'

'You seen any civilians since this war started? Because I haven't. Sometimes it feels as though the whole country is fighting. Men, women and children.'

They saw the smoke long before they reached the factory. The police had barricaded the road and were waving through all the ambulances, and stopping the cars. Bethan tore off her nurse's veil, opened the window and held it aloft.

'Nurse John, straight through. Follow the ambulance.'

She recognised the sergeant from the police station. 'How bad is it?'

'You'll see,' he answered, tight-lipped as he signalled the car behind her to stop.

'Oh dear God!' Haydn stared at the rows of blanket-covered corpses laid out on the concrete apron of the loading bay.

'Find out who's in charge, and ask what you can do to help.' Bethan dived out of the car and looked for Dr John. He was injecting morphine into a patient so badly burned, Bethan couldn't determine age or sex.

'Twenty dead so far, but it's still burning and there's a risk of explosion. Initial estimates are sixty missing, but some of them could be working to clear the explosives from the area. The most severely injured are in this line. There's morphine vials in my bag for the burns victims. Don't send any to the hospital without it, or they might not survive the trip. Check for damaged limbs and severed arteries. I've had to amputate two arms already.'

Bethan turned to see Haydn behind her.

'I can't find anyone.'

She knew that by 'anyone' he meant Jane, not whoever was in charge, but this was no time to look for individuals. 'Huw's behind you. Ask him.' She was already cutting the sleeve of a smouldering overall from a young girl. He heard her murmuring soft words of comfort as he walked away.

'Huw?' Haydn had to touch his arm to gain his attention. 'What can I do?'

'Do?' Huw asked blankly. 'Do you think I'd be handing out tea if there was something I could do? The roof's caved in over the area that housed the assembly line. We know there's at least ten girls trapped beneath it, what we don't know is whether they're alive or dead. Ronnie and Wyn have been trying to get them out since I've been here. The firemen are doing what they can, but they won't let anyone else get near because the whole area's riddled with bins of explosives that could go up at any moment.'

'Jane ...'

'She worked with Myrtle, close to Jenny Powell. They think, although they're not sure, that they are the ones trapped under there.'

'Can you shift it?' Wyn gasped, sliding the torch they had borrowed from a fireman ahead of him, as he slithered sideways on his back. He stopped to push a girder beneath the edge of the section of roof that covered them in the hope that it would raise it higher above their heads.

'This is worse than trying to throw a fat woman out of bed, when you've a ton of eiderdowns pressing down on you.' Ronnie summoned all his strength to push up a section of roof so he could see what lay beyond it.

'You've had experience of pushing fat women out of bed?'

'Only in my dreams.' Ronnie had no difficulty in hearing Wyn's voice. After the din of factory sirens, ambulance bells, and screams in the loading bay, it was miraculously quiet beneath the roof. He tried not to think about the bins of explosives and the fires that still smouldered on what was left of the factory floor. His face contorted as he bared his teeth and steeled his muscles to make one last superhuman effort. 'It's no good. I can't shift the bloody thing.' He reached up, hitting his elbow painfully on the metal ceiling that hung a scant three inches from his face, as he wiped away the sweat that was pouring from his forehead.

'Let me try to get round it.' Wyn slipped his arm into a narrow gap between a bench and a girder. 'I can feel something. An overall, an arm. It's warm.' Bracing his feet against the bench, Wyn pushed upwards, inching his way over the thick carpet of shattered shell casings and splintered metal that surrounded the top of the bench. 'Hand me the torch.' He stretched his arm out behind him. Ronnie pushed it in his direction. 'I can see Jenny's face. Jenny?' he called loudly. 'Can you hear me?'

'Is she injured?'

'Not that I can see, but I can only see her arm and head. She's breathing, and there's another girl behind her.'

'Who is it?'

'God only knows, I can't see a bloody thing beyond the torch beam, and I can't move an inch.'

'Do you think the fire's on top of us? I feel as though I'm being roasted for Sunday dinner.'

'Go back and get a couple more metal bars. If we can prop this section up and get the firemen behind us to form a chain, we might be able to get at the girls and hand them out from one to the other. What do you think?'

'It's better than my idea.'

'What's that?'

'Getting everyone out there who can walk to play sardines under here.'

'Are you ever serious?'

'On the rare occasions I've tried, I've gone mad.'

'If you're going, go.'

'Try singing to whoever's trapped. That should wake them up.' Ronnie crawled out backwards from beneath the roof. As he climbed to his feet he saw that he hadn't been far wrong about the cooking. A pile of overalls had blown on to the roof from the tailor's shop and were smoking in a foul-smelling heap of melting rubber buttons and smouldering wool.

'Any luck?' a fireman asked.

He explained what they intended to do. A

few minutes later, the fireman and three of his colleagues came up with a couple of almost undamaged girders and an extra torch.

Taking a deep breath, Ronnie lay on his stomach and bulldozed his way back beneath the roof. The firemen pushed one of the girders alongside him, waiting for his confirming shout that he'd guided it, before lending it any more momentum. It took him ten minutes to reach the spot where he'd left Wyn. He flashed his torch and called out.

'I'm behind the bench. Don't touch it whatever you do. It's the only thing that's stopping the roof from crashing down on the girls. Go to the top of the bench.'

'My top could be your bottom.'

'I'll push my torch up as far as it will go: work your way towards the light.'

'Hi there, you look good in a spotlight, particularly with a dirty face. Are you going to sing "Mammy"?'

'Ronnie ...'

'I'll be serious.'

'If I pass a girl to you, would you be able to get her out?'

'There's four firemen behind me.'

'Right, first one coming.'

Ronnie heard the murmur of women's voices. 'They're alive?'

'And arguing. Tell them it's easier to get the able-bodied out of the way first.'

'Definitely. And I hate to put a damper on a good argument, but there's a fire on top of us. If we don't move soon we'll end up grilled, and it will be well done, not rare.'

Ronnie held out his arms as Wyn thrust Jenny towards him. Her arm was at a peculiar angle and her face was red raw, but her eyes were open. He turned his head and shouted to the fireman behind, waiting for his answering cry before using the girder as a guide and pushing her down the line.

Haydn was handing out tea and hot soup from a WVS wagon when he saw Bethan racing across the yard. He looked across and saw a fireman carrying a girl. Her dust cap had fallen from her head and he recognised her. There was only one girl in Pontypridd with hair that colour.

'Jenny,' he breathed, remembering Huw's assertion that she worked with Jane. Handing the tea to the person nearest him, he tore across the yard.

'Have you seen Jane?' he demanded breathlessly.

'Steady, Haydn,' Bethan warned. 'She's in shock.'

'There's more alive under the roof,' the fireman confirmed. 'We're getting them out just as fast as we can.'

'Jenny, have you seen Myrtle?' Huw stood beside Haydn.

She tried to focus on them, but the effort proved too much.

'That's enough.' Bethan took charge. 'Get her over to the ambulances,' she ordered the firemen. 'I'll show you the way.'

Ronnie waited. The creaking and groaning of their metal cocoon resounded, more alarming with every passing minute. Wyn had handed out three girls so far. Jenny, Judy, and one he hadn't recognised, but Wyn hadn't said a word for at least two minutes and he was beginning to wonder if there were any more survivors.

'Careful, this one's badly injured.'

Ronnie steeled himself, hoping it wasn't burns. Judy's hand had been burnt, and flakes of her skin still clung to his fingers.

'If we slip another girder under here, it could give you more room,' a voice echoed behind him.

'And it could bring the whole lot down on top of us,' he called back.

'We don't have much option: the fire is getting out of control and coming this way.' A fireman crawled up behind him. 'I'm regular, not factory trained, lad,' he pulled rank on him. 'Leave this to the professionals.'

'Not until my mate gets out of here. Wyn, you all right?' Ronnie shouted.

'I need help.'

'I'm coming.'

Before the fireman could stop him, Ronnie crawled around the top of the bench.

'It's Jane. Both her legs are broken and I'm afraid of hurting her.'

'Here, let me take her by the shoulders, we'll manage between us.'

Ten sweating minutes and six girls later they were alone.

'That's it,' Ronnie said flatly.

'I'll just check down there.'

'I'll wait.'

'No you won't. That fireman's going to burst a blood vessel if he shouts any louder. Ronnie, if I don't get out of here will you take care of Diana?'

'What are you talking about ...'

'Give Billy my gold watch. It's in my locker. Tell him about me, and tell him I was proud to be his father and that I loved him. Take care of Diana, and be good to her and Billy. If you're not, I'll come back to haunt you. And warn Huw the same goes for him with Myrtle.'

'Tell him yourself ...'

The shouts outside grew louder.

'Go, Ronnie.'

'I'm not leaving you.'

'I'm afraid you're going to have to.'

Ronnie shone his torch down the length of Wyn's body. It was then that he saw the steel bar pinning down Wyn's leg, and he understood why Wyn hadn't been able to get the last girls out without help.

'What the hell's going on?' The fireman's head appeared in a pool of torchlight at the top of the bench.

'My mate's trapped.'

'We'll be back with a hoist. If you don't care about yourself, there's four firemen behind you who won't move until you do. Get going, will you? The fire's almost on top of us.'

'Remember, the watch is in my locker, and take care of Diana.' Wyn pushed Ronnie;

the fireman grabbed his shoulders. He was pulled kicking and yelling to the outside. The firemen scrabbled out after him just as the roof shattered, settling in a crackling of flame and sparks to the floor.

Ronnie trawled through the ashes and debris, skirting past two bodies reduced to charred cinders. Stifling his nausea, he covered his hands with the torn sleeves of his overalls and turned them over. The shrivelled remains of dust caps clung to the skulls. Women, not men!

He rose to his feet. Black powder and dust was everywhere. The rank stench of burnt gunpowder and cordite assailed his nostrils. He closed his eyes against the stinging smoke, trying to orientate himself, but now that the sheets of metal had been cooled with hoses and dragged out into the yard, it was difficult to see where he and Wyn had worked to free the women.

He found the blackened remains of what might have been a bench, but was it the bench they had worked behind? There was no body close by, not even a pile of ashes.

'Ronnie?' Bethan stood beside him. 'You did all you could, no one could have possibly done more. The firemen said the girls would have died if it hadn't been for you.'

'Not me, Wyn,' he said harshly. 'And I can't even find his body.'

'We've got to go. The salvage workers are waiting to move in.' Bethan dragged him away, up the ramp that led to the canteen and the cloakroom. The lockers had remained untouched by the explosion and the fire that had followed. He walked along the bank until he came to Wyn's. Turning the handle, he opened it. A pair of singed overalls, half-melted rubber boots and a gold watch lay inside. Nothing else. He picked up the watch.

'He asked me to give it to Billy.'

She nodded.

'Someone's going to have to tell Diana. Do you mind if I do it?'

'The police have been given a list of the dead and injured, they're informing the relatives now.'

He closed the locker door.

'Come on, I'll drive you to the hospital, you need to see a doctor.'

'I'm fine.'

'You're bleeding.'

'I don't think it's my blood. Haven't got a cigarette, have you?'

'In the middle of this powder you want to light up?'

'It's not a good idea?'

Bethan recognised the symptoms of shock and led him across the almost deserted yard to the tea wagon.

Night had fallen, murky and smoke-ridden. She would never have found the wagon if it hadn't been for the white stripes painted around the counter.

'You and Wyn brought out a lot of girls who would have died, Ronnie.'

'I remember Jenny. After that it's all a haze.'

'Jenny's concussed, she's got a broken arm and slight burns but she's going to be fine. They've taken her to the hospital. Here, come and sit in my car and drink this. Then I really do have to take you to the hospital.'

'I'd like to see Diana first.'

'She will have been told by now.'

'You don't understand ...'

'Later, Ronnie. You can see her later.'

'Just one more look? In the cloakroom. I need to pay my respects.'

'Two minutes.'

Curling his fingers around the gold watch in his pocket he walked into the women's cloakroom. It had been turned into a temporary mortuary. Two sappers were already loading the bodies on to the back of a truck. No hearses for wartime casualties, he reflected grimly.

In a corner heaped on a pile of charred bones, was a leg. Firm, rounded, ridiculously pink and unscathed. It bore no signs of fire, yet it was neatly severed, just below the knee.

He crouched beside it.

'It's a wooden one, mate,' one of the sappers shouted. 'We think it belonged to the bloke who got those girls out from under the roof that caved in.'

'You found his body?'

'No, just the leg. It was trapped beneath a girder.'

Ronnie fingered the gold watch as he rose to his feet. It was all so bloody obvious. Why hadn't he thought of it straight away? Wyn's overalls wouldn't have been in his locker if he'd been killed. His suit would have been folded there.

Give Billy my gold watch. It's in my locker. Tell him about me, and tell him I was proud to be his father and that I loved him. Take care of Diana, and be good to her and Billy. If you're not, I'll come back to haunt you. And warn Huw the same goes for him with Myrtle.

'Any haunting you do won't be from the grave,' he murmured to himself.

Turning his back on the dead he walked towards the loading bay and Bethan. The sappers' voices echoed after him.

'Well whether it's sabotage or not, there won't be any more ammunition coming out of this place, that's for sure.'

'Want to make a bet on it?' a factory fireman retorted. 'Manager's just said we'll be back to full production this time next week, and we will. They can't lick Jerry without us.'

CHAPTER 24

Huw sat next to Myrtle's bed, glad that the nurses were too busy to chase him away. He wanted to be the first one to talk to her when she woke. The first to give her the news, and tell her it didn't matter. That nothing could possibly make a difference to the way he felt about her. He looked up and saw Doctor John standing in the doorway.

'Someone told me you two only got engaged yesterday, Constable Davies.'

'That's right. How is she, doctor?'

'As well as can be expected. As soon as her arm heals we'll fit her with a false hand. They're very good these days, and there's all kinds of useful gadgets that can be added to them. She'll need a bit of help to adapt, of course. I take it she was right handed?'

'Yes.'

'Pity.'

'She'll have me to help her.'

'The nurse told you about her sight?'

'She said that you didn't know the extent of the damage.'

'The prognosis isn't good.'

'She's blind?'

'She has certainly lost some function, but she may see light and shadows. Time will tell.'

Huw reached down and gripped Myrtle's

left hand. 'Can I stay with her until she wakes?'

'I don't see why not. Constable Davies,' he paused in the doorway. 'I'm sorry.'

'There's no need to be, doctor. She's still alive.'

'After today I can see why you're grateful for that much.'

Bethan left Ronnie with the casualty nurse and walked down the ward looking for Haydn. Her uniform was filthy, her hands, face and hair covered with smuts and ashes, but no one commented or stopped her. She found them at the end of the ward.

'I could hear you two arguing from the other side of the hospital. Are you ever going to stop?'

'She breaks both her legs and then tells me she's intent on staying in Pontypridd and going back to the factory just as soon as she's fit again.'

'Is that what you want, Jane?' Bethan smiled at her sister-in-law.

'It's what I want, but he wants me to go back to London.'

'Isn't that what you wanted when he brought you to Pontypridd?'

'That was before I started contributing to the war effort. After today they're going to need all the skilled hands they can get.'

Haydn reached out to her and Bethan moved away.

'How many times do you expect me to stand

back and watch you being dug out of bomb craters?'

'This is the last, I promise. I'll take a week or so off as soon as I can walk, and bring Anne down to see you in London.'

'Time the patient was asleep.' A nurse picked up Jane's chart from the foot of the bed.

Haydn leaned over and dropped a kiss on to his wife's forehead. Bethan turned aside, pretending she hadn't seen the tear fall from his eye.

'I really thought she'd be safe here,' he said as they walked down the ward together.

'Tell me anywhere that's safe in this country at the moment and I'll send my children there.'

'I didn't understand. Today, at the factory, those women, Wyn Ronnie ... they were as brave as any soldier I've seen under fire.'

'Don't ask Jane to stay at home and look after Anne again, Haydn. At least not until after the war's over. If you do, you'll lose her.'

'I understand that now. I behaved like an idiot, didn't I?'

'It's not the first time, and knowing you, it won't be the last.'

'Poor Wyn.'

'Poor Diana.'

The lorry ground to a halt at the end of the trading estate. The driver leaned over, opened the passenger door and shouted to the young man leaning on a makeshift crutch fashioned from a piece of steel piping.

'Where are you headed?'

'North?'

'Wales or England?'

'Wales.'

'Hop in. I'm sorry,' the driver apologised as the man limped towards him. 'Trust me to tell a one-legged man to hop. I honestly didn't see.'

'That's not surprising in this blackout.' He tucked away the white handkerchief he'd used to attract attention.

'Can you manage?' the driver asked as the man tossed the metal bar into the cab and heaved himself up, using his hands.

'I'm used to it. It happened a year or so ago.'

'Active service?'

'The blitz.'

'Bloody Jerry.'

'Bloody war.'

'Where exactly are you going?'

'Rhyl. I have a friend there working in munitions. I'm hoping they'll take me on.'

'They will. They're that short they'll take on a one-armed, no-headed monkey, no disrespect intended.'

'And none taken.'

'It's good to have company. It can get lonely on these long night runs. What's your name?'

It was a simple enough question but his passenger hesitated for a moment.

'Glyn, Glyn Powell.'

'Pleased to meet you. Mind you, after today's news you might not be working in munitions for very long.'

'What's happened?'

'Where've you been all day, Glyn?'

'A bit busy.'

'And nowhere near a radio. Haven't you heard? The Japanese bombed Pearl Harbor this morning. The Yanks are coming in on our side. Mind you, I think that's bloody typical. We do all the hard work, then when it looks like we've hit a winning streak they join us and take all the credit.'

'If they help us win the war that bit sooner, it will be worth giving them some of the credit.'

'You're not one of those Communists or pacifists who's prepared to make peace at all costs, are you?'

'No. Just someone who has lost a lot in the two years since the war started.'

'Yes, well. I'm sorry, mate. I didn't mean to offend you. You like films?' he asked settling on what he hoped was a safe topic of conversation. 'What do you think of Gary Cooper? Now there's a hero for you.'

CHAPTER 25

'It was a beautiful service.'

'Yes, wasn't it.' Diana repeated the trite phrase over and over again. She couldn't bear to look at the sofa where Wyn's father was holding court. Dressed in his best suit and wearing his Great War medals on his chest, he was receiving the condolences and congratulations of friends and neighbours on his son's behalf, and she couldn't help feeling that he was prouder of Wyn dead than he ever had been of him alive.

'That medal will be something for Billy to inherit.'

'Yes, thank you.' She turned away from the minister's wife, wondering why on earth she was thanking her.

'Diana?'

She turned to see Ronnie behind her. 'Is there somewhere we can talk?'

'At Wyn's memorial service?'

'Diana, didn't anyone tell you? I was the last person to see him. I have something to give you.'

She looked at the room full of people. Myrtle sitting next to Huw, her arm in a sling, her face half hidden behind the dark glasses the doctor had prescribed to save what was left of her sight.

540

'It's important, Diana.'

'Come through the kitchen into the back garden.'

She crossed the yard and climbed the steps to the small vegetable plot her mother tended.

He walked towards her and opened his hand. 'It's his watch. He wanted Billy to have it.'

She took it from him, staring down at the case through a tear-stained haze.

'He left us something else, Diana.'

'Us? Ronnie, please ...'

'He left us each other. You do know why they didn't find his body, don't you?'

Her eyes told him she already suspected the truth.

'He's not dead. I promise you, he's still alive. There's no way his overalls could have got back into his locker if he'd been killed. He must have wanted to disappear. I have no idea where he's gone, or why ...'

'I do.' She had searched the house for Erik's letter to tell him Wyn had been killed, but it had disappeared, together with photographs of her and Billy, and his mother and Myrtle. She had wondered if he'd been planning it for some time.

Tomorrow she'd walk up to Jacobsdal. Someone there would have Erik's address. There were other things that should be sent on. The bankbook that held his inheritance from his mother. A letter wishing Erik and his new friend, whoever he was, well.

'He told me that if I didn't look after you and Billy he'd come back to haunt me, and the same went for Huw with Myrtle. But he isn't a ghost, Diana.'

She ran her fingers over the engraving on the watch casing. The fine work was slightly worn at the catch.

He reached out and brushed a tear from her cheek. 'I never thought I'd be able to ask you this, but will you marry me? Not now of course, but in a year or so?'

'What about Tony? And Billy and ...'

He wrapped his arms around her, holding her as though he never intended to let go. 'There's no problem we can't face or solve as long as we're together.'

'And Wyn?'

'We'll tell his son what a brave hero he had for a father.'

'Ronnie ...'

'Do you love me?'

'You know I do.'

'That's the only difficult bit. From here on in, everything's going to be perfect. Trust me?' He moved away and held out his hand. She took it. They walked slowly down the steps and back into the house.